Books by
WILLIAM FAULKNER

Soldiers' Pay
Mosquitoes
Sartoris
The Sound and the Fury
As I Lay Dying
Sanctuary
These Thirteen
Light in August
Doctor Martino
Pylon
Absalom, Absalom!
The Unvanquished
The Wild Palms
The Hamlet
Go Down, Moses
Intruder in the Dust
Knight's Gambit
Collected Stories
Requiem for a Nun
A Fable
Big Woods
The Town
The Mansion
The Reivers
Snopes
Essays, Speeches and Public Letters
The Wishing Tree
New Orleans Sketches
Flags in the Dust

POETRY
The Marble Faun and *A Green Bough*

FLAGS IN THE DUST

FLAGS
in the
DUST

WILLIAM
FAULKNER

Edited and with an Introduction
by Douglas Day

VINTAGE BOOKS
A Division of Random House, New York

Library of Congress Cataloging in Publication Data

Faulkner, William, 1897–1962.
    Flags in the dust.
    An uncut version of the work published in 1929 under title: Sartoris.
    I. Title.
[PZ3.F272F 4] [PS3511.A86]   813'.5'2   74–3315
ISBN 0–394–71239–0

Introduction

In the autumn or winter of 1926, William Faulkner, twenty-nine, began work on the first of his novels about Yoknapatawpha County. Sherwood Anderson had told him some time before that he should write about his native Mississippi, and now Faulkner took that advice: he used his own land, and peopled it with men and women who were partly drawn from real life, and partly depicted as they should have been in some ideal mythopoeic structure. A year later, on September 29, 1927, the new novel was completed. It was 596 pages long in transcript, and he called it *Flags in the Dust*. Full of enthusiasm, Faulkner sent *Flags in the Dust* up to Horace Liveright (who had published his first two novels) in New York. Liveright read it, disliked it, and sent it back with his firm recommendation that Faulkner not try to offer it for publication anywhere else: it was too diffuse, too lacking in plot and structure; and, Liveright felt, no amount of revision would be able to salvage it. Faulkner, crushed, showed *Flags in the Dust* to several of his friends, who shared Liveright's opinion.

But he still believed that this would be the book that would make his name as a writer, and for several months he tried to edit it himself, sitting at his worktable in Oxford. Finally, discouraged, he sent a new typescript off to Ben Wasson, his agent in New York.

"Will you please try to sell this for me?" he asked Wasson. "I can't afford all the postage it's costing me." In the meantime, convinced that he would never become a successful novelist, Faulkner began work on a book that he was sure would never mean anything to anyone but himself: *The Sound and the Fury*.

Wasson tried eleven publishers, all of whom rejected *Flags in the Dust*. Finally he gave the typescript to Harrison Smith, then an editor of Harcourt, Brace & Company. Smith liked it, and showed it to Alfred Harcourt, who agreed to publish it, provided that someone other than Faulkner perform the extensive cutting job that Harcourt felt was necessary. For fifty dollars, Wasson agreed to pare down his client's novel. On September 20, 1928, Faulkner received a contract for the book, now to be called *Sartoris* (no one knows who changed its name), which was to be about 110,-000 words long, and which was to be delivered to Harcourt, Brace sixteen days later. Faulkner left immediately for New York, presumably to help Wasson with his revision.

But when he sat down in Wasson's apartment to observe the operation on his novel, Faulkner found himself unable to participate. If it were cut, he felt, it would die. Wasson persisted, however, pointing out that the trouble with *Flags in the Dust* was that it was not one novel, but six, all struggling along simultaneously. This, to Faulkner, was praise: evidence of fecundity and fullness of vision, evidence that the world of Yoknapatawpha was rich enough to last. As he later wrote of his third novel, "I discovered that my own little postage stamp of native soil was worth writing about and that I would never live long enough to exhaust it." Nevertheless, Wasson kept his bargain with Alfred Harcourt. For the next two weeks, while

Faulkner sat nearby writing *The Sound and the Fury*, Wasson went through the typescript of *Flags in the Dust*, making cuts of every sort until almost a fourth of the book had been excised. Harcourt, Brace published this truncated version on January 31, 1929, as *Sartoris* (with a dedication: "To Sherwood Anderson through whose kindness I was first published, with the belief that this book will give him no reason to regret that fact"), and the old *Flags in the Dust* was soon forgotten—by everyone but Faulkner.

He had preserved the original holograph manuscript of *Flags in the Dust*, 237 pages in his neat but minuscule and almost illegible hand, and he had bound together with thin wire the 596 pages of a sort of composite typescript of the novel, produced by the combination of three separate but overlapping typescript drafts. The first of these, 447 pages long, seems to have been begun before he completed his manuscript version. The second, 99 pages of which are in the composite typescript, was probably written after he had completed the manuscript and the first typescript. In the third, 146 pages appear to have been a revision of the second typescript. Why Faulkner should have labored over the reconstruction of this text is not clear: perhaps he thought of his composite typescript as a working draft which would allow him ultimately to restore to his novel that which Wasson had carved from it—or perhaps, fastidious man that he was, he simply could not bring himself to throw away all of those typed pages. In any case, the manuscript and typescript both were eventually deposited at the Alderman Library of the University of Virginia, where they lay more or less undisturbed until Mrs. Jill Summers, Faulkner's daughter, remembered that her late father had spoken often of a restoration of

Flags in the Dust. Mrs. Summers asked this writer and Albert Erskine, editor at Random House, to undertake the task.

The result is, now, *Flags in the Dust*, which aims at being a faithful reproduction of that composite typescript. Certain nonsubstantive alterations in spelling and punctuation have been made, in order to bring this novel into conformity with Faulkner's other books; but wherever possible his many idiosyncrasies, especially those on which he himself insisted during his years of working with editors at Random House, were allowed to stand. The final complete typescript, which must have served as setting copy for the Harcourt, Brace edition of *Sartoris* (and which must have been the draft in which Wasson made his cuts), has not survived. Nor have any galley proofs. All we had to work from, then, was the composite typescript, by any scholar's standards a suspect source. There was no way, finally, to tell which of the many differences between *Flags in the Dust* and *Sartoris* were the result of Faulkner's emendations in the hypothetical setting copy and the galley proofs, and which belonged to Wasson. If there were to be any publication of *Flags in the Dust* at all, then, it had to be what we have here provided.

Whether it is better than *Sartoris*, as Faulkner so firmly believed it to be, is of course a matter of taste. It is tempting to launch into a study of the genesis and development of the novel, from the manuscript version through the typescript of *Flags in the Dust* to the publication of *Sartoris;* but this is not the place to do so. Suffice it here to suggest that whereas *Sartoris* is chiefly about the Sartoris clan, their surly gallantry, and their utter and uncaring inability to adjust to the demands of whatever age they find themselves in, *Flags in the Dust* is far more complicated: primary focus is still on the Sartorises, but Faulkner clearly wished to make of his novel an anatomy of the entire Yoknapatawpha social structure, excluding only the Indians. As foils to the doomed and hawklike Bayard Sartoris, we have not only his dead twin, John, but Horace Benbow, too, as a sort of Delta dilettante; and Buddy MacCallum, the young hillman who possesses all the steady virtues Bayard lacks; Harry Mitchell, as the type of the new southern middle class—and even Byron Snopes, the desperate and reptilian representative of a new class threatening to overthrow the old aristocratic order of the area. All of these are present in *Sartoris*, to be sure; but in *Flags in the Dust* their roles are lengthened and heightened, until we realize that each of them is in his way a commentary not only upon Bayard Sartoris, but also upon the Deep South in the years after the First World War.

Flags in the Dust, then, may or may not be a better work of art than *Sartoris*; but few will dispute that it is a more complete fictional document of a time and place in history—or that it is a better introduction to the grand and complex southern world that William Faulkner was to write about until he died.

DOUGLAS DAY
University of Virginia
February, 1973

FLAGS IN THE DUST

ONE

I

Old man Falls roared: "Cunnel was settin' thar in a cheer, his sock feet propped on the po'ch railin', smokin' this hyer very pipe. Old Louvinia was settin' on the steps, shellin' a bowl of peas fer supper. And a feller was glad to git even peas sometimes, in them days. And you was settin' back agin' the post. They wa'nt nobody else thar 'cep' yo' aunt, the one 'fo' Miss Jenny come. Cunnel had sont them two gals to Memphis to yo' gran'pappy when he fust went away. You was 'bout half-grown, I reckon. How old was you then, Bayard?"

"Fourteen," old Bayard answered.

"Hey?"

"Fourteen," Bayard shouted. "Do I have to tell you that every time you tell me this damn story?"

"And thar you all was a-settin'," old man Falls continued, unruffled, "when they turned in at the gate and come trottin' up the carriage drive.

"Old Louvinia drapped the bowl of peas and let out one squawk, but Cunnel shet her up and tole her to run and git his boots and pistols and have 'em ready at the back do', and you lit out fer the barn to saddle that stallion. And when them Yankees rid up and stopped—they stopped right whar that flower bed is now—they wa'nt nobody on the po'ch but

Cunnel, a-settin' thar like he never even heard tell of no Yankees.

"The Yankees they set thar on the hosses, talkin' 'mongst theyselves if this was the right house or not, and Cunnel settin' thar with his sock feet on the railin', gawkin' at 'em like a hillbilly. The Yankee officer he tole one man to ride back to the barn and look for that 'ere stallion, then he says to Cunnel:

" 'Say, Johnny, whar do the rebel, John Sartoris, live?'

" 'Lives down the road a piece,' Cunnel says, not battin' a eye even. ' 'Bout two mile,' he says. 'But you wont find 'im now. He's away fightin' the Yanks agin.'

" 'Well, I reckon you better come and show us the way, anyhow,' the Yankee officer says.

"So Cunnel he got up slow and tole 'em to let 'im git his shoes and walkin' stick, and limped into the house, leavin' 'em a-settin' thar waitin'.

"Soon's he was out of sight he run. Old Louvinia was waitin' at the back do' with his coat and boots and pistols and a snack of cawn bread. That 'ere other Yankee had rid into the barn, and Cunnel taken the things from Louvinia and wropped 'em up in the coat and started acrost the back yard like he was jest takin' a walk. 'Bout that time the Yankee come to the barn do'.

" 'They aint no stock hyer a-tall,' the Yank says.

" 'I reckon not,' Cunnel says. 'Cap'm says fer you to come on back,' he says, goin' on. He could feel that 'ere Yank a-watchin' 'im, lookin' right 'twixt his shoulder blades, whar the bullet would hit. Cunnel says that was the hardest thing he ever done in his life, walkin' on thar acrost that lot with his back to'ads that Yankee without breakin' into a run. He was aimin' to'ads the corner of the barn, whar he

could git the house between 'em, and Cunnel says hit
seemed like he'd been a-walkin' a year without gittin' no closer and not darin' to look back. Cunnel
says he wasn't even thinkin' of nothin' 'cep' he was
glad the gals wa'nt at home. He says he never give a
thought to yo' aunt back thar in the house, because
he says she was a full-blood Sartoris and she was a
match fer any dozen Yankees.

"Then the Yank hollered at him, but Cunnel kep'
right on, not lookin' back nor nothin'. Then the
Yank hollered agin and Cunnel says he could hyear
the hoss movin' and he decided hit was time to stir
his shanks. He made the corner of the barn jest as the
Yank shot the fust time, and by the time the Yank
got to the corner, he was in the hawg-lot, a-tearin'
through the jimson weeds to'ads the creek whar you
was waitin' with the stallion hid in the willers.

"And thar you was a-standin', holdin' the hoss and
that 'ere Yankee patrol yellin' up behind, until Cunnel got his boots on. And then he tole you to tell yo'
aunt he wouldn't be home fer supper."

As usual old man Falls had brought John Sartoris
into the room with him. Freed as he was of time, he
was a far more definite presence in the room than the
two of them cemented by deafness to a dead time
and drawn thin by the slow attenuation of days. He
seemed to stand above them, all around them, with
his bearded, hawklike face and the bold glamor of his
dream.

Old Bayard sat with his feet braced against the side
of the fireplace, holding the pipe in his hand. The
bowl was ornately carved and it was charred with
much usage, and on the bit were the prints of his father's teeth.

"What're you giving it to me for, after all this
time?" he said.

"Well, I reckon I've kep' it long as Cunnel aimed fer me to," old man Falls answered. "A po' house aint no place fer anything of his'n, Bayard," he added. He sat bent forward, elbows on knees, chewing his tobacco for a while.

"Not fer a pipe of his'n," he said. "Hit 'ud be different ef 'twas him, hisself now. Wouldn't no place be a po' house whar he was at. But that 'ere thing that belonged to him, hit 'ud be takin' a advantage of him atter he's gone." Old man Falls chewed his tobacco for a while. "I'm goin' on ninety-fo' year old, Bayard," he said.

He spat neatly into the fireplace and drew the back of his hand across his mouth.

"A thing he toted in his pocket and got enjoyment outen, in them days. Hit'd be different, I reckon, while we was a-buildin' the railroad. He said often enough in them days we was all goin' to be in the po' house by Saturday night. Or cemetery, mo' likely, him ridin' up and down the track with a saddle-bag full of money night and day, keepin' jest one crosstie ahead of the po' house, like he said. That 'us when hit changed. When he had to start killin' folks. Them two cyarpet-baggers stirrin' up niggers to vote, that he walked right into the room whar they was a-settin' behind a table, with they pistols layin' on the table, and that robber and that other feller he kilt, all with that same dang der'nger. When a feller has to start killin' folks, he 'most always has to keep on killin' 'em. And when he does, he's already dead hisself."

It showed on his brow, the dark shadow of fatality and doom, that night when he sat beneath the candles in his dining room and turned a wine glass in his fingers while he talked to his son. The railroad was finished, and today he had been elected to the legislature after a hard and bitter fight, and on his brow lay the shadow of his doom and a little weariness.

"And so," he said, "Redlaw'll kill me tomorrow, for I shall be unarmed. I'm tired of killing men . . . Pass the wine, Bayard."

After old man Falls had gathered up his small parcels and gone old Bayard sat for some time, the pipe in his hand, rubbing the bowl slowly with his thumb. But presently John Sartoris too had departed; withdrawn rather, to that place where the peaceful dead contemplate their frustrated days, and old Bayard dropped his feet to the floor and rose and thrust the pipe into his pocket and took a cigar from the humidor on the mantel. As he struck the match the door behind him opened and a man wearing a green eyeshade entered and approached.

"Simon's here, Colonel," he said in an inflectionless voice.

"What?" Old Bayard turned his head, the cigar between his teeth and the match in his cupped hands.

"Simon's come," the other shouted flatly.

"Oh. All right." Old Bayard flung the match into the grate and thrust the cigar into his breast pocket. He took his black felt hat from the desk and followed the other and stalked through the lobby of the bank and emerged onto the street, where Simon in a linen duster and an ancient tophat held the matched geldings at the curb.

There was a hitching-post there, which old Bayard retained with a testy disregard of industrial progress, but Simon never used it. Until the door opened and Bayard emerged from behind the drawn green shades, Simon sat on the seat with the reins in his left hand and the thong of the whip caught smartly back in his right and usually the unvarying and seemingly incombustible fragment of a cigar in his mouth, talking to the horses in a steady, lover-like flow. Simon spoiled horses. He admired Sartorises and he had for them a warmly protective tenderness, but he loved horses, and beneath his hands the sorriest beast bloomed and acquired comeliness like a caressed woman, temperament like an opera star.

Bayard crossed to the carriage with that stiff erectness of his which, as a countryman once remarked, was so straight as to almost meet itself walking along the street. One or two passers and a merchant or so in his shop door saluted him with a sort of florid servility, and behind him the shade on one window drew aside upon the disembodied face of the man in the green eyeshade. The book-keeper was a hillman of indeterminate age, a silent man who performed his duties with tedious slow care and who watched Bayard constantly and covertly all the while he was in view.

Nor did Simon dismount even then. With his race's fine feeling for potential theatrics he drew himself up and arranged the limp folds of the duster, communicating by some means the histrionic moment to the horses so that they too flicked their glittering coats and tossed their leashed heads, and into Simon's wizened black face there came an expression indescribably majestical as he touched his hat brim with his whiphand. Bayard got in the carriage and Simon clucked to the horses, and the shade fell before the book-keeper's face, and the bystanders, halted to admire the momentary drama of the departure, fell behind.

There was something different in Simon's air today, however; in the very shape of his back and the angle of his hat: he appeared to be bursting with something momentous and ill-contained. But he withheld it for the time being, and at a dashing, restrained pace he drove among the tethered wagons about the square and swung into a broad street where what Bayard called paupers sped back and forth in automobiles, and withheld it until the town was behind them and they trotted on across burgeoning countryside cluttered still with gasoline-propelled paupers but at greater intervals, and his employer had settled back into that drowsing peace which the rhythmic clopping of the horses and the familiar changeful monotony of the land always gave him. Then Simon slowed to a more sedate pace and turned his head.

Simon's voice was not particularly robust nor resonant, yet somehow he could talk to Bayard without difficulty. Others must shout in order to penetrate that wall of deafness beyond which Bayard lived; yet Simon could and did hold long, rambling conversations with him in that monotonous, rather high singsong of his, particularly while in the carriage, the vibration of which helped Bayard's hearing a little.

"Mist' Bayard done got home," Simon remarked in a conversational tone.

Bayard returned from his region of drowsy abstraction and sat perfectly and furiously still while his heart went on, a little too fast and a little too lightly, cursing his grandson for a furious moment; sat so still that Simon looked back and found him gazing quietly out across the land. Simon raised his voice a little.

"He got offen de two oclock train," he continued. "Jumped off de wrong side and lit out th'ough de woods. Section hand seed 'im. Only he aint never come out home yit when I lef'. I thought he wuz wid you, maybe." Dust spun from beneath the horses' feet and moiled in a sluggish cloud behind them. Against the thickening hedgerows their shadow rushed in failing surges, with twinkling spokes and high-stepping legs in a futility of motion without progress. "Wouldn't even git off at de dee-po," Simon continued, with a kind of fretful exasperation. "De dee-po his own folks built. Jumpin' offen de bline side like a hobo. He never even had on no sojer-clothes," he added with frank injury. "Jes' a suit, lak a drummer er somethin'. And when I 'members dem shiny boots and dem light yeller pants and dat 'ere double-jinted backin'-up strop he wo' home las' year . . ." Simon turned and looked back again, sharply. "Cunnel, you reckon dem war folks is done somethin' ter him?"

"What do you mean?" Bayard demanded. "Is he lame?"

"I mean, him sneakin' into his own town. Sneakin' into de town his own gran'pappy built, on de ve'y railroad his own folks owns, jes' like he wuz trash. Dem foreign white folks done done somethin' ter him, er dey done sot dey po-lice after him. I kep' a-tellin' him when he fust went off to dat 'ere foreign war him and Mr Johnny neither never had no business at—"

"Drive on," Bayard said sharply . . . "Drive on, damn your black hide," he repeated.

Simon clucked to the horses and shook them to a swifter gait. The road went on between hedgerows parallelling them with the senseless terrific antics of their shadow. Beyond the bordering gums and locusts and massed vines, fields new-broken or being broken spread on toward patches of woodland newly green and splashed with dogwood and judas trees. Behind the laborious plows viscid shards of new-turned earth glinted damply in the sun.

This was upland country, lying in tilted slopes against the unbroken blue of the hills, but soon the road dropped sheerly into a valley of good broad fields richly somnolent in the levelling afternoon. This was Bayard Sartoris' land, and as they went on from time to time a negro lifted his hand from the plow handle in salute to the passing carriage. Then the road approached the railroad and crossed it, and a partridge and her brood of tiny dusty balls scuttered in the dust before them; and at last the house John Sartoris had built and rebuilt stood among locusts and oaks where mockingbirds were wont to sing.

There was a bed of salvia where that Yankee patrol had halted on that day long ago. Simon brought up here with a flourish and Bayard descended and Simon clucked to the team again and drove off down the drive, rolling his cigar to a freer angle, and took the road back to town.

Bayard stood for a moment before his house, but the white simplicity of it dreamed unbroken amid its ancient sunshot trees. Wistaria mounting one end of the veranda had bloomed and fallen, and a faint drift of shattered petals lay palely about the dark roots of it and about the roots of a rose trained onto the same frame. The rose was slowly but steadily killing the other vine, and it bloomed now thickly with buds no bigger than a thumbnail and blown flowers no larger than silver dollars, myriad, odorless and unpickable.

But the house itself was still and serenely benignant, and he mounted to the empty, colonnaded veranda and crossed it and entered the high spacious hallway. The house was silent, richly desolate of motion or any sound.

"Bayard."

The stairway with its white spindles and red carpet mounted in a tall slender curve into upper gloom. From the center of the ceiling hung a chandelier of crystal prisms and shades, fitted originally for candles but since wired for electricity; to the right of the entrance, beside folding doors opened upon a room emanating an atmosphere of dim and seldom violated stateliness and known as the parlor, stood a tall mirror filled with grave obscurity like a still pool of evening water. At the end of the hallway checkered sunlight fell in a long slant across the door and the world was drowsily monotonous without, and from somewhere beyond the bar of sunlight a voice rose and fell in a rapid preoccupied minor, like a chant. The words were not always distinguishable, but Bayard Sartoris could not hear them at all. He raised his voice again.

"Bayard."

The chanting ceased, and as he turned toward the stairs a tall mulatto woman appeared in the slanting sunlight without the back door and came sibilantly into the hall. Her faded blue garment was pinned up about her knees and it was darkly and irregularly blotched. Beneath it her shanks were straight and lean as the legs of a tall bird, and her bare feet were pale coffee splashes on the dark polished floor.

"Wuz you callin' somebody, Cunnel?" she said, raising her voice to penetrate his deafness. Bayard Sartoris paused with his hand on the walnut newel post and looked down at the woman's pleasant yellow face.

"Has anybody come in this afternoon?" he asked.

"Why, naw, suh," Elnora answered. "Dey aint nobody here a-tall, dat I knows about. Miss Jenny done gone to huh club-meetin' in town dis evenin'," she added. Bayard Sartoris stood with his foot raised to the step, staring down at her.

"Why in hell cant you niggers tell me the truth about things?" he raged suddenly. "Or not tell me anything at all?"

"Lawd, Cunnel, who'd be comin' out here, lessen you er Miss Jenny sont 'um?" But he had gone on, tramping furiously up the stairs. The woman looked after him, then she called to him: "Does you want Isom, er anything?" But he went on without looking back. Perhaps he had not heard her, and she stood and watched him out of sight. "He's gittin' old," she said to herself quietly, and she turned on her sibilant bare feet and returned down the hall whence she had come.

Bayard Sartoris stopped again in the upper hall. The western windows were closed with latticed blinds, through which sunlight seeped in pale dissolving bars that but served to increase the gloom. At the opposite end a tall door opened upon a shallow grilled balcony which offered the valley and the cradling semicircle of the eastern hills in panorama. On either side of this door was a narrow window set with leaded vari-colored panes that, with the bearer of them, constituted his mother's deathbed legacy to him, which John Sartoris' youngest sister had brought from Carolina in a straw-filled hamper in '69.

This was Virginia Du Pre, who came to them, two years a wife and seven years a widow at thirty—a slender woman with a delicate replica of the Sartoris nose and that expression of indomitable and utter weariness which all Southern women had learned to wear, bringing with her the clothing in which she stood and a wicker hamper filled with colored glass. It was she who told them of the manner of Bayard Sartoris' death prior to the second battle of Manassas. She had told the story many times since (at eighty she still told it, on occasions usually inopportune) and as she grew older the tale itself grew richer and richer, taking on a mellow splendor like wine; until what had been a hair-brained prank of two heedless and reckless boys wild with their own youth, was become a gallant and finely tragical focal-point to which the history of the race had been raised from out the old miasmic swamps of spiritual sloth by two angels valiantly and glamorously fallen and strayed, altering the course of human events and purging the souls of men.

That Carolina Bayard had been rather a handful, even for Sartorises. Not so much a black sheep as a nuisance all of whose qualities were positive and unpredictable. His were merry blue eyes, and his rather long hair fell in tawny curls about his temples. His high-colored face wore that expression of frank and high-hearted dulness which you visualize Richard First as wearing before he went crusading, and he once hunted his pack of fox hounds through a rustic tabernacle in which a Methodist revival was being conducted; and thirty minutes later (having caught the fox) he returned alone and rode his horse into the ensuing indignation meeting. In a spirit of fun purely: he believed too firmly in Providence, as all his actions clearly showed, to have any religious convictions at all. So when Fort Moultrie fell and the governor of South Carolina refused to surrender it, the Sartorises were privately a little glad, for now Bayard would have something to do.

In Virginia, as an A.D.C. of Jeb Stuart's, he found plenty to do. As the A.D.C. rather, for though Stuart had other aides, they were soldiers trying to win a war and needing sleep occasionally: Bayard Sartoris alone was willing, nay eager, to defer sleep and security to that time when monotony should return to the world. But now was a holiday without any restrictions whatever.

The war was also a godsend to Jeb Stuart, and shortly thereafter, against the dark and bloody obscurity of the northern Virginia campaigns, Jeb Stuart at thirty and Bayard Sartoris at twenty-three stood briefly like two flaming stars garlanded with Fame's burgeoning laurel and the myrtle and roses of Death, incalculable and sudden as meteors in General Pope's troubled military sky, thrusting upon him like an unwilling garment that notoriety which his skill as a soldier could never have won him. And still in a spirit of pure fun: neither Jeb Stuart nor Bayard Sartoris, as their actions clearly showed, had any political convictions involved at all.

Aunt Jenny told the story first shortly after she came to them. It was Christmas time and they sat before a hickory fire in the rebuilt library—Aunt Jenny with her sad resolute face and John Sartoris, bearded and hawklike, and his three children and a guest: a Scottish engineer whom John Sartoris had met in Mexico in '45 and who was now helping him to build his railway.

Work on the railroad had ceased for the holiday season and John Sartoris and his engineer had ridden in that dusk from the suspended railhead in the hills to the north, and they now sat after supper in the firelight. The sun had set ruddily, leaving the air brittle as thin glass with frost, and presently Joby came in with an armful of firewood. He put a fresh billet on the fire, and in the dry air the flames crackled and snapped, popping in fading embers outward upon the hearth.

"Chris'mus!" Joby exclaimed with the grave and simple pleasure of his race, prodding at the blazing logs with the Yankee musket-barrel which stood in the chimney corner until sparks swirled upward into the dark maw of the chimney like wild golden veils. "Year dat, chilluns?" John Sartoris' eldest daughter was twenty-two and would be married in June, Bayard was twenty, and the younger girl seventeen; and so Aunt Jenny for all her widowhood was one of the chillen too, to Joby. Then he replaced the musket-barrel in its niche and fired a long pine sliver at the hearth in order to light the candles. But Aunt Jenny stayed him, and he was gone—a shambling figure in an old formal coat too large for him, stooped and gray with age; and Aunt Jenny, speaking always of Jeb Stuart as Mister Stuart, told her story.

It had to do with an April evening, and coffee. Or the lack of it, rather; and Stuart's military family sat in scented darkness beneath a new moon, talking of ladies and dead pleasures and thinking of home. Away in the darkness horses moved invisibly with restful sounds, and bivouac fires fell to glowing points like spent fireflies, and somewhere neither near nor far the General's body servant touched a guitar in lingering random chords. Thus they sat in the poignance of spring and youth's immemorial sadness, forgetting travail and glory, remembering instead other Virginian evenings with fiddles above the myriad candles and slender grave measures picked out with light laughter and lighter feet, thinking *When will this be again? Shall I make one?* until they had talked themselves into a state of savage nostalgia and words grew shorter and shorter and less and less frequent. Then the General roused himself and brought them back by speaking of coffee, or its lack.

This talk of coffee began to end a short time later with a ride along midnight roads and then through woods black as pitch, where horses went at a walk and riders rode with sabre or musket at arm's length before them lest they be swept from their saddles by invisible boughs, and continued until the forest thinned with dawn-ghosts and the party of twenty was well within the Federal lines. Then dawn accomplished itself yet more and all efforts toward concealment were discarded and the horsemen dashed on and crashed through astonished picket-parties returning placidly to camp, and fatigue parties setting forth with picks and shovels and axes in the golden sunrise, and swept yelling up the knoll on which General Pope and his staff sat at breakfast al fresco.

Two men captured a fat staff-major, others pursued the fleeing officers for a short distance into the sanctuary of the woods, but most of them rushed on to Pope's private commissary tent and emerged presently from the cyclonic demolition of it, bearing sundry parcels. Stuart and the three officers with him halted their dancing mounts at the table and one of them swept up a huge blackened coffee pot and tendered it to the General, and while the enemy shouted and let off muskets among the trees, they toasted each other in sugarless and creamless scalding coffee, as with a loving cup.

"General Pope, Sir," Stuart said, bowing in his saddle to the captured officer. He drank and extended the pot.

"I'll drink it, Sir," the major replied, "and thank God he is not here to respond in person."

"I had remarked that he appeared to leave hurriedly," Stuart said. "A prior engagement, perhaps?"

"Yes, Sir. With General Halleck," the major agreed drily. "I am sorry we have him for an opponent instead of Lee."

"So am I, Sir," Stuart replied. "I like General Pope in a war." Bugles were shrilling among the trees far and near, sending the alarm in flying echoes from brigade to brigade lying about the forest, and drums were beating wildly to arms and erratic bursts of musketry surged and trickled along the scattered outposts like the dry clatter of an opening fan, for the name 'Stuart' speeding from picket to picket had peopled the blossoming peaceful woods with grey phantoms.

Stuart turned in his saddle and his men came up and sat their horses and watched him alertly, their spare eager faces like mirrors reflecting their leader's constant consuming flame. Then from the right there came something like a concerted volley, striking the coffee pot from Bayard Sartoris' hand and clipping and snapping viciously among the dappled branches above their heads.

"Be pleased to mount, Sir," Stuart said to the captured officer, and though his tone was exquisitely courteous all levity was gone from it. "Captain Wyatt, you have the heaviest mount: will you—?" The captain freed his stirrup and hauled the prisoner up behind him. "Forward!" the General said and whirled rowelling his bay, and with the thunderous coordination of a single centaur they swept down the knoll and crashed into the forest at the point from which the volley had come before it could be repeated. Blue-clad pigmy shapes plunged scattering before and beneath them, and they rushed on among trees vicious with minies like myriad bees. Stuart now carried his plumed hat in his hand and his long tawny locks, tossing to the rhythm of his speed, appeared as gallant flames smoking with the wild and self-consuming splendor of his daring.

Behind them and on one flank muskets still banged and popped at the flashing phantoms of their passing, and from brigade to brigade lying spaced about the jocund forest bugles shrilled their importunate alarms. Stuart bore gradually to the left, bringing all the uproar into his rear. The country became more open and they swung into column at the gallop. The captured major bounced and jolted behind Captain Wyatt, and the General reined his horse back beside the gallant black thundering along beneath its double burden.

"I am distressed to inconvenience you thus, Sir," he began with his exquisite courtesy. "If you will indicate the general location of your nearest horse picket I shall be most happy to capture a mount for you."

"Thank you, General," the major replied, "but majors can be replaced much easier than horses. I shall not trouble you."

"Just as you wish, Sir," Stuart agreed stiffly. He spurred on to the head of the column again. They now galloped along a faint trace that was once a road. It wound on between vernal palisades of undergrowth and they followed it at a rapid controlled gait and debouched suddenly upon a glade, and a squadron of Yankee cavalry reined back with shocked amazement, then hurled forward again.

Without a break in their speed Stuart whirled his party and plunged back into the forest. Pistol-balls were thinly about their heads and the flat tossing reports were trivial as snapping twigs above the converging thunder of hooves. Stuart swerved from the road and they crashed headlong through undergrowth. The Federal horsemen came yelling behind them and Stuart led his party in a tight circle and halted it panting in a dense copse and they heard the pursuit sweep past.

They pushed on and regained the road and retraced their former course, silently and utterly alert.

To the left the sound of the immediate pursuit crashed and died away. Then they cantered again. Presently the woods thickened and they were forced to slow to a trot, then to a walk. Although there was no more firing and the bugles too had ceased, into the silence, above the strong and rapid breathing of the horses and the sound of their own hearts in their ears, was a nameless something—a tenseness seeping like an invisible mist from tree to tree, filling the dewy morning woods with portent though birds flashed swooping from tree to tree, unaware or disregardful of it.

A gleam of white through the trees ahead; Stuart raised his hand and they halted and sat their horses, watching him quietly and holding their breaths with listening. Then the General advanced again and broke through the undergrowth into another glade and they followed, and before them rose the knoll with the deserted breakfast table and the rifled commissary tent. They trotted across the glade and halted at the table while the General scribbled hastily upon a scrap of paper. The glade dreamed quiet and empty of threat beneath the mounting golden day; laked within it lay a deep and abiding peace like golden wine; yet beneath this solitude and permeating it was that nameless and waiting portent, patient and brooding and sinister.

"Your sword, Sir," Stuart commanded, and the prisoner removed his weapon and Stuart took it and pinned his scribbled note to the table-top with it. The note read:

"General Stuart's compliments to General Pope, and he is sorry to have missed him again. He will call again tomorrow."

Stuart gathered his reins. "Forward," he said.

They descended the knoll and crossed the empty

glade and at an easy canter they took the road they had traversed that dawn—the road that led toward home. Stuart glanced back at his captive, at the gallant black with its double burden. "If you will direct us to the nearest cavalry picket I will provide you with a proper mount," he offered again.

"Will General Stuart, cavalry leader and General Lee's eyes, jeopardise his safety and that of his men and his cause in order to provide for the temporary comfort of a minor prisoner of his sword? This is not bravery: it is the rashness of a heedless and headstrong boy. There are fifteen thousand men within a radius of two miles of this point; even General Stuart cannot conquer that many, though they are Yankees, single-handed."

"Not for the prisoner, Sir," Stuart replied haughtily, "but for the officer suffering the fortune of war. No gentleman would do less."

"No gentleman has any business in this war," the major retorted. "There is no place for him here. He is an anachronism, like anchovies. General Stuart did not capture our anchovies," he added tauntingly. "Perhaps he will send Lee for them in person?"

"Anchovies," repeated Bayard Sartoris who galloped nearby, and he whirled his horse. Stuart shouted at him, but he lifted his reckless stubborn hand and flashed on; and as the General would have turned to follow a Yankee picket fired his musket from the roadside and darted into the woods, shouting the alarm. Immediately other muskets exploded on all sides and from the forest to the right came the sound of a considerable body put suddenly into motion, and behind them in the direction of the knoll, a volley crashed. A third officer spurred up and caught Stuart's bridle.

"Sir, Sir," he exclaimed. "What would you do?"

Stuart held his horse rearing, and another volley rang behind them, dribbling off into single scattered reports, crashed focalized again, and the noise to the right swelled nearer. "Let go, Allan," Stuart said. "He is my friend."

But the other clung on. "It is too late," he said. "Sartoris can only be killed: you would be captured."

"Forward, Sir, I beg," the captive major added. "What is one man, to a paladin out of romance?"

"Think of Lee, for God's sake, General!" the aide implored. "Forward!" he shouted to the troop, spurring his own horse and dragging the General's onward as a body of Federal horse burst from the woods behind them.

"And so," Aunt Jenny finished, "Mister Stuart went on and Bayard rode back after those anchovies, with all Pope's army shooting at him. He rode yelling 'Yaaaiiiih, Yaaaiiiih, come on, boys!' right up the knoll and jumped his horse over the breakfast table and rode it into the wrecked commissary tent, and a cook who was hidden under the mess stuck his arm out and shot Bayard in the back with a derringer.

"Mister Stuart fought his way out and got back home without losing but two men. He always spoke well of Bayard. He said he was a good officer and a fine cavalryman, but that he was too reckless."

They sat quietly for a time, in the firelight. The flames leaped and popped on the hearth and sparks soared in wild swirling plumes up the chimney, and Bayard Sartoris' brief career swept like a shooting star across the dark plain of their mutual remembering and suffering, lighting it with a transient glare like a soundless thunder-clap, leaving a sort of radiance when it died. The guest, the Scottish engineer, had sat quietly, listening. After a time he spoke.

"When he rode back, he was no actually cer-rtain there wer-re anchovies, was he?"

"The Yankee major said there were," Aunt Jenny replied.

"Ay." The Scotsman pondered again. "And did Mister-r Stuart retur-rn next day, as he said in's note?"

"He went back that afternoon," Aunt Jenny answered, "looking for Bayard." Ashes soft as rosy feathers shaled glowing onto the hearth, and faded to the softest gray. John Sartoris leaned forward into the firelight and punched at the blazing logs with the Yankee musket-barrel.

"That was the god-damdest army the world ever saw, I reckon," he said.

"Yes," Aunt Jenny agreed. "And Bayard was the god-damdest man in it."

"Yes," John Sartoris admitted soberly, "Bayard was wild." The Scotsman spoke again.

"This Mister-r Stuart, who said your brother was reckless: Who was he?"

"He was the cavalry general Jeb Stuart," Aunt Jenny answered. She brooded for a while upon the fire; her pale indomitable face held for a moment a tranquil tenderness. "He had a strange sense of humor," she said. "Nothing ever seemed quite so diverting to him as General Pope in his night-shirt." She dreamed once more on some far away place beyond the rosy battlements of the embers. "Poor man," she said. Then she said quietly: "I danced a valse with him in Baltimore in '58," and her voice was proud and still as banners in the dust.

. . . But the door was closed now, and what light passed through the colored panes was richly and solemnly hushed. To his left was his grandsons' room, the room in which his grandson's wife and her child had died last October. He stood beside this door for a moment, then he opened it quietly. The blinds were closed and the room was empty, and he stood on the dark threshold for a while. Then he slammed the door to and tramped on with that heavy-footed obliviousness of the deaf and entered his own bedroom and crashed the door behind him, as was his way of shutting doors.

He sat down and removed his shoes, the shoes that were made to his measure twice a year by a Saint Louis house, then he rose and went in his stockings to the window and looked down upon his saddlemare tethered to a mulberry tree in the back yard and a negro lad lean and fluid of movement as a hound, lounging richly static nearby. From the direction of the kitchen, invisible from this window, Elnora's endless minor ebbed and flowed unheard by him upon the lazy scene.

He crossed to his closet and drew therefrom a pair of scarred and stained riding-boots and stamped into them and took a cigar from the humidor on the table beside his huge walnut bed, and he stood for a time with the cigar clamped between his teeth, having forgotten to light it. Through the cloth of his pocket his hand touched the pipe there, and he took it out and laid it on top of his chest of drawers. Then he quitted the room and banged the door behind him and tramped heavily down the stairs and out the back door.

Isom waked easily and untethered the mare and held the stirrup. He mounted and remembered the cigar at last and fired it. Isom opened the gate into the lot and closed it, and trotted on ahead and opened the gate that let his master into the field beyond, and closed that one. Bayard rode on, trailing his pungent smoke.

Elnora stood barelegged in the center of the kitchen floor and soused her mop into the pail and thumped it on the floor again.

> *"Sinner riz fum de moaner's bench,*
> *Sinner jump to de penance bench;*
> *When de preacher ax'im whut de reason why,*
> *Says 'Preacher got de women jes' de same ez I'.*
> *Oh, Lawd, Oh Lawd!*
> *Dat's whut de matter wid de church today."*

2

Simon's destination was a huge brick house set well up onto the street. The lot had been the site of a fine old colonial house which rose among magnolias and oaks and flowering shrubs. But the house had burned and some of the trees had been felled to make room for an architectural garbling so imposingly terrific as to possess a kind of chaotic majesty. It was a monument to the frugality (and the mausoleum of the social aspirations of his women) of a hillman who had moved in from a small settlement called Frenchman's Bend and who, as Miss Jenny Du Pre put it, had built the handsomest house in Frenchman's Bend on the most beautiful lot in Jefferson. The hillman had stuck it out for two years during which his women-folks sat about the veranda all morning in lace-trimmed "boudoir caps" and spent the afternoons in colored silk riding through the streets in a new rubber-tired surrey; then the hillman sold his house to a newcomer in the town and took his women back to the country and doubtless set them to work again.

A number of motor cars ranked along the street lent a formally festive air to the place, and Simon with his tilted cigar stub wheeled up and drew rein and indulged in a brief colorful altercation with a negro sitting behind the wheel of a car parked before the hitching-block. "Dont block off no Sartoris ca'iage, black boy," he added when the other had moved the motor and permitted Simon access to the post. "Block off de commonality, ef you wants, but dont intervoke no equipage waitin' on Cunnel er Miss Jenny. Dey wont stand for it."

He descended and tethered the team, and his spirit mollified by the rebuke administered and laved with the beatitude of having gained his own way, Simon paused and examined the motor car with curiosity and no little superciliousness tinged faintly with envious awe, and spoke affably with its conductor. But not for long, for Simon had sisters in the Lord in this kitchen, and presently he let himself through the gate and followed the path that led around to the back. He could hear the party going on as he passed beneath the windows: that sustained unintelligible gabbling with which white ladies could surround themselves without effort and which they seemed to consider a necessary (or unavoidable) adjunct to having a good time. The fact that it was a card party would have seemed neither paradoxical nor astonishing to Simon, for time and much absorbing experience had taught him a fine tolerance of white folks' vagaries and for those of ladies of any color.

The hillman had built his house so close to the street that the greater part of the original lawn with its fine old trees lay behind it. There were once crepe-myrtle and syringa and lilac and jasmine bushes without order, and casual stumps and fences with honeysuckle overgrown; and after the original house had burned these had taken the place and made of its shaggy formality a mazed and scented jungle loved of mockingbirds and thrushes, where boys and girls lingered on spring and summer nights among drifting fireflies and quiring whip-poor-wills. Then the hillman had bought it and cut some of the trees in order to build his house near the street after the country fashion, and chopped out the jungle of bushes and vines and whitewashed the remaining trees and ran his barn- and hog- and chicken-lot fences between their ghostly trunks. He didn't remain long enough to learn of garages.

Some of the antiseptic desolation of his tenancy had faded now, and its present owner had set out more shrubbery—jasmine and mock-orange and verbena—with green iron tables and chairs beneath them and a pool and a tennis court; and Simon passed on with discreet assurance, and on a consonantless drone of female voices he rode into the kitchen where a thin woman in a funereal purple turban and poising a beaten biscuit heaped with a mayonnaise-impregnated something in a soiled kid glove, and a mountainous one in the stained apron of her calling and drinking melted ice-cream from a saucer, rolled their eyes at him.

"I seed him on de street yistiddy and he looked bad; he jes' didn't favor hisself," the visitor was saying as Simon entered, but they dropped the theme of conversation immediately and made him welcome.

"Ef it aint Brother Strother," they said in unison. "Come in, Brother Strother. How is you?"

"Po'ly, ladies; po'ly," Simon replied. He doffed his hat and unclamped his cigar and stowed it away in the hat-band. "I'se had a right smart mis'ry in de back. Is y'all kep' well?"

"Right well, I thank you, Brother Strother," the

visitor replied. Simon drew a chair up to the table, as he was bidden.

"Whut you gwine eat, Brother Strother?" the cook demanded hospitably. "Dey's party fixin's, and dey's some cole greens and a little sof' ice-cream lef' f'um dinner."

"I reckon I'll have a little ice-cream and some of dem greens, Sis' Rachel," Simon replied. "My teef aint much on party doin's no mo'." The cook rose with majestic deliberation and waddled across to a pantry and reached down a platter. She was one of the best cooks in Jefferson: no mistress dared protest against the social amenities of Rachel's kitchen.

"Ef you aint de beatin'es' man!" the first guest exclaimed. "Eatin' ice-cream at yo' age!"

"I been eatin' ice-cream sixty years," Simon said. "Whut reason I got fer quittin' now?"

"Dat's right, Brother Strother," the cook agreed, placing the dish before him. "Eat yo' ice-cream when you kin git it. Jes' a minute and I'll—Here, Meloney," she interrupted herself as a young light negress in a smart white apron and cap entered, bearing a tray of plates containing remnants of edible edifices copied from pictures in ladies' magazines and possessing neither volume nor nourishment, with which the party had been dulling its palates against supper, "git Brother Strother a bowl of dat 'ere ice-cream, honey."

The girl clashed the tray into the sink and rinsed a bowl at the water tap while Simon watched her with his still little eyes. She whipped the bowl through a towel with a fine show of derogatory carelessness, and with her nose at a supercilious angle she clattered on her high heels across the kitchen, still under Simon's unwinking regard, and slammed a door behind her. Then Simon turned his head again.

"Yes, ma'am," he repeated, "I been eatin' ice-cream too long to quit at my age."

"Dey wont no vittle hurt you ez long ez you kin stomach 'um," the cook agreed, raising her saucer to her lips again. The girl returned with her head still averted and set the bowl of viscid liquid before Simon who, under cover of this movement, dropped his hand on her thigh. The girl smacked him sharply on the back of his gray head with her flat palm.

"Miss Rachel, cant you make him keep his hands to hisself?"

"Aint you 'shamed," Rachel demanded, but without rancor. "A ole gray-head man like you, wid a family of grown chillen and one foot in de cemetery?"

"Hush yo' mouf, woman," Simon said placidly, spooning spinach into his soft ice-cream. "Aint dey erbout breakin' up in yonder yit?"

"I reckon dey's erbout to," the other guest answered, putting another laden biscuit into her mouth with a gesture of elegant gentility. "Seems like dey's talkin' louder."

"Den dey's started playin' again," Simon corrected. "Talkin' jes' eased off whiles dey et. Yes, suh, dey's started playin' again. Dat's white folks. Nigger aint got sense ernough to play cards wid all dat racket goin' on."

But they were breaking up. Miss Jenny Du Pre had just finished a story which left the three players at her table avoiding one another's eyes a little self-consciously, as was her way. Miss Jenny travelled very little, and in Pullman smokerooms not at all, and people wondered where she got her stories; who had told them to her. And she repeated them anywhere and at any time, choosing the wrong moment and the wrong audience with a cold and cheerful audacity. Young people liked her, and she was much in demand as a chaperone for picnic parties.

She now spoke across the room to the hostess. "I'm going home, Belle," she stated. "I think we are all tired of your party. I know I am." The hostess was a plump, youngish woman and her cleverly rouged face showed now an hysterical immersion that was almost repose, but when Miss Jenny broke into her consciousness with the imminence of departure this faded quickly, and her face resumed its familiar expression of strained and vague dissatisfaction and she protested conventionally but with a petulant sincerity, as a well-bred child might.

But Miss Jenny was adamant and she rose and her slender wrinkled hand brushed invisible crumbs from the bosom of her black silk dress. "If I stay any longer I'll miss Bayard's toddy time," she explained with her usual forthrightness. "Come on, Narcissa, and I'll drive you home."

"I have my car, thank you, Miss Jenny," the young woman to whom she spoke replied in a grave contralto, rising also; and the others rose with sibilant gathering motions above the petulant modulation of the hostess' protestings, and they drifted slowly into the hall and clotted again before mirrors, colorful and shrill. Miss Jenny pushed steadily toward the door.

"Come along, come along," she repeated. "Harry Mitchell wont want to run into all this gabble when he comes home from work."

"Then he can sit in the car out in the garage," the hostess rejoined sharply. "I do wish you wouldn't go. Miss Jenny, I dont think I'll ask you again."

But Miss Jenny only said "Goodbye, goodbye" with cold affability, and with her delicate replica of the Sartoris nose and that straight grenadier's back of hers which gave the pas for erectness to only one back in town—that of her nephew Bayard—she stood at the top of the steps, where Narcissa Benbow joined her, bringing with her like an odor that aura of grave and serene repose in which she dwelt. "Belle meant that, too," Miss Jenny said.

"Meant what, Miss Jenny?"

"About Harry . . . Now, where do you suppose that damn nigger went to?" They descended the steps and from the parked motors along the street came muffled starting explosions, and the two women traversed the brief flower-bordered walk to the curb. "Did you see which way my driver went?" Miss Jenny asked of the negro in the car next her carriage.

"He went to'ds de back, ma'am." The negro opened the door and slid his legs, clad in army o.d. and linoleum putties, to the ground. "I'll go git him."

"Thank you. Well, thank the Lord that's over," she added. "It's too bad folks haven't the sense or courage to send out invitations, then shut up the house and go away. All the fun of parties is in dressing and getting there, I think." Ladies came in steady shrill groups down the walk and got into various cars or departed on foot with bright, not-quite-musical calls to one another. The northward-swinging sun was down beyond Belle's house, and in the shadow of the house the soft silken shades of the women's clothes were hushed delicately until the wearers reached the edge of the shadow and passed into a level spotlight of sun, where they became delicately brilliant as the plumage of paroquets. Narcissa Benbow wore gray and her eyes were violet, and in her face was that serene repose of lilies.

"Not children's parties," she protested.

"I'm talking about parties, not about having a good

time," Miss Jenny retorted. "Speaking of children: What's the news from Horace?"

"Oh, hadn't I told you?" the other said quickly. "I had a wire yesterday. He landed in New York Wednesday. It was such a mixed-up sort of message, I never could understand what he was trying to tell me, except that he would have to stay in New York for a few days. It was over fifty words long."

"Was it a straight message?" Miss Jenny asked, and when the other said Yes, she added: "Horace must have got rich, like the soldiers say all the Y.M.C.A. did. If it has taught a man like him to make money, the war was a pretty good thing, after all."

"Miss Jenny! How can you talk that way, after John's—after—"

"Fiddlesticks," Miss Jenny said. "The war just gave John a good excuse to get himself killed. If it hadn't been that, it would have been some other way that would have been a bother to everybody around."

"Miss Jenny!"

"I know, my dear. I've lived with these bullheaded Sartorises for eighty years, and I'll never give a single ghost of 'em the satisfaction of shedding a tear over him. What did Horace's message say?"

"It was about something he was bringing home with him," the other answered, and her serene face filled with a sort of fond exasperation. "It was such an incoherent message . . . Horace never could say anything clearly from a distance." She mused again, gazing down the street with its tunnel of oaks and elms through which sunlight fell in spaced tiger bars. "Do you suppose he could have adopted a war-orphan?"

"War-orphan," repeated Miss Jenny. "More likely it's some war-orphan's mamma." Simon appeared at the corner of the house, wiping his mouth on the back of his hand, and came with shuffling celerity across the lawn. His cigar was not in view.

"No," the other said quickly, with grave concern. "You dont believe he would have done that? No, no, he wouldn't have. Horace wouldn't have done that. He never does anything without telling me about it first. He would have written: I know he would. You really dont think that sounds like Horace, do you?"

"Humph," Miss Jenny said through her high-bridged Norman nose, "an innocent like Horace straying with that trusting air of his among all those man-starved European wimmen? He wouldn't know it himself, until it was too late; especially in a foreign language. I bet in every town he was in over seven days his landlady or someone was keeping his supper warm on the stove when he was late, or holding sugar out on the other men to sweeten his coffee with. Horace was born to have some woman making a doormat of herself for him, just as some men are born cuckolded . . . How old are you?"

"I'm still twenty-six, Miss Jenny," the younger woman replied equably. Simon unhitched the team and stood at the carriage step in his Miss Jenny attitude. It differed from the bank one; in place of that leashed military imminence, it was now a gallant and slightly patronizing deference. Miss Jenny gazed at the still serenity of the younger woman's face.

"Why dont you get married, and let that baby look after himself for a while? Mark my words, it wont be six weeks before some other woman will be falling all over herself for the privilege of keeping his feet dry, and he wont even miss you."

"I promised mother," the other replied quietly and without offense . . . "I dont see why he couldn't have sent an intelligible message."

"Well." Miss Jenny turned to her carriage. "Maybe it's only an orphan, after all," she said with comfortless reassurance.

"I'll know soon, anyway," the other agreed, and she crossed to a small car at the curb and opened the door. Miss Jenny mounted with Simon's assistance, and Simon got in and gathered up the reins.

"Let us know when he does get home," she called as the carriage moved forward. "Drive out and get some more jasmine when you want it."

"Thank you. Goodbye."

"All right, Simon." The carriage moved on again, and again Simon waited until they were out of town to impart his news.

"Mist' Bayard done come home," he remarked, in his former conversational tone.

"Where is he?" Miss Jenny demanded immediately.

"He aint come out home yit," Simon answered. "I 'speck he went to de graveyard."

"Fiddlesticks," Miss Jenny snapped. "No Sartoris ever goes to the cemetery but one time . . . Does Colonel know he's home?"

"Yessum, I tole him, but he dont ack like he believed I wuz tellin' him de troof."

"You mean, nobody's seen him but you?"

"I aint seed him neither," Simon disclaimed. "Section han' seed him jump off de train and tole me—"

"You damn fool nigger!" Miss Jenny stormed. "And you went and blurted a fool thing like that to Bayard? Haven't you got any more sense than that?"

"Section han' seed him," Simon repeated stubbornly. "I reckon he knowed Mist' Bayard when he seed him."

"Well, where is he, then?"

"He mought have gone out to de graveyard," Simon suggested.

"Drive on!" Miss Jenny said sharply.

Miss Jenny found her nephew sitting with two bird-dogs in his library. The room was lined with book-cases containing rows of heavy legal tomes bound in dun calf and emanating an atmosphere of dusty and undisturbed meditation, and a miscellany of fiction of the historical-romantic school (all Dumas was there, and the steady progression of the volumes now constituted Bayard Sartoris' entire reading, and one volume lay always on the night-table beside his bed) and a collection of indiscriminate objects—small packets of seed, old rusted spurs and bits and harness buckles, brochures on animal and vegetable diseases, ornate tobacco containers which people had given him on various occasions and which he had never used, inexplicable bits of rock and desiccated roots and grain pods—all collected one at a time and for reasons which had long since escaped his mind, yet preserved just the same. The room contained an enormous closet with a padlocked door, and a big table littered with yet other casual objects, and a locked roll-top desk (keys and locks were an obsession with him) and a divan and three big leather chairs. This room was always referred to as the office, and Bayard Sartoris now sat in it with his hat on and still wearing his riding-boots, transferring bourbon whisky from a small compact keg to a silver-stoppered decanter while the two dogs watched him with majestic gravity.

One of the dogs was quite old and nearly blind. It spent most of the day lying in the sun in the back yard, or during the hot summer days, in the cool dusty obscurity beneath the kitchen floor. But toward the middle of the afternoon it went to the front of the house and waited there quietly until it heard the carriage coming up the drive, and when Bayard Sartoris had descended and passed into the house it returned to the back and waited again until Isom led the mare up to the back porch and Bayard Sartoris came out and mounted. Then together they spent the afternoon going quietly and unhurriedly about the grazing meadows and the planting or harvesting fields and the peaceful woodlands in their dreaming seasonal mutations—the man on his horse and the ticked setter gravely beside him, while the descending evening of their lives drew toward its peaceful close upon the kind land that had bred them both. The other dog was a two-year-old; his net was too hasty for the sedateness of their society overlong, and though at times he set forth with them or came quartering up, splashed and eager, from somewhere to join them in mid procession, he never remained very long but must presently dash away with lolling tongue and the tense delicate feathering of his tail in pursuit of the maddening elusive smells with which the world surrounded him and tempted him from beyond every thicket and copse and ravine.

Bayard Sartoris' boots were wet to the tops and the soles were rimmed with mud, and he bent in intense preoccupation above his keg and bottle under the sober curiosity of the two dogs. The keg was propped in another chair with the bung upward and he was siphoning the rich liquor delicately into the decanter through a slender rubber tube. Miss Jenny came straight through the house and entered the library with her black bonnet still perched on the exact top of her trim white head, and the two dogs looked up at her, the older with grave dignity, the younger one more quickly, tapping his tail on the floor with fawning diffidence. But Bayard Sartoris did not raise his head. Miss Jenny closed the door and gazed coldly at his boots.

"Your feet are wet," she stated. Still he didn't look up, but held the tube delicately in the bottle-neck, watching the clear brown liquor mount steadily in the decanter. At times Bayard Sartoris' deafness was very convenient, more convenient than actual, perhaps; but who could know this certainly? "You go upstairs and get those boots off," Miss Jenny commanded, coming into the room. "I'll fill the decanter."

But within the walled serene tower of his deafness his rapt imperturbability did not falter until the decanter was full and he pinched the tube shut and raised it to drain back into the keg. The older dog sat gravely before him, but the younger one had retreated beyond him, where it lay motionless and alert, its head on its crossed forepaws, watching Miss Jenny with one melting unwinking eye. Bayard Sartoris drew the tube from the keg and looked at his aunt for the first time. "What did you say?"

But Miss Jenny had returned and opened the door again and she shouted into the hall, eliciting an alarmed response from the kitchen, followed presently by Simon in the flesh. "Go up and get Colonel's slippers," she directed. When she turned into the room again neither her nephew nor the keg was visible, but from the open closet door there protruded the young dog's interested hind quarters and the tense feathering of his barometric tail; then Bayard Sartoris thrust the dog out of the closet with his foot and emerged himself and locked the door behind him.

"Has Simon come in yet?" he asked.

"He's coming right now," she answered. "I just called him. Sit down and get those wet boots off." At that moment Simon entered, with the slippers, and Bayard Sartoris sat obediently and Simon knelt and drew his boots off under Miss Jenny's martinet eye. "Are his socks dry?" she asked.

"No'm, dey aint wet," Simon answered. But she bent and felt them herself.

"Here," said her nephew testily, but Miss Jenny ran her hand over both his feet with bland imperturbability.

"Precious little fault of his, that they aint," she said across the topless wall of his deafness. "And then you have to come along with that fool yarn of yours about Mr Bayard."

"Section han' seed him," Simon repeated stubbornly, thrusting the slippers onto Bayard Sartoris' feet. "I aint never said I seed him." He stood up and rubbed his hands on his thighs.

Bayard Sartoris stamped his feet into the slippers. "Bring the toddy fixings, Simon." Then to his aunt, in a casual tone: "Simon says Bayard got off the train this afternoon." But Miss Jenny was storming at Simon again.

"Come back here and get these boots and set 'em behind the stove," she added. Simon returned and sidled swiftly to the hearth and gathered up the boots. "And take these dogs out of here, too," she said. "Thank the Lord Bayard hasn't thought about bringing his horse in here, too." Immediately the old dog came to his feet, and followed by the younger one's diffident alacrity, departed with that same assumed

deliberation with which both Bayard Sartoris and
Simon obeyed Miss Jenny's implacable will.

"Simon says—" Bayard Sartoris repeated.

"Simon says fiddlesticks," Miss Jenny snapped.
"Have you lived with Simon sixty years without
learning that he dont know the truth when he sees
it?" And she followed Simon from the room and on
to the kitchen, and while Simon's tall yellow
daughter bent over her biscuit-board and Simon
filled a glass pitcher with fresh water and sliced lemons and set them and a sugar bowl and two tall
glasses on a tray, Miss Jenny stood in the doorway
and curled what remained of Simon's grizzled hair to
tighter kinks yet. She had a fine command of language at all times, but when her ire was aroused she
soared without effort to sublime heights. Hers was a
forceful clarity and a colorful simplicity which De-
mosthenes would have envied and that even mules
comprehended and of whose intent the most obtuse
persons remained not long unawares; and beneath it
Simon's head bobbed lower and lower and the fine
assumption of detached preoccupation moulted like
feathers from about his defenseless self, until he
caught up the tray and ducked from the room. Miss
Jenny's voice followed him, descending easily with a
sweeping comprehensiveness that included a warning
and a suggestion for future conduct for Simon and
Elnora, and all their descendants actual and problem-
atical, for some years.

"And the next time," Miss Jenny finished, "you or
any section hand or brakeman or delivery boy either
sees or hears anything you think will be of interest to
Colonel, you tell me about it first: I'll do all the telling after that." She gave Elnora another glare for
good measure and returned to the library, where her

nephew was stirring sugar and water carefully in the two glasses.

Simon in a white jacket officiated as butler—doubled in brass, you might say, only it was not brass, but silver so fine that some of the spoon handles were worn now almost to paper thinness where fingers in their generations had held them; silver which Simon's grandfather Joby had buried on a time beneath the ammoniac barn floor while Simon, aged three in a single filthy garment, had looked on with a child's grave interest in the curious game.

An effluvium of his primary calling clung about him always, even when he was swept and garnished for church and a little shapeless in a discarded Prince Albert coat of Bayard Sartoris'; and his every advent into the dining room with dishes brought with him, and the easy attitudes into which he fell near the buffet while answering Miss Jenny's abrupt questions or while pursuing some fragmentary conversation which he and Bayard Sartoris had been engaged in earlier in the day disseminated, and his exits left behind him a faint nostalgia of the stables. But tonight he brought dishes in and set them down and scuttled immediately back to the kitchen: Simon realized that again he had talked too much.

Miss Jenny, with a shawl of white wool about her shoulders against the evening's coolness, was doing the talking tonight, immersing herself and her nephew in a wealth of trivialities—petty doings and sayings and gossip—a behavior which was not like Miss Jenny at all. She had opinions, and a pithy, savagely humorous way of putting them into words, but it was very seldom that she descended to gossip. Meanwhile Bayard Sartoris had shut himself up in that walled tower of his deafness and raised the drawbridge and clashed the portcullis to, where you never knew whether he heard you or no, while his corporeal self ate his supper steadily. Presently they had done and Miss Jenny rang the little silver bell beside her and Simon opened the door and received again the cold broadside of her glare, and shut the door and lurked behind it until they had left the room.

Bayard Sartoris lit his cigar in the library and Miss Jenny followed him there and drew her chair up to the table beneath the lamp and opened the daily Memphis newspaper. She enjoyed humanity in its more colorful mutations, preferring lively romance to the most impeccable of dun fact, so she took in the more lurid afternoon paper even though it was yesterday's when it reached her, and read with cold avidity accounts of arson and murder and violent dissolution and adultery; in good time and soon the American scene was to supply her with diversion in the form of bootleggers' wars, but this was not yet. Her nephew sat without the mellow downward pool of the lamp, with his feet braced against the corner of the hearth from which his boot-soles and the boot-soles of John Sartoris before him had long since worn the varnish away, puffing his cigar. He was not reading, and at intervals Miss Jenny glanced above her glasses and across the top of the paper toward him. Then she read again, and there was no sound in the room save the sporadic rustling of the page.

Presently he rose, with one of his sudden plunging movements, and Miss Jenny watched him while he crossed the room and passed through the door and banged it to behind him. She read on for a while longer, but her attention had followed the heavy tramp of his feet up the hall, and when this ceased she rose and laid the paper aside and followed him to the front door.

The moon had gotten up beyond the dark eastern wall of the hills and it lay without emphasis upon the valley, mounting like a child's balloon through the oaks and locusts along the drive. Bayard Sartoris sat with his feet on the veranda rail, in the moonlight. His cigar glowed at spaced intervals, and a shrill monotone of crickets rose from the immediate grass, and further away, from among the trees, a fairy-like piping of young frogs like endless silver small bubbles rising, and a thin sourceless odor of locust drifted up intangible as fading tobacco-wraiths, and from the rear of the house, up the dark hall, Elnora's voice floated in meaningless minor suspense.

Miss Jenny turned aside just within the door and groped about the yawning lesser obscurity of the mirror until she found her nephew's felt hat, and she carried it out to him and put it in his hand. "Dont sit out here too long, now. It aint summer yet."

He grunted indistinguishably, but he put the hat on and she turned away and went back to the library and finished the paper and folded it and laid it on the table. She snapped the light off and mounted the dark stairs to her room. The moon shone above the trees at this height and it fell in broad silver bars through the eastern windows.

Before turning up the light she crossed to the southern wall and raised a window there, upon the crickets and frogs and somewhere a mockingbird. Outside this window was a magnolia tree, but it was not to bloom yet, nor had the honeysuckle massed along the garden fence flowered. But this would be soon, and from here she could overlook the garden, could look down upon Cape jasmine and syringa and calycanthus where the moon lay upon their bronze

and yet unflowered sleep, and upon those other
shoots and graftings from Carolina and Virginian
gardens she had known as a girl.

Just beyond the corner from this window the
kitchen lay, and Elnora's voice welled in mellow
falling suspense. *All folks talkin' 'bout heaven aint
gwine dere* Elnora sang, and presently she and Simon
emerged into the moonlight and took the path to
Simon's house below the barn. Simon had fired his
cigar at last, and the evil smoke of it trailed behind
him, fading; but when they had gone it still seemed
that the rank pungency of it lingered yet within the
sound of the crickets and of the frogs upon the silver
air, mingled and blended inextricably with the dying
fall of Elnora's voice.

All folks talkin' 'bout heaven aint gwine dere

His cigar was cold, and he moved and dug a match
from his waistcoat and relit it and braced his feet
again upon the railing, and again the drifting sharpness of tobacco lay along the windless currents of the
silver air, straying and fading slowly amid locust-
breaths and the ceaseless fairy reiteration of crickets
and frogs. There was a mockingbird somewhere
down the valley, far away, and in a while another
sang from the magnolia at the corner of the garden
fence. An automobile passed along the smooth valley
road, slowed for the railway crossing, then sped on
again, and when the sound of it had died away, the
whistle of the nine-thirty train swelled from among
the hills.

Two long blasts with dissolving echoes, two short
following ones; but before it came in sight his cigar
was cold again, and he sat holding it in his old fingers
and watched the locomotive drag its string of yellow

windows up the valley and into the hills again, where after a time it whistled once more, arrogant and resonant and sad. John Sartoris had sat so on this veranda and watched his two trains emerge from the hills and traverse the valley into the hills again, with lights and smoke and bells and a noisy simulation of speed. But now his railway belonged to a syndicate and there were more than two trains on it, and they ran from Chicago to the Gulf, completing his dream, though John Sartoris himself slept these many years unawares perhaps amid martial cherubim, lapped in the useless vainglory of that Lord which his forefathers had imagined themselves in the rare periods of their metaphysical speculations.

Then his cigar was cold again and he sat and held it in his fingers and watched a tall shape emerge from the lilac bushes along the garden fence and across the patchy moonlight toward the veranda where he sat. His grandson wore no hat and he came on and mounted the steps and stood with the moonlight bringing the hawklike planes of his face into high relief while his grandfather sat holding his dead cigar and looked at him.

"Bayard, son?" old Bayard said. Young Bayard stood in the moonlight. His eyesockets were cavernous shadows.

"I tried to keep him from going up there on that goddam little popgun," he said at last with brooding savageness. Then he moved again and old Bayard lowered his feet from the rail, but his grandson only dragged a chair violently up beside him and flung himself into it. His motions were abrupt also, like his grandfather's, but controlled and flowing for all their violence.

"Why in hell didn't you let me know you were

coming?" old Bayard demanded. "What do you mean, straggling in here like this?"

"I didn't let anybody know." Young Bayard dug a cigarette from his pocket and raked a match on his shoe.

"What?"

"I didn't tell anybody I was coming," he repeated above the cupped match, raising his voice.

"Simon knew it. Do you inform nigger servants of your movements instead of your own gran'daddy?"

"Damn Simon, sir," young Bayard shouted. "Who set him to watching me?"

"Dont yell at me, boy," old Bayard shouted in turn. His grandson flung the match away and drew at the cigarette in deep troubled draughts. "Dont wake Jenny," old Bayard added more mildly, striking a match to his cold and spent cigar. "All right, are you?" Young Bayard saw that his hands were trembling.

"Here," he said, extending his hand. "Let me hold it. You're going to set your moustache on fire." But old Bayard repulsed him sharply and sucked stubbornly and impotently at the match in his unsteady fingers.

"I said, are you all right?" he repeated.

"Why not?" young Bayard snapped. "Takes damn near as big a fool to get hurt in a war as it does in peacetime. Damn fool, that's what it is." He drew at the cigarette again, then he hurled it not half consumed after the match. "There was one I had to lay for four days to catch him. Had to get Sibleigh in an old crate of a D.H. to suck him in for me. Wouldn't look at anything but cold meat, him and his skull and bones. Well, he got it. Stayed on him for six thousand feet, put a whole belt right into his cockpit. You could a covered 'em all with your hat. But the bastard just wouldn't burn." Young Bayard's voice rose again as he talked on. Locust drifted up in sweet gusts upon the air, and the crickets and frogs were clear and monotonous as pipes blown drowsily by an idiot boy. From her silver casement the moon looked down upon the valley dissolving in opaline tranquillity into the serene mysterious infinitude of the hills, and young Bayard's voice went on and on, recounting violence and speed and death.

"Hush," old Bayard said again. "You'll wake Jenny," and his grandson's voice sank obediently; but soon it rose again above the dark and stubborn struggling of his heart, and soon Miss Jenny emerged with her white woolen shawl over her night-dress and came and kissed him.

"I reckon you're all right," she said, "or you wouldn't be in such a bad humor. Tell us about Johnny."

"He was drunk," young Bayard answered harshly. "Or a fool. I tried to keep him from going up there, on that damn Camel. You couldn't see your hand, that morning. Air all full of hunks of cloud and any fool could a known that on their side it'd be full of Fokkers that could reach twenty-five thousand, and him on a damn Camel. But he was hell-bent on going up there, damn near to Lille. I couldn't keep him from it. He shot at me," young Bayard said. "I tried to head him off and drive him back, but he gave me a burst. He was already high as he could get, but they must have been five thousand feet above us when they spotted us. They flew all over him. Hemmed him up like a damn calf in a pen while one of them sat right on his tail until he took fire and jumped. Then they streaked for home." Locust drifted and drifted on the still air, and the silver rippling of the tree frogs. In the magnolia at the corner of the house the mockingbird sang. Down the valley another one replied.

"Streaked for home, with the rest of his gang," young Bayard said. "Him and his skull and bones. It was Ploeckner," he added, and for the moment his voice was still and untroubled with vindicated pride. "He was one of the best they had. Pupil of Richthofen's."

"Well, that's something," Miss Jenny agreed, stroking his head. Young Bayard brooded for a time.

"I tried to keep him from going up there on that goddam little popgun," he burst out again.

"What did you expect, after the way you raised him?" Miss Jenny demanded. "You're the oldest . . . You've been to the cemetery, haven't you?"

"Yessum," he answered quietly.

"What's that?" old Bayard demanded.

"That old fool Simon said that's where you were . . . You come on and eat your supper," she said briskly and firmly, entering his life again without a by-your-leave, taking up the snarled threads of it after her brisk and capable fashion, and he rose obediently.

"What's that?" old Bayard repeated.

"And you come on in, too." Miss Jenny swept him also into the orbit of her will as you gather a garment from a chair in passing. "Time you were in bed." They followed her to the kitchen and stood while she delved into the ice box and set food on the table, and a pitcher of milk, and drew a chair up.

"Fix him a toddy, Jenny," old Bayard suggested. But Miss Jenny vetoed this immediately.

"Milk's what he wants. I reckon he had to drink enough whisky during that war to last him for a while. Bayard used to never come home from his, without wanting to ride his horse up the front steps and into the house. Come on, now," and she drove old Bayard firmly out of the kitchen and up the stairs. "You go on to bed, you hear? Let him alone for a while." She saw his door shut and she entered young Bayard's room and prepared his bed, and after a while from her own room she heard him mount the stairs.

His room too was treacherously illumined by the moon, and the old familiarity of it was sharp with ghosts that neither slept nor waked. Without turning on the light he went and sat on the bed. Outside the windows the interminable crickets and frogs, as though the moon's rays were thin glass impacting among the trees and shrubs and shattering in brittle musical rain upon the ground, and above this and with a deep timbrous quality, the measured respirations of the pump in the electric plant beyond the barn.

He dug another cigarette from his pocket and lit it. But he took only two draughts before he flung it away. And then he sat quietly in the room which he and John had shared in the young masculine violence of their twinship, on the bed where he and his wife had lain the last night of his leave, the night before he went back to England and thence out to the Front again, where John already was. Beside him on the pillow the wild bronze flame of her hair was hushed now in the darkness, and she lay holding his arm with both hands against her breast while they talked quietly, soberly at last.

But he was not thinking of her then. When he thought of her who lay rigid in the dark beside him, holding his arm tightly between her breasts, it was only to be a little savagely ashamed of the heedless thing he had done to her. He was thinking of his

brother whom he had not seen in over a year, thinking that in a month they would see one another
again.

Nor was he thinking of her now, although the
walls held, like a withered flower in a casket, the fra-
grance of that magical chaos in which they had
briefly lived, tragic and transient as a blooming of
honeysuckle. He was thinking of his dead brother;
the spirit of their violent complementing days lay
like a dust everywhere in the room, obliterating the
scent of that other presence, stopping his breathing,
and he went to the window and flung the sash crashing upward and leaned there, gulping air into his
lungs like a man who has been submerged and who
still cannot believe that he has reached the surface
again.

Later, lying naked between the sheets, he waked
himself with his own groaning. The room was filled
now with a gray light, sourceless and chill, and he
turned his head and saw Miss Jenny, the woolen
shawl about her shoulders, sitting in a chair beside
the bed.

"What's the matter?" he said.

"That's what I want to know," Miss Jenny answered. "You make more noise than that water
pump."

"I want a drink."

Miss Jenny leaned forward and raised a glass from
the floor beside her and extended it to him. Bayard
had risen on his elbow. "I said a drink," he said.

"You drink this milk, boy," Miss Jenny commanded. "You think I'm going to sit up all night just
to feed you whisky? Drink it, now."

He took the glass and emptied it obediently and
lay back. Miss Jenny set the glass on the floor.

"What time is it?"

"Hush," she said. She laid her hand on his brow. "Go to sleep."

He rolled his head on the pillow, but he could not evade her hand.

"Get away," he said. "Let me alone."

"Hush," Miss Jenny said. "Go to sleep."

TWO

I

Simon said: "You aint never yit planted nothin' whar hit ought ter be planted." He sat on the bottom step, whetting the blade of his hoe with a file. Miss Jenny stood with her caller at the edge of the veranda above him, in a man's felt hat and heavy gloves. A pair of shears dangled below her waist, glinting in the morning sunlight.

"And whose business is that?" she demanded. "Yours, or Colonel's? Either one of you can loaf on this porch and tell me where a plant will grow best or look best, but if either of you ever grew as much as a weed out of the ground yourselves, I'd like to see it. I dont give two whoops in the bad place where you or Colonel either thinks a flower ought to be planted; I plant my flowers just exactly where I want 'em to be planted."

"And den dares 'um not ter come up," Simon added. "Dat's de way you en Isom gyardens. Thank de Lawd Isom aint got to make his livin' wid de sort of gyardenin' he learns in dat gyarden."

Simon wore a disreputable hat, of a fabric these many years anonymous. Miss Jenny stared coldly down at this hat.

"Isom made his living by being born black," Miss Jenny snapped. "Suppose you quit scraping at that

hoe and see if you cant dare some of the grass in that
salvia bed to come up."

"I got to git a aidge on dis curry-comb," Simon
said. "You go'n out dar to yo' gyarden: I'll git dis
bed cleaned up." He scraped steadily at the hoe-
blade.

"You've been at that long enough to find out that
you cant possibly wear that blade down to the
handle with just a file. You've been at it ever since
breakfast. I heard you. You get out there where
folks passing will think you're working, anyhow."

Simon groaned and spent a half minute laying the
file aside. He laid it on one step, then he picked it up
and moved it to another step. Then he laid it against
the step behind him. Then he ran his thumb along
the blade, examining it with morose hopefulness.

"Hit mought do now," he said. "But hit'll be jest
like weedin' wid a curry-c—"

"You try it, anyway," Miss Jenny said. "Maybe
the weeds'll think it's a hoe. You go give 'em a
chance to, anyhow."

"Ise gwine, Ise gwine," Simon answered pettishly,
rising and hobbling away. "You go'n see erbout dat
place o' yo'n; I'll 'tend to dis."

Miss Jenny and the caller descended the steps and
went on around the corner of the house.

"Why he'd rather sit there and rasp at that new
hoe with a file instead of grubbing up a dozen weeds
in that salvia bed, I cant see," Miss Jenny said. "But
he'll do it. He'd sit there and scrape at that hoe until
it looked like a saw blade, if I'd let him. Bayard
bought a lawn mower three or four years ago—God
knows what for—and turned it over to Simon. The
folks that made it guaranteed it for a year. They
didn't know Simon, though. I often thought, reading

about those devastations and things in the papers last year, what a good time Simon would have had in the war. He could have shown 'em things about devastation they never thought of. Isom!" she shouted.

They entered the garden and Miss Jenny paused at the gate. "You, Isom!"

This time there was a reply, and Miss Jenny went on with her caller and Isom lounged up from somewhere and clicked the gate behind him.

"Why didn't you—" Miss Jenny began, looking back over her shoulder, then she stopped and regarded Isom's suddenly military figure with brief, cold astonishment. For Isom now wore khaki, with a divisional emblem on his shoulder and a tarnished service stripe on his cuff. And it didn't fit him, or rather, it fitted him too well. His lean sixteen-year-old neck rose from the slovenly collar's limp, overlarge embrace, and an astonishing amount of his wrists was visible beneath the cuffs. The breeches bagged hopelessly into the unskillful wrapping of the putties which, with either a fine sense for the unique or a bland disregard of military usage, he had donned prior to his shoes, and the soiled overseas cap came down most regrettably on his bullet head.

"Where did you get those clothes?" Miss Jenny's shears dangled below her waist on a heavy black cord, glinting in the sun, and Miss Benbow in a white dress and a soft straw hat turned also and looked at him with a strange expression.

"Dey's Caspey's," Isom answered. "I jes' bor'd 'um."

"Caspey?" Miss Jenny repeated. "Is he home?"

"Yessum. He got in las' night on de nine-thirty."

"Last night, did he? Where is he now? Asleep, I reckon?"

"Yessum. Dat's whar he wuz when I lef' home."

"And I reckon that's how you borrowed his uniform," Miss Jenny said tartly. "Well, let him sleep this morning. Give him a day to get over the war. But if it made a fool out of him like it did Bayard, he'd better put that thing on again and go back to it. I'll declare, men cant seem to stand anything." She strode on, the other in her straight white dress followed.

"You are awfully hard on men, not to have a husband to worry with, Miss Jenny," she said. "Besides, you're judging all men by your Sartorises."

"They aint my Sartorises," Miss Jenny disclaimed promptly. "I just inherited 'em. But you just wait; you'll have one of your own to bother with soon; you just wait until Horace gets home, then see how long it takes him to get over it. Men cant seem to stand anything," she repeated. "Cant even stand helling around with no worry and no responsibility and no limit to all of the meanness they can think about wanting to do. Do you think a man could sit day after day and month after month in a house miles from anywhere and spend the time between casualty lists tearing up bedclothes and window curtains and table linen to make lint and watching sugar and flour and meat dwindling away and using pine knots for light because there aren't any candles and no candlesticks to put them in, if there were, and hiding in nigger cabins while drunken Yankee generals set fire to the house your great-great-grandfather built and you and all your folks were born in? Dont talk to me about men suffering in war." Miss Jenny snipped larkspur savagely. "Just you wait until Horace comes home; then you'll see. John at least had consideration enough, after he'd gone and gotten himself into something where he had no business, not to come back and worry everybody to death. But Bayard now, coming back in the middle of it and having everybody thinking he was settled down at last, teaching at that Memphis flying school, and then marrying that fool girl."

"Miss Jenny!"

"Well, I dont mean that, but she ought to've been spanked, hard. I know: didn't I do the same thing, myself? It was all that harness Bayard wore. Talk about men being taken in by a uniform!" Miss Jenny clipped larkspur. "Dragging me up there to the wedding, mind you, with a lot of rented swords and some of Bayard's pupils trying to drop roses into the street. I reckon some of 'em were not his pupils, because one of 'em finally did drop a few that missed the houses." Miss Jenny snipped larkspur savagely. "I had dinner with 'em one night. Sat in the hotel an hour until they finally came for me. Then we stopped at a delicatessen and Bayard and Caroline got out and went inside and came back with about a bushel of packages and dumped 'em into the car under my feet. That was the dinner I'd been invited to, mind you; there wasn't a sign of anything that looked or smelt like a stove in the whole place. I didn't offer to help 'em. I told Caroline I didn't know anything about that sort of house-keeping, because my folks were so old-fashioned they cooked food at our house.

"Then the others came in—some of Bayard's soldier friends, and a herd of other folks' wives, near as I could gather. Young women that ought to have been at home, seeing about supper, gabbling and screeching in that silly way young married women have when they're doing something they hope their husbands wouldn't like. They began to unwrap bottles—about a dozen, I reckon, and Bayard and Caroline came in with that silver I gave 'em and mono-grammed napkins and that delicatessen stuff that tasted like wet swamp grass, on paper plates. We ate it there, sitting on the floor or standing up or just wherever you happened to be.

"That was Caroline's idea of keeping house. She said they'd settle down when they got old. About thirty-five, I suppose she meant. Thin as a rail; there wouldn't have been much to spank. But she'd ought to've had it, just the same. Soon as she found out about the baby, she named it. Named it Bayard nine months before it was born and told everybody about it. Used to talk about it like it was her grandfather or something. Always saying Bayard wont let me do this or that or the other."

Miss Jenny continued to clip larkspur, the caller tall in a white dress beside her. The fine and huge simplicity of the house rose among its thickening trees, the garden lay in the sunlight bright with bloom, myriad with scent and with a drowsy hum-ming of bees—a steady golden sound, as of sunlight become audible—all the impalpable veil of the immediate, the familiar; just beyond it a girl with a bronze skirling of hair and a small, supple body in a constant epicene unrepose, a dynamic fixation like that of carven sexless figures caught in moments of action, striving, a mechanism all of whose members must move in performing the most trivial action, her wild hands not accusing but passionate still beyond the veil impalpable but sufficient.

Miss Jenny stooped over the bed of larkspur, her narrow back, though stooping, erect still, indomita-ble. A thrush flashed modestly across the bright air and into the magnolia tree in a dying parabola. "And then, when he had to go back to the war, of course he brought her down here and left her on my hands." The caller stood tall in her white dress, and Miss Jenny said: "No, I dont mean that." She snipped larkspur.

"Poor women," she said. "I reckon we do have to take our revenge wherever and whenever we can get it. Only she ought to've taken it out on Bayard."

"When she died," Narcissa said, "and he couldn't know about it; when he couldn't have come to her if he had? And you can say that?"

"Bayard love anybody, that cold brute?" Miss Jenny clipped larkspur. "He never cared a snap of his fingers for anybody in his life except Johnny." She snipped larkspur savagely. "Swelling around here like it was our fault, like we made 'em go to that war. And now he's got to have an automobile, got to go all the way to Memphis to buy one. An automobile in Bayard Sartoris' barn, mind you; him that wont even lend the bank's money to a man that owns one . . . Do you want some sweet peas?"

"Yes, please," the guest answered. Miss Jenny straightened up, then she stopped utterly still.

"Just look yonder, will you?" she said, pointing with her shears. "That's how they suffer from war, poor things." Beyond a frame of sweet peas Isom in his khaki strode solemnly back and forth. Upon his right shoulder was a hoe and on his face an expression of rapt absorption, and as he reversed at each end of his beat, he mumbled to himself in measured singsong. "You, Isom!" Miss Jenny shouted.

He halted in midstride, still at shoulder arms. "Ma'am?" he answered mildly. Miss Jenny continued to glare at him, and his military bearing faded and he lowered his piece and executed a sort of effacing movement within his martial shroud.

"Put that hoe down and bring that basket over here. That's the first time in your life you ever picked up a garden tool of your own free will. I wish I could discover the kind of uniform that would make you keep both hands on it; I'd certainly buy you one."

"Yessum."

"If you want to play soldier, you go off somewhere with Bayard and do it. I can raise flowers without any help from the army," she added, turning to her guest with her handful of larkspur. "And what are you laughing at?" she demanded sharply.

"You both looked so funny," the younger woman explained. "You looked so much more like a soldier than poor Isom, for all his uniform." She touched her eyes with her fingertips. "I'm sorry: please forgive me for laughing."

"Hmph," Miss Jenny sniffed. She put the larkspur into the basket and went on to the sweet pea frame and snipped again, viciously. The guest followed, as did Isom with the basket; and presently Miss Jenny was done with sweet peas and she moved on again with her train, pausing to cut a rose here and there, and stopped before a bed where tulips lifted their bright bells. She and Isom had guessed happily, this time; the various colors formed an orderly pattern.

"When we dug 'em up last fall," she told her guest, "I'd put a red one in Isom's right hand and a white one in his left, and then I'd say 'All right, Isom, give me the red one.' He'd never fail to hold out his left hand, and if I just looked at him long enough, he'd hold out both hands. 'Didn't I tell you to hold that red one in your right hand?' I'd say. 'Yessum, here 'tis.' And out would come his left hand again. 'That aint your right hand, stupid,' I'd say. 'Dat's de one you said wuz my right hand a while ago,' Mr Isom

says. Aint that so, nigger?" Miss Jenny glared at
Isom, who again performed his deprecatory effacing
movement behind the slow equanimity of his ivory
grin.

"Yessum, I 'speck it is."

"You'd better," Miss Jenny rejoined warningly.
"Now, how can anybody keep a decent garden, with
a fool like that? I expect every spring to find corn or
lespedeza coming up in the hyacinth beds or something." She examined the tulips again, weighing the
balanced colors one against another in her mind.
"No, you dont want any tulips," she decided briskly,
moving on.

"No, Miss Jenny," the guest agreed demurely.
They went on to the gate, and Miss Jenny stopped
again and took the basket from Isom.

"And you go home and take that thing off, you
hear?" she told Isom.

"Yessum."

"And I want to look out that window in a few
minutes and see you in the garden with that hoe
again," she added. "And I want to see both of your
right hands on it and I want to see it moving, too.
You hear me?"

"Yessum."

"And tell Caspey to be ready to go to work in the
morning. Even niggers that eat here have got to
work some." But Isom was gone, and they went on
and mounted the steps. "Dont he sound like that's exactly what he's going to do?" she confided as they
entered the hall. "He knows as well as I do that I
wont dare look out that window, after what I said.
Come in," she added, opening the parlor door.

This room was opened but seldom now, though in
John Sartoris' day it had been constantly in use. He
was always giving dinners, and balls too on occasion,

with the folding doors between it and the dining room thrown open and three negroes with stringed instruments ensconced on the stairway and all the candles burning. For with his frank love of pageantry, as well as his innate sociability, he liked to surround himself with an atmosphere of scent and delicate garments and food and music. He had lain also in this room in his grey regimentals and so brought to a conclusion the colorful, if not always untarnished, pageant of his own career; perhaps ghosts he knew greeted him there again and surrounded him as of old upon the jocund mellowness of his hearth.

But during Bayard's time it was less and less in use, and slowly and imperceptibly it lost its jovial but stately masculinity, becoming by mutual and unspoken agreement a place for his wife and his son John's wife and Miss Jenny to clean thoroughly twice a year and in which, preceded by a ritualistic unswaddling of brown holland, they entertained their more formal callers. This was its status up to the birth of his grandsons and the death of their parents, and it continued thus until his wife died. After that Miss Jenny bothered with formal callers but little and with the parlor not at all. She said it gave her the creeps.

And so it stayed closed nearly all the time and slowly acquired an atmosphere of solemn and macabre fustiness and was referred to as the Parlor with a capital P. Occasionally young Bayard or John would open the door and peer into solemn obscurity in which the shrouded furniture loomed with a sort of ghostly benignance, like albino mastodons. But they did not enter; already in their minds the room was associated with death, an idea which even the holly and tinsel of Christmas tide could not completely obscure. They were away at school by the time they reached party age, but even during vacations, though they had filled the house with the polite bedlam of their contemporaries, the room would be opened only on Christmas eve. And after they had gone to England in '16 it was opened twice a year to be cleaned after the ancient ritual that even Simon had inherited from his forefathers, and to have the piano tuned or when Miss Jenny and Narcissa Benbow spent a forenoon or afternoon there, and formally not at all.

The furniture loomed shapelessly in its dun shrouds; the piano alone was uncovered, and the younger woman drew the bench up and removed her hat and let it slip to the floor beside her. Miss Jenny set her basket down and from the gloom beside the piano she drew a straight, hard chair, uncovered also, and sat down and removed her felt hat from her trim white head. Light came through the open door, and faintly through the heavy maroon-and-lace curtains, but it only served to enhance the obscurity and render more shapeless the hooded anonymous furniture.

But behind these dun bulks and in all the corners of the room there waited, as actors stand within the wings beside the waiting stage, figures in crinoline and hooped muslin and silk; in stocks and flowing coats; in grey too, with crimson sashes and sabres in gallant sheathed repose—Jeb Stuart himself perhaps, on his glittering garlanded bay or with his sunny hair falling upon fine broadcloth beneath the mistletoe and holly boughs of Baltimore in '58. Miss Jenny sat with her uncompromising grenadier's back and held her hat upon her knees and fixed herself to look on.

Narcissa's white dress was pliant as light against the gloom and as serene, and her hands touched chords from the keyboard and drew them together and rolled the curtain back upon the scene.

In the kitchen Caspey was having breakfast while Simon his father, and Elnora his sister, and Isom his nephew (still wearing the uniform) watched him. He had been Simon's understudy in the stables and general handy-man about the place, doing all the work Simon managed, through the specious excuse of decrepitude, to slough off onto his shoulders and that Miss Jenny could devise for him and which he could not evade. Bayard Sartoris also employed him in the fields occasionally. Then the draft had got him and bore him to France and the St. Sulpice docks as one of a labor battalion, where he did what work corporals and sergeants managed to slough off onto his unmilitary shoulders and that white officers could devise for him and which he could not evade.

Thus all the labor about the place devolved upon Simon and Isom, but Miss Jenny kept Isom piddling about the garden so much of the time that Simon was soon as bitter against the War Lords as any professional Democrat. Meanwhile Caspey was working a little and trifling with continental life in its martial mutations rather to his future detriment, for at last the tumult died and the captains departed and left a vacuum filled with the usual bitter bickering of Armageddon's heirs-at-law; and Caspey returned to his native land a total loss, sociologically speaking, with a definite disinclination toward labor, honest or otherwise, and two honorable wounds incurred in a razor-hedged crap game. But return he did, to his father's querulous satisfaction and Elnora's and Isom's admiration, and he now sat in the kitchen, telling them about the war.

"I dont take nothin' f'um no white folks no mo'," he was saying. "War done changed all dat. If us colored folks is good enough to save France f'um de Germans, den us is good enough to have de same rights de Germans has. French folks thinks so, anyhow, and if America dont, dey's ways of learnin' 'um. Yes, suh, it wuz de colored soldier saved France and America bofe. Black regiments kilt mo' Germans dan all de white armies put together, let 'lone unloadin' steamboats all day long fer a dollar a day."

"War aint hurt dat big mouf o' yo'n, anyhow," Simon said.

"War unloosed de black man's mouf," Caspey corrected. "Give him de right to talk. Kill Germans, den do yo' oratin', dey tole us. Well, us done it."

"How many you kilt, Unc' Caspey?" Isom asked deferentially.

"I aint never bothered to count 'um up. Been times I kilt mo' in one mawnin' dan dey's folks on dis whole place. One time we wuz down in de cellar of a steamboat tied up to de bank, and one of dese submareens sailed up and stopped by de boat, and all de white officers run up on de bank and hid. Us boys didn't know dey wuz anything wrong 'twell folks started clambin' down de ladder. We never had no guns wid us at de time, so when we seed dem green legs comin' down de ladder we crope up to de een of de ladder, and as dey come down one of de boys would hit 'um over de haid wid a stick of wood an another would drag 'um outen de way and cut dey th'oat wid a razor. Dey wuz about thirty of 'um . . . Elnora, is dey any mo' of dat coffee lef'?"

"Sho," Simon murmured. Isom's eyes popped quietly and Elnora removed the coffee pot from the stove and refilled Caspey's cup.

Caspey drank coffee for a moment. "And another time me and a boy wuz gwine along a road. We got tired unloadin' steamboats all day long, so one day de Captain's dog-robber foun' whar he kep' dese here unloaded passes and he took a hanful of 'um, and me and him wuz on de road to town when a truck come along and de boy axed us did us want a lif'. He wuz a school boy, so he writ on three of de passes whenever we come to a place dat mought be M.P. invested, and we got along fine, ridin' about de country on dat private truck, 'twell one mawnin' we looked out whar de truck wuz and dey wuz a M.P. settin' on de seat whilst de truck boy wuz tryin' to explain to him. So we turned de other way and lit out walkin'. After dat we had to dodge de M.P. towns, 'case me and de other boy couldn't write on de passes.

"One day we wuz gwine along a road. It wuz a busted-up road and it didn't look much like M.P. country, but dey wuz some of 'um in de las' town us dodged, so we didn't know us wuz so close to whar de fightin' wuz gwine on 'twell we turned a corner onto a bridge and come right onto a whole regiment of Germans, swimmin' in de river. Dey seed us about de same time we seed dem and dived under de water, and me and de other boy grabbed up two machine guns settin' dar and we sot on de bridge rail, and ev'y time a German stuck his haid up to take a new breaf, us shot him. It wuz jes' like shootin' turkles in a slough. I reckon dey wuz clost to a hundred us kilt befo' de machine guns run dry. Dat's whut de Captain give me dis fer." He drew from his pocket a florid plated medal of Porto Rican origin, and Isom came quietly up to see it.

"Umumuh," Simon said. He sat with his hands on his knees, watching his son with rapt astonishment. Elnora came up to see also, with her arms daubed with flour.

"Whut does dey look like?" Elnora asked. "Like folks?"

"Dey's big," Caspey answered. "Sort of pink lookin' and about eight foot tall. Only folks in de whole American war dat could handle 'um wuz de colored regiments." Isom returned to his corner beside the woodbox.

"Aint you got some gyardenin' to do, boy?" Simon demanded of him.

"Naw, suh," Isom answered, his enraptured gaze still on his uncle. "Miss Jenny says us done caught up dis mawnin'."

"Well, dont you come whinin' to me when she jumps on you," Simon warned him. "Whar did you kill de nex' lot?" he asked his son.

"We didn't kill no mo' after dat," Caspey answered. "We decided dat wuz enough and dat we better leave de rest of 'um fer de boys dat wuz gittin' paid fer killin' 'um. We went on 'twell de road played out in a field. Dey wuz some ditches and ole wire fences and holes in de field, wid folks livin' in 'um. De folks wuz white American soldiers and dey egvised us to pick us out a hole and stay dere fer a while, if us wanted de peace and comfort of de war. So we picked out a dry hole and moved in. Dey wasn't nothin' to do all day long but lay in de shade and watch de air balloons and listen to de shootin' about fo' miles up de road. De white boys could write, so dey fixed up de passes and we took time

about gwine up to whar de army wuz and gittin'
grub. When de passes give out we found whar a
French army wid some cannons was livin' over in de
woods a ways, so we went over whar dey wuz and
got grub.

"Dat went on fer a long time, 'twell one day de
balloons wuz gone and de white boys says it wuz
time to move again. But we didn't see no use in
gwine nowhar else, so we stayed, me and de other
colored boy. Dat evenin' we went over to whar de
French army wuz fer some grub, but dey wuz gone
too. De boy wid me says maybe de Germans done
caught 'um, but we didn't know; hadn't heard no big
racket since yistiddy. So we went back to de cave.
Dey wasn't no grub, so we crawled in and went to
bed and slep' dat night, and early de nex' mawnin'
somebody come into de hole and tromped on us and
we woke up. It wuz one of dese army upliftin' ladies
huntin' German bayonets and belt-buckles. She says
'Who dat in here?' and de boy wid me says 'Us shock
troops.' So we got out, but we hadn't gone no piece
befo' here come a wagon-load of M.P.s. And de
passes had done give out."

"Whut you do den?" Simon asked. Isom's eyes
bulged quietly in the gloom behind the woodbox.

"Dey taken and shut us up in de jail-house fer a
while. But de war wuz mos' thu' and dey needed us
to load dem steamboats back up, so dey sont us to a
town name' Bres' . . . I dont take nothin' offen no
white man, M.P. er not," Caspey stated again. "Us
boys wuz in a room one night, shootin' dice. De
bugle had done already played de lights out tune, but
we wuz in de army, whar a man kin do whut he
wants as long as dey'll let him, so when de M.P.
come along and says 'Put out dat light,' one of de
boys says 'Come in here, and we'll put yo'n out.' Dey

wuz two of de M.P.s and dey kicked de do' in and started shootin', and somebody knocked de light over and we run. Dey foun' one of de M.P.s de nex' mawnin' widout nothin' to hole his collar on, and two of de boys wuz dead, too. But dey couldn't fin' who de rest of us wuz. And den we come home."

Caspey emptied his cup. "I dont take nothin' offen no white man no mo', lootenant ner captain ner M.P. War showed de white folks dey cant git along widout de colored man. Tromple him in de dust, but when de trouble bust loose, hit's 'Please, suh, Mr Colored Man; right dis way whar de bugle blowin', Mr Colored Man, you is de savior of de country.' And now de colored race gwine reap de benefits of de war, and dat soon."

"Sho," said Simon, impressed.

"Yes, suh. And de women, too. I got my white in France, and I'm gwine git it here, too."

"Lemme tell you somethin, nigger," Simon said, "de good Lawd done took keer of you fer a long time now, but He aint gwine bother wid you always."

"Den I reckon I'll git along widout Him," Caspey retorted. He rose and stretched. "Reckon I'll go down to de big road and ketch a ride into town. Gimme dem clothes, Isom."

Miss Jenny and her guest stood on the veranda when he passed along beside the house and crossed the lawn toward the drive.

"There goes your gardener," Narcissa said. Miss Jenny looked.

"That's Caspey," she corrected. "Now, where do you reckon he's headed? Town, I'll bet a dollar," she added, watching his lounging khaki back, by means of which he contrived in some way to disseminate a sort of lazy insolence. "You, Caspey!"

He slowed in passing Narcissa's car where it stood on the drive and examined it with a disparagement too lazy to sneer even, then slouched on without quickening his pace.

"You, Caspey!" Miss Jenny called, raising her voice. But he went steadily on down the drive, insolent and slouching and unhurried. "He heard me," she said ominously. "We'll see about this when he comes back. Who was the fool anyway, who thought of putting niggers into the same uniform with white men? Mr Vardaman knew better; he told those fools at Washington at the time that it wouldn't do. But politicians!" She invested the innocent word with an utter and blasting derogation. "If I ever get tired of associating with gentlefolks, I know what I'll do: I'll run for Congress . . . Listen at me! tiradin' again. I declare, at times I believe these Sartorises and all their possessions just set out to plague and annoy me. Thank the Lord, I wont have to live with 'em after I'm dead. I dont know where they'll be, but no Sartoris is going to stay in heaven any longer than he can help."

The other laughed. "You seem very sure of your own destination, Miss Jenny."

"Why shouldn't I be?" Miss Jenny demanded. "Haven't I been storing up crowns and harps for a long time?" She shaded her eyes with her hand and stared down the drive. Caspey had reached the gate and he now stood beside the road, waiting for a ride to town. "Dont you stop for him, you hear?" she said suddenly. "Why wont you stay for dinner?"

"No," the other answered. "I must get on home. Aunt Sally's not well today . . ." She stood for a moment in the sunlight, with her hat and the basket of flowers on her arm, musing. Then with a motion of sudden decision she drew a folded paper from the front of her dress.

"Got another one, did you?" Miss Jenny asked, watching her. "Lemme see it." She took the paper and opened it and stepped back out of the sun. Her nose glasses hung on a slender silk cord that rolled onto a spring in a small gold case pinned to her bosom. She snapped the cord out and set the glasses on her high-bridged nose, and behind them her gray eyes were cold and piercing as a surgeon's.

The paper was a single sheet of unmarked foolscap; it bore writing in a frank, open script that at first glance divulged no individuality whatever; a hand youthful yet at the same time so blandly and neatly unsecretive that presently you speculated a little.

"You did not answer mine of 25th. I did not expect you would yet. You will answer soon. I can wait. I will not harm you. I am square and honest as you will learn when our ways come together. I do not expect you to answer Yet. But you know where."

Miss Jenny refolded the paper with a gesture of fine and delicate distaste. "I'd burn this thing, if it wasn't the only thing we have to catch him with. I'll give it to Bayard tonight."

"No, no," the other protested quickly, extending her hand. "Please, not that. Let me have it and tear it up."

"It's our only evidence, child—this and the other one. We'll get a detective."

"No, no; please! I dont want anybody else to know about it. Please, Miss Jenny." She reached her hand again.

"You want to keep it," Miss Jenny accused coldly.

"Just like a young fool of a woman, to be flattered over a thing like this."

"I'll tear it up," the other repeated. "I would have sooner, but I wanted to tell someone. It—it—I thought I wouldn't feel so filthy, after I had shown it to someone else. Let me have it, please."

"Fiddlesticks. Why should you feel filthy? You haven't encouraged it, have you?"

"Please, Miss Jenny."

But Miss Jenny still held on to it. "Dont be a fool," she snapped. "How can this thing make you feel filthy? Any young woman is liable to get an anonymous letter. And a lot of 'em like it. We all are convinced that men feel that way about us, and we cant help but admire one that's got the courage to tell us about it, no matter who he is."

"If he'd just signed his name. I wouldn't mind who it was. But like this . . . Please, Miss Jenny."

"Dont be a fool," Miss Jenny repeated. "How can we find who it is, if you destroy the letter?"

"I dont want to know." Miss Jenny released the paper and Narcissa tore it into bits and cast them over the rail and rubbed her hands on her dress. "I dont want to know. I want to forget all about it."

"Nonsense. You're dying to know, right now. I bet you look at every man you pass and wonder if it's him. And as long as you dont do something about it, it'll go on. Get worse, probably. You better let me tell Bayard."

"No, no. I'd hate for him to know, to think that I would—might have . . . It's all right: I'll just burn them up after this, without opening them . . . I must really go."

"Of course: you'll throw 'em right into the stove," Miss Jenny agreed with cold irony. Narcissa descended the steps and Miss Jenny came forward into the sunlight again, letting her glasses snap back into the case. "It's your business, of course. But I'd not stand for it, if 'twas me. But then, I aint twenty-six years old . . . Well, come out again when you get another one, or you want some flowers."

"Yes, I will. Thank you for these."

"And let me know what you hear from Horace. Thank the Lord, it's just a glass-blowing machine, and not a war widow."

"Yes, I will. Goodbye." She went on through the dappled shade in her straight white dress and her basket of flowers stippled against it, and got in her car. The top was back and she put her hat on and started the engine, and looked back again and waved her hand. "Goodbye."

The negro had moved down the road, slowly, and had stopped again, and he was watching her covertly as she approached. As she passed him he looked full at her and she knew he was about to hail her. She opened the throttle and passed him with increasing speed and drove swiftly all the way to town, where she lived in a brick house among cedars on a hill.

She was arranging the larkspur in a dull lemon urn on the piano. Aunt Sally rocked steadily in her chair beside the window, clapping her feet flatly on the floor at each stroke. Her work basket sat on the window ledge between the gentle billowing of the curtains, her ebony walking-stick leaned beside it.

"And you were out there two hours," Aunt Sally said, "and you never saw him at all?"

"He wasn't there," Narcissa answered. "He's gone to Memphis."

Aunt Sally rocked steadily. "If I was them, I'd make him stay there. I wouldn't have that boy around me, blood or no blood . . . What did he go to Memphis for? I thought that aeroplane what-do-you-call-it was broke up."

"He went on business, I suppose."

"What business has he got in Memphis? Bayard Sartoris has got more sense than to turn over any business to that wild fool."

"I dont know," Narcissa answered, arranging the larkspur. "He'll be back soon, I suppose. You can ask him then."

"Me ask him? I never said two words to him in his life. And I dont want to. I been used to associating with gentlemen."

Narcissa broke some of the stems, arranging the blooms in a pattern. "What's he done that gentlemen dont do, Aunt Sally?"

"Why, jumping off water tanks and going up in balloons just to scare folks. You think I'd have that boy around me? I'd have him locked up in the insane asylum, if I was Bayard and Jenny."

"He didn't jump off of the tank. He just swung off of it on a rope and dived into the swimming pool. And it was John that went up in the balloon."

"That wasn't what I heard. I heard he jumped off that tank, across a whole line of freight cars and lumber piles and didn't miss the edge of the pool an inch."

"No he didn't. He swung on a rope from the top of a house and then dived into the pool. The rope was tied to the tank."

"Well, didn't he have to jump over a lot of lumber and freight cars? And couldn't he have broken his neck just as easy that way as jumping off the tank?"

"Yes," Narcissa said.

"There! What'd I tell you? And what was the use of it?"

"I dont know."

"Of course you dont know. That was the reason he did it." Aunt Sally rocked triumphantly for a while. Narcissa put the last touches to the blue pattern of the larkspur. A tortoise-shell cat bunched suddenly and silently in the window beside the work basket. Still crouching it blinked into the room for a moment, then it sank to the window sill and with arched neck fell to grooming its shoulder with a narrow pink tongue. Narcissa moved to the window and laid her hand on the creature's sleek back.

"And then, going up in that balloon, when . . ."

"That wasn't Bayard," Narcissa repeated. "That was John."

"That wasn't what I heard. I heard it was the other one and that Bayard and Jenny were both begging him with tears in their eyes not to do it. I heard . . ."

"Neither one of them were there. Bayard wasn't even there. It was John did it. He did it because the man that came with the balloon got sick. John went up in it so the country people wouldn't be disappointed. I was there."

"Stood there and let him do it, did you, when you could a telephoned Jenny or walked across the square to the bank and got Bayard? You stood there and never opened your mouth, did you?"

"Yes," Narcissa answered. Stood there beside Horace in the slow, intent ring of country people, watching the globe swelling and tugging at its ropes, watched John Sartoris in a faded flannel shirt and corduroy breeches, while the carnival man explained the rip-cord and the parachute to him; stood there feeling her breath going out faster than she could draw it in and watched the thing lurch into the air with John sitting on a frail trapeze bar swinging below it, with eyes she could not close, saw the balloon and people and all swirl slowly upward and then found herself clinging to Horace behind the shelter of a wagon, trying to get her breath.

He landed three miles away in a brier thicket and disengaged the parachute and regained the road and hailed a passing negro in a wagon. A mile from town they met old Bayard driving furiously in the carriage and the two vehicles stopped side by side in the road while old Bayard in the one exhausted the accumulate fury of his rage and in the other his grandson sat in his shredded clothes and on his scratched face that look of one who has gained for an instant a desire so fine that its escape was a purifaction, not a loss.

The next day, as Narcissa was passing a store, he emerged with that abrupt violence which he had in common with his brother, pulling up short to avoid a collision with her.

"Oh, ex—Why, hello," he said. Beneath the crisscrosses of tape his face was merry and wild, and his unruly hair was hatless. For a moment she gazed at him with wide, hopeless eyes, then she clapped her hand to her mouth and went swiftly on, almost running.

Then he was gone, with his brother, shut away by that foreign war as two noisy dogs are penned in a kennel far away, the bold, jolly face of him and his rough, shabby clothes. Miss Jenny gave her news of them, of the dull, dutiful letters they wrote home at sparse intervals; then he was dead. But far away beyond seas, and there was no body to be returned clumsily and tediously to earth, and so to her he seemed still to be laughing at that word as he had laughed at all the other mouthsounds that stood for repose, who had not waited for Time and its furniture to teach him that the end of wisdom is to dream high enough not to lose the dream in the seeking of it.

Aunt Sally rocked steadily in her chair.

"Well, it dont matter which one it was. One's bad as the other. But I reckon it aint their fault, raised like they were. Rotten spoiled, both of 'em. Lucy Sartoris wouldn't let anybody control 'em while she lived. If they'd been mine, now . . ." She rocked on. "Beat it out of 'em, I would. Raising two wild Indians like that. But those folks, thinking there wasn't anybody quite as good as a Sartoris. Even Lucy Cranston, come from as good people as there are in the state, acting like it was divine providence that let her marry one Sartoris and be the mother of two more. Pride, false pride."

She rocked steadily in her chair. Beneath Narcissa's hand the cat purred with lazy arrogance.

"It was a judgment on 'em, taking John instead of that other one. John at least tipped his hat to a lady on the street, but that other boy . . ." She rocked monotonously, clapping her feet flatly against the floor. "You better stay away from that boy. He'll be killing you same as he did that wife of his."

"At least, give me benefit of clergy first, Aunt Sally," Narcissa said. Beneath her hand, beneath the cat's sleek hide, muscles flowed suddenly into tight knots, like wire, and the animal's body seemed to elongate as it whipped from beneath her hand and flashed out of sight across the veranda.

"Oh," Narcissa said. Then she whirled and caught up Aunt Sally's stick and ran from the room.

"What—" Aunt Sally said. "You bring my stick back here," she said. She sat staring at the door, hearing the swift clatter of the other's heels in the hall and then on the veranda. She rose and leaned in the window. "You bring my stick here," she shouted.

Narcissa sped across the veranda and to the ground. In the canna bed the cat, crouching, jerked its head back and its yellow unwinking eyes. Narcissa rushed at it, raising the stick.

"Put it down!" she cried. "Drop it!" For another second the yellow eyes glared at her, then the animal ducked its head and lept in a long fluid bound, the bird between its jaws.

"Oh-h-h, damn you! Damn you! You—you Sartoris!" and she hurled the stick after the final tortoise flash as the cat whipped around the corner of the house.

"You get my stick and bring it right back this minute!" Aunt Sally shouted through the window.

She had seen Bayard once from a distance. He appeared as usual at the time—a lean figure in casual easy clothes unpressed and a little comfortably shabby, and with his air of smoldering abrupt violence. He and his brother had both had this, but Bayard's was a cold, arrogant sort of leashed violence, while in John it was a warmer thing, spontaneous and merry and wild. It was Bayard who had attached a rope to a ninety-foot water tank and, from the roof of an adjoining building, swung himself across the intervening fifty yards of piled lumber and freight cars and released the rope and dived into a narrow concrete swimming pool while upturned faces gaped and screamed—a cold nicety of judgment and unnecessary cruel skill; John who, one County Fair day, made the balloon ascension, the aeronaut having been stricken with ptomaine poisoning, that the county people might not be disappointed, and landed three miles away in a brier thicket, losing most of his clothing and skin and returning to town cheerful and babbling in the wagon of a passing negro.

But both of these were utterly beyond her; it was not in her nature to differentiate between motives whose results were the same, and on occasions when she had seen them conducting themselves as civilized beings, had been in the same polite room with them, she found herself watching them with shrinking and fearful curiosity, as she might have looked upon wild beasts with a temporary semblance of men and engaged in human activities, morally acknowledging the security of the cage but spiritually unreassured.

But she had not seen them often. They were either away at school, or if at home they passed their headlong days in the country, coming into town at rare intervals and then on horseback, in stained corduroy and flannel shirts. Yet rumors of their doings came in to her from time to time, causing always in her that shrinking, fascinated distaste, that blending of curiosity and dread, as if a raw wind had blown into that garden wherein she dwelt. Then they would be gone again, and she would think of them only to remember Horace and his fine and electric delicacy, and to thank her gods he was not as they.

Then the war, and she learned without any surprise whatever that they had gone to it. That was exactly what they would do, and her nature drowsed again beneath the serene belief that they had been removed from her life for good and always; to her the war had been brought about for the sole purpose of removing them from her life as noisy dogs are shut up in a kennel afar off. Thus her days. Man became amphibious and lived in mud and filth and died and was buried in it; the world looked on in hysterical amazement. But she, within her walled and windless garden, thought of them only with a sober and pointless pity, like a flower's exhalation, and like the flower, uncaring if the scent be sensed or not. She gave clothing and money to funds, and she knitted things also, but she did not know where Saloniki was and was incurious as to how Rheims or Przemysl were pronounced.

Then Horace departed, with his Snopes, and the war became abruptly personal. But it was still not the same war to which the Sartoris boys had gone; and soon she was readjusted again, with Aunt Sally Wyatt in the house and the steady unemphasis of their feminine days. She joined the Red Cross and various other welfare organizations, and she knitted harsh wool with intense brooding skill and performed other labors while other women talked of their menfolks into her grave receptivity.

There was a family of country people moved recently to town—a young man and his pregnant wife and two infant children. They abode in a rejuvenated rented cabin on the edge of town, where the woman did her own housework, while the man was employed by the local distributor for an oil company, laboring all day with a sort of eager fury of willingness and a desire to get on. He was a steady, exemplary sort, willing and unfailingly good-natured and reliable, so he was drafted immediately and denied exemption and ravished celeritously overseas. His family accompanied him to the station in an automobile supplied by the charity of an old lady of the town and they watched him out of their lives with that tearless uncomplaining gravity of primitive creatures. The Red Cross took charge of the family, but Narcissa Benbow adopted them. She was present when the baby was born two weeks later, she superintended the household—meals and clothing—until the woman was about again, and for the next twelve

months she wrote a monthly letter to the husband
and father who, having no particular aptitude for it
save his unflagging even temper and a ready willingness to do as he was told, was now a company cook
in the S.O.S.

This occupation too was just a grave centering of
her days; there was no hysteria in it, no conviction
that she was helping to slay the biblical Beast, or
laying up treasure in heaven. Horace was away too;
she was waiting for him to return, marking time, as it
were. Then Bayard Sartoris had returned home, with
a wife. She sensed the romantic glamor of this with
interest and grave approval, as of a dramatic scene,
but that was all; Bayard Sartoris went away again.
Narcissa met his wife now and then, and always with
a little curiosity, as though, voluntarily associating so
intimately with a Sartoris, she too must be an animal
with the temporary semblance of a human being.
There was no common ground between them, between Narcissa with her constancy, her serenity
which the other considered provincial and a little
dull, and the other with her sexless vivid unrepose
and the brittle daring of her speech and actions.

She had learned of John Sartoris' death without
any emotion whatever except a faint sense of vindication, a sort of I-told-you-so feeling, which recurred (blended now with a sense of pitying
outrage, blaming this too on Bayard) when Bayard's
wife died in childbirth in October of the same year,
even though she stood with old Bayard's deaf and arrogant back and Miss Jenny's trim indomitability
amid sad trees and streaming marble shapes beneath a
dissolving afternoon. Then November, and bells and
whistles and revolvers. Horace would be coming
home soon now, she thought at the time. Before
Christmas, perhaps. But before he did so she had seen

Bayard once on the street, and later, while she and Miss Jenny sat in Miss Jenny's dim parlor one morning, he came unexpectedly to the door and stood there looking at her with his bleak and brooding gaze.

"It's Bayard," Miss Jenny said. "Come in here and speak to Narcissa, sonny."

He said Hello and she turned on the piano bench, again with that feeling of curiosity and dread. "Who is it?" he said, and he came into the room, bringing with him like a raw wind that cold leashed violence which she remembered.

"It's Narcissa Benbow," Miss Jenny repeated testily. "Go on and speak to her and stop acting like you dont know who she is."

Narcissa gave him her hand and he stood holding it, but he was not looking at her. She withdrew her hand, and he glanced at her again, then away, and he loomed above them and stood rubbing his hand through his hair.

"I want a drink," he said. "I cant find the key to the desk."

"Stop and talk to us a few minutes, and you can have one."

He stood for a moment above them, then he moved abruptly and before Miss Jenny could speak he had dragged the holland envelope from another chair.

"Let that alone, you Indian!" Miss Jenny exclaimed. She rose. "Here, take my chair, if you're too weak to stand up any longer. I'll be back in a minute," she added to Narcissa. "I'll have to get my keys."

He sat laxly in the chair, rubbing his hand through his hair, his gaze brooding somewhere about his booted feet. Narcissa sat utterly quiet, watching him with that blending of shrinking and fascination. She said at last:

"I am so sorry about John and your wife. I asked Miss Jenny to tell you when she wrote . . ."

He sat rubbing his head slowly, in the brooding violence of his temporary repose.

"You aren't married yourself, are you?" he asked. She sat quietly, watching him. "Ought to try it," he added. "Everybody ought to get married once, like everybody ought to go to one war."

Miss Jenny returned with the keys, and he got his long abrupt body erect and left them. After that day, she called on Miss Jenny only when she was sure he was not at home.

2

It was a week before Caspey returned home. In the meantime young Bayard had driven out from Memphis in his car. Memphis was seventy-five miles away and the trip had taken an hour and forty minutes because some of the road was narrow clay country road. The car was long and low and gray; the four-cylinder engine had sixteen valves and eight spark-plugs, and the people had guaranteed that it would run eighty miles an hour, although there was a strip of paper pasted to the windshield, to which he paid no attention whatever, asking him in red letters not to do so for the first five hundred miles.

Miss Jenny was frankly interested: she must get in and sit in it for a while; and though Simon affected to pay it but the briefest derogatory notice, Isom circled quietly about it with an utter and yearning admiration. But old Bayard just looked down at the long, dusty thing from his chair on the veranda, and grunted.

He would not descend to examine it, even, despite Miss Jenny's insistence, and he sat with his feet on the rail and watched Bayard slide in under the wheel and drive slowly off with Miss Jenny beside him; watched them glide noiselessly down the drive and saw the car pass out of sight down the valley. Presently above the trees a cloud of dust rose into the azure afternoon and hung rosily in the sun, and a sound as of leashed thunder died muttering behind it, but this had no significance for him. Isom squatted below him on the steps.

It had no significance even when they returned in twenty minutes; he did not even see the car until it had entered the gate and was swooping up the drive and came to a stop almost in its former tracks. Miss Jenny had no hat, and she was holding her hair in both hands, and when the car stopped she sat for a moment so, then she drew a long breath.

"I wish I smoked cigarettes," she said, and then: "Is that as fast as it'll go?"

"How fer y'all been, Miss Jenny?" Isom asked, rising and circling the car again with his diffident yearning. Miss Jenny opened the door and got out a little stiffly, but her voice was clear as a girl's and her eyes were shining and her dry old cheeks were flushed.

"We've been to town," she answered proudly. Town was four miles away.

After that the significance grew slowly. He received intimations of it from various sources. But because of his deafness, these intimations came slowly since they must come directly to him and not through overheard talk. The actual evidence, the convincing evidence, came from old man Falls. Eight or ten times a year he walked in from the county farm, always stopping in at the bank. Twice a year old Bayard bought him a complete outfit of clothing, and on the other occasions he had always for him a present of tobacco and a small sack of peppermint candy, of which the old fellow was inordinately fond. He would never take money.

Old Bayard's office was also the directors' room. It was a large room containing a long table aligned with chairs, and a tall cabinet in which blank banking forms were kept, and old Bayard's roll-top desk and swivel chair, and a sofa on which he napped occasionally in the hot afternoons. His desk, like the one at home, was cluttered with an astonishing variety of objects which had no relation to the banking business whatever, and the mantel above the fireplace bore yet more objects of an agricultural nature, as well as a dusty assortment of pipes and three or four jars of tobacco which furnished solace for all the banking force and for a respectable portion of the bank's pipe-smoking clientele. Weather permitting, old Bayard spent most of the day sitting in a tilted chair in the bank door, and when these patrons found him there, they would pass on back to the office and fill their pipes. It was a sort of unspoken convention not to take more than a pipeful at a time.

It was to this room that they would retire on old man Falls' visits, and here they would sit (they were both deaf) and shout at one another for half an hour or so, about John Sartoris and crops. You could hear them plainly from the street and through the wall of the store on either side. Old man Falls' eyes were blue and innocent as a boy's and his first act after he and old Bayard were seated, was to open Bayard's parcel and take from it a plug of chewing tobacco, cut off a chew and put it in his mouth, replace the plug and wrap and tie the parcel neatly again. He never cut the string, but always untied the tedious knot with his stiff, gnarled fingers.

And he sat now in his clean, faded overalls, with the small parcel on his knees, telling Bayard about the automobile that had passed him that morning on the road. Everyone had seen or heard of young Bayard's low gray car, but old man Falls was the first to tell his grandfather how he drove it. Old Bayard sat utterly still, watching the other with his fierce old eyes until he had finished.

"Are you sure who it was?" he asked.

"Hit passed me too fast for me to tell whether they was anybody in hit a-tall or not. I asked when I fetched town who 'twas. Seems like ever'body knows how fast he runs hit except you."

Old Bayard sat quietly for a time. He raised his voice:

"Byron."

The door opened quietly and the book-keeper, Snopes, entered—a thin, youngish man with hairy hands and covert close eyes that looked always as though he were just blinking them, though you never saw them closed.

"Yes, sir, Colonel," he said in a slow, nasal voice without inflection.

" 'Phone out to my house and tell my grandson not to touch that car until I come home."

"Yes, sir, Colonel." And he was gone as silently as he entered.

Old Bayard slammed around in his swivel chair again and old man Falls leaned forward, peering at his face.

"What's that 'ere wen you got on yo' face, Bayard?" he asked.

"What?" Bayard demanded, then he raised his hand to a small bump which the suffusion of his face had brought into white relief. "Here? I dont know what it is. It's been there about a week, but I dont reckon it's anything."

"Is it gittin' bigger?" the other asked. He rose and laid his parcel down and extended his hand. Old Bayard drew his head away.

"It's nothing," he repeated testily. "Let it alone." But old man Falls put the other's hand aside and touched the place with his fingers.

"H'm," he said. "Hard's a rock. Hit'll git bigger, too. I'll watch hit, and when hit's right, I'll take hit off. Hit aint ripe, yit." The book-keeper appeared suddenly and without noise beside them.

"Yo' cook says him and Miss Jenny is off car-ridin' somewheres. I left yo' message."

"Jenny's with him, you say?"

"That's what yo' cook says," the book-keeper repeated in his inflectionless voice.

"Well. All right."

The book-keeper withdrew and old man Falls picked up his parcel. "I'll be gittin' on too," he said. "I'll come in next week and take a look at hit. You better let hit alone till I git back." He followed the book-keeper from the room, and presently old Bayard rose and stalked through the lobby and tilted his chair in the door again.

That afternoon when he arrived home, the car was not in sight, nor did his aunt answer his call. He mounted to his room and put on his riding-boots and lit a cigar, but when he looked down from his window into the back yard, neither Isom nor the saddled mare was visible. He tramped down the stairs and on through the house and entered the kitchen, and there Caspey sat, eating and talking to Isom and Elnora.

"And one mo' time me and another boy—" Caspey was saying. Then Isom saw Bayard, and rose from his seat in the woodbox corner and his eyes rolled whitely in his bullet head. Elnora paused also with her broom, but Caspey turned his head without rising, and still chewing steadily he blinked his eyes at Bayard in the door.

"I sent you word a week ago to come on out here at once, or not to come at all," Bayard said. "Did you get it?" Caspey mumbled something, still chewing, and old Bayard came into the room. "Get up from there and saddle my horse."

Caspey turned his back deliberately and raised his glass of buttermilk from the table. "Git on, Caspey," Elnora hissed at him.

"I aint workin' here," he answered, just beneath Bayard's deafness. He turned to Isom. "Whyn't you go'n git his hoss fer him? Aint you workin' here?"

"Caspey, fer Lawd's sake!" Elnora implored. "Yes, suh, Cunnel; he's gwine," she said loudly.

"Who, me?" Caspey said. "Does I look like it?" He raised the glass steadily to his mouth, then Bayard moved again and Caspey lost his nerve and rose quickly before the other reached him, and crossed the kitchen toward the door, but with sullen insolence in the very shape of his back. As he fumbled with the door Bayard overtook him.

"Are you going to saddle that mare?" he demanded.

"Aint gwine skip it, big boy," Caspey answered, just below Bayard's deafness.

"What?"

"Oh, Lawd, Caspey!" Elnora moaned. Isom crouched into his corner. Caspey raised his eyes swiftly to Bayard's face and opened the screen door.

"I says, I aint gwine skip it," he repeated, raising his voice. Simon stood at the foot of the steps, the setter beside him, gaping his toothless mouth up at them, and old Bayard reached a stick of stove wood from the box at his hand and knocked Caspey through the door and down the steps at his father's feet.

"Now, you go saddle that mare," he said.

Simon helped his son to rise and led him, a little unsteadily, toward the barn and out of earshot, while the setter watched them, gravely interested. "I kep' tellin' you dem new-fangled war notions of yo'n wa'n't gwine ter work on dis place," he said angrily. "And you better thank de Lawd fer makin' yo' haid hard ez it is. You go'n and git dat mare, en save dat nigger freedom talk fer town-folks: dey mought stomach it. Whut us niggers want ter be free fer, anyhow? Aint we got ez many white folks now ez we kin suppo't?"

━━➤

That night at supper, old Bayard looked at his grandson across the roast of mutton. "Will Falls told me you passed him on the Poor House hill running forty miles an hour today."

"Forty fiddlesticks," Miss Jenny said promptly, "it was fifty-four. I was watching the—what do you call it, Bayard? speedometer."

Old Bayard sat with his head bent a little, watching his hands trembling on the carving knife and fork; hearing beneath the napkin tucked into his waistcoat, his heart a little too light and a little too fast; feeling Miss Jenny's eyes upon him.

"Bayard," she said sharply. "What's that on your face?" He rose so suddenly at his place that his chair tipped over backward with a crash, and he tramped blindly from the room with his trembling hands and the light swift thudding of his heart.

3

"I know what you want me to do," Miss Jenny told old Bayard across her newspaper. "You want me to let my housekeeping go to the dogs and spend all my time in that car, that's what you want. Well, I'm not going to do it. I dont mind riding with him now and then, but I've got too much to do with my time to spend it keeping him from running that car fast. Neck, too," she added. She rattled the paper crisply.

She said: "Besides, you aint foolish enough to believe he'll drive slow just because there's somebody with him, are you? If you do think so, you'd better send Simon along. Lord knows Simon can spare the time. Since you quit using the carriage, if he does anything at all, I dont know it." She read the paper again.

Old Bayard's cigar smoked in his fingers.

"I might send Isom," he said.

Miss Jenny's paper rattled sharply and she stared at her nephew for a long moment. "God in heaven, man, why dont you put a block and chain on him and have done with it?"

"Well, didn't you suggest sending Simon with him, yourself? Simon has his work to do, but all Isom ever does is saddle my horse once a day, and I can do that myself."

"I was trying to be ironical," Miss Jenny said. "God knows, I should have learned better by this time. But if you've got to invent something new for the niggers to do, you let it be Simon. I need Isom to

keep a roof over your head and food on the table."
She rattled the paper. "Why dont you come right out
and tell him not to drive fast? A man that has to
spend eight hours a day sitting in a chair in that bank
door ought not to have to spend the rest of the afternoon helling around the country in an automobile if
he dont want to."

"Do you think it would do any good to ask him?
There was never a damned one of 'em ever paid any
attention to my wishes yet."

"Ask the devil," Miss Jenny said. "Who said anything about ask? Tell him not to. Tell him that if
you hear again of his going fast in it, that you'll frail
the life out of him. I believe anyway that you like to
ride in that car, only you wont admit it, and you just
dont want him to ride in it when you cant go too."
But old Bayard had slammed his feet to the floor and
risen, and he tramped heavily from the room.

Instead of mounting the stairs, however, Miss
Jenny heard his footsteps die away down the hall,
and presently she rose and followed to the back
porch, where he stood in the darkness there. The
night was dark, myriad with drifting odors of the
spring and with insects. Dark against lesser dark, the
barn loomed upon the sky.

"He hasn't come yet," she said impatiently,
touching his arm. "I could have told you. Go on up
and go to bed, now; dont you know he'll let you
know when he comes in? You're going to think him
into a ditch somewhere, with these fool notions of
yours." Then more gently: "You're too childish
about that car. It's no more dangerous at night than it
is in daylight. Come on, now."

He shook her hand off, but he turned obediently
and entered the house. This time he mounted the
stairs and she could hear him in his bedroom, thump-

ing about. Presently he ceased slamming doors and drawers and lay beneath the reading lamp with his Dumas, and he lay reading quietly. After a time the door opened and young Bayard entered and came into the radius of the light with his bleak eyes.

His grandfather did not remark his presence and he touched old Bayard's arm. Then old Bayard looked up, and when he did so young Bayard turned and quitted the room.

After the shades on the windows were drawn at three o'clock old Bayard retired to his office to wait until his grandson came for him. In the front of the bank the cashier and the book-keeper could hear him clattering and banging around. The cashier paused, a stack of silver clipped neatly in his fingers.

"Hear 'im?" he said. "Something on his mind here, lately. Used to be he was quiet as a mouse back there until they come for him, but last few weeks he tromples and thumps around back there like he was fighting hornets."

The book-keeper said nothing. The cashier set the stack of silver aside, built up another one.

"Something on his mind, lately. That examiner must a put a bug in his ear, I reckon."

The book-keeper said nothing. He swung the adding machine to his desk and clicked the lever over. In the back room old Bayard moved audibly about. The cashier stacked the remaining silver neatly and rolled a cigarette. The book-keeper bent above the steady clicking of the adding machine, and the cashier sealed his cigarette and lit it and waddled to the window and lifted the curtain.

"Simon's brought the carriage, today," he said.

"That boy finally wrecked that car, I reckon. Better call Colonel."

The book-keeper slid from his stool and went to the door to the office and opened it. Old Bayard glanced up from his desk.

"All right, Byron," he said. The book-keeper turned away.

Old Bayard stalked through the bank and opened the street door and stopped utterly, the door knob in his hand.

"Where's Bayard?" he said.

"He aint comin'," Simon answered. Old Bayard crossed the pavement.

"What? Where is he?"

"He en Isom off somewhar in dat cyar," Simon answered. "Lawd knows whar dey is by now. Takin' dat boy away fum his work in de middle of de day, cyar-ridin'. After all de time I spent tryin' to git some sense inter Isom's haid," Simon continued. "Cyar-ridin'," he said. "Cyar-ridin'." Old Bayard got in the carriage.

"I'll be damned," old Bayard said, "if I haven't got the triflingest set of folks to make a living for in the whole damn world. There's just one thing about it: when I finally have to go to the poor house, every damned one of you'll be there when I come."

"Now, here you quoilin' too," Simon said. "Miss Jenny shoutin' at me 'twell I wuz thu de gate, and now you already started at dis eend. But ef Mr Bayard dont leave dat boy alone, he aint gwine to be no better'n a town nigger spite of all I kin do."

"Jenny's already ruined him," old Bayard said. "Bayard cant hurt him much."

"You sho' tole de troof den," Simon agreed. He gathered up the reins. "Come up, dar."

"Here, hold up a minute, Simon," old Bayard said. Simon reined the horses back. "Whut you want now?"

Old Bayard drew another long breath. "Go back to my office and get me a cigar out of that jar on the mantel."

Two days later, as he and Simon tooled sedately homeward through the afternoon, simultaneously almost with the warning thunder of it the car burst upon them on a curve, slewed into the ditch and into the road again and rushed on; and in the flashing instant he and Simon saw the whites of Isom's eyes and the ivory cropping of his teeth behind the steering wheel. When the car returned home that afternoon Simon conducted Isom to the barn and whipped him with a harness strap.

That night they sat in the office after supper. Old Bayard held his cigar unlighted in his fingers. Miss Jenny was immersed in her paper.

Suddenly old Bayard said: "Maybe he'll get tired of it after a while."

Miss Jenny raised her head.

"And when he does," Miss Jenny said, "dont you know what he'll get then? When he finds that car wont go fast enough for him?" she demanded, staring at him across her newspaper. He sat holding his cigar, his head bent a little. "He'll buy an aeroplane," Miss Jenny told him. She rattled the paper and turned a page. "He ought to have a wife," she added in a detached voice, reading again. "Let him get a son, then he can break his neck as soon and as often as he pleases. Providence doesn't seem to have any judgment at all," she said, thinking of the two of them, of his dead brother. She said: "But Lord knows, I'd hate to see any girl I was fond of, married to him." She rattled the paper again, turning another page. "I dont know what else you expect from him. From any Sartoris. You dont waste your afternoons riding in that car because you think it'll keep him from turning it over: you go because when it does happen, you want to be in it, too. So do you think you've got any more consideration for folks than he has?" He sat holding his cigar, his face still averted. Miss Jenny was watching him again across her paper.

"I'm coming down town in the morning, and we're going and have the doctor look at that bump on your face, you hear?"

In his room, as he removed his collar and tie before the chest of drawers, his eye fell upon the pipe which he had laid there four weeks ago, and he put the collar and tie down and picked up the pipe and held it in his hand, rubbing the charred bowl slowly with his thumb.

Then with sudden decision he quitted the room and tramped down the hall. At the end of the hall a stair mounted into the darkness. At the foot he fumbled a light switch and followed the cramped turnings cautiously in the dark, to a door set at a difficult angle, and opened it upon a broad, low room with a pitched ceiling, smelling of dust and silence and ancient disused things.

The room was cluttered with indiscriminate furniture—chairs and sofas like patient ghosts holding lightly in dry and rigid embrace yet other ghosts—a fitting place for dead Sartorises to gather and speak among themselves of glamorous and old disastrous days. The unshaded light swung on a single cord from the center of the ceiling. He unknotted it and drew it to its full length and carried it across to a nail in the wall above a cedar chest. He fastened it here and drew a chair across to the chest and sat down.

The chest had not been opened since 1901, when

his son John had succumbed to yellow fever and an old Spanish bullet-wound. There had been two occasions since, in July and in October of last year, but the other grandson still possessed quickness and all the incalculable portent of his heritage. So he had forborne for the time being, expecting to kill two birds with one stone, as it were.

Thus each opening was in a way ceremonial, commemorating the violent finis to some phase of his family's history, and while he struggled with the stiff lock it seemed to him that a legion of ghosts breathed quietly at his shoulder, and he pictured a double line of them with their arrogant identical faces waiting just beyond a portal and stretching away toward the invisible dais where Something sat waiting the latest arrival among them; thought of them chafing a little and a little bewildered, thought and desire being denied them, in a place where, immortal, there were no opportunities for vainglorious swashbuckling. Denied that Sartoris heaven in which they could spend eternity dying deaths of needless and magnificent violence while spectators doomed to immortality looked eternally on. The Valhalla which John Sartoris, turning the wine glass in his big, well-shaped hand that night at the supper table, had seen in its chaste and fragile bubble.

The lock gave at last and he raised the lid. The ghosts fell away and from the chest there rose a thin exhilarating odor of cedar, and something else: a scent drily and muskily nostalgic, as of old ashes, and his hands, well-shaped but not so large and a shade less capable than his father's, rested for a moment upon a brocade garment. The brocade was richly hushed and the fall of fine Mechlin was dustily yellow, pale and textureless as winter sunlight. He raised the garment carefully. The lace cascaded mellow and pale as spilled wine upon his hands, and he laid it aside and lifted out next a rapier. It was a Toledo, a blade delicate and fine as the prolonged stroke of a violin bow, in a velvet sheath. The sheath was elegant and flamboyant and soiled, and the seams had cracked drily.

Old Bayard held the rapier upon his hands for a while, feeling the balance of it. It was just such an implement as a Sartoris would consider the proper equipment for raising tobacco in a virgin wilderness; it and the scarlet heels and the ruffled wristbands in which he fought his stealthy and simple neighbors. And old Bayard held it upon his two hands, seeing in its stained fine blade and shabby elegant sheath the symbol of his race; that too in the tradition: the thing itself fine and clear enough, only the instrument had become a little tarnished in its very aptitude for shaping circumstance to its arrogant ends.

He laid it aside. Next came a heavy cavalry sabre, and a rosewood box containing two duelling pistols with silver mountings and with the lean, deceptive delicacy of race horses, and what old man Falls had called "that 'ere dang der'nger." It was a stubby, evil-looking thing with its three barrels; viciously and coldly utilitarian, and between the other two weapons it lay like a cold and deadly insect between two flowers.

He lifted out next the blue army forage-cap of the 'forties and a small pottery vessel and a Mexican machete, and a long-necked oil can such as locomotive drivers use. It was of silver, and engraved upon it, surrounded by a carven ornate wreath, was the picture of a locomotive with a huge bell-shaped funnel. Beneath it, the name, "Virginia" and the date, "August 9, 1874."

He laid these aside and with sudden purposefulness

he removed the other objects—a frogged and braided coat of Confederate grey and a gown of sprigged muslin scented faintly of lavender and evocative of old formal minuets and drifting honeysuckle among steady candle flames—and came upon a conglomeration of yellowed papers neatly bound in packets, and at last upon a huge, brass-bound Bible. He raised this to the edge of the chest and opened it. The paper was brown and mellow with years, and it had a texture like that of slightly-moist wood ashes, as though each page were held intact by its archaic and fading print. He turned the pages carefully back to the fly leaves. Beginning near the bottom of the final blank page, a column of names and dates rose in stark, fading simplicity, growing fainter and fainter where time had lain upon them. At the top they were still legible, as they were at the foot of the preceding page. But halfway up this page they ceased, and from there on the sheet was blank save for the faint soft mottlings of time and an occasional brownish penstroke significant but without meaning.

Bayard sat for a long time, regarding the stark dissolving apotheosis of his name. Sartorises had derided Time, but Time was not vindictive, because it was longer than Sartorises. And probably unaware of them. But it was a good gesture, anyway. And he recalled his father's words.

"In the nineteenth century," John Sartoris had said, "chortling over genealogy anywhere is poppycock. But particularly so in America, where only what a man takes and keeps has any significance, and where all of us have a common ancestry and the only house from which we can claim descent with any assurance, is the Old Bailey. Yet the man who professes to care nothing about his forbears is only a little less vain than he who bases all his actions on blood precedent. And a Sartoris is entitled to a little vanity and poppycock, if he wants it."

Yes, it was a good gesture, and Bayard sat and mused quietly on the tense he had unwittingly used. Was. Fatality again: the augury of a man's destiny peeping out at him from the roadside hedge, if he but recognise it; and as he sat and gazed with blind eyes at the page, Time rolled back again and again he ran panting through undergrowth while a Yankee cavalry patrol crashed behind him, crashed fainter and fainter until he crouched with spent, laboring lungs in a bramble thicket and heard their fading thunder along a dim wagon road. Then he crawled forth again and went to a spring he knew that flowed from the roots of a beech tree; and as he leaned his mouth to it the final light of day was reflected onto his face, bringing into sharp relief forehead and nose above the cavernous sockets of his eyes and the panting animal snarl of his teeth, and from the still water there stared back at him for a sudden moment, a skull.

The unturned corners of man's destiny. Well, heaven, that crowded place, lay just beyond one of them, they claimed; heaven, filled with every man's illusion of himself and with the conflicting illusions of him that parade through the minds of other illusions . . . He stirred again and sighed quietly, and took out his fountain pen. At the bottom of the column he wrote:

"John Sartoris. July 5, 1918."

and beneath that:

"Caroline White Sartoris and son. October 27, 1918."

When the ink was dry he closed the book and replaced it and took the pipe from his pocket and put

it in the rosewood box with the duelling pistols and
the derringer and replaced the other things and
closed the chest and locked it again.

Young Bayard drove her to town the next morning.
Old Bayard sat tilted in his chair in the door, and he
looked up at her with a fine assumption of surprise
and his deafness seemed more pronounced than ordinary. But she got him out of his chair with cold im-
placability and led him still grumbling along the
street, where merchants and loungers before the
stores spoke to her as to a martial queen, old Bayard
stalking along beside her with laggard reluctance,
like that of a small boy.

But she carried him firmly on, and at a row of
dingy signs tacked flat to the wall, she turned and
mounted a narrow stairway debouching between
two stores. At the top was a dark corridor with
doors. The nearest door was of pine, its gray paint
scarred at the bottom as though it had been kicked
repeatedly by feet that struck it at the same height
and with the same force. In the door itself, near the
edge, two holes an inch apart bore mute witness to
the missing hasp, and from a staple in the jamb
depended the hasp itself, fixed there by a huge rusty
lock of a pattern which had not been manufactured
in twenty years. Bayard offered to stop here, but
Miss Jenny led him firmly on to the second door
across the hall.

This door was freshly painted and grained to rep-
resent walnut. Into the top half of it was let a pane of
thick, opaque glass bearing a name in raised gilt letters, and two embracing office hours. Miss Jenny
opened this door and Bayard followed her into a
small cubbyhole of a room of spartan but suave asep-

sis. The walls were an immaculate new gray, with an engraved reproduction of a Corot and two spidery dry-points in narrow frames, and it contained a new rug in warm buff tones and a bare table and four chairs in fumed oak—all impersonal and clean and inexpensive, but revealing at a glance the proprietor's soul; a soul hampered now by material strictures, but destined and determined to someday function in its proper surroundings—that of Persian rugs and mahogany or teak, and a single irreproachable print on the chaste wall. A young woman in a starched white dress rose from a smaller table in one corner, patting her hair.

"Good morning, Myrtle," Miss Jenny said. "Tell Dr Alford we'd like to see him, please."

"You have an appointment?" the girl said in a voice without any inflection at all.

"We'll make one now, then," Miss Jenny replied. "You dont mean to say Dr Alford dont come to work before ten oclock, do you?"

"Dr Alford dont—doesn't see anyone without an appointment," the girl parrotted, gazing at a point above their heads. "If you have no appointment, you'll have to have an ap—"

"Tut, tut," Miss Jenny interrupted briskly, "you run and tell Dr Alford Colonel Sartoris wants to see him, there's a good girl."

"Yessum, Miss Jenny," the girl said obediently and she crossed the room, but at the further door she paused again and again her voice became parrot-like. "Wont you sit down? I'll see if the doctor is engaged."

"You go and tell Dr Alford we're here," Miss Jenny repeated affably. "Tell him I've got some shopping to do this morning."

"Yessum, Miss Jenny," the girl agreed, and disappeared, and after a dignified interval she returned, once more clothed faultlessly in her professional manner. "The doctor will see you now. Come in, please," she said, holding the door open and standing aside.

"Thank you, honey," Miss Jenny replied. "Is your mamma still in bed?"

"No'm, she's sitting up now, thank you."

"That's good," Miss Jenny agreed. "Come on, Bayard."

This room was smaller than the other, and brutally carbolized. There was a white enamelled cabinet filled with vicious nickel gleams, and a metal operating table and an array of electric furnaces and ovens and sterilizers. When they entered, the doctor in a linen jacket bent above a small desk, and for a while he proffered them his sleek oblivious profile. Then he glanced up, and rose.

He was in the youthful indeterminate thirties; a newcomer to the town and nephew of an old resident. He had made a fine record in medical school and was of a personable exterior, but there was a sort of preoccupied dignity, a sort of erudite and cold unillusion regarding mankind, about him that precluded the easy intimacy of the small town and caused even those who remembered his visits during his boyhood to his aunt and uncle, to address him as doctor or mister. He had a small moustache and a face like a reposeful mask—a comforting face, but cold; and while Bayard sat restively his dry scrubbed fingers probed delicately at the wen on the other's face. Miss Jenny asked him a question, but he continued his delicate exploration raptly, as though he had not heard, as though she had not even spoken; inserting a small electric bulb, which he first sterilized, into Bayard's mouth and snapping its ruby glow on and off within his cheek. Then he removed it and sterilized it again and returned it to the cabinet.

"Well?" Miss Jenny said impatiently. The doctor shut the cabinet deliberately and dried his hands and came and stood over them, and with his thumbs hooked in his jacket pockets he became solemnly and unctuously technical, rolling the harsh words from his tongue with an epicurean deliberation.

"It should be taken out at once," he finished. "It doesn't pain him now, and that is the reason I advise an immediate operation."

"You mean, it might develop into cancer?" Miss Jenny asked.

"No question about it at all. Course of time. Neglect it, and I can promise you nothing; have it out now, and he need never worry about it." He looked at Bayard again with lingering and chill contemplation. "It will be very simple. I will remove it as easily as that." And he made a short gesture with his hand.

"What's that?" Bayard demanded.

"I say, I can remove that growth so easily you wont know it, Colonel Sartoris."

"I'll be damned if you do!" Bayard rose with one of his characteristic plunging movements.

"Sit down, Bayard," Miss Jenny ordered. "Nobody's going to cut on you without your knowing it. Should it be done right away?" she asked.

"Yes, ma'am. I wouldn't have that thing on my face overnight. Otherwise, it is only fair to warn you that I cannot assume responsibility for it . . . I could remove it in two minutes," he added, looking at Bayard's face again with cold speculation. Then he half turned his head and stopped in a listening attitude, and beyond the thin walls a voice in the other room boomed in rich rolling waves.

"Mawnin', sister," it said. "Didn't I hear Bayard

Sartoris cussin' in here?" The doctor and Miss Jenny held their arrested attitudes, then the door surged open and the fattest man in Yocona county filled it. He wore a shiny alpaca coat over waistcoat and trousers of baggy unpressed black broadcloth; above a plaited shirt the fatty rolls of his neck practically hid his low collar and a black string tie. His Roman senator's head was covered with a vigorous curling of silvery hair. "What the devil's the matter with you?" he boomed, then he sidled into the room, filling it completely, dwarfing its occupants and its furnishings.

This was Doctor Lucius Quintus Peabody, eighty-seven years old and weighing three hundred and ten pounds and possessing a digestive tract like that of a horse. He had practiced medicine in Yocona county when a doctor's equipment consisted of a saw and a gallon of whisky and a satchel of calomel; he had been John Sartoris' regimental surgeon, and up to the day of the automobile he would start out at any hour of the twenty-four in any weather and for any distance, over practically impassable roads in a lopsided buckboard to visit anyone, white or black, who sent for him; accepting for fee usually a meal of corn pone and coffee or perhaps a small measure of corn or fruit, or a few flower bulbs or graftings. When he was young and hasty he had kept a daybook, kept it meticulously until these hypothetical assets totalled $10,000.00. But that was forty years ago, and since then he hadn't bothered with a record at all; and now from time to time a countryman enters his shabby office and discharges an obligation, commemorating sometimes the payor's entry into the world, incurred by his father or grandfather and which Dr Peabody himself had long since forgotten about. Every one in the county knew him, and it was said that he could spend the balance of his days driving about the county in the buckboard he still used, with never a thought for board and lodging and without the expenditure of a penny for either. He filled the room with his bluff and homely humanity, and as he crossed the floor and patted Miss Jenny's back with one flail-like hand the whole building trembled to his tread.

"Mawnin', Jenny," he said. "Havin' Bayard measured for insurance?"

"This damn butcher wants to cut on me," Bayard said querulously. "You come on and make 'em let me alone, Loosh."

"Ten A.M.'s mighty early in the day to start carvin' white folks," Dr Peabody boomed. "Nigger's different. Chop up a nigger any time after midnight. What's the matter with him, son?" he asked of Dr Alford.

"I dont believe it's anything but a wart," Miss Jenny said, "but I'm tired of looking at it."

"It's no wart," Dr Alford corrected stiffly. He recapitulated his diagnosis in technical terms while Dr Peabody enveloped them all in the rubicund benevolence of his presence.

"Sounds pretty bad, dont it?" he agreed, and he shook the floor again and pushed Bayard firmly into the chair again with one huge hand, and with the other he dragged his face up to the light. Then he dug a pair of iron-bowed spectacles from the side pocket of his coat and examined Bayard's wen through them. "Think it ought to come off, do you?"

"I do," Dr Alford answered coldly. "I think it is imperative that it be removed. Unnecessary there. Cancer."

"Folks got along with cancer a long time before

they invented knives," Dr Peabody said drily. "Hold still, Bayard."

And people like you are one of the reasons, was on the tip of the younger man's tongue. But he forbore and said instead: "I can remove that growth in two minutes, Colonel Sartoris."

"Damned if you do," Bayard rejoined violently, trying to rise. "Get away, Loosh."

"Sit still," Dr Peabody said equably, holding him down while he probed at the wen. "Does it hurt any?"

"No. I never said it did. And I'll be damned—"

"You'll probably be damned anyway," Dr Peabody told him. "You'd be about as well off dead, anyhow. I dont know anybody that gets less fun out of living than you seem to."

"You told the truth for once," Miss Jenny agreed. "He's the oldest person I ever knew in my life."

"And so," Dr Peabody continued blandly, "I wouldn't worry about it. Let it stay there. Nobody cares what your face looks like. If you were a young fellow, now, out sparkin' the gals every night—"

"If Dr Peabody is permitted to interfere with impunity—" the younger man began.

"Will Falls says he can cure it," Bayard said.

"With that salve of his?" Dr Peabody asked.

"Salve?" Dr Alford repeated. "Colonel Sartoris, if you let any quack that comes along treat that growth with homemade or patent remedies, you'll be dead in six months. Dr Peabody even will bear me out," he added with fine irony.

"I dont know," Dr Peabody replied slowly. "Will has done some curious things with that salve of his."

"I must protest against this," Dr Alford said. "Mrs Du Pre, I protest against a member of my profession sanctioning even negatively such a practice."

"Pshaw, boy," Dr Peabody answered. "We aint goin' to let Will put his dope on Bayard's wart. It's all right for niggers and livestock, but Bayard dont need it. We'll just let this thing alone, long as it dont hurt him."

"If that growth is not removed immediately, I wash my hands of all responsibility," Dr Alford stated. "To neglect it will be as fatal as Mr Falls' salve. Mrs Du Pre, I ask you to witness that this consultation has taken this unethical turn through no fault of mine and over my protest."

"Pshaw, boy," Dr Peabody said again. "This aint hardly worth the trouble of cuttin' out. We'll save you an arm or a leg as soon as that fool grandson of his turns that automobile over with 'em. Come on, Bayard."

"Mrs Du Pre—" Dr Alford essayed.

"Bayard can come back, if he wants to." Dr Peabody patted the younger man's shoulder with his heavy hand. "I'm going to take him to my office and talk to him a while. Jenny can bring him back if she wants to. Come on, Bayard." And he led Bayard from the room. Miss Jenny rose also.

"That Loosh Peabody is as big a fogy as old Will Falls," she said. "Old people just fret me to death. You wait: I'll bring him right back here, and we'll finish this business." Dr Alford held the door open for her and she sailed in a stiff silk-clad rage from the room and followed her nephew and Dr Peabody across the corridor and through the scarred door with its rusty lock, and into a room resembling a miniature cyclonic devastation mellowed peacefully over with dust ancient and long undisturbed.

"You, Loosh Peabody," Miss Jenny said.

"Sit down, Jenny," Dr Peabody told her, "and be quiet. Unfasten your shirt, Bayard."

"What?" Bayard said belligerently. The other thrust him into a chair.

"Want to see your chest," he explained. He crossed to an ancient roll-top desk and rummaged through the dusty litter which it bore. There was litter and dust everywhere in the huge room. Its four windows gave upon the square, but the elms and mulberry trees ranged along the sides of the square shaded these first-floor offices, so that light entered them but it was tempered, like light which has passed through water. In the corners of the ceiling were spider webs thick and heavy as Spanish moss and dingy as gray lace; and the once-white walls were an even and unemphatic drab save for a paler rectangle here and there where an outdated calendar had hung and been removed. Besides the desk the room contained three or four huge chairs with broken springs, and a rusty stove in a sawdust-filled box, and a leather sofa holding mutely in its worn surface Dr Peabody's recumbent shape; beside it and slowly gathering successive layers of dust, was a stack of lurid paper-covered nickel novels. This was Dr Peabody's library, and on this sofa he passed his office hours, reading them over and over. Other books there were none.

But the waste basket beside the desk and the desk itself and the mantel above the trash-filled fireplace, and the window ledges too were cluttered with circular mail matter and mail-order catalogues and government bulletins of all kinds. In one corner, on an upended packing-box, sat a water cooler of stained oxidized glass; in another corner leaned a clump of cane fishing poles warping slowly of their own weight; and on every horizontal surface rested a collection of objects not to be found outside of a second-hand store—old garments, bottles, a kerosene lamp, a wooden box of tins of axle grease, lacking one, a clock in the shape of a bland china morning-glory supported by four garlanded maidens who had suffered sundry astonishing anatomical mischances, and here and there among their dusty indiscrimination various instruments pertaining to the occupant's profession. It was one of these that Dr Peabody sought now, in the littered desk on which sat a framed photograph of his son, and though Miss Jenny said again, "You, Loosh Peabody, you listen to me," he continued to seek it with undisturbed equanimity.

"You fasten your clothes and we'll go back to that doctor," Miss Jenny said to her nephew. "Neither you nor I can waste any more time with a doddering old fool."

"Sit down, Jenny," Dr Peabody repeated, and he drew out a drawer and removed from it a box of cigars and a handful of faded artificial trout flies and a soiled collar and lastly a stethoscope, then he tumbled the other things back into the drawer and shut it with his knee.

Miss Jenny sat trim and outraged, fuming while he listened to Bayard's heart.

"Well," she snapped, "does it tell you how to take that wart off his face? Will Falls didn't need any telephone to find that out."

"It tells more than that," Dr Peabody answered. "It tells how Bayard'll get rid of all his troubles, if he keeps on riding in that hellion's automobile."

"Fiddlesticks," Miss Jenny said. "Bayard's a good driver. I never rode with a better one."

"It'll take more'n a good driver to keep this"—he tapped Bayard's chest with his blunt finger—"goin', time that boy whirls that thing around another curve or two like I've seen him do."

"Did you ever hear of a Sartoris dying from a natural cause, like anybody else?" Miss Jenny demanded. "Dont you know that heart aint going to take Bayard off before his time? You get up from there, and come on with me," she added to her nephew. Bayard buttoned his shirt, and Dr Peabody sat on the sofa and watched him quietly.

"Bayard," he said suddenly, "why dont you stay out of that damn thing?"

"What?"

"If you dont keep out of that car, you aint goin' to need me nor Will Falls, nor that boy in yonder with all his hand-boiled saws and razors, neither."

"What business is it of yours?" Bayard demanded. "By God, cant I break my neck in peace if I want to?" He rose. He was trembling again, fumbling at his waistcoat buttons, and Miss Jenny rose also and made to button it for him, but he put her roughly aside. Dr Peabody sat quietly, thumping his fat fingers on one fat knee. "I have already outlived my time," Bayard continued more mildly. "I am the first Sartoris there is any record of, who saw sixty years. I reckon Old Marster is keeping me for a reliable witness to the extinction of my race."

"Now," Miss Jenny said icily, "you've made your speech, and Loosh Peabody has wasted the morning for you, so I reckon we can leave now and let Loosh go out and doctor mules for a while, and you can sit around the rest of the day, being a Sartoris and feeling sorry for yourself. Good morning, Loosh."

"Make him let that place alone, Jenny," Dr Peabody said.

"Aint you and Will Falls going to cure it for him?"

"You keep him from letting Will Falls put anything on it," Dr Peabody repeated equably. "It's all right. Just let it alone."

"We're going to a doctor, that's what we're going to do," Miss Jenny replied. "Come on here."

When the door had closed he sat motionless and heard them quarrelling beyond it. Then the sound of their voices moved down the corridor toward the stairs, and still quarrelling loudly and on Bayard's part with profane emphasis, the voices died away. Then Dr Peabody lay back on the sofa shaped already to the bulk of him, and with random deliberation he reached a nickel thriller from the stack at the head of the couch.

4

As they neared the bank Narcissa Benbow came along from the opposite direction, and they met at the door. Old Bayard liked her, liked to rally her in a ponderously gallant way on imaginary affairs of the heart, and she had for him a diffident sort of affection and she stopped in her pale print dress and shouted her grave voice into his deafness, and when he took his tilted chair again Miss Jenny followed her into the bank and to the window. There was no one behind the grille at the moment save the book-keeper. He glanced briefly and covertly over his shoulder at them, then slid from his stool and crossed to the window with his surreptitious tread but without raising his eyes again.

He took Narcissa's check, and while she listened to Miss Jenny's recapitulation of Bayard's and Loosh Peabody's stubborn masculine stupidity, she remarked beneath the brim of her hat his forearms, from which the sleeves had been turned back, and the fine, reddish hair which clothed them down to the second joints of his fingers; and while Miss Jenny ceased momentarily to nurse her sense of helpless outrage, she remarked with a faint distinct distaste and a little curiosity, since it was not particularly warm today, the fact that his arms and hands were beaded with perspiration.

But this was not long in her consciousness, and she took the notes he pushed under the grille to her and opened her bag. From its blue satin maw the corner of an envelope and some of its superscription peeped suddenly, but she crumpled it quickly from sight and put the money in and closed the bag before Miss Jenny had seen. They turned away. At the door she paused again, clothed in her still and untarnished aura, and stood for a moment while old Bayard made her a heavy and involved compliment upon her appearance. Then she went on, surrounded by her grave tranquillity like a visible presence or an odor or a sound.

As long as she was in sight at the door, the bookkeeper stood where she had left him. His head was bent and his hand made a series of neat, meaningless figures on the pad beneath it, until she moved again and went on out of sight. Then he moved, and in doing so he found that the pad had adhered to his sweating wrist, so that when he removed his arm it came away also, then its own weight freed it and it dropped to the floor.

He finished the forenoon stooped on his high stool at his high desk beneath the green-shaded light, penning his neat figures into ledgers and writing words into them in the flowing Spencerian hand he had been taught in a Memphis business college. At times he slid from the stool and crossed to the window with his covert evasive eyes and served a client, then returned to his stool and picked up his pen. The cashier, a rotund man with bristling hair and lapping jowls like a Berkshire hog, returned presently, accompanied by a director, who followed him inside the grille. They ordered Coca-Colas from a neighboring drug store by telephone and stood talking until the refreshment arrived by negro boy. Snopes had been included and he descended again and took his glass. The other two sipped theirs; he spooned the ice from his into a spittoon and emptied it at a draught and replaced the glass on the tray and spoke a general and ignored thanks in his sober country idiom and returned to his desk.

Noon came. Old Bayard rose crashing from his tilted chair and stalked back to his office, where he would eat his frugal cold lunch and then sleep for an hour, and banged the door behind him. The cashier took his hat and departed also; for an hour Snopes would have the bank to himself. Outside the square lay motionless beneath noon; the dinnerward exodus of lawyers and merchants and clerks did not disturb its atmosphere of abiding and timeless fixation; in the elms surrounding the courthouse no leaf stirred in the May sunlight. Across the bank windows an occasional shadow passed, but none turned into the door, and presently the square was motionless as a theatre drop.

Snopes drew a sheet of paper from a drawer and laid it beneath the light and wrote slowly upon it, pausing at intervals, drawing his pen through a sentence or a word, writing again. Someone entered; without looking up he slid the paper beneath a ledger, crossed to the window and served the customer, returned and wrote again. The clock on the wall ticked into the silence and into the slow, mouse-like scratching of the pen. The pen ceased at last, but the clock ticked on like a measured dropping of small shot.

He re-read the first draught, slowly. Then he drew out a second sheet and made a careful copy. When this was done he re-read it also, comparing the two; then he folded the copy again until it was a small square thickness, and stowed it away in the fob-pocket of his trousers. The original he carried across to the cuspidor, and holding it above the receptacle he struck a match to it and held it in his fingers until the final moment. Then he dropped it into the spittoon and when it was completely consumed, he crushed the charred thing to powder. Quarter to one. He returned to his stool and opened his ledgers again.

At one the cashier with a toothpick appeared at the door talking to someone, then he entered and went to old Bayard's office and opened the door. "One oclock, Colonel," he shouted into the room, and old Bayard's heels thumped heavily on the floor. As the Snopes took his hat and emerged from the grille old Bayard stalked forth again and tramped on ahead and took the tilted chair in the doorway.

There is in Jefferson a boarding house known as the Beard hotel. It is a rectangular frame building with a double veranda, just off the square, and it is conducted theoretically by a countryman, but in reality by his wife. Beard is a mild, bleached man of indeterminate age and of less than medium size, dressed always in a collarless shirt and a black evil pipe. He also owns the grist mill near the square, and he may be found either at the mill, or on the outskirts of the checker-game in the courthouse yard, or sitting in his stocking feet on the veranda of his hostelry. He is supposed to suffer from some obscure ailment puzzling to physicians, which prevents him exerting himself physically. His wife is a woman in a soiled

apron, with straggling, damp grayish hair and an air
of spent but indomitable capability. They have one
son, a pale, quiet boy of twelve or so, who is always
on the monthly honor roll at school; he may be seen
on spring mornings schoolward bound with a bouquet of flowers. His rating among his contemporaries
is not high.

Men only patronize the Beard hotel. Itinerant
horse- and cattle-traders; countrymen in town overnight during court or the holiday season or arrested
perhaps by inclement weather, stop there; and juries
during court week—twelve good men and true
marching in or out in column of twos, or aligned in
chairs and spitting across the veranda rail with solemn and awesome decorum; and two of the town
young bloods keep a room there, in which it is ru-
mored dice and cards progress Sundays and drinking is
done. But no women. If a skirt (other than Mrs
Beard's gray apron) so much as flashes in the vicinity
of its celibate portals, the city fathers investigate immediately, and woe to the peripatetic Semiramis if
she be run to earth. Here, in company with a number of other bachelors—clerks, mechanics and such—
the book-keeper Snopes lives.

And here he repaired when the bank day was
finished. The afternoon was a replica of the morning.
Then at three oclock the green shades were drawn
upon door and windows, and Snopes and the cashier
went about striking a daily balance. At 3:30 young
Bayard arrived in his car and old Bayard stalked
forth and got in it and was driven away. Presently
thereafter the janitor, an ancient, practically incapac-
itated negro called Doctor Jones, came in and
doddered futilely with a broom. By 4:30 he was
done, and the cashier locked the vault and switched

on the light above it, and he and the book-keeper emerged and locked the front door, and the cashier shook it experimentally.

Snopes crossed the square and passed through the courthouse and entered a street. It was a tawdry street, lined with shabby and odorous stores. Into one of these he turned. This was a restaurant, a concrete-floored space bounded by a wooden counter polished by eating elbows and lined with a row of backless and excruciating stools. It was owned and operated by a cousin Snopes, and here he purchased fifteen cents' worth of gaudy stale candy.

He recrossed the square and entered the Beard hotel. The hall was empty; it smelled of damp, harsh soap, and its linoleum floor covering gleamed, still wet. From the rear came the unmistakable sounds of Mrs Beard's ceaseless and savage activity, and he followed these sounds and she ceased mopping and looked across her gray shoulder at him, sweeping her lank hair aside with a reddened forearm.

"Evenin', Miz Beard," he said. "Virgil come home yet?"

"He was through here a minute ago," she answered. "If he aint out front, I reckon he aint fur. You got some mo' work fer him?"

"Yessum. You dont know which-a-way he went?"

"Call him in the back yard. He dont usually go fur away." She dragged her dank hair aside again; shaped long to labor, her muscles were restive under inaction. She grasped the mop again.

He thanked her and went on, and stood on the kitchen steps above a yard barren of grass and containing a chicken pen also grassless, in which a few fowls huddled or moved about in forlorn distraction in the dust. On one hand was a small kitchen garden

in orderly, tended rows. In the corner of the fence
was an outhouse of some sort, of weathered boards.

"Virgil," he called. The yard was desolate with
ghosts; ghosts of discouraged weeds, of food in the
shape of tin cans, broken boxes and barrels, a pile of
stove wood and a chopping block across which lay
an axe whose helve had been mended with rusty wire
amateurishly wound. Presently he descended into it,
and the chickens remarked him and raised a discordant clamor, anticipating food, doubtless.

"Virgil."

Sparrows found sustenance of some sort in the dust
among the fowls, but the fowls, perhaps with a foreknowledge of doom, huddled back and forth along
the wire, discordant and distracted, watching him
with predatory importunate eyes. He was about to
turn and reenter the kitchen when the boy appeared
silently and innocently from the outhouse, with his
straw-colored hair and his bland eyes. His mouth was
pale and almost sweet, but secretive at the corners.
His chin was negligible.

"Hi, Mr Snopes, you calling me?"

"Yes, if you aint doin' anything special," Snopes
answered, and they reentered the house and passed
the room where the boy's mother labored with drab
fury, and mounted a stairs carpeted too with linoleum fastened to each step by a treacherous sheet-
iron strip treated to resemble brass and scuffed and
scarred by tired or careless feet. Snopes' room
contained a bed, a chair, a dressing table and a wash-
stand with a slop-jar beside it. The floor was covered
with straw matting frayed in places. The single light
hung unshaded from a greenish-brown cord; upon
the wall above the paper-filled fireplace a framed
lithograph of an Indian maiden in immaculate buck-

skin leaned her naked bosom above a formal moonlit pool of Italian marble. She held a guitar and a rose, and dusty sparrows sat on the window ledge and watched them brightly through the dusty screen.

The boy entered politely; nevertheless his pale eyes took in the room and its contents at a comprehensive glance. He said: "That air gun aint come yet, has it, Mr Snopes?"

"No, it aint," Snopes answered. "It'll be here soon, though."

"You ordered off after it a long time, now."

"That's right. But it'll be here soon. Maybe they haven't got one in stock, right now." He crossed to the dresser and took from a drawer a few sheets of foolscap and laid them on the dresser top, and drew the chair up and dragged his suitcase from beneath the bed and set it in the chair. Then he took a fountain pen from his pocket and uncapped it and laid it beside the paper. "It ought to be here any day, now."

The boy seated himself on the suitcase and took up the pen. "They got 'em at Watts' hardware store," he suggested.

"If the one we ordered dont come soon, we'll git one there," Snopes said. "When did we order it, anyway?"

"Week ago Tuesday," the boy answered glibly. "I wrote it down."

"Well, it'll be here soon. You ready?"

The boy squared himself before the paper. "Yes, sir." Snopes took a folded paper from the top pocket of his trousers and spread it open.

"Code number forty-eight. Mister Joe Butler, Saint Louis, Missouri," he read, then he leaned over the boy's shoulder, watching the pen. "That's right: up close to the top," he commended. "Now." The boy dropped down the page about two inches, and as

Snopes read, he transcribed in his neat, copybook hand, pausing only occasionally to inquire as to the spelling of a word.

" 'I thought once I would try to forget you. But I cannot forget you because you cannot forget me. I saw my letter in your hand satchel today. Every day I can put my hand out and touch you you do not know it. Just to see you walk down the street To know what I know what you know. Some day we will both know to gether when you got use to it. You kept my letter but you do not anser. That is a good sign you do—' " The boy had reached the foot of the page. Snopes removed it, leaving the next sheet ready. He continued to read in his droning, inflectionless voice:

" '—not forget me you would not keep it. I think of you at night the way you walk down the street like I was dirt. I can tell you something you will be surprised I know more than watch you walk down the street with cloths. I will some day you will not be surprised then. You pass me you do not know it I know it. You will know it some day. Be cause I will tell you.' Now," he said, and the boy dropped on to the foot of the page. " 'Yours truly Hal Wagner. Code number twenty-four.' " Again he looked over the boy's shoulder. "That's right." He blotted the final sheet and gathered it up also. The boy recapped the pen and thrust the chair back, and Snopes produced a small paper bag from his coat.

The boy took it soberly. "Much obliged, Mr Snopes," he said. He opened it and squinted into it. "It's funny that air gun dont come on."

"It sure is," Snopes agreed. "I dont know why it dont come."

"Maybe it got lost in the post office," the boy suggested.

"It may have. I reckon that's about what happened to it. I'll write 'em again, tomorrow."

The boy rose, but he stood yet with his straw-colored hair and his bland, innocent face. He took a piece of candy from the sack and ate it without enthusiasm. "I reckon I better tell papa to go to the post office and ask 'em if it got lost."

"No, I wouldn't do that," Snopes said quickly. "You wait; I'll 'tend to it. We'll get it, all right."

"Papa wouldn't mind. He could go over there soon's he comes home and see about it. I could find him right now, and ask him to do it, I bet."

"He couldn't do no good," Snopes answered. "You leave it to me. I'll get that gun, all right."

"I could tell him I been working for you," the boy pursued. "I remember them letters."

"No, no, you wait and let me 'tend to it. I'll see about it first thing tomorrow."

"All right, Mr Snopes." He ate another piece of candy, without enthusiasm. He moved toward the door. "I remember ever' one of them letters. I bet I could sit down and write 'em all again. I bet I could. Say, Mr Snopes, who is Hal Wagner? Does he live in Jefferson?"

"No, no. You never seen him. He dont hardly never come to town. That's the reason I'm 'tending to his business for him. I'll see about that air gun, all right."

The boy opened the door, then he paused again. "They got 'em at Watts' hardware store. Good ones. I'd sure like to have one of 'em. Yes, sir, I sure would."

"Sure, sure," Snopes repeated. "Our'n'll be here tomorrow. You just wait: I'll see you git that gun."

The boy departed. Snopes locked the door, and for a while he stood beside it with his head bent, his hands slowly knotting and writhing together. Then he burned the folded sheet over his hearth and ground the carbonized paper to dust under his heel. With his knife he cut the fictitious address from the top of the first sheet, the signature from the bottom of the second, then he folded them and inserted them in a cheap envelope. He sealed this and stamped it, and took out his pen and with his left hand he addressed it with labored printed letters. That night he took it to the station and mailed it on the train. In the meantime he stopped in at Watts' and bought an air rifle.

5

At times, as Simon puttered about the place during the day, he could look out across the lot into the pasture and see the carriage horses growing daily shabbier and less prideful with idleness and the cessation of their once daily grooming, or he would pass the carriage motionless in its shed, its tongue propped at an accusing angle on the wooden mechanism he had invented for that purpose, and in the harness room the duster and tophat gathered slow dust on the nail in the wall, holding too in their mute waiting a patient and questioning uncomplaint. And at times when he stood shabby and stooped a little with stubborn bewilderment and age on the veranda with its ancient roses and wistaria and all its unchangeable and steadfast serenity and watched Sartorises come and go in a machine a gentleman of his day would have scorned and which any pauper could own and only a fool would ride in, it seemed to him that John Sartoris stood beside him with his bearded, hawklike face and an expression of haughty and fine contempt.

And standing so, with the afternoon slanting athwart the southern end of the porch and the heady and myriad odors of the ripening spring and the drowsy hum of insects and the singing of birds steady upon it, Isom rolling his eyes in the dark, cool doorway or near the corner of the house would hear his grandfather mumbling in a monotonous singsong in which was incomprehension and the petulant querulousness of age, and Isom would withdraw to the kitchen where his mother labored steadily with her placid yellow face and her endless crooning song.

"Pappy out dar talkin' ter Marse John agin," Isom told her. "Gimme dem cole 'taters, mammy."

"Aint Miss Jenny got some work fer you dis evenin'?" Elnora demanded, pausing to give him the cold potatoes.

"No'm. She gone off in de cyar agin."

"Hit's de Lawd's blessin' you and her aint bofe out in it, like you is whenever Mist' Bayard'll let you. You git on outen my kitchen, now. I got dis flo' mopped and I dont want it tracked up."

Quite often these days Isom could hear his grandfather talking to John Sartoris as he labored about the stable or the flower beds or the lawn, mumbling away to that arrogant ghost which dominated the house and its occupants and the whole scene itself across which the railroad he had built ran punily with distance but distinct, as though it were a stage set for the diversion of him whose stubborn dream, flouting him so deviously and cunningly while the dream was impure, had shaped itself fine and clear now that the dreamer was purged of the grossness of pride with that of flesh.

"Gent'mun equipage," Simon mumbled. He was working again with his hoe in the salvia bed at the top of the drive. "Ridin' in dat thing, wid a gent'-mun's proper equipage goin' to rack and ruin in de barn." He wasn't thinking of Miss Jenny. It didn't make much difference what women rode in, their menfolks permitting of course. They only showed off a gentleman's equipage anyhow; they were but the barometers of a gentleman's establishment, the glass of his gentility: horses themselves knew that. "Yo' own son, yo' own twin grandson ridin' right up in yo' face in a contraption like dat," he continued, "and you lettin' 'um do it. You bad as dey is. You jes' got ter lay down de law ter 'um, Marse John; wid all dese foreign wars and sich de young folks is growed away fum de correck behavior; dey dont know how ter conduck deyselfs in de gent'mun way. Whut you reckon folks gwine think when dey sees yo' own folks ridin' in de same kine o' rig trash rides in? You jes' got ter resert you'self, Marse John. Aint Sarto-rises set de quality in dis country since you wuz bawn? And now jes' look at 'um."

He leaned on his hoe and watched the car swing up the drive and stop before the house. Miss Jenny and young Bayard got out and mounted to the ve-randa. The engine was still running, a faint shimmer of exhaust drifted upon the bright forenoon. Simon came up with his hoe and peered at the array of dials and knobs on the dash. Bayard turned in the door and spoke his name.

"Cut the switch off," he ordered.

"Cut de which whut off?" Simon asked.

"That little bright-colored lever by the steering wheel there. Turn it down."

"Naw, suh," Simon answered, backing away. "I aint gwine tech it. I aint gwine have it blowin' up in my face."

"It wont hurt you," Bayard said impatiently. "Just put your hand on it and pull it down. That little bright jigger there."

Simon peered doubtfully at the gadgets and things, but without coming any nearer, then he craned his neck further and stared over into the car. "I dont see nothin' but dis yere big lever stickin' up thoo de flo'. Dat aint de one you mentionin', is it?" Bayard descended in two strides and leaned across the door and cut the switch under Simon's curious blinking regard. The purr of the engine ceased.

"Well, now," Simon said. "Is dat de one you wuz talkin' erbout?" He stared at the switch for a time, then he straightened up and stared at the hood. "She's quit b'ilin' under dar, aint she? Is dat de way you stops her?" But Bayard had mounted the steps again and entered the house. Simon lingered a while longer, examining the gleaming long thing, dynamic as a motionless locomotive and a little awesome, touching it lightly with his hand, then rubbing his hand on his thigh. He walked all around it, slowly, and touched the tires, mumbling to himself and shaking his head, then he returned to his salvia bed, where Bayard emerged presently and found him.

"Want to take a ride, Simon?" he asked.

Simon's hoe ceased and he straightened up. "Who, me?"

"Sure. Come on." Simon stood with his static hoe and rubbed his head slowly. Bayard continued to cajole him. "Come on; we'll just go down the road a piece. It wont hurt you."

"Naw, suh, I dont reckon it's gwine ter hurt me," he agreed. But he allowed himself to be drawn gradually toward the car, staring at its various members with slow blinking speculation, now that it was about to become an actual quantity in his life. At the door and with one foot raised to the running board he made a final stand against the subtle powers of evil judgment. "You aint gwine run it thoo de bushes like you and Isom done dat day y'all passed Cunnel and me on de road, is you?"

Bayard reassured him, and he got in slowly, with mumbled sounds of anticipatory concern, and he sat forward on the seat with his feet drawn under him, clutching the door with one hand and a lump of shirt on his chest with the other as the car moved down the drive. They passed through the gates and onto the road and still he sat hunched forward on the seat, as the car gained speed, and with a sudden convulsive movement he caught his hat just as it blew off his head.

"I 'speck dis is fur ernough, aint it?" he suggested, raising his voice. He pulled his hat down on his head, but as he released it he had to clutch wildly at it again, and he removed it and clasped it beneath his arm, and again his hand fumbled at his breast and became motionless clamped tightly about a lump of his shirt. "I got to weed dat bed dis mawnin'," he said, louder still. "Please, suh, Mist' Bayard," he added and his wizened old body sat yet further forward on the seat and he cast quick covert glances at the steadily increasing rush of hedgerow beside the road.

Then Bayard leaned forward and Simon watched his forearm tauten, and then they shot forward on a roar of sound like blurred thunderous wings. Earth, the unbelievable ribbon of the road, crashed beneath them and away behind into dust convolvulae: a dun moiling nausea of speed, and the roadside greenery was a tunnel rigid and streaming and unbroken. But he said no other word, and when Bayard glanced the lipless cruel derision of his teeth at him presently, Simon knelt in the floor, his old disreputable hat under his arm and his hand clutching a fold of his shirt on his breast. Later the white man glanced at him again, and Simon was watching him and the blurred irises of his eyes were no longer a melting pupilless brown: they were red, and in the blast of wind they were unwinking and in them was that mindless phosphorescence of an animal's. Bayard jammed the throttle down to the floor.

The wagon was moving drowsily and peacefully along the road. It was drawn by two mules and was filled with negro women asleep in chairs. Some of them wore drawers. The mules themselves didn't wake at all, but ambled sedately on with the empty wagon and the overturned chairs, even when the car crashed into the shallow ditch and surged back onto the road again and thundered on without slowing. The thunder ceased, but the car rushed on, and still under its own momentum it began to sway from side to side as Bayard tried to drag Simon's hands from the switch. But Simon knelt in the floor with his eyes shut tightly and the air blast toying with the grizzled remnant of his hair, holding the switch off with both hands.

"Turn it loose!" Bayard shouted.

"Dat's de way you stops it, Lawd! Dat's de way you stops it, Lawd!" Simon chanted, keeping the switch covered with his hands while Bayard hammered them with his fist. And he clung to it until the car slowed and stopped. Then he fumbled the door open and descended to the ground. Bayard called to him, but he went on back along the road at a limping rapid shuffle.

"Simon!" Bayard called, but Simon's shabby figure went on stiffly, like a man who has been deprived of the use of his legs for a long time. "Simon!" Bayard called again, but he neither slowed nor looked back, and Bayard started the car again and drove on until he could turn it about. Simon now stood in the ditch at the roadside, and his head was bent above something that engaged his hands when Bayard overtook him and stopped.

"Come on here and get in," he commanded.

"Naw, suh. I'll walk," Simon answered.

"Jump in, now," Bayard said sharply. He opened the door, but Simon stood in the ditch with his hand thrust inside his shirt, and Bayard could see that he was shaking uncontrollably. "Come on, you old fool; I'm not going to hurt you."

"I'll walk home," Simon repeated stubbornly but without heat. "You git on wid dat thing."

"Ah, get in, Simon. I didn't know I'd scared you that bad. I wont do it again."

"You git on home," Simon said again. "Dey'll be worried erbout you. You kin tell 'um whar I'm at."

Bayard watched him a moment, but Simon was not looking at him, and presently he slammed the door and went on. Nor did Simon look up even then, even when the car burst again into the thunder of roaring wings within a swirling cloud of dust that hung sluggishly after the thunder had died. Soon the wagon emerged from the dust, the mules now at a high flop-eared trot, and jingled past him, leaving behind it upon the dusty insect-rasped air a woman's voice in a quavering wordless hysteria, passive and quavering and sustained. This faded slowly down the shimmering flat reaches of the valley and Simon removed from the breast of his shirt an object hung on a cord about his neck. It was small, vaguely globular and desiccated and was covered with soiled napped fur: the first joint of the hind leg of a rabbit, caught supposedly in a graveyard in the dark of the moon, and Simon rubbed it through the sweat on his forehead and on the back of his neck, then he returned it to his bosom. His hands were still trembling, and he put his hat on and got back onto the road and turned toward home through the dusty noon.

He drove on down the valley toward town, passing the never-closed iron gates and the serene white house among its old trees, and went on at speed. The sound of the unmuffled engine crashed into the dust and swirled it into lethargic bursting shapes, and faded punily across the fecund valley quick with cotton and corn. Just outside of town he came upon another negro, in a wagon, and he held the car straight upon the vehicle until the mules reared, tilting the wagon for an instant. Then he swerved and whipped past with not an inch to spare, so close that the yelling negro in the wagon could see the lipless and savage derision of his teeth.

He went on, then in a mounting swoop like a niggard zoom the cemetery with his great-grandfather in pompous effigy gazing out across the valley and his railroad, flashed past, and he thought of old Simon trudging along the dusty road toward home, clutching his rabbit's foot, and again he felt savage and ashamed.

Then town among its trees, its shady streets like green tunnels along which tight lives accomplished their peaceful tragedies, and he closed the muffler and at a sedate pace he approached the square. The clock on the courthouse raised its four faces above the bowering elms, in glimpses seen between arching vistas of bordering oaks. Ten minutes to twelve. At twelve exactly his grandfather would repair to his office in the rear of the bank and there he would drink the pint of buttermilk which he brought in

with him every morning in a vacuum bottle, then for
an hour he would sleep on the sofa in a dark corner
of the room. As Bayard turned onto the square the
tilted chair in the bank door was already vacant, and
he slowed his car and eased it into the curb before a
propped sandwich board. Fresh Catfish Today the
board stated in letters of liquefied chalk, and through
the screen doors behind it came a smell of refrig-
erated food—cheese and pickle, with a faint overtone
of fried grease.

He stood for a moment on the sidewalk while the
noon throng parted and flowed about him. Negroes
slow and aimless as figures of a dark placid dream,
with an animal odor, murmuring and laughing
among themselves. There was in their consonantless
murmuring something ready with mirth, in their
laughter something grave and sad; country people—
men in overalls or corduroy or khaki and without
neckties, women in shapeless calico and sunbonnets
and snuff-sticks; groups of young girls in stiff mail-
order finery, the young heritage of their bodies'
grace dulled already by self-consciousness and labor
and unaccustomed high heels and soon to be obscured forever by child-bearing; youths and young
men in cheap tasteless suits and shirts and caps,
weather-tanned and clean-limbed as race horses and
a little belligerently blatant. Against the wall squatting a blind negro beggar with a guitar and a wire
frame holding a mouthorgan to his lips, patterned the
background of smells and sounds with a plaintive reiteration of rich monotonous chords, rhythmic as a
mathematical formula but without music. He was a
man of at least forty and his was that patient resigna-
tion of many sightless years, yet he too wore filthy
khaki with a corporal's stripes on one sleeve and a
crookedly sewn Boy Scout emblem on the other, and

on his breast a button commemorating the fourth
Liberty Loan and a small metal brooch bearing two
gold stars, obviously intended for female adornment.
His weathered derby was encircled by an officer's
hat cord, and on the pavement between his feet sat a
tin cup containing a dime and three pennies.

Bayard sought a coin in his pocket, and the beggar
sensed his approach and his tune became a single repeated chord but without a break in the rhythm until
the coin clinked into the cup, and still without a
break in the monotony of his strumming and the
meaningless strains of his mouthorgan, his left hand
dropped groping a little to the cup and read the coin
in a single motion, then once more the guitar and
mouthorgan resumed their blended pattern. As Bayard turned away someone spoke at his side—a broad
squat man with a keen weathered face and gray temples. He wore corduroys and boots, and his body was
the supple body of a horseman and his brown still
hands were the hands that horses love. MacCallum
his name, one of a family of six brothers who lived
eighteen miles away in the hills, and with whom
Bayard and John hunted foxes and 'coons during
their vacations.

"Been hearing about that car of yours," MacCallum said. "That's her, is it?" He stepped down from
the curb and moved easily about the car, examining
it; his hands on his hips. "Too much barrel," he said,
"and she looks heavy in the withers. Clumsy. Have
to use a curb on her, I reckon?"

"I dont," Bayard answered. "Jump in and I'll
show you what she'll do."

"No, much obliged," the other answered. He
stepped onto the pavement again, among the negroes
gathered to stare at the car. Along the street there
came now in small groups children going home from

school during the noon recess—little girls with colored boxes and books and skipping-ropes and talking sibilantly among themselves of intense feminine affairs, and boys in various stages of deshabille shouting and scuffling and jostling the little girls, who shrank together and gave the boys cold reverted glares. "Going to eat a snack," he explained. He crossed the pavement and opened the screen door. "You ate yet?" he asked, looking back. "Come on in a minute, anyway." And he patted his hip significantly.

The store was half grocery and confectionery and half restaurant. A number of customers stood about the cluttered but clean front section, with sandwiches and bottles of soda water, and the proprietor bobbed his head with flurried, slightly distrait affability above the counter to them. The rear half of the room was filled with tables at which a number of men and a woman or so, mostly country people, sat eating with awkward and solemn decorum. Next to this was the kitchen, filled with frying odors and the brittle hissing of it, where two negroes moved about like wraiths in a blue floating lethargy of smoke. They crossed this room also and MacCallum opened a door set in an outthrust angle of the wall and they entered a smaller room, or rather a large disused closet. There was a small window high in the wall, and a bare table and three or four chairs, and presently the younger of the two negroes followed them.

"Yes, suh, Mr MacCallum and Mr Sartoris." He set two freshly rinsed glasses, to which water yet adhered in sliding drops, on the table and stood drying his hands on his apron. He had a broad untroubled black face, a reliable sort of face.

"Lemons and sugar and ice," MacCallum said.

"You dont want none of that soda pop, do you?" he asked Bayard. The negro bowed and was turning away when MacCallum addressed Bayard, whereupon he paused with his hand on the door.

"No," Bayard answered. "Rather have a toddy myself."

"Yes, suh," the negro agreed. "Y'all wants a toddy." Someway he contrived to imply a grave approval, a vindication, and he bowed again with a sort of suave sense of the fine moment and turned doorward again. Then he stepped aside as the proprietor in a fresh apron entered at his customary distracted trot and stood rubbing his hands on his thighs.

"Morning, morning," he said. "How're you, Rafe? Bayard, I saw Miss Jenny and the old Colonel going up to Dr Alford's office the other day. Aint nothing wrong, is there?" His head was like an inverted egg; his hair curled meticulously away from the part in the center into two careful reddish-brown wings, like a toupee, and his eyes were a melting passionate brown.

"Come in here and shut that door," MacCallum ordered, drawing the other into the room. He produced from beneath his coat a bottle of astonishing proportions and set it on the table. It contained a delicate amber liquid and the proprietor rubbed his hands on his thighs and his hot mild gaze gloated upon it.

"Great Savior," he said, "where'd you have that demijohn hid? in your pants leg?" MacCallum uncorked the bottle and extended it and the proprietor leaned forward and smelled it, his eyes closed. He sighed.

"Henry's," MacCallum said. "Best run he's made yet. Reckon you'd take a drink if Bayard and me was to hold you?" The other cackled loudly, unctuously.

"Aint he a comical feller, now?" he asked Bayard. "Some joker, aint he?" He glanced at the table. "You aint got but two glasses. Wait till I—" Someone tapped at the door: the proprietor leaned his conical head to it and waggled his hand at them. MacCallum concealed the bottle without haste as the proprietor opened the door. It was the negro, with another glass, and lemons and sugar and a cracked bowl of ice. The proprietor admitted him.

"If they want me up front, tell 'em I've stepped out but I'll be back in a minute, Houston."

"Yes, suh," the negro replied, setting the things on the table. MacCallum produced the bottle again.

"What do you keep on telling your customers that old lie for?" he asked. "Everybody knows what you are doing."

The proprietor cackled again, gloating upon the bottle. "Yes, sir," he repeated, "he's sure some joker. Well, you boys have got plenty of time, but I got to get on back and keep things running."

"Go ahead," MacCallum told him, and the proprietor made himself a toddy. He raised the glass, stirring it and sniffing it alternately while the others mixed lemons and whisky and water. Then he removed his spoon and put it on the table.

"Well, I hate to hurry a good thing mighty bad," he said, "but business dont wait on pleasure, you know."

"Work does interfere with a man's drinking," MacCallum agreed.

"Yes, sir, it sure does," the other replied. He lifted his glass. "Your father's good health," he said. He drank. "I dont see the old gentleman in town much, nowadays."

"No," MacCallum answered. "He aint never got over Buddy being in the Yankee army. Claims he aint coming to town again until the Democratic party denies Woodrow Wilson."

"It'll be the best thing they ever done, if they was to recall him and elect a man like Debs or Senator Vardaman president," the proprietor agreed sagely. "Well, that sure was fine," he added. "Henry's sure a wonder, aint he?" He set his glass down and turned to the door. "Well, you boys make yourselves at home. If you want anything, just call Houston." And he bustled out at his distracted trot.

"Sit down," MacCallum said. He drew up a chair, and Bayard drew another up opposite him across the table. "Deacon sure ought to know good whisky. He's drunk enough of it to float his counters right on out the front door." He filled his glass and pushed the bottle across to Bayard, and they drank again, quietly.

"You look bad, son," MacCallum said suddenly, and Bayard raised his head and found the other examining him with his keen steady eyes. "Overtrained," he added, and Bayard made an abrupt gesture of negation and raised his glass again, but he could still feel the other watching him intently but without rudeness. "Well, you haven't forgot how to drink good whisky, anyhow . . . Why dont you come out and take a week's hunt? Got an old red we been saving for you. Been running him off and on for two years, now, with the young dogs. Aint put old General on him yet, because the old feller'll nose him out, and I wanted to save him for you boys. John would have enjoyed that fox. You remember that night John cut across down to Samson's bridge ahead of the dogs, and when we got to the river here come him and the fox floating along on that drift log, the fox on one end and John on the other, singing that fool song as loud as he could yell? John would

have enjoyed this here fox. He outsmarts them young
dogs every time. But old General'll get him."

Bayard sat with his head bent, turning his glass in
his hand. He reached a packet of cigarettes from his
jacket and shook a few of them onto the table at his
hand and flipped the packet across the table to the
other. But MacCallum made no move to take it. He
drank his toddy steadily and refilled his glass and
stirred his spoon slowly in it. Bayard lit one of his
cigarettes and emptied his glass and reached for the
bottle. "You look like hell, boy," MacCallum repeated.

"Dry, I reckon," Bayard answered in a voice as
level as the other's. He made himself another toddy,
his cigarette smoking on the table edge beside him.
He raised his glass, but instead of drinking he held it
for a moment to his nose, and the small muscles at
the base of his nostrils tautened whitely, then he
swung the glass from him and with a steady hand he
emptied it onto the floor. The other watched him
quietly while he picked up the bottle again and
poured the glass half full of raw liquor and sloshed a
little water into it and tilted it down his throat. "I've
been good too damn long," he said aloud, and he fell
to talking of the war. Not of combat, but rather of a
life peopled by young men like fallen angels, and of
a meteoric violence like that of fallen angels, beyond
heaven or hell and partaking of both: doomed immortality and immortal doom.

MacCallum sat and listened quietly, drinking his
whisky steadily and slowly and without appreciable
effect, as though it were milk he drank; and Bayard
talked on and presently found himself without surprise eating food. The bottle was now less than half
full. The negro Houston had brought the food in
and had his drink, taking it neat and without batting

an eye. "Ef I had a cow dat give dat, de calf wouldn't git no milk a-tall," he said, "and I wouldn't never churn. Thank'ee, Mr MacCallum, suh."

Then he was out, and Bayard's voice went on, filling the cubby-hole of a room, surmounting the odor of cheap food too quickly cooked and of sharp spilt whisky, with ghosts of a thing high-pitched as a hysteria, like a glare of fallen meteors on the dark retina of the world. Again a light tap at the door, and the proprietor's egg-shaped head and his hot diffident eyes.

"You gentlemen got everything you want?" he asked, rubbing his hands on his thighs.

"Come and get it," MacCallum said, jerking his head toward the bottle, and the other made himself a toddy in his stale glass and drank it and stood while Bayard finished his tale of himself and an Australian major and two ladies in the Leicester lounge one evening (the Leicester lounge being out of bounds, and the Anzac lost two teeth and his girl, and Bayard himself got a black eye), watching the narrator with round melting astonishment.

"Great Savior," he said, "the av'aytors was sure some hellraisers, wadn't they? Well, I reckon they're wanting me up front again. You got to keep on the jump to make a living, these days." And he scuttled out again.

"I've been good too goddam long," Bayard repeated harshly, watching MacCallum fill the two glasses. "That's the only thing Johnny was ever good for. Kept me from getting in a rut. Bloody rut, with a couple of old women hanging around me, and nothing to do except scare old niggers." He drank his whisky and set the glass down on the table, still clutching it. "Damn ham-handed Hun," he said. "He never could learn to fly properly. I kept trying to keep him from going up there on that goddam popgun," and he cursed his dead brother savagely. Then he raised his glass again, but halted it half way to his mouth. "Where in hell did my drink go?"

MacCallum reached the bottle and emptied it into Bayard's glass, and he drank and banged the thick tumbler on the table and rose and lurched back against the wall. His chair crashed backward, and he braced himself, staring at the other. "I kept on trying to keep him from going up there, on that Camel. But he gave me a burst. Right across my nose."

MacCallum rose also. "Come on here," he said quietly, and he offered to take Bayard's arm, but Bayard evaded him and they passed through the kitchen and traversed the long tunnel of the store. Bayard walked steadily enough, and the proprietor bobbed his head at them across the counter.

"Call again, gentlemen," he said. "Call again."

"All right, Deacon," MacCallum answered. Bayard strode on without turning his head. As they passed the soda fountain a young lawyer standing beside a stranger, addressed him.

"Captain Sartoris, shake hands with Mr Gratton here. Gratton was up on the British front for a while last year." The stranger turned and extended his hand, but Bayard stared at him bleakly and walked so steadily on that the other involuntarily gave back a pace in order not to be overborne.

"Why, goddam his soul," he said to Bayard's back. The lawyer grasped his arm.

"He's drunk," he whispered quickly, "he's drunk."

"I dont give a damn," the other exclaimed loudly. "Because he was a goddam shave-tail he thinks—"

"Shhhh, shhhh," the lawyer hissed. The proprietor appeared at the corner of his candy case, peering out with hot round alarm.

"Gentlemen, gentlemen!" he exclaimed. The stranger made another violent movement, and Bayard stopped.

"Wait a minute while I bash his face in," he told MacCallum, turning. The stranger thrust the lawyer aside and stepped forward.

"You never saw the day—" he began. MacCallum took Bayard's arm firmly and easily.

"Come on here, boy."

"I'll bash his bloody face in," Bayard stated equably, watching the angry stranger with his bleak eyes. The lawyer grasped his companion's arm again.

"Get away," the other said, flinging him off. "Just let him try it. Come on, you limey—"

"Gentlemen! Gentlemen!" the proprietor implored.

"Come on here, boy," MacCallum said. "I've got to look at a horse."

"A horse?" Bayard repeated. He turned obediently, then as an afterthought he paused and looked back. "Cant bash your face in now," he told the stranger. "Sorry. Got to look at a horse. Call for you at the hotel later." But the stranger's back was turned, and behind it the lawyer grimaced at MacCallum and waggled his hand.

"Get him away, MacCallum, for God's sake."

"Bash his face in later," Bayard repeated. "Cant bash yours, though, Eustace," he told the lawyer. "Taught us in ground-school never seduce a fool nor hit a cripple."

"Come on, here," MacCallum repeated, leading him away. At the door Bayard must stop again to light a cigarette, then they went on. It was three oclock and again they walked among school children in released surges, sibilant with temporary freedom. Bayard strode steadily enough, and a little bellig-

erently, and presently MacCallum turned into a side
street and they went on before negro shops, and between a busy grist mill and a silent cotton gin they
turned into a lane filled with tethered horses and
mules. From the end of the lane a blacksmith's anvil
clanged, but they passed its ruby glow and the
squatting overalled men along the shady wall, and
came next to a high barred gate backing a long dun-
colored brick building smelling of ammonia. A few
men sat on the top of the gate, others leaned their
crossed arms upon it, and from the paddock itself
came voices, then through the slatted gate gleamed a
haughty motionless shape of burnished flame.

The stallion stood against the yawning cavern of
the livery stable door like a motionless bronze flame,
and along its burnished coat ran at intervals little
tremors of paler flame, little tongues of nervousness
and pride. But its eye was quiet and arrogant, and occasionally and with a kingly air its gaze swept along
the group at the gate with a fine disdain, without
seeing them as individuals at all, and again little
tongues of paler flame rippled flicking along its coat.
About its head was a rope hackamore; it was tethered
to a door post, and in the background a white man
moved about at a respectful distance with a proprietorial air: beside him, a negro hostler with a tow sack
tied about his middle with a string. MacCallum and
Bayard halted at the gate, and the white man circled
the stallion's haughty immobility and crossed to
them. The negro hostler came forth also, with a soft
dirty cloth and chanting in a sad mellow singsong.
The stallion permitted him to approach and suffered
him to erase with his rag the licking nervous little
flames that ran in renewed ripples under its skin.

"Aint he a picture, now?" the white man demanded of MacCallum, leaning his elbow on the

gate. A cheap nickel watch was attached to his suspender loop by a length of rawhide lace leather worn black and soft with age, and his shaven beard was heaviest from the corners of his mouth to his chin; he looked always as though he were chewing tobacco with his mouth open. He was a horse trader by profession, and he was usually engaged in litigation with the railroad company over the violent demise of some of his stock by its agency. "Look at that nigger, now," he added. "He'll let Tobe handle him like a baby. I wouldn't get within ten foot of him, myself. Dam'f I know how Tobe does it. Must be some kin between a nigger and a animal, I always claim."

"I reckon he's afraid you'll be crossing the railroad with him some day about the time 39 is due," MacCallum said drily.

"Yes, I reckon I have the hardest luck of any feller in this county," the other agreed. "But they got to settle this time: I got 'em dead to rights this time."

"Yes," MacCallum said. "The railroad company ought to furnish that stock of your'n with time tables." The other onlookers guffawed.

"Ah, the company's got plenty of money," the trader rejoined. Then he said: "You talk like I might have druv them mules in front of that train. Lemme tell you how it come about—"

"I reckon you wont never drive him in front of no train." MacCallum jerked his head toward the stallion. The negro burnished its shimmering coat, crooning to it in a monotonous singsong. The trader laughed.

"I reckon not," he admitted. "Not less'n Tobe goes, too. Just look at him, now. I wouldn't no more walk up to that animal than I'd fly."

"I'm going to ride that horse," Bayard said suddenly.

"What hoss?" the trader demanded, and the other onlookers watched Bayard climb the gate and vault over into the lot. "You let that hoss alone, young feller," the trader added. But Bayard paid him no heed. He turned from the gate, the stallion swept its regal gaze upon him and away. "You let that hoss alone," the trader shouted, "or I'll have the law on you."

"Let him be," MacCallum said.

"And let him damage a fifteen hundred dollar stallion? That hoss'll kill him. You, Sartoris!"

MacCallum drew a wad of bills enclosed by a rubber band from his hip pocket. "Let him be," he repeated. "That's what he wants."

The trader glanced at the money with quick calculation. "I take you gentlemen to witness—" he began loudly, then he ceased and they watched tensely as Bayard approached the stallion. The beast swept its haughty glowing eye upon him again and lifted its head without alarm and snorted, and the negro crouched against its shoulder and his crooning chant rose to a swifter beat. Then the beast snorted again and swept its head up, snapping the rope like a gossamer thread, and the negro grasped at the flying rope-end.

"Git away, whitefolks," he said hurriedly. "Git away, quick."

But the stallion eluded his hand. It cropped its teeth in a vicious arc and the negro leaped sprawling as the animal's whole body soared like a bronze explosion. But Bayard had dodged beneath the sabring hooves and as the horse swirled the myriad flicking tongues of its glittering coat the spectators saw that the man had contrived to take a turn with the rope-end about its jaws, then they saw the animal rear again, dragging the man from the ground and whipping his body like a rag upon its flashing arc. Then it stopped trembling as Bayard closed its nostrils with the twisted rope, and suddenly he was upon its back while still it stood with lowered head and rolling eyes, rippling its burnished coat into quivering tongues of flame before exploding again.

The beast burst like unfolding bronze wings: a fluid desperation; the onlookers tumbled away from the gate and hurled themselves to safety as the gate splintered to matchwood beneath its soaring volcanic thunder. Bayard crouched on its shoulders and dragged its mad head around and they swept down the lane, spreading pandemonium among the horses and mules tethered and patient before the blacksmith shop and among the wagons there. Where the lane debouched into the street a group of negroes scattered before them, and without a break in its stride the stallion soared over a small negro child clutching a stick of striped candy directly in its path. A wagon drawn by mules was turning into the lane: these reared madly before the wild slack-jawed face of the white man in the wagon, and again Bayard dragged his thunderbolt around and headed it away from the square. Down the lane behind him, through the dust the spectators ran, shouting, the trader among them, and Rafe MacCallum still clutching his roll of money.

The stallion moved beneath him like a tremendous mad music, uncontrolled, splendidly uncontrollable. The rope served only to curb its direction, not its speed, and among shouts from the pavement on either side he swung the animal into another street that broke suddenly upon his vision. This was a quieter street; soon they would be in the country and the stallion could exhaust its rage without the added hazards of motors and pedestrians. Voices faded behind him into the thunder of shod hooves: "Runaway! Runaway!" but this street was deserted save for a small automobile going in the same direction, and further along beneath the slumbrous tunnel of the trees, bright small spots of color scuttled out of the street and clotted on one side. Children. Hope they stay there, he said to himself. His eyes were streaming a little; beneath him the surging lift and fall; in his nostrils a pungent sharpness of rage and energy and heat like smoke from the animal's body, and he swept past the motor car, remarking for a flashing second a woman's face and a mouth partly open and two eyes round with a serene astonishment. But the face flashed away without registering on his mind and he saw the children, small taut shapes of fear in bright colors, and on the other side of the street a negro man playing a hose onto the sidewalk, and beside him a second negro with a pitchfork.

Someone screamed from a neighboring veranda, and the group of children broke, shrieking; a small figure in a white shirt and diminutive pale blue pants darted from the curb into the street, and Bayard leaned forward and dragged at the rope, swerving the beast toward the opposite sidewalk, where the two negroes stood. The small figure came on, flashed safely behind, then rushing green beneath the stallion's feet; a tree trunk like a wheel spoke in reverse, and the animal struck clashing fire from wet concrete, slipped, lunged, then crashed down; and for Bayard, a red shock, then blackness. The horse scrambled to its feet and whirled and struck viciously at the prone rider with its forefeet, but the negro with the pitchfork drove it away, whereupon it trotted stiffly back up the street and passed the slowing motor car with the woman driver. At the end of the street it submitted docilely to capture by the negro hostler. Rafe MacCallum still clutched his roll of bills.

6

They gathered him up and brought him to town in a commandeered motor car and roused Dr Peabody from slumber. Dr Peabody profanely bandaged Bayard's unconscious head and, when he came to, gave him a drink from the bottle which resided in the littered waste basket and threatened to telephone Miss Jenny if Bayard didn't go straight home. Rafe MacCallum promised to see that he went, and the owner of the impressed automobile offered to drive him. It was a Ford body with, in place of a tonneau, a miniature one-room cabin of sheet iron and larger than a dog kennel, in each painted geometrical window of which a painted housewife simpered benignantly above a painted sewing machine, and into which an actual sewing machine neatly fitted, borne thus about the countryside by the agent. The agent's name was V. K. Suratt and he now sat with his shrewd plausible face behind the wheel. Bayard with his humming head sat beside him, and to the fender clung a youth with brown forearms and a slanted extremely new straw hat, who let his limber body absorb the jolts with negligent young skill as they rattled sedately out of town on the valley road.

The drink Dr Peabody had given him, instead of quieting his jangled nervous system, rolled sluggishly and hotly in his stomach and served only to nauseate him a little, and against his closed eyelids red antic shapes rolled in throbbing and tedious cycles. He watched them dully and without astonishment as they emerged from blackness and whirled sluggishly and consumed themselves and reappeared, each time a little fainter as his mind cleared. And yet, somewhere blended with them, yet at the same time apart and beyond them with a serene aloofness and steadfast among their senseless convolutions, was a head with twin dark wings of hair. It seemed to have some relation to the instant itself as it culminated in crashing blackness; at the same time it seemed, for all its aloofness, to be a part of the whirling ensuing chaos which now enveloped him; a part of it, yet bringing into the vortex a sort of constant coolness like a faint, shady breeze. So it remained, aloof and not quite distinct, while the coiling shapes faded into a dull unease of physical pain from the jolting of the car, leaving about him like an echo that cool serenity and something more—a sense of shrinking yet fascinated distaste, of which he or something he had done, was the object.

It was getting well into evening. On either hand cotton and corn showed in green spears upon the rich, dark soil, and in the patches of green woodland doves called moodily. After a time Suratt turned from the highway into a faint, rutted wagon road between a field and a patch of woods and they drove straight into the sun, and Bayard held his hat before his face.

"Sun hurt yo' head?" Suratt asked beside him. "'Taint long, now," he added. The road wound presently into the woods where the sun was intermittent, and it rose gradually toward a low crest on which trees stood like a barred grate against the western sky. They crossed this hill and the land fell away in ragged ill-tended fields, and beyond them in a clump of fruit trees and a grove of silver poplars pale as absinthe and twinkling ceaselessly without wind, a weathered small house squatted. Beyond it and much larger loomed a barn gray and gaunt with age. The road forked here. One faint arm curved sandily away toward the house; the other went on between rank weeds toward the barn. The youth on the fender leaned his head into the car. "Drive on to the barn," he directed.

Suratt obeyed. Beyond the bordering weeds a fence straggled in limp dilapidation, and from the weeds the handles of a plow stood at a gaunt angle while its shard rusted peacefully in the undergrowth, and other implements rusted half concealed in the growth—skeletons of labor healed over by the earth they were to have violated, kinder than they. The fence turned at an angle and Suratt stopped the car and the youth stepped down and opened a warped wooden gate and Suratt drove on into the barnyard where stood a wagon with drunken wheels and a home-made bed, and the rusting skeleton of a Ford car. Low down upon its domed and hoodless radiator the two lamps gave it an expression of beetling patient astonishment, like a skull, and a lean cow ruminated and watched them without interest.

The barn doors sagged drunkenly from broken hinges, held to the posts with twists of baling wire; beyond, the cavern of the hallway yawned in stale desolation—a travesty of earth's garnered fulness and its rich inferences. Bayard sat on the fender and leaned his bandaged head back against the car body and watched Suratt and the youth enter the barn and disappear slowly upward on invisible ladder rungs. The cow stood yet in ruminant dejection, and upon the yellow surface of a pond enclosed by banks of trodden and sun-cracked clay beneath a clump of locust shrubs and willows, geese drifted like small muddy clouds. The sun fell in a long slant upon their rumps and their suave necks and upon the cow's lean rhythmically twitching flank, ridging her visible ribs with dingy gold. Presently Suratt's legs fumbled into sight, followed by his cautious body, and after him the youth with his slanted hat slid easily down the perpendicular ladder, letting his body from rung to rung in easy one-handed swoops.

He emerged carrying an earthen jug close against his leg. Suratt followed in his neat tieless blue shirt and jerked his head at Bayard, and they turned the corner of the barn and retreated along the wall, among waist-high jimson weeds. Bayard rose and followed and overtook them as the youth with his jug slid with an agile unceasing motion between two lax strands of barbed wire. Suratt stooped through more sedately and held the top strand taut and pressed the lower one down with his foot until Bayard was through. Behind the barn the land descended into shadow toward a junglish growth of willow and elder, against which a huge beech and a clump of saplings stood like mottled ghosts, and from which a cool dankness rose like a breath to meet them. The spring welled from the roots of the beech into a wooden frame buried to the edge in white sand that quivered ceaselessly and delicately beneath the water's limpid unrest, and strayed on away into the willow and elder growth without a sound.

The earth about the spring was trampled smooth and packed as an earthen floor. Near the spring a blackened iron pot sat on four bricks, beneath it was a heap of pale wood ashes and a litter of extinct brands and charred fagot-ends. Against the pot leaned a scrubbing board with a ridged metal face polished to a dull even gleam like old silver, and a rusty tin cup hung from a nail in the beech tree above the spring. The youth set the jug down and he and Suratt squatted gravely beside it.

"I dont know if we aint a-goin' to git in trouble, givin' Mr Bayard whisky, Hub," Suratt said. "Still, Doc Peabody give him one dram hisself, so I reckon we kin give him one mo'. Aint that right, Mr Bayard?" Squatting he glanced up at Bayard with his shrewd affable face. Hub twisted the corncob stopper from the jug and passed it to Suratt, who tendered it to Bayard. "I been knowin' Mr Bayard ever since he was a chap in knee pants," Suratt confided to Hub, "but this is the first time me and him ever taken a drink together. Aint that so, Mr Bayard? . . . I reckon you'll want a drinkin' cup, wont you?" But Bayard was already drinking, with the jug tilted across his horizontal forearm and the mouth held to his lips by the same hand, as it should be done. "He knows how to drink outen a jug, dont he?" Suratt added. "I knowed he was all right," he said in a tone of confidential vindication. Bayard lowered the jug and returned it to Suratt, who offered it formally to Hub.

"Go ahead," Hub said. "Hit it." Suratt did so, with measured pistonings of his taut throat in relief against the brooding green of the jungle wall. Above the stream gnats whirled and spun in a levelling ray of sunlight like erratic golden chaff. Suratt lowered the jug and passed it to Hub and wiped his mouth on the back of his hand.

"How you feel now, Mr Bayard?" he asked. Then he said heavily: "You'll have to excuse me. I reckon I ought to said Captain Sartoris, oughtn't I?"

"What for?" Bayard asked. He squatted also on his heels, against the bole of the tree beside the limpid soundless laughing of the spring. The rising slope of ground behind them hid the barn and the house, and the three of them squatted in a small bowl of peacefulness remote from the world and its rumors, filled with the cool unceasing breathing of the spring and a seeping of sunlight among the elders and willows like a thinly diffused wine. On the surface of the spring the sky lay reflected, stippled with windless beech leaves. Hub squatted leanly with his brown forearms clasped about his knees, smoking a cigarette beneath the downward tilt of his straw hat. Suratt was across the spring from him. He wore a faded clean blue shirt, and in contrast to it his hands and face were a rich even brown, like mahogany. The jug sat rotundly, benignantly between them.

"Yes, sir," Suratt repeated, "I always find the best cure for a wound is plenty of whisky. Doctors, these here fancy young doctors, 'll tell a feller different, but old Doc Peabody hisself cut off my gran'pappy's leg while gran'pappy laid back on the dinin' table with a demijohn in his hand and a mattress and a chair across his laigs and fo' men a-holdin' him down, and him cussin' and singin' so scandalous the women-folks and the chillen went down to the pasture behind the barn and waited. Take some mo'," he said, and he reached the jug across the spring and Bayard drank again. "Reckon you're beginnin' to feel pretty fair, aint you?"

"Damned if I know," Bayard answered. "It's dynamite, boys."

Suratt with the lifted jug guffawed, then he lipped it and his Adam's apple pumped again in arched relief against the wall of elder and willow. The elder would soon flower, with pale clumps of tiny blooms. Miss Jenny made a little wine of it every year. Good wine, if you knew how and had the patience. Elder flower wine. Like a ritual for a children's game; a game played by little girls in small pale dresses, between supper and twilight. Above the bowl where sunlight yet came in a levelling beam, gnats whirled and spun like dust-motes in a quiet disused room. Suratt's voice went on affably, ceaselessly recapitulant, in polite admiration of the hardness of Bayard's head and the fact that this was the first time he and Bayard had ever taken a drink together. They drank again, and Hub began to borrow cigarettes of Bayard and he became also a little profanely and robustly anecdotal in his country idiom, about whisky and girls and dice; and presently he and Suratt were arguing amicably about work. They seemed to be able to sit tirelessly and without discomfort on their heels, but Bayard's legs had soon grown numb and he straightened them, tingling with released blood, and he now sat with his back against the tree and his long legs straight before him, hearing Suratt's voice without listening to it.

His head was now no more than a sort of taut discomfort; at times it seemed to float away from his shoulders and hang against the wall of green like a transparent balloon within which or beyond which that face that would neither emerge completely and distinguishably nor yet fade completely away and so trouble him no longer, lingered with shadowy exasperation—two eyes round with a grave shocked astonishment, two lifted hands flashing behind little white shirt and blue pants swerving into a lifting rush plunging clatter crash blackness . . .

Suratt's slow plausible voice went on steadily, but without any irritant quality. It seemed to fit easily into the still scene, speaking of earthy things. "Way I learnt to chop cotton," he was saying, "my oldest brother taken and put me in the same row ahead of him. Started me off, and soon's I taken a lick or two, here he come behind me. And ever' time my hoe chopped once I could year his'n chop twice. I never had no shoes in them days, neither," he added drily.

"So I had to learn to chop fast. But I swo' then, come what mought, that I wouldn't never plant nothin' in the ground, soon's I could he'p myself. It's all right for folks that owns land, but folks like my folks was dont never own no land, and ever' time we made a furrow, we was scratchin' earth for somebody else." The gnats danced and whirled more madly yet in the sun above the secret places of the stream, and the sun's light was taking on a rich copper tinge. Suratt rose. "Well, boys, I got to be gittin' back to'ds town, myself." He looked at Bayard again with his shrewd talkative face. "I reckon Mr Bayard's clean got over that knock he taken, aint he?"

"Dammit," Bayard said, "quit calling me Mr Bayard."

Suratt picked up the jug. "I knowed he was all right, when you got to know him," he said to Hub. "I been knowin' him since he was knee-high to a grasshopper, but me and him jest aint been throwed together like this. I was raised a pore boy, fellers, while Mr Bayard's folks has lived on that 'ere big place with plenty of money in the bank and niggers to wait on 'em. But he's all right," he repeated. "He aint goin' to say nothin' about who give him this here whisky."

"Let him tell, if he wants," Hub answered. "I dont give a damn."

They drank again. The sun was almost gone and from the secret marshy places of the stream came a fairy-like piping of young frogs. The gaunt invisible cow lowed barnward, and Hub replaced the corncob in the mouth of the jug and drove it home with his palm and they mounted the slope above the spring and crawled through the fence. The cow stood in the barn door and watched them approach and lowed again, moody and mournful, and the geese had

left the pond and they now paraded sedately across
the barnyard toward the house, in the door of which,
framed by two crepe-myrtle bushes, a woman stood.

"Hub," she said in a flat country voice.

"Goin' to town," Hub answered shortly. "Sue'll
have to milk."

The woman stood quietly in the door. Hub carried
the jug into the barn. The cow turned and followed
him, but he heard her and turned and gave her a resounding kick in her gaunt ribs and cursed her without heat. Presently he reappeared and went on to the
gate and opened it and stood so until Suratt drove
through. Then he closed it and wired it to again and
swung onto the fender. But Bayard moved over in
the seat and Hub got inside. The woman stood yet in
the door, watching them quietly. About the doorstep
the geese surged erratically with discordant cries,
their necks undulant and suave as formal gestures in
a pantomime.

The shadow of the poplar grove fell long across
the untidy fields, and the car pushed its elongated
shadow before it like the shadow of a huge
humpshouldered bird. They mounted the sandy hill
in the last of the sun among the trees, and dropped
downward out of sunlight and into violet dusk. The
road was soundless with sand and the car lurched in
the worn and shifting ruts and so out of the woods,
between tilled fields again and onto the broad valley
road.

The waxing moon stood overhead. As yet it gave
off no light though, and they drove on toward town,
passing an occasional belated country wagon homeward bound; these Suratt greeted with a grave gesture of his brown hand, and presently where the road
crossed a wooden bridge among more willow and
elder where dusk was yet denser and more palpable,

Suratt stopped the car and climbed out over the door. "You fellers set still," he said. "I wont be but a minute." They heard him at the rear of the car, then he reappeared with a tin bucket and he let himself gingerly down the rank roadside bank beside the bridge. Water chuckled and murmured beneath the bridge, invisible with twilight, its murmur burdened with the voice of cricket and frog. Above the willows that marked its course gnats still spun and whirled, for bullbats appeared from nowhere in long swoops, in midswoop vanished, then appeared again against the serene sky swooping, silent as drops of water on a pane of glass, swift and noiseless and intent as though their wings were feathered with twilight and with silence.

Suratt scrambled up the bank, with his pail, and he removed the radiator cap and tilted the bucket above the mouth of it. The moon stood yet without emphasis overhead, yet a faint shadow of the bucket fell upon the hood of the car and upon the pallid planking of the bridge the leaning willow fronds were repeated, faintly but delicately distinct. The last of the water gurgled with faint rumblings into the engine's interior and Suratt replaced the bucket and climbed over the blind door again. The lights operated from a generator; he turned these on now. While the car was in low speed the lights glared to a soundless crescendo, but when he let the clutch in they dropped to a wavering glow no more than a luminous shadow on the unrolling monotonous ribbon of the road.

Night was an accomplished thing before they reached town. Across the unemphatic land the lights on the courthouse clock were like yellow beads suspended above the trees, on the dark horizon line, and upon the green afterglow in the west a column of smoke stood like a balanced plume. Suratt put them out at the restaurant and drove on, and they entered and the proprietor lifted his conical head and his round melting eyes from behind the soda fountain.

"Great Savior, boy," he exclaimed. "Aint you gone home yet? Doc Peabody's been huntin' you ever since four oclock, and Miss Jenny drove to town in the carriage, lookin' for you. You'll kill yourself."

"Get to hell back yonder, Deacon," Bayard answered, "and bring me and Hub about two dollars' worth of ham and eggs."

Later they returned for the jug in Bayard's car, Bayard and Hub and a third young man, freight agent at the railway station, with three negroes and a bull fiddle in the rear seat. But they drove no further than the edge of the field above the house and stopped here while Hub went on afoot down the sandy weed-hedged road toward the barn in its looming silver solitude. The moon stood pale and cold overhead, and on all sides insects shrilled in the dusty undergrowth. In the rear seat the negroes murmured among themselves.

"Fine night," Mitch, the freight agent, suggested. But Bayard smoked his cigarette moodily, his head closely helmeted in its white bandage. Moon and insects were one, audible and visible, dimensionless and unsourced.

After a while Hub materialized against the dissolving vagueness of the road, crowned by the silver gleam of his hat, and he swung the jug onto the door and removed the stopper. Mitch passed it to Bayard.

"Drink," Bayard said shortly, and Mitch did so, then the others drank.

"We aint got nothin' for the niggers to drink out of," Hub said.

"That's so," Mitch agreed. He turned in his seat. "Aint one of you boys got a cup or something?" The negroes murmured again, questioning one another in mellow consternation.

"I know," Bayard said. He got out and lifted the hood and removed the cap from the breather-pipe. "It'll taste a little like oil for a drink or two, but you boys wont notice it after that."

"Naw, suh," the negroes agreed in chorus. One took the cup and wiped it out with the corner of his coat, and they too drank in turn, with smacking expulsions of breath. Then Bayard replaced the cap and got into his seat.

"Anybody want another right now?" Hub asked, poising the corncob above the jug mouth.

"Give Mitch another," Bayard directed. "He'll have to catch up."

Mitch drank again briefly. Then Bayard took the jug and tilted it. The others watched him respectfully.

"Dam'f he dont drink it," Mitch murmured. "I'd be afraid to hit it so often, if I was you."

"It's my damned head." Bayard lowered the jug and passed it to Hub. "I keep thinking another drink will ease it off some."

"Doc put that bandage on too tight," Hub said. "You want it loosened a little?"

"I dont know." Bayard lit another cigarette and threw the match away. "I believe I'll take it off. It's been on there long enough." He raised his hands and fumbled at the bandage.

"You better let it alone," Mitch said. But Bayard fumbled at the fastening, then he slid his fingers beneath a turn of the cloth and tugged at it savagely.

One of the negroes leaned forward with a pocket knife and severed it, and they watched quietly while Bayard stripped it off and flung it away.

"You ought not to done that," Mitch told him.

"Ah, let him take it off, if he wants," Hub said. "He's all right." He got in and stowed the jug away between his knees. Bayard backed the car around. The sandy road hissed beneath its broad tires and rose shaling into the woods again where the dappled moonlight was intermittent, treacherous with dissolving vistas of shadow and formless growth. Invisible and sourceless among the shifting patterns of light and shade whip-poor-wills were like flutes tongued liquidly. The road passed out of the woods and descended, with sand in shifting and silent lurches, and they emerged between fields flattening away to the straight valley road and turned onto it and away from town.

The car swept onward, borne on the sustained hiss of its muffled intake like a dry sibilance of sand in a huge hour glass. The negroes in the back murmured quietly among themselves in mellow snatches, mellow snatches of laughter whipped from their lips like scraps of torn paper swirling away behind. They passed the iron gates and Bayard's home dreaming serenely in the moonlight among its trees, and the silent boxlike flag station and the metal-roofed cotton gin on the railroad siding. Then the road rose into the hills. It was broad and smooth and empty for all its winding, and the negroes sat now a little tensely anticipatory. But Bayard drove at a steady smooth gait, not slow, but not anything like what they had expected of him. Twice more they stopped and drank, and then from an ultimate hilltop they looked downward upon clustered lights again. Hub produced the breather cap and they drank once more.

Through streets identical with those at home they moved smoothly, toward an identical square. People along the streets turned and looked after them curiously. They crossed the square without stopping and into another quiet street. There were no arc lights at the street intersections, since there was a moon, and they went on between broad lawns and shaded windows, and presently beyond an iron fence and set well back among ancient trees, lighted windows hung in ordered tiers like rectangular lanterns strung among the branches.

They stopped here in shadow. The negroes descended and lifted the bass viol out, and a guitar. The third negro held a slender tube frosted over with keys upon which the intermittent moon glinted in hushed glints, and they stood with their heads together, murmuring among themselves and touching plaintive muted chords from the strings. Then the one with the clarinet raised it to his lips.

The tunes were old tunes. Some of them were sophisticated tunes and formally intricate, but in the rendition this was lost and all of them were imbued instead with a plaintive similarity, a slurred and rhythmic simplicity, and they drifted in rich plaintive chords upon the silver air fading, dying in minor reiterations along the treacherous vistas of moon and shadow. They played again, an old waltz. The college Cerberus came across the dappled lawn to the fence, but without antagonistic intent. Across the street, in the shadows there, other listeners stood; a car approached and slowed into the curb and shut off motor and lights, and in the tiered windows heads leaned, aureoled against the lighted rooms behind, without individuality at this distance but feminine and delicately and divinely young.

At last they played "Home, Sweet Home" and

when the rich minor died away, across to them came a soft clapping of slender palms. Then Mitch sang "Goodnight, Ladies" in his true, oversweet tenor, and the young hands were more importunate; and as they drove away the slender heads leaned aureoled with bright hair in the lighted windows and the soft clapping drifted after them for a long while, fainter and fainter in the silver silence.

At the top of the first hill out of town they stopped and Hub removed the breather cap. Behind them random lights among the trees, and it was as though there came yet to them across the hushed world that sound of young palms like flung delicate flowers before their youth and masculinity, and they drank without speaking, lapped yet in the fading magic of the lost moment. Mitch sang to himself softly; the car slid purring on again. The road dropped curving smoothly, empty and blanched. Bayard broke the spell.

"Cut out, Hub," he said. Hub bent forward and reached under the dash and the car slid on with a steady leashed muttering like waking thunderous wings, then the road flattened in a long swoop toward another rise and the muttering lept to crescendo and the car shot forward with neck-snapping violence. The negroes' murmur ceased, then one of them raised a wailing shout.

"Reno lost his hat," Hub said, looking back.

"He dont need it," Bayard shouted in reply. The car roared up this hill and rushed across the crest of it and flashed around a tight banked curve.

"Oh, Lawd," the negro wailed. "Mr Bayard!" His words whipped away behind like stripped leaves. "Lemme out, Mr Bayard!"

"Jump out, then," Bayard answered. The road fell from beneath them like a tilting floor and away across a valley, straight now as a string. The negroes crouched with their eyes shut against the air blast, clutching their instruments. The speedometer showed 55 and 60 and turned slowly on. Mad rushing miles sped beneath them, sparse houses loomed into the headlights' sweep, flashed slumbering away, and fields and patches of woodland like tunnels, and still they roared on beneath the silver night across the black and silver land.

The road wound among the hills. Whip-poor-wills called on either side, one to another in quiring liquid astonishment at their thunderous phantom; at intervals when the headlights swept in the road's abrupt windings two spots of pale fire blinked in the dust before the bird blundered awkwardly somewhere beneath the radiator. The ridge rose steadily, with wooded slopes falling away on either hand. Sparse negro cabins squatted upon the slopes or beside the road, dappled with shadow and lightless and profound with slumber; beneath trees before them wagons stood or warped farm implements leaned, shelterless, after the shiftless fashion of negroes.

The road dipped, then rose again in a long slant broken by another dip; then it stood directly before them like a wall. The car shot upward and over the dip, left the road completely, then swooped dreadfully on, and the negroes' concerted wail whipped forlornly away. Then the ridge attained its crest and the car's thunder ceased and it came slowly to a stop. The negroes sat now in the bottom of the tonneau.

"Is dis heaven?" one murmured after a time.

"Dey wouldn't let you in heaven, wid licker on yo' breaf and no hat, feller," another said.

"Ef de Lawd dont take no better keer of me dan He done of dat hat, I dont wanter go dar, noways," the first rejoined.

"Mmmmmmm," the second agreed. "When us come down dat 'ere las' hill, dis yere cla'inet almos' blowed clean outen my han', let 'lone my hat."

"And when us jumped over dat 'ere lawg er whut-ever it wuz back dar," the third one added, "I thought for a minute dis whole auto'bile done blowed outen my han'."

They drank again. It was high here, and the air moved with gray coolness. On either hand lay a valley filled with shadow and with ceaseless whip-poor-wills; beyond these valleys the silver earth rolled on into the sky. Across it, sourceless and mournful and far, a dog howled. Before them the lights on the courthouse clock were steadfast and yellow and unwinking in the dissolving distance, but in all other directions the world rolled away in slumbrous ridges, milkily opaline. Bayard's head felt as cool and clear as a clapperless and windless bell. Within it that head emerged clearly at last, those two eyes round with grave astonishment, winged serenely by two dark wings of hair. He sat for a while in the motionless car, gazing into the sky.

"It was that Benbow girl," he said to himself quietly.

All of her instincts were antipathetic toward him, toward his violence and his brutally obtuse disregard of all the qualities which composed her being. His idea was like a trampling of heavy feet in those cool corridors of hers, in that grave serenity in which her days accomplished themselves; at the very syllables of his name her instincts brought her upstanding and under arms against him, thus increasing, doubling the sense of violation by the act of repulsing him and by the necessity for it. And yet, despite her armed senti-

nels, he still crashed with that hot violence of his
through the bastions and thundered at the very in-
most citadel of her being. Even chance seemed to
abet him, lending to his brutal course a sort of
theatrical glamor, a tawdry simulation of the virtues
which the reasons (if he had reasons) for his actions
outwardly ridiculed. That mad flaming beast he rode
almost over her car and then swerved it with an utter
disregard of consequences to himself onto a wet sidewalk in order to avoid a frightened child; the pallid,
suddenly dreaming calm of his bloody face from
which violence had been temporarily wiped as with
a damp cloth, leaving it still with that fine bold austerity of Roman statuary, beautiful as a flame shaped
in bronze and cooled: the outward form of its energy but without its heat.

Her appetite was gone at supper, and Aunt Sally
mouthed her prepared soft food and mumbled querulously at her because she would not eat. But eat she
could not; there was still between her and any desire
for food the afternoon's experience like a recurring
echo in her violated corridors—the mad rush of the
beast and its rider like a bronze tidal wave, into
which the small running figure in white and pale
blue was sucked and overwhelmed and spewed forth
again unscathed while the wave spent its blind fury
and ebbed, leaving the rider prone on the wet sidewalk while the horse stood erect like a man and
struck at him with its forefeet. And partly because
that with recurrence of the picture her sense of irre-
mediable violation increased and partly through
irritation and anger with herself because it did, food
choked her; she could not swallow it.

Later Aunt Sally sat and talked monotonously
above her interminable fancy-work. Aunt Sally
would never divulge what is was to be when com-

pleted, nor for whom, and she had been working on it for fifteen years, carrying always about with her a shapeless bag of dingy threadbare brocade containing odds and ends of colored fabric in all possible shapes. She could never bring herself to trim any of them to any pattern, so she shifted and fitted and mused and shifted them like pieces of a puzzle picture, trying to fit them to a pattern or to create a pattern about them without cutting them, smoothing her colored scraps on a cardtable with flaccid, patient putty-colored fingers, shifting and shifting them. From the bosom of her dress the needle Narcissa had threaded for her dangled its spidery skein.

Across the room Narcissa sat on her curled legs, with a book. Aunt Sally's voice droned on with bland querulous interminability, and Narcissa turned the pages restively under her unseeing eyes. Suddenly she rose and laid the book down and crossed the hall into another room and sat in the half-light at her piano. But still between herself and the familiar keyboard the thunderous climacteric of the afternoon's moment recurred and she saw his calm and bloodless face as a piece of flotsam unwelcome and too heavy to move, washed onto the grave unshadowed beach of her days, disrupting that serene constancy to which she clung so fiercely; and at last she rose with abrupt decision and went to the telephone.

Miss Jenny thanked her for her solicitude tartly, and dared to say that Bayard was all right, still an active member of the so-called human race, that is, since they had received no official word from the coroner. No, she had heard nothing of him since Loosh Peabody had 'phoned her at four oclock that Bayard was on his way home with a broken head. The broken head she readily believed, but the other part of the message she had put no credence in whatever, having lived with those damn Sartorises eighty years and knowing that home would be the last place in the world a Sartoris with a broken head would ever consider going. No, she was not even interested in his present whereabouts, and she hoped he hadn't injured the horse? Horses were valuable animals.

Well, if Miss Jenny wasn't alarmed, she certainly had no call to be, and she returned to the living room and explained to Aunt Sally whom she had been talking to and why, and drew a low chair to the lamp and picked up her book. She put the afternoon from her mind deliberately, and for a while and with a sort of detachment she watched her other self sink further and further into the book, until at last the book absorbed her attention. But then the vacuum of her relaxed will roused her again, and although she read deliberately on, a minor part of her consciousness probed ceaselessly, seeking the reason, until with a stabbing rush like a touched nerve it filled her mind again—the bronze fury of them, the child become an intent and voiceless automaton of fear, Bayard's bleeding head chiselled and calm and cold. Then the long effort of thrusting him without her bastions again.

Aunt Sally fumbled her colored scraps together and returned them to their receptacle and rose and said goodnight and hobbled from the room. Narcissa sat and turned the pages on, hearing the other mount the stairs with measured laborious tappings of her ebony stick, and for a while longer she read with a mounting crescendo of nervous effort. For a paragraph or two, sometimes for a page, the book would absorb her; then again she would find her muscles tensing as she relived the afternoon. She flung the book away and returned to the piano again, determined to exorcise it, but Aunt Sally thumped on the floor overhead with her stick, and she desisted and returned to her discarded book. So it was with actual relief that she greeted Dr Alford shortly after.

"I was passing and heard your piano," he said. "You haven't stopped?"

She explained that Aunt Sally had gone to bed, and he sat formally and talked to her in his cultured pedantic voice on cold and erudite subjects for two hours. Then he departed and she stood in the door and watched him down the drive. The moon stood in the sky; along the drive cedars in a grave descending curve were pointed inky and motionless on the pale, faintly spangled sky, and upon the unstirring silver air the thin stringent odor of them lay like an exhalation.

She returned to the living room and got her book and turned out the lights and mounted the stairs. Across the corridor Aunt Sally snored with genteel placidity, and Narcissa stood for a moment, listening to the homely noise. I will be glad when Horry gets home, she thought going on.

She turned on her light and undressed and took her book to bed, where she again held her consciousness deliberately submerged as you hold a puppy under water until its body ceases to resist. And after a time her mind surrendered wholly to the book and she read on, pausing to think warmly of sleep, reading a page more. And so when the negroes first blended their instruments beneath her window, she paid them only the most perfunctory notice. Why in the world are those jelly-beans serenading me? she thought with faint amusement, visioning immediately Aunt Sally in her night-cap leaning from a window and shouting them away.

But in the midst of this amusing picture she sat

bolt upright, with a sharp and utter certainty; then she rose and entered the adjoining room and looked out the window.

The negroes were grouped on the lawn, in the moonlight: the frosted clarinet, the guitar, the grave comic bulk of the viol. At the street entrance to the drive a motor car loomed in shadow, whose and occupied by whom she could not discern. The musicians played once, then they retreated across the lawn and down the drive, and presently the car drove on, without lights. It was he: no one else would play one tune beneath a lady's midnight window, just enough to waken her from sleep, then go away.

She returned to her room. The book lay face downward on the bed. But the labor was undone again, and she stood for a while at her window, between the parted curtains, looking out upon the black and silver world and the peaceful night. The air moved upon her face and amid the fallen dark wings of her hair with grave coolness, but inwardly . . . "The beast, the beast," she whispered to herself. She let the curtains fall and on her silent feet she descended the stairs again and sought the telephone in the darkness. She miffled its bell with her fingers when she rang.

Miss Jenny's voice came out of the night with its usual brisk and cold asperity, and without surprise or curiosity. No, he had not returned home, for he was now safely locked up in jail, she believed, unless the city officers were too corrupted to obey a lady's request. Serenading? Fiddlesticks. What would he want to go serenading for? he couldn't injure himself serenading, unless someone killed him with a flat iron or an alarm clock. And why was she concerned about him?

Narcissa hung up, and for a moment she stood in the darkness, beating her fists on the telephone's unresponsive box. The beast, the beast.

She had received three callers that night. One came formally and with intent; the second came informally and without any particular effort to remain anonymous or otherwise; the third came anonymously and with calculated intent. The garage which sheltered her car was a small brick building surrounded by evergreens. One side of it was a continuation of the garden wall. Beyond the wall a grass-grown lane led back to another street. The garage was about fifteen yards from the house and its roof rose to the level of the second story of the house. Narcissa's bedroom windows looked out upon the slate roof of it.

This third caller entered by the lane and mounted onto the wall and thence onto the garage roof, where he now lay in the shadow of a cedar branching above it, sheltered so from the moon. He had lain there for a long time. The room facing him was dark when he arrived, but he had lain in his fastness quiet as an animal and with an animal's patience, without movement save to occasionally raise his head and reconnoiter the immediate scene with covert dartings of his eyes.

But the room facing him remained dark after the first hour had passed. In the meantime a car entered the drive (he recognised it; he knew every car in town) and a man entered the house. The second hour passed and the room was still dark and still the car stood in the drive. Then the man emerged again and drove away, and a moment later the window facing him glowed suddenly and beyond the sheer cur-

tains her figure moved across his vision. He watched
her move about the room beyond the gauzy veil of
the curtains, watched the shadowy motions of her
disrobing. Then she passed out of his vision. But the
light still burned and he lay with a still and infinite
patience, lay so while another hour passed and another car stopped in the street and three men
carrying an awkwardly shaped burden came up the
drive and stepped into the moonlight beneath her
window and stopped there; lay so until they played
their music and went away again. When they had
gone she came to the window and parted the curtains
and stood for a while in the dark fallen wings of her
hair, looking directly into his hidden eyes.

Then the curtains fell again, and once more she
was a shadowy movement beyond them. Then the
light went off, and he lay face down on the steep
pitch of the garage roof, utterly motionless for a long
time, darting from beneath his hidden face covert
ceaseless glances, quick and darting and all-
embracing as those of an animal.

To Narcissa's house they came finally. They had visited the dark homes of all the other unmarried girls
one by one and sat in the car while the negroes stood
on the lawn with their blended instruments. Heads
had appeared at darkened windows, sometimes lights
went up; once they were invited in, but Hub and
Mitch hung diffidently back, once refreshment was
sent out to them, once they were heartily cursed by
a young man who happened to be sitting with the
young lady on the dark veranda. In the meantime
they had lost the breather cap, and as they moved
from house to house all six of them drank fraternally
from the jug, turn and turn about. At last they

reached the Benbows' and the negroes crossed the lawn and played beneath the cedars. There was a light yet in one window, but none came to it.

The moon stood far down the sky. Its light was now a sourceless silver upon things, spent and a little coldly wearied, and the world was empty for them as they rolled without lights along a street lifeless and fixed in black-and-silver as any street in the moon itself. Beneath stippled intermittent shadows they passed, crossed quiet intersections of streets dissolving away, occasionally a car motionless at the curb before a house. A dog crossed the street ahead of them trotting, and went on across a lawn and so from sight, intently but without haste, but saving this there was no movement anywhere. The square opened spaciously about the absinthe-cloudy mass of elms that framed the courthouse. Among them the round spaced globes were more like huge pallid grapes than ever. Above the exposed vault in each of the banks burned a single bulb; inside the hotel lobby, before which a few cars were aligned with their rears outward, another burned with a hushed glow. Other lights there were none.

They circled the courthouse, and a shadow moved near the hotel door and detached itself from shadow and came to the curb and stood there, its white shirt glinting dully between the lax wings of dark coat, and as the slow car swung away toward another street, the man hailed them. Bayard slowed and stopped and the man came through the blanched dust and laid his hand on the door.

"Hi, Buck," Mitch said. "You're up pretty late, aint you?"

The man had a sober, good-natured horse's face and he wore a metal star on his unbuttoned waistcoat. His coat humped slightly on his hip.

"What you boys doin'?" he asked. "Been to a dance?"

"Having a little party," Bayard answered. "Want a drink, Buck?"

"No, much obliged." He stood with his hand on the door, gravely and good-naturedly serious. "Aint you fellers out kind of late, yourselves?"

"It is gettin' on," Mitch agreed. The marshal lifted his foot to the running board. Beneath his hat his eyes were in shadow. "We're going in now," Mitch said. The other mused quietly, and Bayard added:

"Sure; we're on our way home now."

The officer stood quietly for a moment. Then he moved his head slightly and spoke to the negroes.

"I reckon you boys are about ready to turn in, aint you?"

"Yes, suh," the negroes answered in chorus, and they got out and lifted the bass viol out. Bayard gave Reno a bill and they thanked him and picked up the viol and departed quietly down a side street. The officer paid them no further heed.

"Aint that yo' car in front of Rogers' cafe, Mitch?" he asked.

"I reckon so. That's where I left it."

"Well, suppose you run Hub out home, lessen he's goin' to stay in town tonight. Bayard better come with me."

"Aw, hell, Buck," Mitch protested.

"What for?" Bayard demanded.

"His folks are worried about him," the other said, addressing Mitch and Hub. "They aint seen hide nor hair of him since that stallion fell with him. Where's yo' bandage, Bayard?"

"Took it off," he answered shortly. "See here, Buck, we're going to put Mitch out and then Hub and me are going straight home."

"You been on yo' way home ever since fo' oclock, Bayard," the officer replied soberly, "but you dont seem to git no nearer there. I reckon you better come with me tonight, like yo' aunt said."

"Did Aunt Jenny tell you to arrest me?"

"They was worried about you, son. Miss Jenny just 'phoned and asked me to kind of see if you was all right until mawnin'. So I reckon we better. You ought to went on home this evenin'."

"Aw, have a heart, Buck," Mitch repeated.

"I ruther make Bayard mad than Miss Jenny," the other answered patiently. "You boys go on, and Bayard better come with me."

Mitch and Hub got out and Hub lifted out his jug and they said goodnight and crossed the square to where Mitch's Ford stood before the restaurant. The marshal got in beside Bayard, and he drove on. The jail was not far. It loomed presently above its walled court, square and implacable, its slitted upper windows brutal as sabre blows. They turned into an alley and the marshal got out and opened a gate. Bayard drove into the grassless littered court and stopped while the other crossed the yard to a small garage in which stood a Ford car. He backed this out and motioned Bayard forward. The garage was built to the Ford's dimensions, and when the nose of Bayard's long car touched the back wall, a good quarter of it was still out of doors.

"Better'n nothin', though," the marshal said. "Come on." They entered through the kitchen, into the jailkeeper's living quarters, and Bayard stood in a dark passage while the other fumbled with hushed sounds ahead of him. Then a light came on, and they entered a bleak neat room, with spare conglomerate furniture and a few articles of masculine apparel about.

"Say," Bayard objected, "aren't you giving me your bed?"

"Wont need it befo' mawnin'," the other answered. "You'll be gone, then. Want me to he'p you off with yo' clothes?"

"No. I'm all right." Then, more graciously: "Goodnight, Buck, and much obliged."

"Goodnight," the marshal answered. He closed the door behind him and Bayard removed his coat and shoes and his tie and snapped the light off and lay on the bed. Moonlight seeped into the room impalpably, refracted and sourceless; the night was without any sound. Beyond the window a cornice rose in successive shallow steps; beyond that the sky was opaline and dimensionless. His head was clear and cold. The whisky he had drunk was completely dead. Or rather, it was as though his head were one Bayard who watched curiously and impersonally that other Bayard who lay in a strange bed and whose alcohol-dulled nerves radiated like threads of ice through that body which he must drag forever about a bleak and barren world with him. "Hell," he said, lying on his back, staring out the window where nothing was to be seen, waiting for sleep, not knowing if it would come or not, not caring a particular damn either way. Nothing to be seen, and the long long span of a man's natural life. Three score and ten years, to drag a stubborn body about the world and cozen its insistent demands. Three score and ten, the Bible said. Seventy years. And he was only twenty-six. Not much more than a third through it. Hell.

THREE

I

Horace Benbow in his clean, wretchedly fitting khaki which but served to accentuate his air of fine and delicate futility, and laden with an astonishing impedimenta of knapsacks and kitbags and paper-wrapped parcels, got off the two-thirty train. His sister called to him across the tight clotting of descending and ascending passengers, and he roved his distraught gaze like a somnambulist rousing with an effort to avoid traffic, about the agglomerate faces. "Hello, hello," he said, then he thrust himself clear and laid his bags and parcels on the edge of the platform and moved with intent haste up the train toward the baggage car.

"Horace!" his sister called again, running after him. The station agent emerged from his office and stopped him and held him like a finely bred restive horse and shook his hand, and thus his sister overtook him. He turned at her voice and came completely from out his distraction and swept her up in his arms until her feet were off the ground, and kissed her on the mouth.

"Dear old Narcy," he said, kissing her again. Then he set her down and stroked his hands on her face, as a child would. "Dear old Narcy," he repeated, touching her face with his fine spatulate hands, gazing at her as though he were drinking that constant serenity of hers through his eyes. He continued to repeat Dear old Narcy, stroking his hands on her face, utterly oblivious of his surroundings until she recalled him.

"Where in the world are you going, up this way?"

Then he remembered, and released her and rushed on, she following, and stopped again at the door of the baggage car, from which the station porter and a trainhand were taking trunks and boxes as the baggage clerk tilted them out.

"Cant you send down for it?" she asked. But he stood peering into the car, oblivious of her again. The two negroes returned and he stepped aside, still looking into the car with peering, birdlike motions of his head. "Let's send back for it," his sister said again.

"What? Oh. I've seen it every time I changed cars," he told her, completely forgetting the sense of her words. "It'd be rotten luck to have it go astray right at my doorstep, wouldn't it?" Again the negroes moved away with a trunk, and he stepped forward again and peered into the car. "That's just about what happened to it; some clerk forgot to put it on the train at M— There it is," he interrupted himself. "Easy now, cap," he called in the country idiom, in a fever of alarm as the clerk slammed into the door a box of foreign shape and stencilled with a military address. "She's got glass in her."

"All right, colonel," the baggage clerk agreed, "we aint hurt her none, I reckon. If we have, all you got to do is sue us." The two negroes backed up to the door and Horace laid his delicate impractical hands on the box as the clerk tilted it expertly outward. "Easy now, boys," he repeated nervously, and he trotted beside them to the platform. "Set it down easy, now. Here, sis, lend a hand, will you?"

"We got it all right, cap'm," the station porter said. "We aint gwine drop it." But Horace continued to dab at it with his hands, and as they set it down he leaned his head to it, listening. "She's all right on de inside, aint she?"

"It's all right," the train porter assured him. He turned away. "Le's go," he called.

"I think it's all right," Horace agreed, his ear against the box, "I dont hear anything. It's packed pretty well." The engine blew two blasts and Horace sprang erect, digging into his pocket, and ran to the moving cars. The porter was just closing the vestibule, but he leaned down to Horace's extended hand and straightened up and touched his cap. Horace returned to his box and gave another coin to the station porter. "Put it inside for me, careful, now. I'll be back for it soon."

"Yes, suh, Mr Benbow. I'll look out fer it."

"I thought it was lost, once," he confided, slipping his arm inside his sister's, and they retraced their steps toward the car. "It was delayed at Brest and didn't come until the next boat. I had the first outfit I got—a small one—with me, and I pretty near lost that one, too. I was blowing a small one in my cabin on the boat one afternoon, when the whole thing, cabin and all, took fire. The captain decided that I'd better not try it again until we got ashore, with all the men on board. The vase turned out pretty well, though," he babbled. "Lovely little thing. I'm catching on; I really am. Venice is a lovely place," he added. "Must take you there, some day." Then he squeezed her arm and fell to repeating Dear old Narcy, as though the homely sound of the nickname on his tongue was a taste he loved and had not forgotten. A few people still lingered about the station. Some of them spoke to him and he stopped to shake their hands, and a marine private with the Second Division Indian head on his shoulder remarked the triangle on Horace's sleeve and made a vulgar sound of derogation through his pursed lips.

"Howdy, buddy," Horace said, turning upon the other his shy startled gaze.

"Evenin', general," the marine answered. He spat, not exactly at Horace's feet, and not exactly anywhere else. Narcissa clamped her brother's arm against her side with her elbow.

"Do come on home and get into some decent clothes," she said in a lower tone, hurrying him along.

"Get out of uniform?" he said. "I rather fancied myself in khaki," he said, a little hurt. "You really think I am ridiculous in this?" he asked quietly.

"Of course not," she answered immediately, squeezing his hand. "I'm sorry I said that. You wear it just as long as you want to."

"It's a good uniform," he said soberly. "People will realize that in about ten years, when noncombatants' hysteria has worn itself out and the individual soldiers realize that the A.E.F. didn't invent disillusion."

"What did it invent?" she asked, holding his arm against her, surrounding him with the fond, inattentive serenity of her affection.

"God knows . . . Dear old Narcy," he said again, and they crossed the side track and approached her car. "So you have dulled your palate for khaki."

"Of course not," she answered, shaking his arm a little. "You wear it just as long as you want to." She opened the car door. Someone called after them and they looked back and saw the porter trotting after them with Horace's hand-luggage, which he had walked off and left lying on the platform.

"Oh, Lord," Horace said, "I worry with it for four

thousand miles, then lose it on my own doorstep. Much obliged, Sol." He extended his hands, but the porter came up and stowed the things in the car. "That's the first outfit I got," he added to his sister. "And the vase I blew on shipboard. I'll show it to you when we get home."

His sister got in under the wheel. "Where are your clothes? In the box?"

"I haven't got any. Had to throw most of 'em away to make room for the other stuff. No room for anything else."

Narcissa looked at him for a moment with fond fretted annoyance. "What's the matter?" he asked innocently. "Forget something yourself?"

"No. Get in. Aunt Sally's waiting to see you."

They drove on and mounted the shady gradual hill toward the square, and Horace looked about happily upon familiar quiet scenes. Some new tight little houses with minimum of lawn—homes built by country-bred people and set close to the street after the country fashion; occasionally a house going up on a lot that was vacant sixteen months ago when he went away. Other streets stretched away, shadier, with houses a little older and a little more imposing as they got away from the station's vicinity; and pedestrians, usually old men bound townward after their naps, to spend the afternoon in grave futile absorptions.

The hill flattened away into the plateau on which the town proper had been built these hundred and more years ago, and the street became definitely urban presently with garages and small new shops with merchants in shirt-sleeves and customers; the picture show with its lobby plastered with life in colored lithographic mutations. Then the square, with its unbroken low skyline of old weathered brick and fading dead names stubborn yet beneath the super-imposed recenter ones, and drifting negroes in casual o.d. garments worn by both sexes and country people in occasional khaki too; and their more brisk urban brethren weaving among their placid chewing unhaste and among the sitting groups in chairs before certain stores.

The courthouse was of brick too, with stone arches rising among elms, and among the trees the monument of the Confederate soldier stood like a white candle. Beneath the porticos of the courthouse and upon benches about the green, the city fathers sat and talked and drowsed, in uniform too, now and then. But it was the grey of Jackson and Beauregard and Johnston, and they sat in a sedate gravity of minor political sinecures, murmuring and smoking and spitting about unhurried checker-boards. When the weather was bad they moved inside to the circuit clerk's office.

It was here that the young men loafed also, pitching dollars or tossing baseballs back and forth or lying on the grass until the young girls in their little colored dresses and cheap nostalgic perfume came trooping down town through the late afternoon to the drug store. When the weather was bad the young men loafed in the drug stores or in the barber shop.

"Lots of uniforms yet," Horace said. "All be home by June. Have the Sartoris boys come home yet?"

"John is dead," his sister answered. "Didn't you know?"

"No," he answered quickly, with swift concern. "Poor old Bayard. Rotten luck they have. Funny family. Always going to wars, and always getting killed. And Bayard's wife died, you wrote me."

"Yes. But Bayard's here. He's got a racing automobile and he spends all his time tearing around the country. We are expecting every day to hear he's killed himself in it."

"Poor devil," Horace said, and again: "Poor old Colonel. He used to hate an automobile like a snake. Wonder what he thinks about it."

"He goes with him."

"What? Old Bayard in a motor car?"

"Yes. Miss Jenny says it's to keep Bayard from breaking his fool neck. But she says Colonel Sartoris doesn't know it, but that Bayard would just as soon break both their necks. That he probably will before he's done." She drove on across the square, among tethered wagons and cars parked casually and without order. "I hate Bayard Sartoris," she said with sudden vehemence. "I hate all men." Horace looked at her quickly.

"What's the matter? What's Bayard done to you? No, that's backward. What have you done to Bayard?" But she didn't answer. She turned into another street bordered by negro stores of one story and shaded by metal awnings beneath which negroes lounged, skinning bananas or small florid cartons of sweet cakes; and then a grist mill driven by a spasmodic gasoline engine. It oozed chaff and a sifting dust mote-like in the sun, and above the door a tediously hand-lettered sign: W. C. BEARDS MILL. Between it and a shuttered and silent gin draped with feathery soiled festoons of old lint, an anvil clanged at the end of a short lane filled with wagons and horses and mules, and shaded by mulberry trees beneath which countrymen in overalls squatted. "He ought to have more consideration for the old fellow than that," Horace said fretfully. "Still, they've just gone through with an experience that pretty well shook the verities and the humanities, and whether they know it or not, they've got another one ahead of 'em that'll finish the business. Give him a little time . . . But I personally cant see why they dont let him go ahead and kill himself, if that's what he wants. Sorry for Miss Jenny, though."

"Yes," his sister agreed, quietly again, "they're worried about Colonel Sartoris' heart, too. Everybody except him and Bayard, that is. I'm glad I have you instead of one of those Sartorises, Horry." She laid her hand quickly and lightly on his thin knee.

"Dear old Narcy," he said, then his face clouded again. "Damn scoundrel," he said. "Well, it's their trouble. How's Aunt Sally been?"

"All right." And then: "I *am* glad you're home again."

The shabby small shops were behind, and now the street opened away between old shady lawns, spacious and quiet. These homes were quite old, in actuality, or appearance at least, and, set well back from the street and its dust, they emanated a gracious and benign peace, steadfast as a windless afternoon in a world without motion or sound. Horace looked about him and drew a long breath.

"Perhaps this is the reason for wars," he said. "The meaning of peace."

The meaning of peace. They turned into an intersecting street narrower but more shady and even quieter, with a golden Arcadian drowse, and drove through a gate in a honeysuckle-covered fence of iron pickets. From the gate the cinder-packed drive rose in a grave curve between cedars. The cedars had been set out by an English architect of the 'forties, who had built the house (with the minor concession of a veranda) in the funereal light Tudor which the young Victoria had sanctioned; and beneath and among them, even on the brightest days, lay a resinous exhilarating gloom. Mockingbirds loved them, and catbirds, and thrushes demurely mellifluous in the late afternoon; but the grass beneath them was sparse or not at all and there were no insects save fireflies in the dusk.

The drive ascended to the house and curved before it and descended again to the street in an unbroken arc of cedars. Within the arc rose a lone oak tree, broad and huge and low; around its trunk ran a wooden bench. About this halfmoon of lawn and without the arc of the drive, were bridal wreath and crepe-myrtle bushes old as time, and huge as age, would make them. Big as trees they were, and in one fence corner was an astonishing clump of stunted banana palms and in the other a lantana with its clotted wounds, which Francis Benbow had brought home from Barbados in a tophat-box in '71.

About the oak and from the funereal scimitar of the drive, lawn flowed streetward with good sward broken by random clumps of jonquil and narcissus and gladiolus. Originally the lawn was in terraces and the flowers constituted a formal bed on the first terrace. Then Will Benbow, Horace and Narcissa's father, had had the terraces obliterated. It was done with plows and scrapers and the lawn was seeded anew with grass, and he had supposed the flower bed destroyed. But the next spring the scattered bulbs sprouted again, and now every year the lawn was stippled with bloom in yellow, white and pink without order. Neighbors' children played quietly beneath the cedars, and a certain few young girls asked and received permission to pick some of the flowers each spring. At the top of the drive, where it curved away descending again, sat the brick doll's house in which Horace and Narcissa lived, surrounded always by that cool, faintly-stringent odor of cedar trees.

It was trimmed with white and it had mullioned casements brought out from England; along the veranda eaves and above the door grew a wistaria vine like heavy tarred rope and thicker than a man's wrist. The lower casements stood open upon gently billowing curtains of white dimity; upon the sill you expected to see a scrubbed wooden bowl, or at least an immaculate and supercilious cat. But the window sill held only a wicker work basket from which, like a drooping poinsettia, spilled an end of patchwork in crimson and white; and in the doorway Aunt Sally, a potty little woman in a lace cap, leaned upon a gold-headed ebony walking-stick.

Just as it should be, and Horace turned and looked back at his sister crossing the drive with the parcels he had forgotten again. The meaning of peace.

He banged and splashed happily in his bathroom, shouting through the door to his sister where she sat on his bed. His discarded khaki lay upon a chair, holding yet through long association, in its harsh drab folds, something of his taut and delicate futility. On the old marble-topped dresser lay the crucible and tubes of his glass-blowing outfit, the first one he had bought, and beside it the vase he had blown on shipboard—a small chaste shape in clear glass not four inches high, fragile as a silver lily and incomplete.

"They work in caves," he was shouting through the door, "down flights of stairs underground. You feel water seeping under your foot while you are

reaching for the next step, and when you put your
hand out to steady yourself against the wall, it's wet
when you take it away. It feels just like blood."

"Horace!"

"Yes, magnificent. And way ahead you see the
glow. All of a sudden the tunnel comes glimmering
out of nothing, then you see the furnace, with things
rising and falling in front of it, cutting the light off,
and the walls go glimmering again. At first they're
just shapeless things hunching about. Antic, with
shadows on the wet walls, red shadows; a dull red
gleam, and black shapes like cardboard cut-outs rising and falling like a magic-lantern shutter. And then
a face comes out, blowing, and the other faces sort of
swell out of the red dark like painted balloons.

"And the things themselves! Sheerly and tragically
beautiful. Like preserved flowers, you know. Macabre and inviolate; purged and purified as bronze, yet
fragile as soap bubbles. Sound of pipes crystallized.
Flutes and oboes, but mostly reeds. Oaten reeds.
Dammit, they bloom like flowers right before your
eyes. Midsummer night's dream to a salamander."
His voice became unintelligible, soaring into phrases
which she did not herself recognise, but from the
pitch of his voice she knew were Milton's archangels
in their sonorous plunging ruin.

Presently he emerged, in a white shirt and serge
trousers but still borne aloft on his flaming verbal
wings, and while his voice chanted in measured syllables she fetched a pair of shoes from the closet, and
while she stood holding the shoes, he ceased and
touched her face again with his hands after that
fashion of a child.

At supper Aunt Sally broke into his staccato babbling.

"Did you bring your Snopes back with you?" she asked. This Snopes was a young man, member of a seemingly inexhaustible family which for the last ten or twelve years had been moving to town in driblets from a small settlement known as Frenchman's Bend. Flem, the first Snopes, had appeared unheralded one day and without making a ripple in the town's life, behind the counter of a small restaurant on a side street, patronized by country people. With this foothold and like Abraham of old, he led his family piece by piece into town. Flem himself was presently manager of the city light and water plant, and for the following few years he was a sort of handy-man to the city government; and three years ago, to old Bayard Sartoris' profane surprise and unconcealed disapproval, he became vice-president of the Sartoris bank, where already a relation of his was a book-keeper.

He still retained the restaurant, and the canvas tent in the rear of it in which he and his wife and baby had passed the first few months of their residence in town, and it served as an alighting-place for incoming Snopeses, from which they spread to small third-rate businesses of various kinds—grocery stores, barber shops (there was one, an invalid of some sort, with a second-hand peanut parcher)— where they multiplied and flourished. The older residents, from their Jeffersonian houses and genteel stores and offices, looked on with amusement at first. But this was long since become something like consternation.

The Snopes to which Aunt Sally referred was named Montgomery Ward and he had just turned twenty-one in '17, and just before the draft law went into effect he applied to a recruiting officer in Memphis and was turned down because of his heart. Later, somewhat to everyone's surprise, particularly that of Horace Benbow's friends, he departed with Horace to a position in the Y.M.C.A. Later still it was told of him that he had travelled all the way to Memphis on that day he offered himself for service, with a plug of chewing tobacco beneath his left arm-pit. But he and his patron had already gone when that story got out.

"Did you bring your Snopes back with you?" Aunt Sally asked.

"No," he answered, and his thin, nerve-sick face clouded with a fine cold distaste. "I was very much disappointed in him. I dont even care to talk about it."

"Anybody could have told you that when you left," Aunt Sally said, chewing slowly above her plate. Horace brooded for a moment, his thin hand tightened slowly about his fork.

"It's individuals like that, parasites—" he began, but his sister interrupted.

"Who cares about an old Snopes, anyway?" she said. "Besides, it's too late at night to talk about the horrors of war." Aunt Sally made a moist sound through her food, of vindicated superiority.

"It's the generals they have nowadays," she said. "General Johnston or General Forrest wouldn't have took a Snopes in his army." Aunt Sally was no relation at all. She lived next door but one with two maiden sisters, one younger and one older than she. She had been in and out of the house ever since Horace and Narcissa could remember, having arrogated to herself certain rights in their lives before they could walk; rights which were never expressed and which she never availed herself of, yet the mutual understanding of which she never permitted to fall

into desuetude. She would walk into any of the
rooms unannounced, and she liked to talk tediously
and a little tactlessly of Horace's and Narcissa's in-
fantile ailments. It was said that she had once 'made
eyes' at Will Benbow although she was a woman of
thirty-four or -five when Will married; and she still
spoke of him with a faintly disparaging possessive-
ness, and of his wife she spoke nicely, too. "Julia was
a right sweet-natured girl," Aunt Sally would say.

So when Horace went off to the war Aunt Sally
moved over to keep Narcissa company: no other arrangement had ever occurred to any one of the three
of them. Aunt Sally was a good old soul, but she
lived much in the past, shutting her intelligence with
a bland finality to anything which had occurred
since 1901. For her, time had gone out drawn by
horses, and into her stubborn and placid vacuum the
squealing of automobile brakes had never penetrated.
Aunt Sally had a lot of the crudities which old people are entitled to. She liked the sound of her own
voice and she didn't like to be alone in the house
after dark, and as she had never got accustomed to
her false teeth and so never touched them other than
to change occasionally the water in which they sat,
she ate unprettily of unprepossessing but easily mal-
leable foods. Narcissa reached her hand beneath the
table and squeezed her brother's knee.

"I *am* glad you're home, Horry."

He looked at her quickly, and the cloud faded
from his face as suddenly as it had come, and he let
himself slip, as into water, into the constant serenity
of her affection again.

He was a lawyer, principally through a sense of duty
to the family tradition, and though he had no partic-

ular affinity to it other than a love for printed words, for the dwelling-places of books, he contemplated returning to his musty office with a glow of . . . not eagerness: no; of deep and abiding unreluctance, almost of pleasure. The meaning of peace. Old unchanging days; unwinged, perhaps, but undisastrous, too. You dont see it, feel it, save with perspective. Fireflies had not yet come, and the cedars flowed unbroken on either hand down to the street, like a curving ebony wave with rigid unbreaking crests pointed on the sky. Light fell outward from the casement, across the porch and upon a bed of cannas, hardy, bronze-like—none of your flowerlike fragility, theirs; and within the room Aunt Sally's quavering monotone. Narcissa was there too, beside the lamp with a book, filling the room with her still and constant presence like the odor of jasmine, watching the door; and Horace stood on the dark veranda with his cold pipe, surrounded by that cool, faintly-stringent scent of cedar trees like another presence. The meaning of peace, he said to himself again, releasing the grave words one by one within the cool bell of silence into which he had come at last again, hearing them linger with a dying fall pure as silver and crystal struck lightly together.

"How's Belle?" he asked on the evening of his arrival home.

"They're all right," his sister answered. "They have a new car."

"Dare say," Horace agreed with detachment. "The war should certainly have accomplished that much." Aunt Sally had left them at last and tapped her slow bedward way. Horace stretched his serge legs luxuriously and for a while he ceased striking matches to his stubborn pipe and sat watching his sister's dark head bent above the magazine upon her knees, lost from lesser and inconstant things. Her hair was smoother than any reposing wings, sweeping with burnished unrebellion to a simple knot low on her neck. "Belle's a rotten correspondent," he added. "Like all women."

She turned a page, without looking up. "Did you write to her often?"

"It's because they realize that letters are only good to bridge intervals between actions, like the interludes in Shakespeare's plays," he went on, oblivious. "And did you ever know a woman who read Shakespeare without skipping the interludes? Shakespeare himself knew that, so he didn't put any women in the interludes. Let the men bombast to one another's echoes while the ladies were backstage washing the dinner dishes or putting the children to bed."

"I never knew a woman who read Shakespeare," Narcissa corrected. "He talks too much."

Horace rose and stood above her and patted her dark head.

"O profundity," he said. "You have reduced all wisdom to a phrase, and measured your sex by the stature of a star."

"Well, they dont," she repeated, raising her head.

"No? why dont they?" He struck another match to his pipe, watching her across his cupped hands as gravely and with poised eagerness, like a striking bird. "Your Arlens and Sabatinis talk a lot, and nobody ever had more to say and more trouble saying it than old Dreiser."

"But they have secrets," she explained. "Shakespeare doesn't have any secrets. He tells everything."

"I see. Shakespeare had no sense of discrimination and no instinct for reticence. In other words, he wasn't a gentleman," he suggested.

"Yes . . . That's what I mean."

"And so, to be a gentleman, you must have secrets."

"Oh, you make me tired." She returned to her magazine and he sat beside her on the couch and took her hand in his and stroked it upon his cheek and upon the fine devastation of his hair.

"It's like walking through a twilit garden," he said happily. "The flowers you know are all there, in their shifts and with their hair combed out for the night, but you know all of them. So you dont bother 'em, you just walk on and sort of stop and turn over a leaf occasionally, a leaf you didn't notice before; perhaps you find a violet under it, or a bluebell or a lightning bug; perhaps only another leaf or a blade of grass. But there's always a drop of dew on it." He continued to stroke her hand upon his face. With her other hand she turned the magazine slowly on, listening to him with her fond serene detachment.

"Did you write to Belle often?" she repeated. "What did you say to her?"

"I wrote what she wanted to read. What all women want in letters. People are really entitled to half of what they think they ought to have, you know."

"What did you tell her?" Narcissa persisted, turning the pages slowly, without looking up, her passive hand in his, following the stroking movement of his.

"I told her I was unhappy. Perhaps I was," he added. His sister freed her hand quietly and laid it on the page. He said: "I admire Belle. She's so cannily stupid. Once I feared her. Perhaps . . . No, I dont. I am immune to destruction: I have a magic. Which is a good sign that I am due for it, say the sages," he added lightly. "But then, acquired wisdom is a dry thing; it has a way of crumbling to dust where a sheer and blind coursing of stupid sap is impervious." He sat without touching her, in a rapt and instantaneous repose. "Not like yours, O Serene," he said, waking again. Then he fell to saying Dear old Narcy, and again he took her hand. It did not withdraw; neither did it wholly surrender.

"I dont think you ought to say I'm dull so often, Horry," she said soberly.

"Neither do I," he agreed. "But I must take some sort of revenge on perfection."

Later she lay in her dark room. Across the corridor Aunt Sally snored with placid regularity; in the adjoining room Horace lay while that wild fantastic futility of his voyaged in lonely regions of its own beyond the moon, about meadows nailed with firmamented stars to the ultimate roof of things, where unicorns filled the neighing air with galloping, or grazed or lay supine in latent and golden-hooved repose.

Horace was seven when she had been born. In the background of her sober babyhood were three beings whose lives and conduct she had adopted with rapt intensity—a lad with a wild thin face and an unflagging aptitude for tribulation; a darkly gallant shape romantic with smuggled edibles and with strong hard hands smelling always of a certain thrilling carbolic soap—a being something like Omnipotence but without awesomeness; and lastly, a gentle figure without legs or any inference of locomotion, like a minor shrine, surrounded always by an aura of gentle melancholy and an endless delicate manipulation of colored silken thread. This last figure was constant with a gentle and melancholy unassertion; the second revolved in an orbit which bore it at regular intervals into outer space, then returned it with its strong and jolly virility into her intense world again; but the first she had made her own by a sober and maternal perseverance. And so by the time she was five or six, people coerced Horace by threatening to tell Narcissa on him.

Julia Benbow died genteelly and irreproachably when Narcissa was seven and Horace fourteen, had been removed from their lives as a small sachet of lavender is removed from a chest of linen, leaving a delicate lingering impalpability; and slept now amid pointed cedars and doves and serene marble shapes. Thus Narcissa acquired two masculine destinies to control and shape, and through the intense maturity of seven and eight and nine she cajoled and threatened and commanded and (very occasionally) stormed them into concurrence. And so through fourteen and fifteen and sixteen, while Horace was first at Sewanee and later at Oxford. Then Will Benbow's time came, and he joined his wife Julia among the marbles and the cedars and the doves, and the current of her maternalism had now but a single channel. For a time this current was dammed by a stupid mischancing of human affairs, but now Horace was home again and lay now beneath the same roof and the same recurrence of days, and the channel was undammed again.

"Why dont you marry, and let that baby look after himself for a while?" Miss Jenny Du Pre had demanded once, in her cold, abrupt way. Perhaps when she too was eighty, all men would be Sartorises to her, also. But that was a long time away. Sartorises. She thought of Bayard, but briefly, and without any tremor at all. He was now no more than the shadow of a hawk's flight mirrored fleetingly by the windless surface of pool, and gone; where, the pool knew and cared not, leaving no stain.

2

He settled into the routine of days between office and home. The musty, solemn familiarity of calf-bound and never-violated volumes on whose dusty bindings prints of Will Benbow's dead fingers could yet have been found; a little tennis in the afternoons, usually on Harry Mitchell's fine court; cards in the evenings, also with Belle and Harry usually, or again and better still, with the ever accessible and never-failing magic of printed pages while his sister beyond the lamp from him filled the room with that constant untroubling serenity of hers in which his spirit drowsed like a swimmer on a tideless summer sea.

Aunt Sally had returned home, with her bag of colored scraps and her false teeth, leaving behind her a fixed impalpability of a nebulous but definite obligation conferred at some personal sacrifice, as was her way, and a faint odor of old female flesh which faded from the rooms slowly, lingering yet in unexpected places, so that at times Narcissa, waking and lying for a while in the darkness, in the sensuous pleasure of having Horace home again, imagined that she could hear yet in the dark myriad silence of the house Aunt Sally's genteel and placid snores.

At times it would be so distinct that she would pause suddenly and speak Aunt Sally's name into an empty room. And sometimes Aunt Sally replied, having availed herself again of her prerogative of coming in at any hour the notion took her, unannounced, to see how they were getting along and to

complain querulously of her own household. She was
old, too old to react easily to change, and it was hard
for her to readjust herself to her sisters' ways again
after her long sojourn in a household where everyone gave in to her regarding all domestic affairs. At
home her older sister ran things in a capable shrewish
fashion; she and the third sister persisted in treating
Aunt Sally like the child she had been sixty-five
years ago, whose diet and clothing and hours must be
rigorously and pettishly supervised.

"I cant even go to the bathroom in peace," she
complained querulously. "I'm a good mind to pack
up and move back over here, and let 'em get along
the best way they can." She rocked fretfully in the
chair which by unspoken agreement was never dis-
puted her, looking about the room with her bleared
old eyes. "That nigger dont half clean up, since I
left. That furniture, now . . . a damp cloth . . ."

"I wish you would take her back," Miss Sophia,
the elder sister, told Narcissa. "She's got so crochety
since she's been with you that there's no living with
her. What's this I hear Horace's taken up? making
glassware?"

His proper crucibles and retorts had arrived intact.
At first he had insisted on using the cellar, clearing
out the lawn mower and the garden tools and all the
accumulate impedimenta, and walling up the windows so as to make a dungeon of it. But Narcissa had
finally persuaded him upon the upper floor of the garage and here he had set up his furnace and had had
four mishaps and produced one almost perfect vase
of clear amber, larger, more richly and chastely serene and which he kept always on his night table and
called by his sister's name in the intervals of apostro-
phising both of them impartially in his moments of
rhapsody over the realization of the meaning of

peace and the unblemished attainment of it, as Thou still unravished bride of quietude.

At times he found himself suddenly quiet, a little humble in the presence of the happiness of his winged and solitary cage. For a cage it was, barring him from freedom with trivial compulsions; but he desired a cage. A topless cage, of course, that his spirit might wing on short excursions into the blue, but far afield his spirit did not desire to go: its direction was always upward plummeting, for a plummeting fall.

Still unchanging days. They were doomed days; he knew it, yet for the time being his devious and uncontrollable impulses had become one with the rhythm of things as a swimmer's counter muscles become one with a current, and cage and all his life grew suave with motion, oblivious of destination. During this period not only did his immediate days become starkly inevitable, but the dead thwarted ones with all the spent and ludicrous disasters which his nature had incurred upon him, grew lustrous in retrospect and without regret, and those to come seemed as undeviating and logical as mathematical formulae beyond an incurious golden veil.

At Sewanee, where he had gone as his father before him, he had been an honor man in his class. As a Rhodes Scholar he had gone to Oxford, there to pursue the verities and humanities with that waiting law office in a Mississippi country town like a gate in the remote background through which he must someday pass, thinking of it not often and with no immediate perspective, accepting it with neither pleasure nor regret. Here, amid the mellow benignance of these walls, was a perfect life, a life accomplishing itself placidly in a region remote from time and into which the world's noises came only from afar and with only that glamorous remote significance of a parade passing along a street far away, with inferences of brass and tinsel fading beyond far walls, into the changeless sky. Here he developed a reasonably fine discrimination in alcohol and a brilliant tennis game, after his erratic electric fashion; but save for an occasional half sophomoric, half travelling-sales-manish sabbatical to the Continent in company with fellow-countrymen, his life was a golden and purposeless dream, without palpable intent or future with the exception of that law office to which he was reconciled by the sheer and youthful insuperability of distance and time.

There had come a day on which he stood in that mild pleasurable perplexity in which we regard our belongings and the seemingly inadequate volume of possible packing space, coatless among his chaotic possessions, slowly rubbing the fine unruly devastation of his head. About the bedroom bags and boxes gaped, and on the bed, on chairs, on the floor, were spread his clothes—jackets and trousers of all kinds and all individual as old friends. A servant moved about in the next room and he entered, but the man ignored him with silent and deft efficiency, and he went on to the window. The thin curtains stirred to a faint troubling exhalation of late spring. He put their gentle billowing aside and lit a cigarette and idly watched the match fall, its initial outward impulse fading into a wavering reluctance, as though space itself were languid in violation. Someone crossing the quad called up to him indistinguishably. He waved his hand vaguely in reply and sat on the window sill.

Outward, above and beyond buildings peaceful and gray and old, within and beyond trees in an untarnished and gracious resurgence of green, afternoon was like a blonde woman going slowly in a windless garden; afternoon and June were like blonde sisters in a windless garden-close, approaching without regret the fall of day. Walking a little slower, perhaps; perhaps looking backward, but without sadness, untroubled as cows. Horace sat in the window while the servant methodically reduced the chaos of his possessions to the boxes and bags, gazing out across ancient gray roofs, and trees which he had seen in all their seasonal moods, in all moods matching his own. Had he been younger he would have said goodbye to them secretively or defiantly; older, he would have felt neither the desire to nor the impulse to suppress it. So he sat quietly in his window for the last time while the curtains stirred delicately against his hair, brooding upon their dreaming vistas where twilight was slowly finding itself and where, beyond dissolving spires, lingered grave evening shapes; and he knew a place where, had he felt like walking, he could hear a cuckoo, that symbol of sweet and timeless mischief, that augur of the fever renewed again.

All he wanted anyway was quiet and dull peace and a few women, preferably young and good looking and fair tennis players, with whom to indulge in harmless and lazy intrigue. So his mind was made up, and on the homeward boat he framed the words with which he should tell his father that he was going to be an Episcopal minister. But when he reached New York the wire waited him saying that Will Benbow was ill, and all thoughts of his future fled his mind during the journey home and during the two subsequent days that his father lived. Then Will Benbow was buried beside his wife, and Aunt Sally Wyatt was sombrely ubiquitous about the house and talked with steady macabre complacence of Will at meals and snored placidly by night in the guest room. The next day but one Horace opened his father's law office again.

His practice, what there was of it, consisted of polite interminable litigation that progressed decorously and pleasantly from conference to conference, the greater part of which were given to discussions of the world's mutations as exemplified by men or by printed words; conferences conducted as often as not across pleasant dinner tables or upon golf links or, if the conferee were active enough, upon tennis courts —conferences which wended their endless courses without threat of consummation or of advantage or detriment to anyone involved.

There reposed also in a fire-proof cabinet in his office—the one concession Will Benbow had ever made to progress—a number of wills which Horace had inherited and never read, the testators of which accomplished their lives in black silk and lace caps and an atmosphere of formal and timeless desuetude in stately, high-ceiled rooms screened from the ceaseless world by flowering shrubs and old creeping vines; existences circumscribed by church affairs and so-called literary clubs and a conscientious, slightly contemptuous preoccupation with the welfare of remote and obtusely ungrateful heathen peoples. They did not interest themselves in civic affairs. To interfere in the lives or conduct of people whom you saw daily or who served you in various ways or to whose families you occasionally sent food and cast-off clothing was not genteel. Besides, the heathen was far enough removed from his willy nilly elevation to annoy no one save his yet benighted brethren. Clients upon whom he called at rare intervals by formal and unnecessary request and who bade fair to outlive him as they had outlived his father and to be heired in turn by some yet uncorporeal successor to him. As if God, Circumstance, looking down upon the gracious if faintly niggard completeness of their lives, found not the heart to remove them from surroundings tempered so peacefully to their requirements, to any other of lesser decorum and charm.

The meaning of peace; one of those instants in a man's life, a neap tide in his affairs, when, as though with a premonition of disaster, the moment takes on a sort of fixed clarity in which his actions and desires stand boldly forth unshadowed and rhythmic one with another like two steeds drawing a single chariot along a smooth empty road, and during which the I in him stands like a tranquil deciduated tree above the sere and ludicrous disasters of his days.

3

Narcissa had failed to call at the office for him and he walked home and changed to flannels and the blue jacket with the Oxford club insignia embroidered upon the breast pocket, and removed his racket from its press. In trees and flower beds spring was accomplishing itself more and more with the accumulating days, and he walked on with the sunlight slanting into his hair, toward Belle's. He strode on, chanting to himself, walking a little faster until the majestic monstrosity of the house came into view.

Someone piped thinly to him from beyond the adjoining fence; it was Belle's eight-year-old daughter, her dress of delicate yellow a single note in a chord of other small colored garments engaged in the intense and sober preoccupations of little girls. Horace waved his racket and went on and turned into Belle's drive.

The gravel slipped with short sibilance beneath his rubber soles. He did not approach the house but followed instead along the drive toward the rear, where already against further sunshot green he saw a figure in white tautly antic with motion. They were playing already. Belle would be there, already ensconced in her usual chair: Ahenobarbus' vestal, proprietorial and inattentive, preeningly dictatorial; removed from the dust and the heat and the blood; disdainful and the principal actor in the piece, O thou grave myrtle shapes amid which petulant Death

But Belle was the sort of watcher he preferred, engaged as she would be in that outwardly faultless immersion, in the unflagging theatrics of her own part in the picture, surrounding him as she would with that atmosphere of surreptitious domesticity. Belle didn't play tennis herself: her legs were not good, and Belle knew it; but sat instead in a tea gown of delicate and irreproachable lines at a table advantageously placed and laden with books and magazines and the temporarily discarded impedimenta of her more Atalanta-esque sisters. There was usually a group around Belle's chair—other young women or a young man or so inactive between sets, with an occasional older woman come to see just exactly what was going on or what Belle wore at the time; watching Belle's pretty regal airs with the young men. "Like a moving picture," Aunt Sally Wyatt said once, with cold and curious interest.

And presently Meloney would bring tea out and lay it on the table at Belle's side. Between the two of them, Belle with her semblance of a peahen suave and preening and petulant upon clipped sward, before marble urns and formal balustrades, and Meloney in her starched cap and apron and her lean shining legs, they made a rite of the most casual gathering; lending a sort of stiffness to it which Meloney seemed to bring in on her tray and beneath which the calling ladies grew more and more reserved and coldly watchful and against which Belle flowered like a hothouse bloom, brilliant and petulant and perverse.

It had taken Belle some time to overcome Jefferson's prejudice against a formal meal between dinner and supper and to educate the group in which she moved to tea as a function in itself and not as something to give invalids or as an adjunct to a party of some sort. But Horace had assisted her, unwittingly and without self-consciousness; and there had been a youth, son of a carpenter, of whom Belle had made a poet and sent to New Orleans and who, being a conscientious objector, had narrowly escaped prison during the war and who now served in a reportorial capacity on a Texas newspaper, holding the position relinquished by a besotted young man who had enlisted in the Marine Corps early in '17.

But educate them she did. Certain young matrons took to the idea and emulated her, and even her husband himself had learned to take his cup.

Horace passed on around the house and there came into view the entire court with its two occupants in fluid violent action. Beneath an arcade of white pilasters and vine-hung beams Belle was ensconced like a colorful butterfly, surrounded by the fragile, harmonious impedimenta of the theatric moment. Two sat with her; above the group a crepe-myrtle flowered already. The other woman (the third member of the group was a young girl in white and with a grave molasses bang and a tennis racket across her knees) spoke to him, and Belle greeted him with a sort of languid possessive desolation. Her hand was warm, prehensile, like mercury in his palm exploring softly with delicate bones and petulant scented flesh. Belle's eyes were like hothouse grapes and her mouth was redly mobile, rich with discontent; but waked now from its rouged repose, this was temporarily lost. She had lost Meloney, she told him.

"Meloney saw through your gentility," Horace said. "You grew careless, probably. Your elegance is much inferior to Meloney's. You surely didn't expect to always deceive anyone who can lend as much rigid discomfort to the function of eating and drinking as Meloney could, did you? Or has she got married some more?"

"She's gone in business," Belle answered fretfully. "A beauty shop. And why, I cant for the life of me see. Those things never do last, here. Can you imagine Jefferson women supporting a beauty shop, with the exception of us three? Mrs Marders and I might; I'm sure we need it, but what use has Frankie for one?"

"What seems curious to me," the other woman said, "is where the money came from. People thought that perhaps you had given it to her, Belle."

"Since when have I been a public benefactor?" Belle rejoined coldly. Horace grinned faintly. Mrs Marders said:

"Now, Belle, we all know how kindhearted you are; dont try to conceal it."

"I said a public benefactor," Belle repeated. Horace said quickly:

"Well, Harry would swap a handmaiden for an ox, any day. At least, he can save a lot of wear and tear on his cellar, not having to counteract your tea in a lot of unrelated masculine tummies. I suppose there'll be no more tea out here, will there?"

"Don't be silly," Belle said.

Horace said: "I realize now that it is not tennis that

I came here for, but for the incalculable amount of uncomfortable superiority I always get when Meloney serves me tea . . . I saw your daughter as I came along," he added.

"She's somewhere around, I suppose," Belle agreed indifferently. "You haven't had your hair cut yet," she stated. "Why is it that men have no sense about barbers?" she addressed the other two. The older woman watched them brightly, coldly across her two flaccid chins. The young girl sat quietly in her simple virginal white, her racket on her lap and one brown hand lying upon it like a sleeping tan puppy. She was watching Horace with sober interest but without rudeness, as children do. "They either wont go to the barber at all, or they insist on having their heads all gummed up with pomade and things," Belle added.

"Horace is a poet," the other woman said in an admonitory tone. Her flesh draped loosely from her cheek-bones like rich, slightly soiled velvet; her eyes were like the eyes of an old turkey, mucous and predatory and unwinking. "Poets must be excused for what they do. You should remember that, Belle." Horace bowed in her direction.

"Your race never fails in tact, Belle," he said. "Mrs Marders is one of the few people I know who give the law profession its true evaluation."

"It's like any other business, I suppose," Belle said. "You are late today. Why didn't Narcissa come?"

"I mean, dubbing me a poet," Horace explained. "The law, like poetry, is the final resort of the lame, the halt, the imbecile and the blind. I dare say Caesar invented the law business to protect himself against poets."

"You're so clever," Belle said. The young girl spoke suddenly:

"Why do you bother about what men put on their hair, Miss Belle? Mr Mitchell's bald."

The other woman laughed, unctuously, steadily, watching them with her lidless unlaughing eyes. She watched Belle and Horace and still laughed steadily, brightly and cold. " 'Out of the mouths of babes—' " she quoted. The young girl glanced from one to another with her clear sober eyes. She rose.

"I guess I'll see if I cant get a set now," she said.

Horace moved also. "Let's you and I—" he began. Without turning her head Belle touched him with her hand.

"Sit down, Frankie," she commanded. "They haven't finished the game yet. You shouldn't laugh so much on an empty stomach," she told the other woman. "Do sit down, Horace."

The girl still stood with slim and awkward grace, holding her racket. She looked at Belle a moment, then she turned her head toward the court again. Horace took the chair beyond Belle; her hand dropped hidden into his, with that secret movement, then it grew passive; it was as though she had turned a current off somewhere. Like one entering a dark room in search of something, finding it and pressing the light off again.

"Dont you like poets, Frankie?" Horace asked across Belle's body.

"They cant dance," the girl answered, without turning her head. "I guess they are all right, though. They went to the war, the good ones did. There was one was a good tennis player, that got killed. I've seen his picture, but I dont remember his name."

"Oh, dont start talking about the war, for heaven's sake," Belle said. Her hand stirred in Horace's but did not withdraw. "I had to listen to Harry for two years. Explaining why he couldn't go. As if I cared whether he did or not."

"He had a family to support," Mrs Marders suggested brightly. Belle half reclined, her head against the chair-back, her hidden hand moving slowly in Horace's, exploring, turning, ceaselessly like a separate volition curious but without warmth.

"Some of them were aviators," the girl continued. She now turned the pages of the magazine upon the table. She stood with one little unemphatic hip braced against the table-edge, her racket clasped beneath her arm. Then she closed the magazine and again she watched the two figures leanly antic upon the court. "I danced with one of those Sartoris boys once. I was too scared to know which one it was. I wasn't anything but a baby, then."

"Were they poets?" Horace asked. "I mean, the one that got back. I know the other one, the dead one, was."

"He sure can drive that car of his," she answered, still watching the game, her straight hair (hers was the first bobbed head in town) not brown not gold, her brief nose in profile, her brown still hands clasping her racket. Belle stirred and freed her hand.

"Do go on and play, you all," she said. "You make me nervous." Horace rose with alacrity.

"Come on, Frankie," he said. "Let's you and I take 'em on."

The girl looked at him. "I'm not so hot," she said soberly. "I hope you wont get mad."

"Why? If we get beat?" They moved together toward the court where the two players were now exchanging sides. "Do you know what the finest sensation of all is?" Her straight brown head moved just at his shoulder. It's her dress that makes her arms and hands so brown, he thought. Little. He could not remember her at all sixteen months back, when he had gone away. They grow up so quickly, though, after a certain age. Go away again and return, and find her with a baby, probably.

"Good music?" she suggested tentatively, after a time.

"No. It's to finish a day and say to yourself: Here's one day during which I have accomplished nothing and hurt no one and had a whale of a good time. How does it go? 'Count that day lost whose low descending sun—'? Well, they've got it exactly backward."

"I dont know. I learned it in school, I guess," she answered indifferently. "But I dont remember it now. D'you reckon they'll let me play? I'm not so hot," she repeated.

"Of course they will," Horace assured her. And soon they were aligned: the two players, the bookkeeper in the local department store and a youth who had been recently expelled from the state university for a practical joke (he had removed the red lantern from the barrier about a street excavation and hung it above the door of the girls' dormitory) against Horace and the girl. Horace was an exceptional player, electric and brilliant. One who knew tennis and who had patience and a cool head could have defeated him out of hand by letting him beat himself. But not these. The points see-sawed back and forth, but usually Horace managed to retrieve the advantage with stroking or strategy so audacious as to obscure the faultiness of his tactics.

Meanwhile he could watch her; her taut earnestness, her unflagging determination not to let him down, her awkward virginal grace. From the back line he outguessed their opponents with detached

and impersonal skill, keeping the point in abeyance
and playing the ball so as to bring her young intent
body into motion as he might pull a puppet's strings.
Hers was an awkward speed that cost them points,
but from the base line Horace retrieved her errors
when he could, pleasuring in the skimpy ballooning
of her little dress moulded and dragged by her arms
and legs, watching the taut revelations of her
speeding body in a sort of ecstasy. Girlwhite and all
thy little Oh. Not pink, no. For a moment I thought
she'd no. Disgraceful, her mamma would call it. Or
any other older woman. Belle's are pink O muchly
"Oaten reed above the lyre," Horace chanted,
catching the ball at his shoe-tops with a full swing,
watching it duck viciously beyond the net. Oaten
reed above the lyre. And Belle like a harped gesture,
not sonorous. Piano, perhaps. Blended chords, anyway. Unchaste   ? Knowledgeable better.
Knowingly wearied. Weariedly knowing. Yes, piano.
Fugue. Fugue of discontent. O moon rotting waxed
overlong too long

Last point. Game and set. She made it with savage
awkwardness; and turned at the net and stood with
lowered racket as he approached. Beneath the simple
molasses of her hair she was perspiring a little. "I
kept on letting 'em get my alley," she explained.
"You never bawled me out a single time. What ought
I to do, to break myself of that?"

"You ought to run in a cheese-cloth shimmy on
hills under a new moon," Horace told her. "With
chained ankles, of course. But a slack chain. No, not
the moon; but in a dawn like pipes. Green and gold,
and maybe a little pink. Would you risk a little
pink?" She watched him with grave curious eyes as
he stood before her lean in his flannels and with his
sick brilliant face and his wild hair. "No," he cor-

rected himself again. "On sand. Blanched sand, with dead ripples. Ghosts of dead motion waved into the sand. Do you know how cold the sea can be just before dawn, with a falling tide? Like lying in a dead world, upon the dead respirations of the earth. She's too big to die all at once. Like elephants . . . How old are you?" Now all at once her eyes became secretive, and she looked away. "Now what?" he demanded. "What did you start to say then?"

"There's Mr Mitchell," she said. Harry Mitchell had come out, in tight flannels and a white silk shirt and new ornate sport shoes that cost twenty dollars per pair. With a new racket in a patent case and press, standing with his squat legs and his bald bullet head and his undershot jaw of rotting teeth beside the studied picture of his wife. Presently, when he had been made to drink a cup of tea, he would gather up all the men present and lead them through the house to his bathroom and give them whisky, pouring out a glass and fetching it down to Rachel. He would give you the shirt off his back. He was a cotton speculator and a good one; he was ugly as sin and kindhearted and dogmatic and talkative, and he called Belle "little mother" until she broke him of it. Belle lay yet in her chair; she was watching them as they turned together from the court.

"What was it?" Horace persisted.

"Sir?"

"What you started to say just then."

"Nothing," she answered. "I wasn't going to say anything."

"Oh, that's too feminine," Horace said. "I didn't expect that of you, after the way you play tennis." They moved on under the veiled contemplation of Belle's gaze.

"Feminine?" Then she added: "I hope I can get another set soon. I'm not a bit tired, are you?"

"Yes. Any woman might have said that. But maybe you're not old enough to be a woman."

"Horace," Belle said.

"I'm seventeen," the girl answered. "Miss Belle likes you, dont she?"

Belle spoke his name again, mellifluously, lazily peremptory. Mrs Marders sat now with her slack chins in a raised teacup. The girl turned to him with polite finality. "Thanks for playing with me," she said. "I'll be better someday, I hope. We beat 'em," she said generally.

"You and the little lady gave 'em the works, hey, big boy?" Harry Mitchell said, showing his discolored teeth. His heavy prognathous jaw narrowed delicately down, then nipped abruptly off into pugnacious bewilderment.

"Mr Benbow did," the girl corrected in her clear voice, and she took the chair next Belle. "I kept on letting 'em get my alley."

"Horace," Belle repeated, "your tea is getting cold."

It had been fetched by the combination gardenerstableman-chauffeur, temporarily impressed and smelling of vulcanized rubber and ammonia. Mrs Marders removed her chins from her cup. "Horace plays too well," she said, "really too well. The other men cant compete with him. You were lucky to have him for a partner, child."

"Yessum," the girl agreed. "I guess he wont risk me again."

"Nonsense," Mrs Marders rejoined, "Horace enjoyed playing with you. Didn't you notice it, Belle?"

Belle made no reply. She poured Horace's tea, and

at this moment Belle's daughter came across the lawn in her crocus-yellow dress. Her eyes were like stars, more soft and melting than any deer's and she gave Horace a swift shining glance.

"Well, Titania?" he said.

Belle half turned her head, still with the teapot raised, and Harry set his cup on the table and went and knelt on one knee in her path, as if he were cajoling a puppy. The child came up, still watching Horace with her radiant and melting diffidence, and permitted her father to embrace her and fondle her with his short, heavy hands. "Daddy's gal," Harry said. She submitted to having her prim little dress mussed, pleasurably but a little restively; her eyes flew shining again.

"Dont muss your dress, sister," Belle said, and the child evaded her father's hands with a prim movement. "What is it now?" Belle asked. "Why aren't you playing?"

"Nothing. I just came home." She came and stood diffidently beside her mother's chair.

"Speak to the company," Belle said. "Dont you know better than to come where older people are, without speaking to them?" The little girl did so, shyly and faultlessly, greeting them in rotation, and her mother turned and pulled and patted at her straight soft hair. "Now, do go and play. Why do you always want to come where grown people are? You're not interested in what we're doing."

"Ah, let her stay, mother," Harry said. "She wants to watch her daddy and Horace play tennis."

"Run along, now," Belle added with a final pat, paying no attention to Harry. "And do keep your dress clean."

"Yessum," the child agreed, and she turned obediently, giving Horace another quick shining look. He watched her and saw Rachel stand presently in the kitchen door and speak to her, and she turned and mounted the steps and entered the door which Rachel held open.

"What a beautifully mannered child," Mrs Marders said. "How do you do it, Belle?"

"They're so hard to do anything with," Belle said. "She has some of her father's traits. Drink your tea, Harry."

Harry took his cup from the table and sucked its lukewarm contents into himself noisily and dutifully. "Well, big boy," he said to Horace, "how about a set? These squirrels think they can beat us."

"Frankie wants to play again," Belle said. "Do let the child have the court for a little while."

"What?" Harry was busy evolving his racket from its intricate and expensive casing. He paused and raised his savage undershot face and his dull kind eyes.

"No, no," the girl protested quickly, "I've had enough. I'd rather look on a while."

"Dont be silly," Belle said. "They can play any time."

"Sure the little lady can play," Harry said. "Here, you jelly-beans, how about fixing up a set with the little lady?" He restored his racket, with ostentatious care.

"Please, Mr Mitchell," the girl said.

"Dont mind him," Belle told her. "He and Horace can play some other time. You children go on and play. He'll have to make the fourth, anyway."

The ex-student spoke: "Sure, Mr Harry, come on. Me and Frankie'll play you and Joe."

"You folks go ahead and play a set," Harry repeated. "I've got a little business to talk over with Horace. You all go ahead." He insisted, overrode their polite protests until they took the court. Then he jerked his head significantly at Horace.

"Go on with him," Belle said. "The baby." Without looking at him, without touching him, she enveloped him with rich and smoldering promise. Mrs Marders sat across the table from them, curious and bright and cold with her teacup. "Unless you want to play with that silly child again."

"Silly?" Horace repeated. "She's too young to be unconsciously silly yet."

"Run along," Belle told him. "And hurry back. Mrs Marders and I are tired of one another."

Horace followed his host into the house, followed his short rolling gait and the bald indomitability of his head. From the kitchen, as they passed, little Belle's voice came steadily, recounting some astonishment of the day, with an occasional mellow ejaculation from Rachel for antistrophe. In the bathroom Harry got a bottle from a cabinet, and preceded by labored heavy footsteps mounting, Rachel entered without knocking, bearing a pitcher of ice water. "Whyn't y'all g'awn and play, ef you wants?" she demanded. "Whut you let that 'oman treat you and that baby like she do, anyhow?" she demanded of Harry. "You ought to take and lay her out wid a stick of wood. Messin' up my kitchen at fo' oclock in de evenin'. And you aint helpin' none, neither," she told Horace. "Gimme a dram, Mr Harry, please, suh."

She took her glass and waddled heavily out; they heard her descend the stairs slowly and heavily on her fallen arches. "Belle couldn't get along without Rachel," Harry said, rinsing two glasses. "She talks too much, like all niggers. To listen to her you'd think Belle was some kind of a wild animal, wouldn't you? A dam tiger or something. But Belle and I understand each other. You've got to make allowances for women, anyway. Different from men. Born contrary; complain when you dont please 'em and complain when you do." Then he said, with astonishing irrelevance: "I'd kill the man that tried to wreck my home like I would a dam snake. Well, let's take one, big boy."

Presently he sloshed ice water into his empty glass and gulped that, too, and he reverted to his former grievance.

"Cant get to play on my own dam court," he said. "Belle gets all these dam people here every day. What I want is a court where I can come home from work and get in a couple of fast sets every afternoon. Appetizer before supper. But every dam day I get home from work and find a lot of young girls and jelly-beans, using it like it was a public court." Horace drank his more moderately, and Harry lit a cigarette and threw the match onto the floor and hung his leg across the lavatory. "I reckon I'll have to build another court for my own use and put a hogwire fence around it with a Yale lock, so Belle cant give picnics on it. There's plenty of room down there by the lot fence. No trees, too. Put it out in the dam sun, and I reckon Belle'll let me use it now and then. Well, suppose we get on back."

He led the way through his bedroom and stopped to show Horace a new repeating rifle he had just bought, and to press upon him a package of cigarettes which he imported from South America, and they descended and emerged into afternoon become later. The sun was level now across the court where three players leaped and sped with soft quick slapping of rubber soles, following the fleeting impact of the ball. Mrs Marders sat yet with her ceaseless chins, although she was speaking of departure as they came up. Belle turned her head against the chair-back, but Harry led Horace on.

"We're going to look over a location for a tennis court. I think I'll take up tennis myself," he told Mrs Marders with clumsy irony.

Horace halted in his loose, worn flannels, with his thin face brilliant and sick with nerves, smoking his host's cigarettes and watching his hopeless indomitable head and his intent, faintly comical body as he paced off dimensions and talked steadily in his harsh voice; paced back and forth and planned and calculated with something of a boy's fine ability for fabling, for shaping the incontrovertible present to a desire which he will presently lose in a recenter one and so forget.

Presently Harry was satisfied, and they returned. It was later still. Mrs Marders was gone and Belle sat alone, immersed in a magazine. A youth in a battered Ford had called for Frankie, but another young man had dropped in, and when Horace and Harry came up the three youths clamored politely for Harry to join them.

"Take Horace here," Harry said, obviously pleased. "He'll give you a run for your money." But Horace demurred and the three continued to importune Harry. "Lemme get my racket," he said finally, and Horace followed the heavy scuttling of his backside across the court. Belle glanced up at them briefly.

"Did you find a place?" she asked.

"Yes," Harry answered, uncasing his racket again. "Where I can play by myself, sometimes. A place too far from the street for everybody that comes along to see it and stop." But Belle was reading again. Harry unscrewed his racket press and removed it.

"I'll go in one set, then you and I can get in a fast one before dark," he told Horace.

"Yes," Horace agreed. He sat down and watched Harry stride heavily onto the court and take his position, watched the first serve. Then Belle's magazine rustled and slapped onto the table.

"Come," she said, rising. Horace rose too, and Belle preceded him and they crossed the lawn and entered the house. Rachel moved about in the kitchen, and they went on through the house, where all noises were remote and the furniture gleamed peacefully indistinct in the dying evening light. Belle slid her soft prehensile hand into his, clutching his hand against her softly clothed thigh, and led him into a room beyond folding doors. This room too was quiet and empty and here she stopped against him half turning, and they kissed. But she freed her mouth presently and led him on in the rising dusk and he drew the piano bench out and they sat on opposite sides of it and kissed again. "You haven't told me you love me," Belle said, touching his face with her fingertips, and the fine devastation of his hair. "Not in a long time."

"Not since yesterday," Horace agreed, but he told her, she leaning her breast against him and listening with a sort of rapt voluptuous inattention, like a great still cat; and when he had done and sat touching her face and her hair with his delicate wild hands, she removed her breast and opened the piano and touched the keys. Saccharine melodies she played, from memory and in the current mode, that you might hear on any vaudeville stage, and with shallow skill, a sense for their oversweet nuances. They sat thus for some time, Belle in another temporary vacuum of discontent, building with her hands and for herself an edifice, a world in which she moved romantically, finely and a little tragical; while Horace sat beside her and watched both Belle in her self-imposed and tragic role, and himself performing like the old actor whose hair is thin and whose profile is escaping him via his chin, but who can play to any cue at a moment's notice while the younger men chew their bitter thumbs in the wings.

Presently the rapid heavy concussions of Harry's feet thumped again on the stairs mounting, and the harsh wordless uproar of his voice as he led someone else in the back way and up to his bathroom. Belle ceased her hands and leaned her body against him and kissed him again, clinging. "This is intolerable," she said, freeing her mouth with a movement of her head. For a moment she resisted against his arm, then her hands crashed discordantly upon the keys and slid through Horace's hair and down his cheeks tightening. She freed her mouth again. "Now, sit over there," she directed.

From his chair, she at the piano was half in shadow. Twilight was deeper yet; only the line of her bent head and her back, tragic and still, somehow young. We do turn corners upon ourselves, like suspicious old ladies spying on servants, Horace thought. No, like boys trying to head off a parade. "There's always divorce," he said.

"To marry again?" Her hands trailed off into chords; they merged and faded again into a minor motif in one hand. Overhead Harry moved with his heavy staccato tread, shaking the house. "You'd make a rotten husband."

"I wont as long as I'm not married," Horace answered.

She said, "Come here," and he rose, and in the dusk she was again tragic and young and familiar, and he knew the sad fecundity of the world, and time's hopeful disillusion that fools itself. "I want to have your child, Horace," she said, and then her own child came up the hall and stood diffidently in the door.

For a moment Belle was an animal awkward and mad with fear. She surged away from him with a mad spurning movement; her hands crashed on the keys before she controlled her instinctive violent escape and left in the dusk a mindless protective antagonism, pervading, in steady cumulate waves, directed at Horace as well.

"Come in, Titania," Horace said.

The little girl stood diffidently in silhouette. Belle's voice was sharp with relief. "Well, what do you want? Sit over there," she hissed at Horace. "What do you want, Belle?" Horace drew away a little, but without rising.

"I've got a new story to tell you, soon," he said. But little Belle stood yet, as though she had not heard, and her mother said:

"Go on and play, Belle. Why did you come in the house? It isn't supper time, yet."

"Everybody's gone home," she answered. "I haven't got anybody to play with."

"Go to the kitchen and talk to Rachel then," Belle said. She struck the keys again, harshly. "You worry me to death, hanging around the house." The little girl looked at them for a moment, then she turned obediently and went away. "Sit over there," Belle repeated. Horace resumed his chair and Belle sat in the twilight and played loudly and swiftly, with cold and hysterical skill. Overhead he heard Harry again, heard them descend the stairs. Harry was talking again; the voices passed on toward the rear, ceased. Belle continued to play. It was dance music in the new jazz tradition; still about him in the dark room that mindless protective antagonism like a muscular contraction that remains after the impulse of fright has faded. Without ceasing she said:

"Are you going to stay for supper?"

He was not, he answered, waking suddenly. She did not rise with him, did not turn her head again, and he let himself out of the house and descended into the violet dusk of late spring, where was already a faint star above the windless trees. On the drive just without the garage Harry's new car stood. At the moment he was doing something to the engine of it while the house-yard-stable boy held a patent trouble-lamp over the bald crag of his head and his daughter and Rachel peered across his bent back, leaning their intent and dissimilar faces into the soft bluish glare of the light. Horace went on homeward and supperward. Before he reached the narrow street on which he lived the street lamps sputtered and failed, then glared beneath the dark boughs of trees, beneath delicate motionless veils of leaves.

4

"General William Booth has gotten a leprechaun on Uriah's wife." Horace told himself, and gravely presented the flowers he had brought, and received in return the starry incense of her flying eyes. Mrs Marders was among the group of Belle's more intimate familiars in this room, affable and brightly cold, a little detached and volubly easy; she admired little Belle's gifts one by one with impeccable patience. Belle's voice came from the adjoining room where the piano was bowered for the occasion by potted plams and banked pots and jars of bloom, and where yet more ladies were sibilantly crescendic with an occasional soberly clad male on the outer fringe of their colorful chattering like rocks dumbly imponderable about the cauldron where seethed an hysterical tideflux. These men spoke to one another from the sides of their mouths and, when addressed by the ladies, with bleak and swift affability, from the teeth outward. Harry's bald bullet head moved among his guests, borne hither and yon upon the harsh uproar of his voice; presently, when the recital would have gotten underway and the ladies engaged, he would begin to lead the men one by one and on tiptoe from the room and up the back stairs to his apartments.

But now the guests stood and drifted and chattered, anticipatory and unceasing, and every minute or two Harry gravitated again to the dining room, on the table of which his daughter's gifts and flowers were arrayed and beside which little Belle in her pale lilac dress stood in a shining-eyed and breathless ecstasy.

"Daddy's gal," Harry, in his tight, silver-gray gabardine suit and his bright tie with the diamond stud, chortled, putting his short thick hands on her; then together they examined the latest addition to the array of gifts with utter if dissimilar sincerity—little Belle with quiet and shining diffidence, her father stridently, tactlessly overloud. Harry was smoking his cigarettes steadily, scattering ash; he had receptacles of them open on every available flat surface throughout the lighted rooms. "How's the boy?" he added, shaking Horace's hand.

"Will you look at that sumptuous bouquet Horace has brought your daughter," Mrs Marders said. "Horace, it's really a shame. She'd have appreciated a toy or a doll much more, wouldn't you, honey? Are you trying to make Belle jealous?"

Little Belle gave Horace her flying stars again. Harry squatted before her.

"Did Horace bring daddy's gal some flowers?" he brayed. "Just look at the flowers Horace brought her." He put his hands on her again. Mrs Marders said quickly:

"You'll burn her dress with that cigarette, Harry."

"Daddy's gal dont care," Harry answered. "Buy her a new dress tomorrow." But little Belle freed herself, craning her soft brown head in alarm, trying to see the back of her frock, and then Belle entered in pink beneath a dark blue frothing of tulle, and the rich bloody auburn of her hair. Little Belle showed her Horace's bouquet, and she knelt and fingered and patted little Belle's hair, and smoothed her dress.

"Did you thank him?" she asked. "I know you didn't."

"Of course she did," Horace interposed. "Just as you thank providence for breath every time you breathe." Little Belle looked up at him with her grave ecstatic shining. "We think girls should always have flowers when they play music and dance," he explained, gravely too. "Dont we?"

"Yes," little Belle agreed breathlessly.

"Yes, sir," Belle corrected fretfully. Patting and pulling at her daughter's delicate wisp of dress, with its tiny embroidered flowers at the yoke. Belle kneeling in a soft swishing of silk, with her rich and smoldering unrepose. Harry stood with his squat, tightly clothed body, looking at Horace with the friendly, bloodshot bewilderment of his eyes.

"Yes, sir," little Belle piped obediently.

Belle rose, swishing again. "Come on, sister. It's

time to begin. And dont forget and start pulling at your clothes."

The indiscriminate furniture—dining-room chairs, rockers, sofas and all—were ranged in semicircular rows facing the corner where the piano was placed. Beside the piano and above little Belle's soft brown head and her little sheer frock and the tense, impotent dangling of her legs, the music teacher, a thin passionate spinster with cold thwarted eyes behind nose glasses, stood. The men clung stubbornly to the rear row of chairs, their sober decorum splotched sparsely among the cacophonous hues of the women's dresses. With the exception of Harry, that is, who now sat with the light full on his bald crag. Just beyond him and between him and Mrs Marders, Horace could see Narcissa's dark burnished head. Belle sat on the front row at the end, turned sideways in her chair. The other ladies were still now, temporarily, in a sort of sibilant vacuum of sound into which the tedious labored tinkling of little Belle's playing fell like a fairy fountain.

The music tinkled and faltered, hesitated, corrected itself to the intent nodding of little Belle's head and the strained meagre gestures of the teacher, tinkled monotonously and tunelessly on while the assembled guests sat in a sort of bland, waiting inattention; and Horace speculated on that persevering and senseless urge of parents (and of all adults) for making children a little ridiculous in their own eyes and in the eyes of other children. The clothes they make them wear, the stupid mature things they make them do. And he found himself wondering if to be cultured did not mean to be purged of all taste; civi-

lized, to be robbed of all fineness of objective judgment regarding oneself. Then he remembered that
little Belle also had been born a woman.

The music tinkled thinly, ceased; the teacher
leaned forward with a passionate movement and removed the sheet from the rack, and the room swelled
with a polite adulation of bored palms. Horace too;
and little Belle turned on the bench, with her flying
eyes, and Horace grinned faintly at his own masculine vanity. Sympathy here, when she was answering
one of the oldest compulsions of her sex, a compul-
sion that taste nor culture nor anything else would
ever cause to appear ridiculous to her. Then the
teacher spoke to her and she turned on the bench
again, with her rapt laborious fingers and the brown,
intent nodding of her head.

Belle sat sideways in her chair. Her head was bent
and her hands lay idle upon her lap and she sat
brooding and remote. Horace watched her, the line
of her neck, the lustrous stillness of her arm; trying
to project himself into that region of rich and smoldering immobility into which she had withdrawn for
the while. But he could not; she did not seem to be
aware of him at all; the corridors where he sought her
were empty, and he moved quietly in his seat beneath the thin tinkling of the music and looked about
at the other politely attentive heads and beyond
them, in the doorway, Harry making significant covert signs in his direction. Harry jerked his thumb toward his mouth and moved his head meaningly, but
Horace flipped his hand briefly in reply, without
moving. When he looked doorward again Harry was
gone.

Little Belle ceased again. When the clapping died
the heavy thump-thump-thump of Harry's heels
sounded on the ceiling above. Ridiculous, like the in-

nocent defenseless backside of a small boy caught delving into an apple barrel, and a few of the guests cast their eyes upward in polite astonishment. Belle raised her head sharply, with an indescribable gesture, then she looked at Horace with cold and blazing irritation, enveloping, savage, disdainful of who might see. The thumping ceased, became a cautious clumsy tipping, and Belle's anger faded, though her gaze was still full upon him. Little Belle played again and Horace looked away from the cold fixity of Belle's gaze, a little uncomfortably, and so saw Harry and one of the men guests enter surreptitiously and seat themselves; he turned his head again. Beneath the heavy shadow of her hair Belle still watched him, and he shaped three words with his lips. But Belle's mouth did not change its sullen repose, nor her eyes, and then he realized that she was not looking at him at all, perhaps had never been.

Later Belle herself went to the piano and played a trite saccharine waltz and little Belle danced to it with studied, meaningless gestures too thinly conceived and too airily executed to be quite laughable, and stood with her diffident shining among the smug palms. She would have danced again, but Belle rose from the piano, and the guests rose also with prompt unanimity and surrounded her in laudatory sibilance. Belle stood moodily beside her daughter in the center of it, and little Belle pleasurably. Horace rose also. Above the gabbling of the women he could hear Harry again overhead: thump-thump-thump, and he knew that Belle was also listening although she responded faultlessly to the shrill indistinguishable compliments of her guests. Beside little Belle the teacher stood, with her cold, sad eyes, proprietorial and deprecatory, touching little Belle's hair with a meagre passionate hand.

Then they drifted doorward, with their shrill polite uproar. Little Belle slid from among them and came, a little drunk with all the furore and her central figuring in it, and took Horace's hand. "What do you think was the best," she asked, "when I played, or when I danced?"

"I think they both were," he answered.

"I know. But what do you *think* was the best?"

"Well, I think the dancing was, because your mamma was playing for you."

"So do I," little Belle agreed. "They could see all of me when I was dancing, couldn't they? When you are playing, they cant see but your back."

"Yes," Horace agreed. He moved toward the door, little Belle still clinging to his hand.

"I wish they wouldn't go. Why do they have to go now? Cant you stay a while?"

"I must take Narcissa home. She cant go home by herself, you know."

"Yes," little Belle agreed. "Daddy could take her home in our car."

"I expect I'd better do it. But I'll be coming back soon."

"Well, all right, then." Little Belle sighed with weary contentment. "I certainly do like parties; I certainly do. I wish we had one every night." The guests clotted at the door, evacuating with politely trailing phrases into the darkness. Belle stood responding to their recapitulations with smoldering patience. Narcissa stood slightly aside, waiting for him, and Harry was among them again, strident and affable.

"Daddy's gal," he said. "Did Horace see her playing the piano and dancing? Want to go up and take one before you leave?" he asked Horace in a jarring undertone.

"No, thanks. Narcissa's waiting for me. Some other time."

"Sure, sure," Harry agreed, and Horace was aware of Belle beside him, speaking to little Belle, but when he turned his head she was moving away with her silken swishing and her heavy, faint scent. Harry was still talking. "How about a couple of sets tomorrow? Let's get over early, before Belle's gang comes, and get in a couple of fast ones, then let 'em have the court."

"All right," Horace agreed, as he always did to this arrangement, wondering as usual if that boy's optimism of Harry's really permitted him to believe that they could or would follow it out, or if he had just said the phrase so many times that the juxtaposition of the words no longer had any meaning in his liquor-fuddled brain. Then Narcissa was beside him, and they were saying Goodnight, and the door closed upon little Belle, and Harry's glazed squat dome and upon Belle's smoldering and sullen rage. She had said no word to him all evening.

He turned away and found that his sister had descended the steps and was half way down the dark walk to the street. "If you're going my way, I'll walk along with you," he called to her. She made no reply, neither did she slacken her pace, nor did she increase it when he joined her.

"Why is it," he began, "that grown people will go to so much trouble to make children do ridiculous things, do you suppose? Belle had a house full of people she doesn't care anything about and most of whom dont approve of her, and kept little Belle up three hours past her bedtime; and the result is

Harry's about half tight, and Belle is in a bad humor, and little Belle is too excited to go to sleep, and you and I wish we were home and are sorry we didn't stay there."

"Why do you go there, then?" Narcissa asked coldly. Horace was suddenly stilled. They walked on through the darkness, toward the next street light. Against it branches hung like black coral in a silver sea.

"Oh," Horace said. Then: "I saw that old cat talking with you."

"Why do you call Mrs Marders an old cat? Because she told me something that concerns me and that everybody else seems to know?"

"So that's who told you, is it? I wondered . . ." He slid his arm within her unresponsive one. "Dear old Narcy." They passed through the dappled shadows beneath the light, went on in the darkness again.

"Is it true?" she asked after a time.

"You forget that lying is a struggle for survival," he said. "Little puny man's way of dragging circumstance about to fit his preconception of himself as a figure in the world. Revenge on the sinister gods."

"Is it true?" she persisted. They walked on, arm in arm, she grave and constant and waiting; he shaping and discarding phrases in his mind, finding time to be amused at his own fantastic impotence in the presence of her constancy.

"People dont usually lie about things that dont concern them," he answered wearily. "They are impervious to the world, even if they aren't to life. Not when fact is so much more diverting than their imaginings could be," he added. Narcissa freed her arm with grave finality.

"Narcy—"

"Dont," she said. "Dont call me that." The next corner, beneath the next light, was theirs; they would turn there. Above the arching feathery canyon of the street the sinister gods stared down with their yellow, unwinking eyes. Horace thrust his hands into his jacket pockets, and for a space he was stilled again while his fingers learned the unfamiliar object they had found there. Then he drew it forth: a sheet of heavy notepaper, folded twice and tinged with a fading heavy scent, a scent as of flowers that bloom richly at night. A familiar scent, yet baffling too for the moment, like a face watching him from an arras. He knew the face would emerge in a moment, but as he held the note in his fingers and sought the face through the corridors of his present distraction, his sister spoke suddenly and hard at his side.

"You've got the smell of her all over you. Oh, Horry, she's dirty!"

"I know," he answered unhappily, and the face emerged clearly, and he was suddenly empty and cold and sad. "I know." It was like a road stretching on through darkness, into nothingness and so away; a road lined with black motionless trees O thou grave myrtle shapes amid which Death. A road along which he and Narcissa walked like two children drawn apart one from the other to opposite sides of it; strangers, yet not daring to separate and go in opposite ways, while the sinister gods watched them with cold unwinking eyes. And somewhere, everywhere, behind and before and about them pervading, the dark warm cave of Belle's rich discontent and the tiger-reek of it.

But the world was opening out before him fearsome and sad and richly moribund, as though he were again an adolescent, and filled with shadowy shapes of dread and of delight not to be denied: he must go on, though the other footsteps sounded fainter and fainter in the darkness behind him and then not at all. Perhaps they had ceased, or turned into a byway.

This byway led her back to Miss Jenny. It was now well into June, and the scent of Miss Jenny's transplanted jasmine drifted steadily into the house and surrounded it with constant cumulate waves more grave and simple than a fading resonance of viols. The earlier flowers were gone, and the birds had finished eating the strawberries and now sat about the fig bushes all day, waiting for them to ripen; zinnia and delphinium bloomed without any assistance from Isom who, since Caspey had more or less returned to normalcy (with the exception of Saturday nights) and laying-by time was yet a while away, now spent the lazy long days sleeping peacefully with a cane fishing pole on the creek bank. Old Simon pottered querulously about the place. His linen duster and tophat gathered chaff on the nail in the harness room and the carriage horses waxed fat and insolent and lazy in the pasture. The duster and hat came down from their nail and the horses were harnessed to the carriage but once a week, now—on Sundays, to drive in to town to church. Miss Jenny said she was too far along to risk salvation by driving to church at fifty miles an hour; that she had as many sins as her ordinary behavior could take care of, particularly as she had old Bayard's soul to get into heaven somehow, also, what with him and young Bayard tearing around the country every afternoon at the imminent risk of their necks. About young

Bayard's soul Miss Jenny did not alarm herself at all: he had no soul.

Meanwhile he rode about the farm and harried the negro tenants in his cold fashion, and in two-dollar khaki breeches and a pair of field boots that had cost him fourteen guineas he tinkered with farming machinery and with the tractor he had persuaded old Bayard to buy: for the time being he had become almost civilized again. He went to town only occasionally now, and often on horseback, and all in all his days had become so usefully innocuous that both his aunt and his grandfather were growing a little nervously anticipatory.

"Mark my words," Miss Jenny told Narcissa on the day she drove out again. "He's storing up devilment that's going to burst loose all at once, someday, and then there'll be hell to pay. Lord knows what it'll be—maybe he and Isom will take his car and that tractor and hold a steeple chase with 'em . . . What did you come out for? Got another letter?"

"I've got several more," Narcissa answered lightly. "I'm saving them until I get enough for a book, then I'll bring them all out for you to read." Miss Jenny sat opposite her, erect as a crack guardsman, with that cold briskness of hers that caused agents and strangers to stumble through their errands with premonitions of failure ere they began. But to Narcissa it was like emerging into the fresh air from a stale room. "I just came to see you," she added, and for a moment her serene face held such grave and still despair that Miss Jenny sat more erect yet and stared at her guest with her piercing eyes.

"Why, what is it, child? Did the man walk into your house?"

"No, no." The look was gone, but still Miss Jenny

watched her with those keen old eyes that seemed to see so much more than you thought—or hoped. "Shall I play a while? It's been a long time, hasn't it?"

"Well," Miss Jenny agreed, "if you want to."

There was dust on the piano; Narcissa opened it with a fine gesture, and brushed her fingertips on her skirt. "If you'll let me get a cloth—"

"Here, lemme dust it," Miss Jenny said, and she caught up her skirt by the hem and mopped the keyboard violently. "There, that'll do." Then she drew her chair from behind the instrument and seated herself. She still watched the other's profile with cold speculation, but presently the old tunes stirred her memory again, and in a while her eyes grew more and more remote and the other and the trouble that had shown momentarily in her face, was lost in Miss Jenny's own dead young nights and days and vanquished abiding griefs, and it was some time before she realized that the other was weeping quietly while she played.

Without rising Miss Jenny leaned forward and touched Narcissa's arm. "Now, you tell me what it is," she commanded. And Narcissa told her, quietly in her grave contralto while her eyes still wept.

"Hmph," Miss Jenny said. "That's to be expected of a man that hasn't any more to do than Horace. I dont see why you are so upset over it."

"But that woman," Narcissa wailed suddenly, like a little girl, burying her face in her hands. "She's so dirty!"

Miss Jenny dug into the pocket of her skirt and handed the other a man's handkerchief.

"What do you mean?" she asked. "Dont she wash often enough?"

"Not that way. I m-mean she's—she's—" Narcissa turned suddenly and laid her head on the piano.

"Oh," Miss Jenny said. "All women are, if that's what you mean." She sat stiffly indomitable, musing on the younger woman's shaking shoulders. "Hmph," she said again, "Horace has spent so much time being educated that he never has learned anything . . . Why didn't you break it up in time? Didn't you see it coming?"

The other wept more quietly now. She sat up and dried her eyes on Miss Jenny's handkerchief. "It started before he went away. Dont you remember?"

"That's so. I do sort of remember a lot of women's gabble. Who told you about it, anyway? Horace?"

"Mrs Marders did. And then Horace did. But I never thought that he'd—I never thought—" again her head dropped to the piano, hidden in her arms. "I wouldn't have treated Horace that way."

"Sarah Marders, was it? I might have known . . . I admire strong character, even if it is bad," Miss Jenny stated. "Well, crying wont help any." She rose briskly. "We'll think what to do about it. Only I'd let him go ahead; it'll do him good if she'll just turn around and make a doormat of him . . . Too bad Harry hasn't got spunk enough to . . . But I reckon he'll be glad; I know I would—There, there," she said, at the other's movement of shocked alarm, "I dont reckon Harry'll hurt him. Dry your face, now. You better go to the bathroom and fix up. Bayard'll be coming in soon, and you dont want him to see you've been crying, you know." Narcissa glanced swiftly and a little fearfully toward the door and dabbed hastily at her cheeks with Miss Jenny's handkerchief.

At times the dark lifted, the black trees were no longer sinister, and then Horace and Narcissa walked the road in sunlight, as of old. Then he would seek her through the house and cross the drive and descend the lawn in the sunny afternoon to where she sat in the white dresses he loved beneath the oak into which a mockingbird came each afternoon and sang, bringing her the result of his latest venture in glass-blowing. He had five now, in different colors and all nearly perfect, and each of them had a name. And as he finished them and before they were scarce cooled, he must bring them across the lawn to where she sat with a book or with a startled caller perhaps, in his stained dishevelled clothes and his sooty hands in which the vase lay demure and fragile as a bubble, and with his face blackened too with smoke and a little mad, passionate and fine and austere.

But then the dark would descend once more, and beyond the black and motionless trees Belle's sultry imminence was like a presence, like the odor of death. And then he and Narcissa were strangers again, tugging and straining at the shackles of custom and old affection that bound them with slipping bonds.

And then they were no longer even side by side. At times he called back to her through the darkness, making no sound and receiving no reply; at times he hovered distractedly like a dark bird between the two of them. But at last he merged with himself, fused in the fatalism of his nature, and set his face steadily up the road, looking not back again. And then the footsteps behind him ceased.

5

For a time the earth held him in a smoldering hiatus that might have been called contentment. He was up at sunrise, planting things in the ground and watching them grow and tending them; he cursed and harried niggers and mules into motion and kept them there, and put the grist mill into running shape and taught Caspey to drive the tractor, and came in at mealtimes and at night smelling of machine oil and of stables and of the earth and went to bed with grateful muscles and with the sober rhythms of the earth in his body, and so to sleep. But he still waked at times in the peaceful darkness of his familiar bed and without previous warning, tense and sweating with old terror; and always and constant beneath activity and bodily fatigue and sleep and all, that stubborn struggling of his heart which would not wear away.

But his days were filled, at least, and he discovered pride again. Nowadays he drove the car into town to fetch his grandfather from habit alone, and though he still considered forty-five miles an hour merely cruising speed, he no longer took cold and fiendish pleasure in turning curves on two wheels or in detaching mules from wagons by striking the whiffletrees with his bumper in passing. Old Bayard still insisted on riding with him when he must ride, but with freer breath; and once he aired to Miss Jenny his growing belief that at last young Bayard had outworn his seeking for violent destruction.

Miss Jenny, being a true optimist—that is, expecting the worst at all times and so being daily agreeably surprised—promptly disillusioned him. Meanwhile she made young Bayard drink plenty of milk and otherwise superintended his diet and hours in her martinettish way, and at times she entered his room at night and sat for a while quietly beside the bed where he slept.

Nevertheless, young Bayard improved in his ways. Without being aware of the progress of it, he had become submerged in a monotony of days, had been snared by a rhythm of activities repeated and repeated until his muscles grew so familiar with them as to get his body through the days without assistance from him at all. He had been so neatly tricked by earth, that ancient Delilah, that he was not aware that his locks were shorn, was not aware that Miss Jenny and old Bayard were wondering how long it would be before they grew out again. He needs a wife, was Miss Jenny's thought. Then maybe he'll stay sheared. "A young person to worry with him," she said to herself. "Bayard's too old, and I've got too much to do, to worry with the long devil."

He saw Narcissa about the house now and then, sometimes at the table, and he was aware of her shrinking and of her distaste. But not for long at a time and with no other emotion save a mild curiosity as to why she had not married. Miss Jenny told him that she was twenty-six, the same age as himself.

Then sowing time was over, and it was summer. Cotton and corn was out of the ground and laid-by; the grist mill was ready to run and the gin had been overhauled, and one day he found himself with nothing to do. It was like coming dazed out of sleep, out of the warm, sunny valleys where people lived; and again the cold peak of his stubborn despair stood bleakly among black and savage stars and the valleys were obscured by shadow.

The road descended in a quiet red curve between pines through which the hot July winds swelled with a long sound like a far away passing of trains, descended to a mass of lighter green of willows, where a creek ran beneath a stone bridge. At the top of the grade the scrubby, rabbit-like mules stopped and the younger negro got down and lifted a gnawed white-oak sapling from the wagon and locked the off rear wheel by wedging the pole between the warped wire-bound spokes of it and across the axle tree. Then he climbed into the crazy wagon again, where the other negro sat motionless with the lifted rope-spliced reins in his hand and his head tilted creek-ward. "Whut 'uz dat?" he said.

"Whut 'uz whut?" the other asked. But his father sat yet in his attitude of motionless grave attention, and the younger negro listened also. But there was no further sound save the long sough of the wind among the sober pines and the liquid whistling of a quail somewhere among them. "Whut you hear, pappy?" he repeated.

"Somethin' busted down dar. Tree fell, mebbe." He jerked the reins. "Hwup, mules." The mules flapped their jackrabbit ears and lurched the wagon into motion, and they descended among the cool dappled shadows, on the jarring scrape of the locked wheel that left behind it a glazed bluish ribbon in the soft red dust. At the foot of the hill the road crossed the bridge and went on mounting again; beneath the bridge the creek rippled and flashed brownly among willows, and beside the bridge and bottom up in the creek, a motor car lay. Its front wheels were still spinning and the engine yet ran at idling speed, trailing a faint shimmer of exhaust. The older negro drove onto the bridge and stopped, and the two of them sat and stared quietly down upon the car's long belly. The younger negro spoke suddenly:

"Dar he is! He in de water under hit. I kin see his foots stickin' out."

"He liable to drown, dar," the other said, with static interest, and they descended from the wagon. The younger one slid down the creek bank; the other wrapped the reins about one of the stakes that held the bed on the wagon frame and thrust his peeled hickory goad beneath the seat and circled the wagon without haste and dragged the white-oak pole free of the locked wheel and put it in the wagon. Then he also slid gingerly down the creek bank to where his son squatted, peering at young Bayard's submerged legs.

"Dont you git too clost to dat thing, boy," he commanded. "Hit mought blow up. Dont you year hit still grindin' in dar?"

"We got to git dat man out," the younger one replied. "He gwine drown."

"Dont you tech 'im. White folks'll be sayin' we done it. We gwine wait right heer 'twell some white man comes erlong."

"He'll drown 'fo' dat," the other said, "layin' in dat water." He was barefoot, and he stepped into the water and stood again with brown flashing wings of water stemming about his lean black calves.

"You, John Henry!" his father said. "You come 'way f'um dat thing."

"We got to git 'im outen dar," the boy repeated, and the one in the water and the other on the bank, they wrangled amicably while the water rippled about Bayard's boot toes. Then the younger negro approached warily and caught Bayard's leg and tugged at it. The body responded, shifted, stopped again, and grunting querulously the older one removed his shoes and stepped into the water also. "He hung again," John Henry said, squatting in the water and searching beneath the car with his hand. "He hung under de guidin' wheel. His haid aint quite under water, dough. Lemme git de pole."

He mounted the bank and got the sapling from the wagon bed and returned and joined his father where the other stood in sober, curious disapproval above Bayard's legs, and with the pole they lifted the car enough to drag Bayard free of it. They lifted him onto the shelving bank and he sprawled there in the sun, with his calm face and his matted hair, while water drained out of his boots, and they stood above him on alternate legs while they wrung out their overalls.

"Hist's Cunnel Sartoris's boy, aint it?" the elder said at last, and he lowered himself stiffly to the sand, groaning and grunting, and donned his shoes.

"Yessuh," John Henry answered. "Is he daid, pappy?"

"Co'se he is," the other answered petulantly. "Atter that otto'bile jumped offen dat bridge wid 'im? Whut you reckon he is, ef he aint daid? And whut you gwine say when de law axes how come you de onliest one dat found 'im daid? Tell me dat."

"Tell 'um you holp me."

"Hit aint none of my business. I never run dat thing offen de bridge. Listen at it, dar, mumblin' and grindin' yit. You git on 'fo' hit blows up."

"We better git 'im into town," John Henry said. "Dey mought not be nobody else comin' 'long today." He stooped and raised Bayard's shoulders and tugged him to a sitting position. "He'p me git 'im up de bank, pappy."

"Hit aint none of my business," the other repeated, but he bent and picked up Bayard's legs and they lifted him, and he groaned without waking.

"Dar, now," John Henry exclaimed. "Year dat? He aint daid." But he might well have been, with his long inert body and his head wrung excruciatingly against John Henry's shoulder. They shifted their grips and turned toward the road. "Hah," said John Henry. "Le's go!"

They struggled up the shaling treacherous bank with him and onto the road, where the elder let his end of the burden slip to the ground. "Whuf," he expelled his breath sharply. "He heavy ez a flou' bar'l."

"Come on, pappy," John Henry said, "Le's git 'im in de waggin." The other stooped again, with bared teeth, and they raised Bayard with dust caked redly on his wet thighs, and heaved him by panting stages into the wagon bed. "He looks lak a daid man," John Henry added, "and he sho' do ack lak one. I'll ride back here and keep his haid f'um bumpin'."

"Git dat brakin' pole you lef' in de creek," his father ordered, and John Henry descended and retrieved the sapling and got in the wagon again and lifted Bayard's head onto his knees, and his father unwrapped the reins from the stanchion and mounted to the sagging seat and picked up his peeled hickory wand.

"I dont lak dis kind o' traffickin'," he repeated. "Hwup, mules." The mules lurched the wagon into motion once more, and they went on. Behind them the car lay on its back in the creek, its engine still muttered and rumbled at idling speed.

Its owner lay in the springless wagon, jolting laxly and inert, oblivious of it and of John Henry's dark compassionate face above him. Thus for some miles, while John Henry kept the sun from Bayard's face with the shadow of his hat, then their jolting progress penetrated into that region to which he had withdrawn and he groaned again. "Drive slower, pappy," John Henry said. "De joltin' wakin' 'im up."

"I caint he'p dat," the elder replied, "I never run dat otto'bile offen dat bridge. I got to git on into town and git back home. Git on dar, mules."

John Henry tried to ease him to the jolting, and

Bayard groaned again and lifted his hand to his chest, and moved and opened his eyes. But he closed them immediately against the sun and he lay on John Henry's knees, cursing. Then he moved again, trying to sit up. John Henry restrained him, firmly yet diffidently, and he opened his eyes again, struggling.

"Let go, goddam you!" he said. "I'm hurt."

"Yessuh, captain; ef you'll jes' lay still—"

Bayard heaved himself violently, clutching his side; his teeth shone between his drawn, bloodless lips and he gripped John Henry's shoulder with a clutch like steel hooks. "Stop," he shouted. "Stop him; make him stop! He's driving my damn ribs right through me." He cursed again, trying to get onto his knees, gripping John Henry's shoulder, clutching his side with his other hand. The older negro turned and looked back at him. "Hit him with something," Bayard shouted. "Make him stop. I'm hurt, goddam it!"

The wagon stopped. Bayard was now on his hands and knees, bending lower and lower on all fours, like a wounded beast. The two negroes watched him quietly, and still clutching his side he moved and essayed to climb out of the wagon. John Henry jumped down and helped him, and he got slowly out and leaned against the wheel, with his sweating, bloodless face and the dry grinning of his teeth.

"Git back in de waggin, captain, and le's git to town to de doctor," John Henry said.

Bayard stared at him, moistening his lips with his tongue. Then he moved again and crossed to the roadside and sat down, fumbling at the buttons of his shirt. The two negroes watched him.

"Got a knife, son?" he asked presently.

"Yessuh." John Henry produced his knife, and by Bayard's direction he slit the other's shirt off. Then the two of them bound it tightly about Bayard's body, and he got to his feet.

"Got a cigarette?" he asked.

John Henry had not. "Pappy got some chewin' terbacker," he suggested.

"Gimme a chew, then." They gave him a chew and helped him back into the wagon and onto the seat, and drove on again. They jingled and rattled interminably onward in the red dust, through shadow and sunlight and up hill and down, while Bayard alternately chewed and swore. On and on, and at every jolt, with every breath he took, his broken ribs stabbed and probed into his flesh.

Then a final hill, and the road emerged from the trees and crossed the flat valley and joined the highway, and here they stopped while the sun blazed down on Bayard's naked shoulders and bare head while he and the old negro wrangled as to whether they should drive him home or not, and Bayard swore and raged and suffered. At last he took the reins from the elder negro's hands and swung the mules about himself. The negro continued to protest, querulously, until Bayard dug a banknote from his trousers and gave it to him and surrendered the lines, and they went on.

This last mile was the worst of all. On all sides of them cultivated fields spread away to the shimmering hills: earth was saturated with heat and broken and turned and saturated again and drunken with it, exuding heat like an alcoholic's breath. The trees along the road were sparse and but half grown, and the mules moved at a maddening walk in their own dust. His nerves had become inured to pain and had surrendered to it; he was conscious only of dreadful thirst and he knew that he was becoming light headed. The negroes too realized that he was going out of his head, and the younger one crawled precariously forward and offered him his frayed straw hat. Bayard accepted it and put it on.

The mules with their comical, overlarge ears assumed fantastic shapes, merged into other shapes without significance or meaning; shifted and changed again. At times it seemed to him that they were travelling backward, that they would crawl terrifically past the same tree or telephone post time after time; and it seemed to him that the three of them and the rattling wagon and the two beasts were caught in a ceaseless and senseless treadmill, a motion without progress, forever and to no escape.

But at last and without his being aware of it, the wagon turned in between the iron gates, and shadow fell gratefully upon his naked shoulders, and he opened his eyes and his home swam and floated in a pale mirage like a huge serene shape submerged in water. The jolting stopped and the two negroes helped him down. He mounted the steps and crossed the veranda; in the hallway, after the outer glare, he could see nothing at all for a moment and he stood, a little dizzy and nauseated, blinking. Then Simon's eyeballs rolled out of the obscurity.

"Whut in de Lawd's name," said Simon, "is you been into now?"

"Simon?" he said. He swayed a little; to keep on his feet he strode on again and blundered into something. "Simon?"

Simon moved swiftly and touched him. "I kep' tellin' you dat car 'uz gwine to kill you; I kep' tellin' you!" Simon slid his arm about Bayard and they went on. At the stairs he tried to turn Bayard, but Bayard wouldn't be turned. He continued on down the hall and entered his grandfather's study and stopped, leaning against a chair-back.

"Keys," he said thickly. "Aunt Jenny. Got to have drink."

"Miss Jenny done gone to town wid Miss Benbow," Simon answered. "Dey aint nobody here, aint nobody here a-tall 'cep' de niggers. I kep' a-tellin' you!" he moaned again, pawing at Bayard. "Dey aint no blood, dough. Come to de sofa and lay down, Mist' Bayard."

Bayard moved again, and Simon supported him, and Bayard lurched around the chair and slumped into it, clutching his chest. "Dey aint no blood," Simon babbled.

"Keys," Bayard said again. "Get the keys."

"Yessuh, I'll git 'um." Simon flapped his distracted hands about Bayard. Bayard swore at him, and still moaning Dey aint no blood, he turned and scuttled from the room. Bayard sat forward, clutching his chest, and heard Simon mount the stairs, heard him on the floor overhead. Then he was back, and Bayard watched him open the desk and extract the silver-stoppered decanter and scuttle out again and return with a glass, to find Bayard leaning against the desk, drinking from the decanter. Simon helped him back to the chair and poured him a drink into the glass. Then he fetched him a cigarette and hovered futilely and distractedly about him. "Lemme git de doctuh, Mist' Bayard."

"No. Gimme another drink."

Simon obeyed. "Dat's three, already. Lemme go git Miss Jenny en de doctuh, Mist' Bayard, please, suh."

"No. Leave me alone. Get out of here."

He drank that one. The nausea, the mirage shapes, were gone, and he felt better. At every breath his side stabbed him with hot needles, so he was careful to breathe shallowly. If he could only remember that . . . Yes, he felt much better, so he rose carefully and went to the desk and had another drink. Yes, that was the stuff for a wound, like Suratt had said. Like that time last year when he got that tracer in his belly and nothing would stay on his stomach except gin-and-milk. And this, this wasn't anything: just a few caved slats. Patch his fuselage with a little piano wire in ten minutes. Not like Johnny. They were all going right into his thighs. Damn butcher wouldn't even raise his sights a little. He'd have to remember to breathe shallowly.

He crossed the room slowly but steadily enough. Simon flitted in the dim hall before him, and he mounted the stairs slowly, holding to the rail while Simon watched him with strained distraction. He entered his room, the room that had been his and John's, and stood for a while until he could breathe shallowly again. Then he crossed to the closet and opened it, and kneeling carefully, with his hand to his side, he opened the chest which was there. There was not much in it: a garment; a small leather-bound book; a shotgun shell to which was attached by a piece of wire a withered bear's paw. It was John's first bear, and the shell with which he had killed it in the river bottom near MacCallum's when he was twelve years old. The book was a New Testament; on the flyleaf in faded brown: 'To my son, John, on his seventh birthday, March 16, 1900, from his Mother.' He had one exactly like it; that was the year grandfather had arranged for the morning local freight to stop and pick them up and carry them to town to start to school. The garment was a canvas hunting coat, stained and splotched with what had once been blood and scuffed and torn with briers and smelling yet faintly of salt-peter.

Still kneeling, he lifted the objects out one by one

and laid them on the floor. He picked the coat up again, and its fading stale acridity drifted in his nostrils. "Johnny," he whispered, "Johnny." Suddenly he raised the garment toward his face but halted it as sharply, and with the coat half raised he looked swiftly over his shoulder. But immediately he recovered himself and turned his head and lifted the garment and laid his face against it, defiantly and deliberately, and knelt so for a time.

Then he rose and gathered up the book and the trophy and the coat and crossed to his chest of drawers and took from the top of it a photograph. It was a picture of John's Princeton eating club group, and he gathered this also under his arm and descended the stairs and passed out the back door. As he emerged Simon was just crossing the yard with the carriage, and as he passed the kitchen Elnora was crooning one of her mellow endless songs.

Behind the smoke-house squatted the black pot and the wooden tubs where Elnora did her washing in fair weather. She had been washing today; the clothes line swung with limp damp garments, and beneath the pot smoke yet curled from the soft wood ashes. He thrust the pot over with his foot and rolled it aside, and from the woodshed he fetched an armful of rich pine kindling and laid it on the ashes. Soon a blaze, pale in the sunny air; and when the wood was burning strongly he laid the coat and the Bible and the trophy and the photograph on the flames and prodded them and turned them until they were consumed. In the kitchen Elnora crooned mellowly as she labored; her voice came rich and plaintful and sad along the sunny reaches of the air. He must remember to breathe shallowly.

• • •

Simon drove rapidly on to town, but he had been forestalled. The two negroes had told a merchant about finding Bayard on the roadside and the news had reached Colonel Sartoris at the bank, who had sent for Dr Peabody. But Dr Peabody was gone fishing, so he took Dr Alford instead, and the two of them in Dr Alford's car passed Simon just as he drove into town. He turned around and followed them, but by the time he arrived home they had young Bayard anaesthetized and temporarily incapable of further harm; and when Miss Jenny and Narcissa Benbow drove unsuspectingly up the drive an hour later, he was bandaged and conscious again. They had not heard of it, and Dr Alford's car was the first intimation. Although Miss Jenny did not recognise the car, she knew immediately what it meant. "That fool has killed himself at last," she said, and got out and sailed into the house.

Bayard lay white and still and a little sheepish in his bed. Old Bayard and the doctor were just leaving, and Miss Jenny waited until they were out of the room, then she raged and stormed at him and stroked his face and his hair, while Simon bobbed and mowed in the corner between bed and wall. "Dasso, Miss Jenny, dasso! I kep' a-tellin' 'im!"

And so, having eased her soul, she descended to the veranda where Dr Alford stood in impeccable departure. Old Bayard sat in the car waiting for him, and on Miss Jenny's appearance he became his stiff self again and completed his departure, and he and old Bayard drove away.

Miss Jenny also looked up and down the veranda, then into the hall. "Where—" she said, then she called: "Narcissa." A reply; and she added: "Where are you?" The reply came again and Miss Jenny re-entered the house and saw Narcissa's white dress in the gloom where she sat on the piano bench. "He's awake," Miss Jenny said. "You can come up and see him." The other rose and turned into the light. "Why, what's the matter? You look lots worse than he does. You're white as a sheet."

"Nothing," Narcissa answered. "I—" She stared at Miss Jenny a moment, clenching her hands at her sides. "I must go," she said, and she emerged from the parlor. "It's late, and Horace . . ."

"You can come in and speak to him, cant you?" Miss Jenny asked, watching the other curiously. "There's not any blood, if that's what you are afraid of."

"It isn't that," Narcissa answered. "I'm not afraid." But she was rigid with repressed trembling; Miss Jenny could see her teeth clenched upon her lower lip.

"Why, all right," Miss Jenny agreed kindly, "if you'd rather not. I just thought perhaps you'd like to see he is all right, as long as you are here. But dont, if you dont feel like it."

"Yes. Yes. I feel like it. I want to." She passed Miss Jenny and went on down the hall. At the foot of the stairs she halted until Miss Jenny came up behind her, and they mounted together, although she kept a step ahead and with her face averted from Miss Jenny's probing eyes.

"What's the matter?" Miss Jenny demanded, still watching the other. "What happened to you? Have you fallen in love with him?"

"In love . . . him? Bayard?" She swayed against the rail beside her and paused, and slid her hand along the rail and drew herself onward. She began to laugh thinly, repressing hysteria. Miss Jenny mounted beside her, piercing and curious and cold; Narcissa hurried on. At the stair head she stopped

again, holding to the railing, and permitted Miss
Jenny to precede her; and just without the door to
Bayard's room she stopped yet again and leaned
against it, throttling her laughter and her trembling.
Then she entered the room, where Miss Jenny stood
beside the bed with head reverted.

For a moment she could see nothing for the swelling convolutions of laughter in her throat, and she
was conscious only of her need to repress them and
of a sickly-sweet lingering of ether as she approached
the bed and stood blindly beside it, with her hidden
writhing hands. On the pillow Bayard's head lay as
she had remembered it on that former day—pallid
and calm, like a chiselled mask brushed lightly over
with the shadow of his spent violence. He was
watching her, and for a while she gazed at him, and
Miss Jenny and the room and all, swam away.

"You beast, you beast," she said thinly. "Why must
you always do these things where I've got to see
you?"

"I didn't know you were there," Bayard answered
weakly, with mild astonishment.

But this was gone soon; nor did it return. Every few
days, by Miss Jenny's request, she came out and sat
beside his bed and read to him, bringing into the
room her outward untroubled serenity. He cared
nothing at all about books; it is doubtful if he had
ever read a book on his own initiative; but he would
lie motionless in his cast while her grave contralto
voice went on and on in the drowsy room. Sometimes he tried to talk to her, but she ignored his
attempts and read on; if he persisted, she went away
and left him. So he soon learned to lie, usually with
his eyes closed, voyaging alone in the bleak and bar-

ren regions of his despair, while her voice flowed and
ebbed above the remoter sounds that surrounded
them—Miss Jenny scolding Simon or Isom downstairs or in the garden; the twittering of birds in the
tree just beyond the window; the ceaseless rhythmic
monotone of the water pump below the barn. At
times she would cease and look at him and find that
he was peacefully sleeping.

6

Old man Falls came through the lush green of early
June, came into town through the yet horizontal
sunlight of morning, and in his dusty neat overalls he
now sat opposite old Bayard in immaculate linen and
a geranium like a merry wound. The room was cool
and still, reposeful with dingy light and the casual
dust of a negro janitor's casual and infrequent disturbing. Now that old Bayard was aging, and what
with the deaf tenor of his stiffening ways, he was
showing more and more a desire to surround himself
with things of a like undeference; showing an in-
credible aptitude for choosing servants who circled
about him in a sort of pottering and bland futility.
The janitor, who dubbed old Bayard General and
whom old Bayard and the other clients for whom he
performed seemingly interminable duties of a slovenly
and minor nature, addressed as Dr Jones, was one of
these. He was black and stooped with querulousness
and age, and he took advantage of everyone who
would permit him, and old Bayard swore at him constantly and permitted him to steal his tobacco and the
bank's winter supply of coal and peddle it to other
negroes.

The windows behind which old Bayard and his

caller sat gave upon a vacant lot of rubbish and dusty weeds. It was bounded by the weathered rears of sundry one-story board buildings within which small businesses—repair- and junk-shops and such—had their lowly and ofttimes anonymous being. The lot itself was used by day by country people as a depot for their wagons and teams; already some of these were tethered somnolent and ruminant there, and about the stale ammoniac droppings of their patient generations sparrows swirled in garrulous clouds, or pigeons slanted with sounds like rusty shutters, or strode and preened in burnished and predatory pomposity, crooning among themselves with guttural unemphasis.

Old man Falls sat on the opposite side of the trash-filled fireplace, mopping his face with a blue-figured bandana.

"It's my damned old legs," he explained, faintly apologetic. "Use to be I'd walk twelve fifteen mile to a picnic or a singin' with less study than that 'ere little old three mile into town gives me now." He mopped the handkerchief about that face of his, browned and cheerful these many years with the simple and abounding earth. "Looks like they're fixin' to give out on me, and I aint but ninety-three, neither." He held his parcel in his other hand, but he continued to mop his face, making no motion to open it nor to ascertain its contents.

"Why didn't you wait on the roadside until a wagon came along?" old Bayard demanded in that overloud tone of the deaf. "Always some damn feller with a field full of weeds coming to town."

"I reckon I mought," the other agreed. "But gittin' here so quick would spile my holiday. I aint like you town-folks. I aint got so much time I kin hurry it." He stowed the handkerchief away and rose and laid his parcel carefully on the mantel, and from his shirt he produced a small object wrapped in a clean frayed rag. Beneath his tedious and unhurried fingers there emerged a tin snuff-box polished long since to the dull soft sheen of satin or silver by handling and age. Old Bayard sat in his white linen and watched, watched him quietly as he removed the cap of the box and laid this, too, carefully aside.

"Now, turn yo' face to the light," old man Falls directed.

"Loosh Peabody says that stuff will give me blood poisoning, Will."

The other continued his slow preparations, his blue innocent eyes steadily following the movement of his hands. "Loosh Peabody never said that," he corrected quietly. "One of them young doctors told you that, Bayard. Lean yo' face to the light." But old Bayard sat yet well back in his chair, his hands on the arms of it, watching the other with his piercing old eyes soberly, a little wistful; eyes filled with unnameable things like the eyes of old lions, and intent.

Old man Falls poised a dark gob of his ointment on one finger and raised his head. Then he set the box carefully on his vacated chair and he put his hand on old Bayard's face. But old Bayard still resisted, though passively, watching him with his unutterable things; and the other drew him firmly but gently nearer the light.

"Come on, here. I'm too old to waste any time hurtin' folks. Hold still, now, so' I wont spot yo' face. My hand aint steady enough to lift a rifle ball offen a hot stove no mo'."

He submitted then, and old man Falls patted the salve onto the wen with small deft touches. Then he took up the bit of cloth and removed the surplus from the wen and wiped his fingers and dropped the

rag onto the hearth and knelt stiffly and touched a
match to it. "We allus do that," he explained. "My
granny got that 'ere from a Choctaw woman nigh a
hundred year ago. Aint none of us never told what
hit air nor left no after trace." He rose stiffly again
and dusted his knees. He recapped the box with the
same unhurried laborious care and put it away and
raised his parcel from the mantel and resumed his
chair.

"Hit'll turn black, and long's hit's black, hit's
workin'. Dont put no water on yo' face befo'
mawnin', and I'll come in again in ten days and dose
hit again, and on the—" He brooded a moment,
computing slowly on his gnarled fingers; his lips
moved, but with no sound. "—the ninth day of July,
hit'll drap off. And dont you let Miss Jenny nor none
of them doctors worry you about it."

He sat with his overalled knees close together. The
package lay on his knees and he now opened it after
the ancient laborious ritual, picking with a sort of patient indomitability at the pink knot of the cord until
a younger person would have screamed. Old Bayard
merely lit a cigar and propped his feet on the fireplace, and in good time old man Falls solved the knot
and removed the string and laid it across his chair-
arm. It fell to the floor and he bent and fumbled it
into his blunt fingers and laid it again across the
chair-arm and watched it a while lest it fall again,
then he opened the parcel. First was his carton of tobacco, and he removed a plug and sniffed it, turned it
about in his hand and sniffed it again. But without
biting into it he laid it and its fellows aside and
delved further yet. He spread open the throat of the
resulting paper bag, and his innocent boy's eyes
gloated soberly into it.

"I'll declare," he said. "Sometimes I'm right

ashamed for havin' sech a consarned sweet tooth. Hit dont give me no rest a-tall." Still carefully guarding the other objects on his close knees he tilted the sack and shook two or three of the striped, shrimp-like things into his palm, returned all but one, which he put into his mouth. "I'm afeard now I'll be loosin' my teeth someday and I'll have to start gummin' 'em or eatin' soft ones. I never did relish soft candy." His leathery cheek bulged slightly, with slow regularity like a respiration as he chewed against the hard substance. He peered into the sack again, and he sat weighing it in his hand.

"They was times back in sixty-three and -fo' when a feller could a bought a section of land and a nigger with this yere bag of candy. Lots of times I mind, with ever'thing goin' agin us like, and sugar and cawfee gone and food scace, eatin' stole cawn when they was any to steal and ditch weeds ef they wa'nt; bivouacin' at night in the rain, more'n like . . ." His voice trailed away among ancient phantoms of the soul's and the body's tribulations, into those regions of glamorous and useless endeavor where such ghosts abide. Then he chuckled and chewed his peppermint again.

"I mind that day we was a-dodgin' around Grant's army, headin' nawth. Grant was at Grenada then, and Colonel had rousted us boys out and we taken hoss and jined Van Dorn's cavalry down that-a-way. That was when Colonel had that 'ere silver stallion. Grant was still at Grenada, but Van Dorn lit out one day, headin' nawth; why, us boys didn't know. Colonel mought have knowed, but he never told us. Not that we keered much, long's we was headin' to'ds home.

"So our comp'ny was ridin' along to ourselves, goin' to jine up with the balance of 'em later. Leastways the rest of 'em thought we was goin' to jine 'em. But Colonel never had no idea of doin' that; his cawn hadn't been laid by yit, and he was goin' home fer a spell. We wasn't runnin' away," he explained. "We knowed Van Dorn could handle 'em all right fer a week or two. He usually done it. He was a putty good man," old man Falls said. "A putty good man."

"They were all pretty good men in those days," old Bayard agreed. "But you damn fellers quit fighting and went home too often."

"Well," old man Falls replied defensively, "even ef the hull country's overrun with bears, a feller cant hunt bears all the time. He's got to quit once in a while, ef hit's only to feed and rest up the dogs and hosses. But I reckon them dogs and hosses could stay on the trail long as any. 'Course ever'body couldn't keep up with that 'ere mist-colored stallion. They wa'nt but one animal in the Confedrit army could tech him—that last hoss Zeb Fothergill fotch back outen one of Sherman's cavalry pickets on his last trip into Tennessee.

"Nobody never did know what Zeb done on them trips of his'n; Colonel claimed hit was jest to steal hosses. But he never got back with lessen one. One time he come back with seven of the orneriest critters that ever walked, I reckon. He tried to swap 'em fer meat and cawn-meal, but wouldn't nobody have 'em; then he tried to give 'em to the army, but even the army wouldn't have 'em. So he finally turned 'em loose and requisitioned to Joe Johnston's haidquarters fer ten hosses sold to Forrest's cavalry. I dont know ef he ever got air answer. Nate Forrest wouldn't a had them hosses. I doubt ef they'd even a et 'em in Vicksburg . . . I never did put no big reliability in Zeb Fothergill, him comin' and goin' by hisself like he done. But he knowed hosses, and he usually fotch a good 'un home ever' time he went away to'ds the war. But he never got another'n like this befo'.'"

The bulge receded from his cheek and he produced his pocket knife and cut a neat segment from his plug of tobacco and put it in his mouth. Then he rewrapped his parcel and tied the string about it again. The ash of old Bayard's cigar trembled delicately about its glowing heart, but did not fall; his crossed elastic-sided boots gleamed against the hearth edge.

Old man Falls spat neatly and brownly into the cold fireplace. "That day we was in Calhoun county," he continued. "Hit was as putty a summer mawnin' as you ever see; men and hosses rested and fed and feelin' peart, trottin' along the road through the woods and fields whar birds was a-singin' and young rabbits lopin' across the road. Colonel and Zeb was ridin' along side by side on them two hosses, Colonel on Jupiter and Zeb on that sorrel two-year-old, and they was a-braggin' as usual. We all knowed Colonel's Jupiter, but Zeb kep' a-contendin' he wouldn't take no man's dust. The road was putty straight across the bottom to'ds the river and Zeb kep' on aggin' the Colonel fer a race, until Colonel said All right. He told us boys to come on and him and Zeb would wait fer us at the river bridge 'bout fo' mile ahead, and him and Zeb lit out.

"Them hosses was the puttiest livin' things I ever seen. They went off together like two birds, neck and neck. They was outen sight in no time, with dust swirlin' behind, but we could foller 'em fer a ways by the dust they left, watchin' it kind of suckin' on down the road like one of these here ottomobiles was in the middle of it. When they come to whar the road drapped down to the river Colonel had Zeb beat

by about three hundred yards. Thar was a crick jest
under the ridge, and when Colonel sailed over the
rise and come in sight of the crick, thar was a
comp'ny of Yankee cavalry with their hosses picket-
ted and their muskets stacked, eatin' dinner by the
bridge. Colonel says they was a-settin' thar gapin' at
the rise when he come over hit, holdin' cups of cawfee and hunks of bread in their hands and their
muskets stacked about forty foot away, buggin' their
eyes and mouths at him.

"It was too late fer him to turn back, anyhow, but
I dont reckon he would ef they'd been time. He jest
spurred down the ridge and in amongst 'em, scat-
terin' cook-fires and guns and men, shoutin' 'Surround 'em, boys! Ef you move, you air dead men.'
One or two of 'em made to break away, but Colonel
drawed his pistols and let 'em off, and they come
back and scrouged in amongst the others, and thar
they set, still a-holdin' their cups and dinner, when
Zeb come up. And that was the way we found 'em
when we got thar ten minutes later." Old man Falls
spat again, neatly and brownly, and he chuckled. His
eyes shone like periwinkles. "That cawfee was sho'
mighty fine," he said.

"And thar we was, with a passel of prisoners we
didn't have no use fer. We held 'em all that day and
et their grub; and when night come we taken and
throwed their muskets into the crick and taken their
ammunition and the rest of the grub and put a guard
on their hosses, then the rest of us laid down. And all
that night we laid thar in them fine Yankee blankets,
listenin' to them prisoners sneakin' away one at a
time, slippin' down the bank into the crick and
wadin' off. Time to time one would slip or make a
splash er something, then they'd all git right still fer
a spell. But pretty soon we'd hear 'em at it again,

crawlin' through the bushes to'ds the crick, and us layin' with blanket aidges held to our mouths. Hit was nigh dawn 'fore the last one had snuck off in a way that suited him.

"Then Colonel from whar he was a-layin' let out a yell them pore critters could hear fer a mile.

" 'Go it, Yank,' he says, 'and look out fer moccasins!'

"Next mawnin' we saddled up and loaded our plunder and ever' man taken him a hoss, and lit out fer home. We'd been home two weeks and Colonel had his cawn laid by, when we heard 'bout Van Dorn ridin' into Holly Springs and burnin' Grant's sto's. Seems like he never needed no help from us, noways." He chewed his tobacco for a time, quietly retrospective, reliving in the company of men now dust with the dust for which they had, unwittingly perhaps, fought, those gallant, pinch-bellied days into which few who now trod that earth and drew breath, could enter into with him.

Old Bayard shook the ash from his cigar. "Will," he said, "what the devil were you folks fighting about, anyhow?"

"Bayard," old man Falls answered, "damned ef I ever did know."

After old man Falls had departed with his small parcel and his innocently bulging cheek, old Bayard sat and smoked his cigar. He knew now a sense of finality, of peace; like that of the man who has made his final cast with the dice and from whom all initiative is lifted, leaving him no more than a vegetable until they cease rolling, let them show what they may. He had crossed the Rubicon . . . but had he? He raised his hand and touched the wen again, but lightly, recalling old man Falls' parting stricture; and recalling this, the thought that it might not yet be too late, that he might yet remove the paste with water, followed.

He rose and crossed to the lavatory in the corner of the room. Above it was fixed a small cabinet with a mirror in the door, and in it he examined the black spot on his face, touching it again with his fingers, then staring at his hand. Yes, it might still come off . . . But be damned if he would; be damned to a man who didn't know his own mind. And Will Falls, too; Will Falls, hale and sane and sound as a dollar; Will Falls who, as he himself had said, was too old to have any reason for injuring anyone. He flung his cigar away and quitted the room and tramped through the lobby toward the door where his chair sat. But before he reached the door he stopped and turned and came up to the teller's window, behind which the cashier sat in a green eyeshade.

"Res," he said.

The cashier looked up. "Yes, Colonel?"

"Who is that damn boy that hangs around here, looking through that window all the time?" old Bayard demanded, lowering his voice within a pitch or so of an ordinary conversational tone.

"What boy, Colonel?" Old Bayard pointed, and the cashier raised himself on his stool and peered over the partition and saw without the indicated window a boy of ten or twelve watching him with an innocently casual air. "Oh. That's Will Beard's boy, from up at the boarding house," he shouted. "Friend of Byron's, I think."

"What's he doing, then? Every time I walk through here, there he is looking in that window. What does he want?"

"Maybe he's a bank robber," the cashier suggested.

"What?" Old Bayard cupped his ear fiercely in his palm.

"Maybe he's a bank robber," the other shouted, leaning forward on his stool. Old Bayard snorted and tramped violently away and slammed his chair back against the door. The cashier sat lumped and shapeless on his stool, rumbling deep within his gross body. He said, without turning his head: "Colonel's let Will Falls treat that thing on his face with that salve." The Snopes at his desk made no reply; did not raise his head. After a time the boy moved, and drifted casually and innocently away.

Virgil Beard now possessed, besides the air rifle, a pistol that projected a stream of ammoniac water excruciatingly painful to the eyes, a small magic lantern, and an ex-candy showcase in which he kept birds' eggs and an assortment of insects that had died slowly on pins, and a modest hoard of nickels and dimes and quarters. With a child's innocent pleasure he divulged to his parents the source of this beneficence, and his mother took Snopes to her gray heart, fixing him special dishes and performing trifling acts to increase his creature comfort with bleak and awkward gratitude.

At times the boy, already dressed and with his bland shining face, would enter his room and waken him from his troubled sleep and sit on a chair while Snopes donned his clothing, talking politely and vaguely of certain things he aimed to do, and of what he would require to do them successfully with. Or if not this, he was on hand at breakfast while his harried gray mother and the slatternly negress bore dishes back and forth from the kitchen, quiet but proprietorial; blandly and innocently portentous.

And all during the banking day (it was summer now, and school was out) Snopes never knew when he would look over his shoulder and find the boy lounging without the plate glass window of the bank, watching him with profound and static patience. Presently he would take himself away, and for a short time Snopes would be able to forget him until, wrapped in his mad unsleeping dream, he mounted the boarding house veranda at supper time and found the boy sitting there and waiting patiently his return; innocent and bland, steadfast and unassertive as a minor but chronic disease. "Got another business letter to write tonight, Mr Snopes?"

And sometimes after he had gone to bed and his light was out, he lay in the mad darkness against his sleepless desire moiled in obscene images and shapes, and heard presently outside his door secret, rat-like sounds; and lay so tense in the dark, expecting the door to open and, preceded by breathing above him sourceless and invisible: "Going to write another letter, Mr Snopes?" And he waked sweating from dreams in which her image lived and moved and thwarted and mocked him, with the pillow crushed against his mean, half-insane face, while the words produced themselves in his ears: "Got air other letter to write yet, Mr Snopes?"

So he changed his boarding house. He gave Mrs Beard an awkward, stumbling explanation; vague, composed of sentences with frayed ends. She was sorry to see him go, but she permitted him to pack his meagre belongings and depart without either anger or complaint, as is the way of country people. He went to live with a relation, that I. O. Snopes who ran the restaurant—a nimble, wiry little man with a talkative face like a nutcracker, and false merry eyes—in a small frame house painted a sultry prodigious yellow, near the railway station. Snopeses did not trust one another enough to develop any intimate relations, and he was permitted to go and come when he pleased. So he found this better than the boarding house, the single deterrent to complete satisfaction being the hulking but catlike presence of I.O.'s son Clarence. But, what with his secretive nature, it had even been his custom to keep all his possessions under lock and key, so this was but a minor matter. Mrs Snopes was a placid mountain of a woman who swung all day in a faded wrapper, in the porch swing. Not reading, not doing anything: just swinging.

He liked it here. It was more private; no transients appearing at the supper table and tramping up and down the hallways all night; no one to try to engage him in conversation on the veranda after supper. Now, after supper he could sit undisturbed on the tight barren little porch in the growing twilight and watch the motor cars congregating at the station across the way to meet the 7:30 train; could watch the train draw into the station with its rows of lighted windows and the hissing plume from the locomotive, and go on again with bells, trailing its diminishing sound into the distant evening, while he sat on the dark porch with his desperate sleepless lust and his fear. Thus, until one evening after supper he stepped through the front door and found Virgil Beard sitting patiently and blandly on the front steps in the twilight.

So he had been run to earth again, and drawn, and hounded again into flight. Yet outwardly he pursued the even tenor of his days, unchanged, performing his duties with his slow meticulous care. But within him smoldered something of which he himself grew afraid, and at times he found himself gazing at his idle hands on the desk before him as though they were not his hands, wondering dully at them and at what they were capable, nay importunate, to do. And day by day that lust and fear and despair that moiled within him merged, becoming desperation—a thing blind and vicious and hopeless, like that of a cornered rat. And always, if he but raised his head and looked toward the window, there was the boy watching him with bland and innocent eyes beneath the pale straw of his hair. Sometimes he blinked; then the boy was gone; sometimes not. So he could never tell whether the face had been there at all, or whether it was merely another face swum momentarily from out the seething of his mind. In the meanwhile he wrote another letter.

7

Miss Jenny's exasperation and rage when old Bayard arrived that afternoon was unbounded. "You stubborn old fool," she stormed. "Cant Bayard kill you fast enough, that you've got to let that old quack of a Will Falls give you blood poisoning? After what Dr Alford told you, when even Loosh Peabody, who thinks a course of quinine or calomel will cure anything from a broken neck to chilblains, agreed with him? I'll declare, sometimes I just lose all patience with you folks; wonder what crime I seem to be expiating by having to live with you. Soon as Bayard sort of quiets down and I can quit jumping every time the 'phone rings, you have to go and let that old pauper daub your face up with axle grease and lamp black. I'm a good mind to pack up and get out, and start life over again in some place where they never heard of a Sartoris." She raged and stormed on; old Bayard raged in reply, with violent words and profane, and their voices swelled and surged through the house until Simon and Elnora in the kitchen moved about with furtive hushed sounds. Finally old Bayard tramped from the house and mounted his horse and rode away, leaving Miss Jenny to wear her rage out upon the empty air, and then there was peace for a time.

But at supper the storm brewed and burst again. Simon within the butler's pantry could hear them beyond the swing door, and young Bayard's voice too, trying to shout them down. "Let up, let up," he howled. "For God's sake. I cant hear myself chew."

"And you're another one." Miss Jenny turned promptly on him. "You're just as trying as he is. You and your stiff-necked, sullen ways. Helling around the country in that car just because you think there may be somebody who cares whether or not you break your worthless neck, and then coming into the supper table smelling like a stable-hand! Just because you went to a war. Do you think nobody else ever went to a war? Do you reckon that when my Bayard came back from The War, he made a nuisance of himself to everybody that had to live with him? But he was a gentleman: he raised the devil like a gentleman, not like you Mississippi country people. Clodhoppers. Look what he did with just a horse," she added. "He didn't have any flying machine."

"Look at the little two-bit war he went to," young Bayard rejoined. "A war that was so sorry that grandfather wouldn't stay up there in Virginia where it was, even."

"And nobody wanted him at it," Miss Jenny retorted. "A man that would get mad just because his men deposed him and elected a better colonel in his place. Got mad and came back to the country to lead a bunch of brigands."

"Little two-bit war," young Bayard repeated. "And on a horse. Anybody can go to a war on a horse. No chance for him to do anything much."

"At least he got himself decently killed," Miss Jenny snapped. "He did more with a horse than you could do with that aeroplane."

"Sho'," Simon breathed against the pantry door. "Aint dey gwine it? Takes white folks to sho' 'nough quoil." And so it surged and ebbed through the succeeding days; wore itself out, then surged again when old Bayard returned home with another application of old man Falls' paste. But by this time Simon was having troubles of his own, troubles which he finally consulted old Bayard about one afternoon. Young Bayard was laid up in bed with his crushed ribs, with Miss Jenny mothering him with violent and cherishing affection, and Miss Benbow to visit with him and read aloud to him; and Simon came into his own again. The tophat and the duster came down from the nail, and old Bayard's cigars depleted daily by one, and the fat matched horses spent their accumulated laziness and insolence between home and the bank, before which Simon swung them to a halt each afternoon as of old, with his clamped cigar and his smartly furled whip and all the theatrics of the fine moment. "De ottomobile," Simon philosophised, "is all right for pleasure and excitement, but fer de genu-wine gen'lmun tone, dey aint but one thing: dat's hosses."

Thus Simon's opportunity came ready to his hand, and once they were clear of town and the team had settled into its gait, he took advantage of it.

"Well, Cunnel," he began, "looks lak me en you's got to make some financial 'rangements."

"What?" Old Bayard brought his attention back from where it wandered about the familiar landscape of planted fields and blue shining hills beyond them.

"I says, it looks lak me en you's goin' ter have to arrange about a little cash money."

"Much obliged, Simon," old Bayard answered, "but I dont need any money right now. I'm much obliged, though."

Simon laughed heartily, from the teeth out. "I declare, Cunnel, you sho' is comical. Rich man lak you needin' money!" And he laughed again, with unctuous and abortive heartiness. "Yes, suh, you sho' is comical." Then he ceased laughing and became engrossed with the horses for a moment. Twins they were, Roosevelt and Taft, with sleek hides and broad, comfortable hips. "You, Taf', lean on dat collar! Laziness gwine go in on you someday, and kill you, sho'." Old Bayard sat watching his apelike head and the swaggering tilt of the tophat. Then Simon turned his wizened, plausible face over his shoulder. "But sho' 'nough, now, we is got to quiet dem niggers somehow."

"What have they done? Cant they find anybody to take their money?"

"Well, suh, hit's lak dis," Simon explained. "Hit's kind of all 'round cu'i's. You see, dey been collectin' buildin' money fer dat church whut burnt down, and ez dey got de money up, dey turnt hit over to me, whut wid my 'ficial position on de church boa'd and bein' I wuz a member of de bes' fambly 'round here. Dat 'uz erbout las' Chris'mus time, and now dey wants de money back."

"That's strange," old Bayard said.

"Yessuh," Simon agreed readily. "Hit struck me jes' 'zackly dat way."

"Well, if they insist, I reckon you'd better give it back to 'em."

"Now you's gittin' to it." Simon turned his head again; his manner was confidential, and he exploded his bombshell in a hushed melodramatic tone: "De money's gone."

"Dammit, I know that," old Bayard answered pettishly. "Where is it?"

"I went and put it out," Simon told him, and his tone was still confidential, with a little pained astonishment at the world's obtuseness. "And now dem niggers 'cusin' me of stealin' it."

"Do you mean to tell me that you took charge of money belonging to other people, and then went and loaned it to somebody else?"

"You does de same thing ev'y day," Simon answered. "Aint lendin' out money yo' main business?"

Old Bayard snorted violently. "You get that money back and give it to those niggers, or you'll be in jail, you hear?"

"You talks jes' lak dem uppity town niggers," Simon told him. "Dat money done been put out, now," he reminded his patron.

"Get it back. Haven't you got collateral for it?"

"Is I got which?"

"Something worth the value of the money, to keep until the money is paid back."

"Yessuh, I got dat." Simon chuckled again, a satyrish chuckle, with smug and complacent innuendo. "Yessuh, I got dat, all right. Only I never heard it called collateral befo'. Naw, suh, not dat."

"Did you give that money to some nigger wench?" Old Bayard demanded.

"Well, suh, hit's lak dis—" Simon began, but the other interrupted him.

"Ah, the devil. And now you expect me to pay it back, do you? How much is it?"

"I dont rightly remember. Dem niggers claims hit wuz sevemty er ninety dollars er somethin'. But dont you pay 'um no mind; you jes' give 'um what ever you think is right: dey'll take it."

"I'm damned if I will. They can take it out of your worthless hide, or send you to jail—whichever they want to, but I'm damned if I'll pay a cent of it."

"Now, Cunnel," Simon said, "you aint gwine let dem town niggers 'cuse a member of yo' fambly of stealin', is you?"

"Drive on!" old Bayard shouted. Simon turned on the seat and clucked to the horses and drove on, his cigar tilted toward his hatbrim, his elbows out and the whip caught smartly back in his hand, glancing now and then at the field niggers laboring among the cotton rows with tolerant and easy scorn.

Old man Falls replaced the cap on his tin of salve, wiped the tin carefully with the bit of rag, then knelt on the cold hearth and held a match to the rag.

"I reckon them doctors air still a-tellin' you hit's gwine to kill you, aint they?" he said.

Old Bayard propped his feet against the hearth, cupping a match to his cigar, cupping two tiny matchflames in his eyes. He flung the match away and grunted.

Old man Falls watched the rag take fire sluggishly, with a pungent pencil of yellowish smoke that broke curling in the still air. "Ever' now and then a feller has to walk up and spit in deestruction's face, sort of, fer his own good. He has to kind of put a aidge on hisself, like he'd hold his axe to the grindstone," he said, squatting before the pungent curling of the smoke as though in a pagan ritual in miniature. "Ef a feller'll show his face to deestruction ever' now and then, deestruction'll leave 'im be 'twell his time comes. Deestruction likes to take a feller in the back."

"What?" old Bayard said.

Old man Falls rose and dusted his knees carefully.

"Deestruction's like ary other coward," he roared. "Hit wont strike a feller that's a-lookin' hit in the face lessen he pushes hit too clost. Your paw knowed that. Stood in the do' of that sto' the day them two cyarpet-baggers brung them niggers in to vote that day in '72. Stood thar in his Prince Albert coat and beaver hat, with his arms folded, when ever'body else had left, and watched them two Missouri fellers herdin' them niggers up the road to'ds the sto'; stood right in the middle of the do' while them two cyarpet-baggers begun backin' away with their hands in their pockets until they was clar of the niggers, and cussed him. And him standin' thar jest like this." He crossed his arms on his breast, his hands in sight, and for a moment old Bayard saw, as through a cloudy glass, that arrogant and familiar shape which the old man in shabby overalls had contrived in some way to immolate and preserve in the vacuum of his own abnegated self.

"Then, when they was gone on back down the road, Cunnel reached around inside the do' and lifted out the ballot box and sot hit between his feet.

" 'You niggers come hyer to vote, did you?' he says. 'All right, come up hyer and vote.'

"When they had broke and scattered he let off that 'ere dern'ger over their haids a couple of times, then he loaded hit again and marched down the road to Miz Winterbottom's, whar them two fellers boa'ded.

" 'Madam,' he says, liftin' his beaver, 'I have a small

matter of business to discuss with yo' lodgers. Permit me,' he says, and he put his hat back on and marched up the stairs steady as a parade, with Miz Winterbottom gapin' after him with her mouth open. He walked right into the room whar they was a-settin' behind a table facin' the do', with their pistols layin' on the table.

"When us boys outside heard the three shots we run in. Thar wuz Miz Winterbottom standin' thar, a-gapin' up the stairs, and in a minute hyer comes Cunnel with his hat cocked over his eye, marchin' down the stairs steady as a co't jury, breshin' the front of his coat with his hank'cher. And us standin' thar, a-watchin' him. He stopped in front of Miz Winterbottom and lifted his hat again.

" 'Madam,' he says, 'I was fo'ced to muss up yo' guest room right considerable. Pray accept my apologies, and have yo' nigger clean it up and send the bill to me. My apologies agin, madam, fer havin been put to the necessity of exterminating vermin on yo' premises. Gentlemen,' he says to us, 'good mawnin'.' And he cocked that 'ere beaver on his head and walked out.

"And, Bayard," old man Falls said, "I sort of envied them two nawthuners, be damned ef I didn't. A feller kin take a wife and live with her a long time, but after all they aint no kin. But the feller that brings you into the world or sends you outen hit . . ."

Lurking behind the pantry door Simon could hear the steady storming of Miss Jenny's and old Bayard's voices; later when they had removed to the office and Elnora and Isom and Caspey sat about the table in the kitchen waiting for Simon, the concussion of

Miss Jenny's raging and old Bayard's rock-like stubbornness came in muffled surges, as of far away surf.

"Whut dey quoilin' about now?" Caspey asked. "Is you been and done somethin'?" he demanded of his nephew.

Isom rolled his eyes quietly above his steady jaws. "Naw, suh," he mumbled. "I aint done nothin'."

"Seems like dey'd git wo' out, after a while. Whut's pappy doin', Elnora?"

"Up dar in de hall, listenin'. Go tell 'im to come on and git his supper, so I kin git done, Isom."

Isom slid from his chair, still chewing, and left the kitchen. The steady raging of the two voices increased; where the shapeless figure of his grandfather stood like a disreputable and ancient bird in the dark hallway Isom could distinguish words: . . . poison . . . blood . . . think you can cut your head off and cure it? . . . fool put it on your foot, but . . . face, head . . . dead and good riddance . . . fool of you dying because of your own bullheaded folly . . . you first sitting in a chair, though . . .

"You and that damn doctor are going to worry me to death." Old Bayard's voice drowned the other temporarily. "Will Falls wont have a chance to kill me. I cant sit in my chair in town without that damn squirt sidling around me and looking disappointed because I'm still alive on my feet. And when I come home to get away from him, you cant even let me eat supper in peace. Have to show me a lot of damn colored pictures of what some fool thinks a man's insides look like."

"Who gwine die, pappy?" Isom whispered.

Simon turned his head. "Whut you hangin' eround here fer, boy? Go'n back to dat kichen, whar you belongs."

"Supper waitin'," Isom said. "Who dyin', pappy?"

"Aint nobody dyin'. Does anybody soun' dead? You git on outen de house, now."

Together they returned down the hall and entered the kitchen. Behind them the voices raged and stormed, blurred a little by walls, but dominant and unequivocal.

"Whut dey fightin' erbout, now?" Caspey, chewing, asked.

"Dat's white folks' bizness," Simon told him. "You tend to yo'n, and dey'll git erlong all right." He sat down and Elnora rose and filled a cup from the coffee pot on the stove and brought it to him. "White folks got dey troubles same as niggers is. Gimme dat dish o' meat, boy."

In the house the storm ran its nightly course, ceased as though by mutual consent, both parties still firmly entrenched; resumed at the supper table the next evening. And so on, day after day, until the second week in July and six days after young Bayard had been fetched home with his chest crushed, Miss Jenny and old Bayard and Dr Alford went to Memphis to consult a well-known authority on blood and glandular diseases with whom Dr Alford, with some difficulty, had made a formal engagement. Young Bayard lay upstairs in his cast, but Simon and Elnora would be about the house all day, and Narcissa Benbow had agreed to come out and keep him company.

Between the two of them they got old Bayard on the early train, still protesting profanely like a stubborn and bewildered ox. There were others who knew them in the car. These stopped and spoke to them, and remarking Dr Alford's juxtaposition, became curious and solicitous. Old Bayard took these opportunities to assert himself again, with violent rumbling, but Miss Jenny hushed him coldly and implacably.

They took him, like a sullen small boy, in a cab to the clinic where the specialist waited them, and in a room resembling an easy and informal hotel lobby they sat among other consultants and an untidy clutter of magazines and papers, waiting for the specialist to arrive. They waited a long time. Meanwhile Dr Alford from time to time assaulted the impregnable affability of the woman at the telephone switchboard, was repulsed and returned and sat stiffly beside his patient, aware that with every minute they waited, he was losing ground in Miss Jenny's opinion of him. Old Bayard was cowed too, by this time, though occasionally he rumbled at Miss Jenny with stubborn and hopeless optimism. "Oh, stop swearing at me," she interrupted him. "You cant walk out now. Here, here's the morning paper—take it and be quiet."

Then the specialist entered briskly and crossed to the switchboard woman, where Dr. Alford saw him and rose and crossed to him. The specialist turned—a brisk, dapper man, who moved with arrogant jerky motions, as though he were exercising with a small sword, and who in turning, almost stepped on Dr Alford. He shook Dr Alford's hand and broke into a high, desiccated stream of rapid words. "On the dot, I see. Promptness. Promptness. That's good. Patient here? Asked for a room yet?"

"Yes, Doctor, he's—"

"Good; good. Undressed her already, eh?"

"The patient is a m—"

"Just a moment." The specialist turned. "Oh, Mrs Smith."

"Yes, Doctor." The woman at the switchboard did not raise her head, and at that moment another specialist of some sort, a large one, with a profound, surreptitious air like a royal undertaker, entered and stopped Dr Alford's, and for a while the two of them alternately rumbled and rattled at one another while Dr Alford stood ignored nearby, fuming stiffly and politely, feeling himself sinking lower and lower in Miss Jenny's opinion of his professional status. Then the two specialists had done, and Dr Alford led his man toward his patient.

"Got the patient all ready, you say? Good; good; save time. Lunching down town today. Had lunch yourself?"

"No, Doctor. But the patient is a—"

"Daresay not," the specialist agreed. "Plenty of time, though." He turned briskly toward a curtained exit, but Dr Alford took his arm firmly but courteously and halted him. Old Bayard was reading the paper. Miss Jenny was watching them with cold and smoldering disapproval.

"Mrs Du Pre, Colonel Sartoris," Dr Alford said, "this is Dr Brandt. Colonel Sartoris is your p—"

"How d'ye do? How d'ye do?" the specialist said affably. "Come along with the patient, eh? Daughter? Granddaughter?" Old Bayard looked up.

"What?" he said, cupping his ear, and found the specialist staring at his face with abrupt interest.

"What's that on your face?" he demanded, jerking his hand forth and touching the blackened scabby excrescence. When he did so, the thing came off in his fingers, leaving on old Bayard's withered but unblemished cheek a round spot of skin rosy and fair as any baby's.

On the train that evening old Bayard, who had sat for a long time in deep thought, spoke suddenly.

"Jenny, what day of the month is this?"

"The ninth," Miss Jenny answered. "Why?"

Old Bayard sat for a while longer. Then he rose. "Think I'll go up and smoke a cigar," he said. "I reckon a little tobacco wont hurt me, will it, Doctor?"

Three weeks later they got a bill from the specialist for fifty dollars. "Now I know why he's so well known," Miss Jenny said acidly. Then to old Bayard: "You'd better thank your stars it wasn't your hat he lifted off."

Toward Dr Alford her manner is fiercely and belligerently protective; to old man Falls she gives the briefest and coldest nod and sails on with her nose in air; but to Loosh Peabody she does not speak at all.

8

She passed from the fresh, hot morning into the cool hall, where Simon uselessly and importantly proprietorial with a duster, bobbed his head to her. "Dey done gone to Memphis today," he told her, "but Mist' Bayard waitin' fer you. Walk right up, missy."

"Thank you," she said, and she went on and mounted the stairs and left him busily wafting dust from one surface to another and then back again. The stairs curved onward into the upper hall and she mounted into a steady drift of air that blew through the open doors at the end of the hall; through these doors she could see a segment of blue dissolving hills and salt-colored sky. At Bayard's door she stopped and stood there for a time, clasping the book to her breast.

The house, despite Simon's activity in the hall below, was a little portentously quiet, without the reassurance of Miss Jenny's bustling presence and the cold ubiquity of her scolding. Faint sounds reached her from far away—out-of-doors sounds whose final drowsy reverberations drifted into the house on the vivid July air; sounds too somnolent and remote to die away.

But from the room before her no sound came at all. Perhaps he was asleep; and the initial impulse— her given word, and the fortitude of her desperate heart which had enabled her to come out despite Miss Jenny's absence—having served its purpose and deserted her, she stood just without the door, hoping that he was asleep, that he would sleep all day. Thus she found that she could still hope, and found in this fact a thin and derisive amusement.

But she would have to enter the room in order to find out if he slept, so she touched her hands to her face, as though by that she would restore to it its wonted serene repose for him to see, and entered.

"Simon?" Bayard said, having felt her presence through that sharpened sixth sense of the sick. He lay on his back, his hands beneath his head, gazing out the window, and she paused again just inside the door. At last, roused by her silence, he turned his head and his bleak gaze. "Well, I'll be damned. I didn't believe you'd come out today."

"Yes," she answered. "How do you feel?"

"Not after the way you sit with one foot in the hall all the time Aunt Jenny's out of the room," he continued. "Did she make you come out?"

"She asked me to come out. She doesn't want you to be alone all day, with just Simon in the house. Do you feel better today?"

"So?" he drawled. "Wont you sit down, then?" She crossed to where her customary chair had been moved into a corner and drew it across the floor. He lay with his head cradled in his hands, watching her as she turned the chair about and seated herself. "What do you think about it?"

"About what?"

"About coming out to keep me company?"

"I've brought a new book," she said evasively. "One H—one I just got. I hope you'll like this one."

"I hope so," he agreed, but without conviction. "Seems like I'd like one after a while, doesn't it? But what do you think about coming out here today?"

"I dont think a sick person should be left alone with just negroes around. The name of this one is—"

"Why not send a nurse out, then? No use your coming way out here." She met his gaze at last, with her grave desperate eyes. "Why do you come, when you dont want to?" he persisted.

"I dont mind," she answered hopelessly. She freed her gaze with an effort and opened the book. "The name of this one is—"

"Dont," he interrupted. "I'll have to listen to that damn thing all day. Let's talk a while." But she presented him now the dark crown of her head, and her hands were motionless upon the book on her knees. "What makes you afraid to talk to me?" he demanded.

"Afraid?" she repeated, with her head bent above the book. "Had you rather I'd go?"

"What? No, dammit. I want you to be human for one time and talk to me. Come over here." She would not look at him, but she could feel the moody, leashed violence of him like a steady glare of light beneath which she shrank and recoiled, and despite the assurance of his helpless immobility she was swept by sudden and unreasoning fear, and she raised her hands between them though he lay two yards away and helpless on his back. "Come over here closer," he commanded. She rose, clutching the book.

"I'm going," she said. "I'll tell Simon to stay where he can hear you call. Goodbye."

"Here," he exclaimed. She went swiftly to the door.

"Goodbye."

"After what you just said, about leaving me alone with just niggers on the place?" She paused at the door, and he added with cold cunning: "After what Aunt Jenny told you? What'll I tell her, tonight? Why are you afraid of a man flat on his back, in a damn cast-iron strait-jacket, anyway?" But she only looked at him with her desperate, hopeless eyes. "All right, dammit," he said violently. "Go, then." And he jerked his head savagely on the pillow and stared again out the window while she returned to her chair. He said, mildly: "What's the name of this one?" She told him. "Let her go, then. I reckon I'll be asleep soon, anyway."

She opened the book and began to read, swiftly, as though she were crouching behind the screen of words her voice raised between them. She read steadily on, her head bent over the book. She finished a sentence and stopped and sat utterly still above the book, but almost immediately he spoke. "Go on; I'm still here. Better luck next time."

The forenoon passed on. Somewhere a clock rang the quarter hours, but saving this there was no sound from the other parts of the house. Simon's activity below stairs had long ceased, but a murmur of voices reached her at intervals from somewhere, murmurously indistinguishable. The leaves on the tree beyond the window did not stir in the hot air, and upon it a myriad noises blended in a drowsy monotone— the negroes' voices, sounds of stock from the barnyard, the rhythmic groaning of the water pump; a sudden cacophony of fowls in the garden beneath the window, interspersed with Isom's meaningless cries as he drove them out.

He was asleep now, and as she realized this she realized also that she did not know just when she had stopped reading. And she sat with the page open upon her knees, a page whose words left no echoes whatever in her mind, watching his calm face. It was again like a bronze mask, purged by illness of the heat of its violence, yet with the violence still slumbering there and only refined a little.

She sat with the book open upon her lap, her hands lying motionless upon the opened page, gazing out the window. The curtains stirred faintly, and in the branches of the tree athwart the window the leaves twinkled lightly beneath the intermittent fingers of the sun.

The clock rang again: a sound cool as stroked silver in the silent house, and preceded by cautious, stertorious breathing someone crept up the stairs, and after more surreptitious sounds Simon peered his disembodied head, like that of the curious and wizened grandfather of all apes, around the door. "Is you 'sleep, Mist' Bayard?" he said in a loud, rasping tone.

"Shhhhhhhh," she cautioned him. "What is it?"

"Ef he 'sleep, I dont reckon he wants no dinner now, do he?" Simon rasped.

"Be quiet. You'll have to keep it until he wakes."

"Yessum, I 'speck so," Simon agreed, lowering his voice a little. He entered on tiptoe, and while Narcissa watched him in mounting exasperation and alarm, he scuffed across to the table with sounds as of a huge rat.

"What are you going to do?" she whispered. "You'd better go and tell Elnora to keep his dinner for him. I'll call you when he wakes."

"Yessum, I 'speck so," Simon agreed again. He now busied himself at the table, upon which the books they had read during the past two weeks were stacked one upon another; and as she rose swiftly and quietly he toppled the stack over and lunged clumsily at it and succeeded in knocking it to the floor with a random crash. Bayard opened his eyes.

"Good Lord," he said. "Why cant you stay out of here?"

"Well, now!" Simon exclaimed in ready dismay. "Ef we aint woke 'im up! Yes, suh, me en Miss Benbow done woke 'im up. We wuz gwine save yo' dinner, Mist' Bayard, but I reckon you mought jes' well eat it, long ez you 'wake."

"I reckon so," Bayard agreed. "Bring it up, then. But damned if I wouldn't like to know what objection you have to my sleeping. Thank God you were not born in a drove, like mosquitoes."

"Des lissen at 'im! Wake up quoilin'. You'll feel better when you et some dinner," he told the patient. Then to Narcissa: "Elnora got a nice dinner fer y'all."

"Bring Miss Benbow's up too," Bayard directed. "She can eat here. Unless you'd rather go down?"

In all his movements Simon was a caricature of himself, and he paused in an attitude of shocked reproof. "Dinin' room mo' suitable fer comp'ny," he said.

"Yes, I'll go down," she decided promptly. "I wont put Simon to that trouble."

" 'Taint no trouble," Simon disclaimed. "I jes' thought you mought like to git out fer a while, whar he cant quoil at you. I'm gwine put it on de table right away, missy. You kin walk right down."

"Yes, I'll come right down." He departed, and she laid the book aside. "I tried to keep—"

"I know," Bayard interrupted. "He wont let anybody sleep through mealtime. And you'd better go

and have yours, or he'll carry everything back to the
kitchen. And you dont have to hurry back just on
my account," he added.

"Dont have to hurry back?" She paused at the
door and looked back at him. "What do you mean?"

"I thought you might be tired of reading."

"Oh," she said, and looked away and stood for a
moment clothed in her grave tranquillity.

"Look here," he said suddenly. "Are you sick or
anything? Had you rather go home?"

"No," she answered, rousing. "I'll be back soon."

She had her meal in lonely state in the sombre dining room while Simon, having dispatched Bayard's
tray by Isom, moved about the table and pressed
dishes upon her with bland insistence or leaned
against the sideboard and conducted a rambling
monologue that seemed to have had no beginning
and held no prospect of an end. It still flowed easily
behind her as she went up the hall; as she stood in the
door it was still going on, volitionless, as though en-
tranced with its own existence and feeding on its own
momentum. The salvia bed lay in an unbearable glare
of white light, in clamorous splashes. Beyond it the
drive shimmered with heat until, arched over with
locust and oak, it descended in a cool green tunnel to
the gates and the sultry ribbon of the highroad. Beyond the road fields stretched away shimmering,
broken here and there by motionless clumps of trees,
on to the hills dissolving bluely behind the July haze.

She leaned for a while against the door, in her
white dress, her cheek against the cool, smooth plane
of the jamb, in a faint draft that came steadily from
somewhere, though no leaf stirred. Simon had
finished in the dining room and a drowsy murmur of
voices came up the hall from the kitchen, borne

upon a thin stirring of air too warm to be called a breeze and upon which not even the cries of birds came.

At last she heard a movement from above stairs and she remembered Isom with Bayard's tray, and she turned and slid the parlor door ajar and entered. The shades were drawn closely, and the crack of light that followed her but deepened the gloom. She found the piano and stood beside it for a while, touching its dusty surface and thinking of Miss Jenny erect and indomitable in the gloom beside it. She heard Isom descend the stairs; soon his footsteps died away down the hall, and she drew out the bench and sat down and laid her arms along the closed lid.

Simon entered the dining room again, mumbling to himself and followed presently by Elnora, and they clashed dishes and talked again with a mellow rise and fall of consonantless and indistinguishable words. Then they went away, but still she sat with her arms along the cool wood, in the dark quiet room where even time stagnated a little.

The clock rang again, and she moved. I've been crying, she thought. "I've been crying," she said in a sad whisper that savored its own loneliness and its sorrow. At the tall mirror beside the parlor door she stood and peered at her dim reflection, touching her eyes with her fingertips. Then she went on, but paused again at the stairs, listening, then she mounted briskly and entered Miss Jenny's room and went on to her bathroom and bathed her face.

Bayard lay as she had left him. He was smoking a cigarette now. Between puffs he dabbed it casually at a saucer on the bed beside him. "Well?" he said.

"You're going to set the house on fire that way," she told him, removing the saucer. "You know Miss Jenny wouldn't let you do that."

"I know it," he agreed, a little sheepishly, and she dragged the table over and set the saucer on it.

"Can you reach it now?"

"Yes, thanks. Did they give you enough to eat?"

"Oh, yes. Simon's very insistent, you know. Shall I read some more, or had you rather sleep?"

"Read, if you dont mind. I think I'll stay awake, this time."

"Is that a threat?" He looked at her quickly as she seated herself and took up the book.

"Say, what happened to you?" he demanded. "You acted like you were all in before dinner. Simon give you a drink, or what?"

"No, not that bad." And she laughed, a little wildly, and opened the book. "I forgot to mark the place," she said, turning the pages swiftly. "Do you remember—No, you were asleep. Shall I go back to where you stopped listening?"

"No, just read anywhere. It's all about alike, I guess. If you'll move a little nearer, I believe I can stay awake."

"Sleep, if you want to. I dont mind," she answered.

"Meaning you wont come any nearer?" he asked, watching her with his bleak gaze. She moved her chair nearer and opened the book again and turned the pages on, slowing and scanning them.

"I think it was about here," she said, with indecision. "Yes." She read to herself for a line or two, then she began aloud, read to the end of the page, where her voice trailed off and she creased her brow; turned the next page then flipped it back. "I read this once; I remember it now." And she turned onward again, with frowning indecision. "I must have been asleep too," she said, and she glanced at him with ludicrous and friendly bewilderment. "I seem to have read pages and pages . . ."

"Oh, begin anywhere," he repeated.

"No: wait; here it is." She read again, and he lay watching her. At times she raised her eyes swiftly and found his eyes upon her face, bleakly but quietly. After a while he was no longer watching her, and at last, finding that his eyes were closed, she thought he slept. She finished the chapter and stopped.

"No," he said drowsily. "Not yet." Then, when she failed to resume, he opened his eyes and asked for a cigarette. She laid the book aside and struck a match for him, then picked up the book again.

So the afternoon wore away. The negroes had gone, and no sound was in the house save that of her voice, and the clock at quarter hour intervals; outside the shadows slanted more and more, peaceful harbingers of evening. Bayard was asleep now, despite his contrary conviction, and after a while she ceased and laid the book away. The long shape of him lay stiffly in its cast beneath the sheet, and she examined his bold immobile face with a little shrinking and yet with fascination, and her own patient and hopeless sorrow overflowed (there was enough of it to anneal the world) in pity for him. He was so utterly without any affection for any place or person or thing at all; too—too . . . hard (no, that's not the word—but cold eluded her; she could comprehend hardness, but not coldness) to find relief by crying, even. Better to have lost it, than never to have had it at all, at all.

The afternoon drew on; evening was finding itself. She sat musing and still and quiet, gazing out of the window where no wind yet stirred the leaves, as though she were waiting for someone to tell her what to do next, and she lost all account of time other than as a dark unhurrying stream into which she gazed until the mesmerism of water conjured the water itself away. Lost, lost; yet never to have had it at all . . .

He made an indescribable sound, and she turned her head quickly and saw his body straining terrifically in its cast, and his clenched hands and the snarl of his teeth beneath his lifted lip, and as she sat blanched and incapable of further movement he made the sound again. His breath hissed between his teeth and he screamed, a wordless sound that sank into a steady violence of profanity; and when she rose at last and stood over him with her hands against her mouth, his body relaxed and from beneath his sweating brow he watched her with wide intent eyes in which terror lurked, and mad, cold fury, and questioning despair.

"He damn near got me, then," he said in a dry, light voice, still watching her from beyond the fading agony in his widely opened eyes. "There was a sort of loop of 'em around my chest, and every time he fired, he twisted the loop a little tighter . . ." He fumbled at the sheet and tried to draw it up to his face. "Can you get me a handkerchief? Some in that top drawer there."

"Yes," she said, "yes," and she crossed to the chest of drawers and held her trembling body upright by clinging to it, and found a handkerchief and returned. She tried to dry his brow and face, but finally he took the handkerchief from her and did it himself. "You scared me," she moaned. "You scared me so bad. I thought . . ."

"Sorry," he said shortly. "I dont do that on purpose. I want a cigarette."

She gave it to him and struck the match, and he had to grasp her hand to hold the flame steady, and still holding her wrist he drew deeply several times. She tried to free her wrist, but he held it in his hard fingers, and her trembling body betrayed her and she sank into her chair again, staring at him with ebbing terror and dread. He consumed the cigarette in deep, troubled draughts, and still holding her wrist, he began talking of his dead brother, without preamble, brutally. It was a brutal tale, without beginning, and crassly and uselessly violent and at times profane and gross, though its very wildness robbed it of offensiveness just as its grossness kept it from obscenity. And beneath it all, the bitter struggling of his stubborn heart; and she sitting with her arm taut in his grasp and her other hand pressed against her mouth, watching him with terrified fascination.

"He was zig-zagging: that was the reason I couldn't get on the Hun. Every time I got my sights on him, John'd barge in the way again. Then he quit zig-zagging. Soon as I saw him side-slip I knew it was all over. Then I saw the flame streaming out along his wing, and he was looking back at me. The Hun stopped shooting then, and all of us just lay there for a while. I couldn't tell what John was up to until I saw him swing his legs outside. Then he thumbed his nose at me like he always was doing and flipped his hand at the Hun and kicked his machine out of the way and jumped. He jumped feet first. You cant fall far feet first, you know, and so pretty soon he sprawled out flat. There was a bunch of cloud right under us by that time, and he smacked on it right on his belly, like what we used to call gut-busters in swimming. But I never could pick him up below the cloud. I know I was below it before he could have come out, because after I was down there his machine came diving out right at me, burning good. I pulled away from it, but the damn thing did a split-turn and rushed at me again, and I had to dodge. And so I never could pick him up when he came out of the cloud. I went down fast, until I knew I was below him, then I looked again. But I couldn't find him, and I thought maybe I hadn't gone low enough, so I dived again. But I couldn't pick him up. Then they started shooting at me from the ground—"

He talked on and her hand came away from her mouth and slid down her other arm and tugged at his fingers. "Please," she whispered. "Please!" He ceased and looked at her and his fingers shifted, and just as she thought she was free they clamped again, and now both of her wrists were prisoners. She struggled, staring at him dreadfully, but he grinned his white cruel teeth at her and pressed her crossed arms down upon the bed beside him. "Please, please," she implored, struggling; she could feel the flesh of her wrists, feel the bones turn in it like a loose garment; could see his bleak eyes and the cruel derision of his teeth, and suddenly she swayed forward in her chair and her head dropped between her prisoned arms and she wept with hopeless and dreadful hysteria.

After a while there was no sound in the room again, and he looked at the dark crown of her head, and he lifted his hand and saw the bruised discolorations where his hands had gripped her. But she did not move even then, and he dropped his hand upon her wrists again and lay quietly, and after a while even her trembling had ceased. "I'm sorry," he said. "I wont do it again." He could see only the top of her dark head, and her hands lay quietly beneath his. "I'm sorry," he repeated. "I wont do that anymore."

"You wont drive that car fast again?" she asked. With infinite small pains and slowly he turned himself, cast and all, by degrees onto his side, chewing his lip and swearing under his breath, and laid his other hand on her hair.

"What are you doing?" she said, but without moving. "You'll break your ribs again."

"Yes," he agreed, stroking her hair awkwardly.

"That's the trouble, right there," she said. "That's the way you act: doing things that—that—You do things to hurt yourself just to worry people. You dont get any fun out of doing them."

"No," he agreed, and he lay with his chest full of hot needles, stroking her dark head with his hard, awkward hand. Far above him now the peak among the black and savage stars, and about him the valleys of tranquillity and of peace. It was later still; already shadows were growing in the room, and beyond the window sunlight was a diffused radiance, sourceless yet palpable; from somewhere cows lowed one to another, placidly and mournfully. At last she sat up.

"You're all twisted. You'll never get well, if you dont behave yourself. Turn on your back, now." He obeyed, slowly and painfully, his lip between his teeth and faint beads on his forehead, while she watched him with grave anxiety. "Does it hurt?"

"No," he answered, and his hand shut again on her wrists that made no effort to withdraw. Then the sun was gone, and twilight, foster-dam of quietude and peace, filled the fading room and evening had found itself.

"And you wont drive that car fast anymore?" she persisted from the dusk.

"No," he answered.

9

Meanwhile she had received another letter from her anonymous correspondent. Horace when he came in one night, had brought it in to her as she lay in bed with a book; tapped at her door and opened it and stood for a moment diffidently, and for a while they looked at one another across the barrier of their estrangement and their stubborn pride.

"Excuse me for disturbing you," he said stiffly. She lay beneath the shaded light, with the dark splash of her hair upon the pillow, and only her eyes moved as he crossed the room and stood above her where she lay with her lowered book, watching him with sober interrogation.

"What are you reading?" he asked. For reply she shut the book on her finger, with the jacket and its colored legend upward. But he did not look at it. His shirt was open beneath his silk dressing gown and his thin hand moved among the objects on the table beside the bed; picked up another book. "I never knew you to read so much."

"I have more time for reading, now," she answered.

"Yes." His hand still moved about the table, touching things here and there. She lay waiting for him to speak. But he did not, and she said:

"What is it, Horry?"

Then he ceased, and he came and sat on the edge of the bed. But still her eyes were gravely interrogatory and the shadow of her mouth was stubbornly cold. "Narcy?" he said. She lowered her eyes to the book, and he added: "First, I want to apologise for leaving you alone so often at night."

"Yes?"

He laid his hand on her knee. "Look at me." She raised her face, and the antagonism of her eyes. "I want to apologise for leaving you alone at night," he repeated.

"Does that mean you aren't going to do it anymore, or that you're not coming in at all?"

For a time he sat, brooding upon the wild repose of his hand upon her covered knee. Then he rose and stood beside the table again, touching the objects there, then he returned and sat on the bed. She was reading again, and he tried to take the book from her hand. She resisted.

"What do you want, Horace?" she asked impatiently.

He mused again while she watched him. Then he looked up. "Belle and I are going to be married," he blurted.

"Why tell me? Harry is the one to tell. Unless you all are going to dispense with the formality of divorce."

"Yes," he said. "He knows it." He laid his hand on her knee again, stroking it through the covers. "You aren't even surprised, are you?"

"I'm surprised at you, but not at Belle. Belle has a backstairs nature."

"Yes," he agreed; then: "Who said that to you? You didn't think of that." She lay with her book half raised, watching him. He took her hand roughly; she tried to free it, but he held on. "Who was it?" he demanded.

"Nobody told me. Dont, Horace."

He released her hand. "I know who it was. It was Mrs Du Pre."

"It wasn't anybody," she repeated. "Go away and leave me alone, Horace." And behind the antagonism her eyes were hopeless and desperate. "Dont you see that talking doesn't help any?"

"Yes," he said wearily, but he sat for a while yet, stroking her knee. Then he rose, but turning, he paused again. "Here's a letter for you. I forgot it this afternoon. Sorry."

But she was reading again. "Put it on the table," she said, without raising her eyes. He laid it on the table and went out. At the door he looked back, but her head was bent over her book.

As he removed his clothes it did seem that that heavy fading odor of Belle's body clung to them, and to his hands even after he was in bed; and clinging, shaped in the darkness beside him Belle's rich voluption, until within that warm, not-yet-sleeping region where dwells the mother of dreams, Belle grew palpable in ratio as his own body slipped away from him. And Harry too, with his dogged inarticulateness and his hurt groping which was partly damaged vanity and shock, yet mostly a boy's sincere bewilderment, that freed itself terrifically in the form of movie subtitles. Just before he slept his mind, with the mind's uncanny attribute of irrelevant recapitulation, reproduced with the startling ghostliness of a dictaphone, an incident which at the time he had considered trivial. Belle had freed her mouth, and for a moment, with her body still against his, she held his face in her two hands and stared at him with intent questioning eyes. "Have you plenty of money, Horace?" And "Yes," he had answered immediately. "Of course I have." And then Belle again, enveloping him like a rich and fatal drug, like a motionless and cloying sea in which he watched himself drown.

● ● ●

The letter lay on the table that night, forgotten; it was not until the next morning that she discovered it and opened it.

"I am trying to forget you I cannot forget you Your big eyes your black hair how white your black hair will make you look. And how you walk I am watching you and a smell you give off like a flowr. Your eyes shine with mystry and how you walk makes me sick like a fever all night thinking how you walk. I could touch you you would not know it Every day. But I can not I must pore out on paper must talk You do not know who. Your lips like cupids bow when the day comes when I will press them to mine like I dreamed like a fever from heaven to hell. I know what you do I know more than you think I see men visting you with bitter twangs. Be careful I am a desprate man Nothing is any more to me now If you unholy love a man I will kill him.

"You do not answer. I know you got it I saw one in your hand. You better answer soon I am a desprate man eat up with fever I can not sleep for. I will not hurt you but I am desprate. Do not forget I will not hurt you but I am a desprate man."

Meanwhile the days accumulated. Not sad days nor lonely: they were too feverish to be sorrowful, what with the violated serenity of her nature torn in two directions, and the walls of her garden cast down, and she herself like a night animal or bird caught in a beam of light and trying vainly to escape. Horace had definitely gone his way; they could no longer hear one another's feet on the dark road; and like two strangers they followed the routine of their days, in an unbending estrangement of long affection and similar pride beneath a shallow veneer of polite trivialities. She sat with Bayard almost every day now, but at a discreet distance of two yards. At first he tried to override her with bluster, then with cajolery. But she was firm and at last he desisted and lay gazing quietly out the window or sleeping while she read. From time to time Miss Jenny would come to the door and look in at them and go away. Her shrinking, her sense of dread and unease while with him, was gone now, and at times instead of reading they talked, quietly and impersonally, with that ghost of that other afternoon between them, though neither referred to it. Miss Jenny had been a little curious about that day, but Narcissa was gravely and demurely noncommittal about it; nor had Bayard ever talked about it, and so there was another bond between them, but unirksome. Miss Jenny had heard gossip about Horace and Belle, but on this subject also Narcissa would not talk.

"Have it your own way," Miss Jenny said tartly. "I can draw my own conclusions. I imagine Belle and Horace can produce quite a mess together. And I'm glad of it. That man is making an old maid out of you. It isn't too late now, but if he'd waited five years later to play the fool, there wouldn't be anything left for you except to give music lessons. But you can get married, now."

"Would you advise me to marry?" Narcissa asked.

"I wouldn't advise anybody to marry. You wont be happy, but women haven't got civilized enough yet to be happy unmarried, so you might as well try it. We can stand anything, anyway. And change is good for folks. They say it is, that is."

But Narcissa didn't believe that. I shall never marry, she told herself. Men . . . that was where unhappiness lay. And if I couldn't keep Horace, loving him as I did . . . Bayard slept. She picked up the book and read on to herself, about antic people in an antic world where things happened as they should. The shadows lengthened eastward. She read on, lost from mutable things.

After a while Bayard waked, and she fetched him a cigarette and a match. "You wont have to do this anymore," he said. "I reckon you're glad."

His cast would come off tomorrow, he meant, and he lay smoking his cigarette and talking of what he would do when he was about again. He would see about getting his car repaired first thing; have to take it to Memphis, probably. And he planned a trip for the three of them—Narcissa, Miss Jenny and himself —while the car was in the shop. "It'll take about a week," he added. "She must be in pretty bad shape. Hope I haven't hurt her guts any."

"But you aren't going to drive it fast anymore," she reminded him. He lay still, his cigarette burning in his fingers. "You promised," she insisted.

"When did I promise?"

"Dont you remember? That . . . afternoon, when they were . . ."

"When I scared you?" She sat watching him with her grave troubled eyes. "Come here," he said. She rose and went to the bed and he took her hand.

"You wont drive it fast again?" she persisted.

"No," he answered, "I promise." And they were still so, her hand in his. The curtains stirred in the breeze, and the leaves on the branch beyond the window twinkled and turned and lisped against one another. Sunset was not far away; it would cease then. He moved.

"Narcissa," he said, and she looked at him. "Lean your face down here."

She looked away, and for a while there was no movement, no sound between them.

"I must go," she said at last, quietly, and he released her hand.

His cast was gone, and he was up and about again, moving a little gingerly, it is true; but already Miss Jenny was beginning to contemplate him a little anxiously. "If we could just arrange to have one of his minor bones broken every month or so, just enough to keep him in the house . . ." she said.

"That wont be necessary," Narcissa told her. "He's going to behave from now on."

"How do you know?" Miss Jenny demanded. "What in the world makes you think that?"

"He promised he would."

"He'll promise anything when he's flat on his back," Miss Jenny retorted. "They all will; always have. But what makes you think he will?"

"He promised me he would," Narcissa answered serenely.

His first act was to see about his car. It had been pulled into town and patched up after a fashion until it would run under its own power, but it would be necessary to take it to Memphis to have the frame straightened and the body repaired. Bayard was all for doing this himself, fresh-knit ribs and all, but Miss Jenny put her foot down and after a furious half hour, he was vanquished. And so the car was driven in to Memphis by a youth who hung around one of the garages in town. "Narcissa'll take you driving in her car, if you must ride," Miss Jenny told him.

"In that little peanut parcher?" Bayard said derisively. "It wont do more than twenty-one miles an hour."

"No, thank God," Miss Jenny answered. "And I've written to Memphis and asked 'em to fix yours so it'll run just like that, too."

Bayard stared at her with slow and humorless bleakness. "Did you do any such damn thing as that?"

"Oh, take him away, Narcissa," Miss Jenny exclaimed. "Get him out of my sight. I'm so tired of looking at you."

But he wouldn't ride in Narcissa's car at first. He missed no opportunity to speak of it with heavy, facetious disparagement, but he wouldn't ride in it. Dr Alford had evolved a tight rubber bandage for his chest so that he could ride a horse, but he had developed an astonishing propensity for lounging about the house when Narcissa was there. And Narcissa came quite often. Miss Jenny thought that it was on Bayard's account and pinned the guest down in her forthright way; whereupon Narcissa told her about Horace and Belle while Miss Jenny sat indomitably erect on her straight chair beside the piano.

"Poor child," she said, and "Lord, aint they fools?" and then: "Well, you're right; I wouldn't marry one of 'em either."

"I'm not," Narcissa answered. "I wish there weren't any of them in the world."

Miss Jenny said, "Hmph."

And then one afternoon they were in Narcissa's car and Bayard was driving, over Narcissa's protest at first. But he was behaving himself quite sensibly, and at last she relaxed. They drove down the valley road and turned off toward the hills, where the road mounted presently in long curves among dark pines in the slanting afternoon. The road wound on, with changing sunshot vistas of the valley and the opposite hills beyond at every turn, and always the sombre pines and their faint exhilarating odor. At last they topped a hill. Below them the road sank, then flattened away toward a line of willows, crossed a stone bridge and rose again curving redly from sight among the pines.

"There's the place," he said.

"The place?" she repeated dreamily, rousing; then as the car rolled forward again, gaining speed, she understood. "You promised," she cried, but he jerked the throttle all the way down its ratchet and she clutched him and tried to scream. But she could make no sound, nor could she shut her eyes as the narrow bridge hurtled dancing toward them. And then her heart stopped and her breath as they flashed with a sharp reverberation like hail on a tin roof, between willows and a crashing glint of water and shot on up the next hill. The small car swayed on the curve, lost its footing and went into the ditch, bounded out and hurled across the road. Then Bayard straightened it out and with diminishing speed it rocked on up the hill, and at the top he stopped it. She sat beside him, with her bloodless mouth open, beseeching him with her wide hopeless eyes. Then she caught her breath, wailing.

"I didn't mean—" he began awkwardly. "I just wanted to see if I could do it," and he put his arms around her and she clung to him, moving her hands crazily about his shoulders. "I didn't mean—" he essayed again, and then her crazed hands were on his face and she was sobbing wildly against his mouth.

10

Through the morning hours and following his sleepless night, he bent over his desk beneath the greenshaded light, penning his neat, meticulous figures into the ledgers. The routine of the bank went on; old Bayard sat in his tilted chair in the fresh August morning while passers went to and fro, greeting him with florid cheerful gestures and receiving in return his half military salute—people cheerful and happy with their orderly affairs; the cashier served the morning line of depositors and swapped jovial anecdote with them. For this was the summer cool spell and there was a vividness in the air, a presage of the golden days of frost and yellowing persimmons in the worn-out fields, and of sweet small grapes in the matted vines along the sandy branches, and the scent of cooking sorghum upon the smoky air. But the Snopes crouched over his desk after his sleepless night, with jealousy and thwarted desire and furious impotent rage in his vitals.

His head felt hot and dull, and heavy, and to the cashier's surprise, he offered to buy the Coca-Colas, ordering two for himself, drank them one after the other and returned to his ledgers. So the morning wore away. His neat figures accumulated slowly in the ruled columns, steadily and with a maddening aloofness from his own turmoil and without a mistake although his mind coiled and coiled upon itself, tormenting him with fleeing obscene images in which she moved with another. He had thought it dreadful when he was not certain that there was another; but now to know it, to find knowledge of it on every tongue . . . and young Sartoris, at that: a man whom he had hated instinctively with all his sense of inferiority and all the venom of his worm-like nature. Married, married. Adultery, concealed if suspected, he could have borne; but this, boldly, in the world's face, flouting him with his own impotence . . . He dug a cheap, soiled handkerchief from his hip pocket and wiped the saliva from his jaws.

By changing his position a little he could see old Bayard, could catch a glint of his white suit where he sat oblivious in the door. There was a sort of fascination in the old fellow now, serving as he did as an object upon which the Snopes could vent the secret, vicarious rage of his half-insane mind. And all during the morning he watched the other covertly; once old Bayard entered the cage and passed within arm's length of him, and when he moved his hand to wipe his drooling mouth, he found that the page had adhered to his wrist, blotting the last entry he had made. With his knife blade he erased the smear and rewrote it.

So the morning wore away. He ordered more Coca-Colas and consumed his and returned to his desk. Toward mid-morning the first fury that had raged in him had worn itself away. The images still postured in his mind, but they were now so familiar as to be without personal significance. Or rather, his dulled senses no longer responded so quickly; and one part of him labored steadily on with steady neat care while the other jaded part reviewed the coiling shapes with a sort of dull astonishment that they no longer filled his blood with fire-maenads. It was a sort of stupor, and he wrote on and on, and it was some time before his dulled nerves reacted to a fresh threat and caused him to raise his head. Virgil Beard was just entering the door.

He slid hurriedly from his stool and slipped around a cabinet and darted through the door of old Bayard's office. He crouched within the door, heard the boy ask politely for him, heard the cashier say that he was there a minute ago but that he reckoned he had stepped out; heard the boy say well, he reckoned he'd wait for him. And he crouched within the door, wiping his drooling mouth with his handkerchief.

After a while he opened the door cautiously and peered out. The boy squatted patiently and blandly on his heels against the wall, and Snopes stood again with his clenched trembling hands. He did not curse: his desperate fury was beyond words; but his breath came and went with a fast ah-ah-ah sound in his throat and it seemed to him that his eyeballs were being drawn back and back into his skull, turning further and further until the cords that drew them reached the snapping point. Then he opened the door and went out.

"Hi, Mr Snopes," the boy said genially, rising; but Snopes strode on and into the cage and approached the cashier.

"Res," he said, in a voice scarcely articulate, "gimme five dollars."

"What?" the cashier said.

"Gimme five dollars," he repeated hoarsely. The cashier did so, scribbled a notation and speared it on the file at his elbow. The boy had come up to the second window, but Snopes passed on without looking at him, and he followed the man to the rear and into the office again, his bare feet hissing on the linoleum floor.

"I tried to find you last night," he explained, "but

you warn't at home." Then he looked up and saw
Snopes' face, and after a moment he screamed and
broke his trance and turned to flee. But Snopes
caught him, and he writhed and twisted, screaming
steadily with utter terror as the man dragged him
across the office and opened the door that gave onto
the vacant lot. Snopes was trying to say something in
his mad, shaking voice, but the boy screamed steadily. He had lost all control of his body and he hung
limp in the man's hand while Snopes thrust the bill
into his pocket. Then he released the boy, who stag-
gered away, found his legs, and fled.

"What were you whuppin' that boy, for?" the
cashier asked curiously, when he returned to his
desk.

"For not mindin' his own business," Snopes
snapped, opening his ledger again.

During the hour the cashier was out to lunch the
Snopes was his outward usual self—uncommunicative
but efficient, a little covertly sullen, with his mean,
close-set eyes and his stubby features; patrons remarked nothing unusual in his bearing. Nor did the
cashier when he returned, sucking a toothpick and
belching at intervals. But instead of going home to
dinner, Snopes repaired to a street occupied by negro
stores and barber shops and inquired from door to
door. After a half-hour search he found the negro he
sought, held a few minutes' conversation with him,
then returned across town to his cousin's restaurant
and had a platter of hamburger steak and a cup of
coffee. At two oclock he was back at his desk.

The afternoon passed. Three oclock came; he
went around and touched old Bayard's shoulder and
he rose and dragged his chair inside and the Snopes
closed the doors and drew the green shades upon the
windows. Then he totalled his ledgers while the

cashier counted the cash. In the meantime Simon
drove up to the door and presently old Bayard
stalked forth and got in the carriage and was driven
off. Snopes and the cashier compared notes and
struck a balance, and while the other stacked the
money away in receptacles he carried his ledgers one
by one into the vault. The cashier followed with the
cash and put it away and they emerged and the cashier was about to close the vault, when Snopes stopped
him. "Forgot that cash-book," he explained. The
cashier returned to his window and Snopes carried
the book into the vault and put it away and emerged
and clashed the door to, and hiding the dial with his
body, he rattled the knob briskly. The cashier had
his back turned, rolling a cigarette.

"See it's throwed good," he said. Snopes rattled the
knob again, then shook the door.

"That's got it." They took their hats and emerged
from the cage and locked it behind them, and passed
through the front door, which the cashier closed and
shook also. He struck a match to his cigarette.

"See you tomorrow," he said.

"All right," Snopes agreed, and he stood looking
after the other's shapeless back in its shabby alpaca
coat. He produced his soiled handkerchief and wiped
his mouth again.

That evening about eight oclock he was back down
town. He stood for a time with the group that sat
nightly in front of the drug store on the corner;
stood quietly among them, listening but saying nothing, as was his way. Then he moved on, without
being missed, and walked slowly up the street and
stopped at the bank door. One or two passers spoke
to him while he was finding his key and opening the

door; he responded in his flat country idiom and entered and closed the door behind him. A single bulb burned above the vault. He raised the shade on the window beside it and entered the grilled cage and turned on the light above his desk. Here passers could see him, could have watched him for several minutes as he bent over his desk, writing slowly. It was his final letter, in which he poured out his lust and his hatred and his jealousy, and the language was the obscenity which his jealousy and desire had hoarded away in his temporarily half-crazed mind and which the past night and day had liberated. When it was finished he blotted it carefully and folded it and put it in his pocket, and snapped his light off. He entered the directors' room and in the darkness he unlocked the door which gave onto the vacant lot, closed it and left it unlocked.

He returned to the front and drew the shade on the window, and drew the other shades to their full extent, until no crack of light showed at their edges, emerged and locked the door behind him. On the street he looked casually back at the windows. The shades were close; the interior of the bank was invisible from the street.

The group still talked in front of the drug store and he stopped again on the outskirts of it. People passed back and forth along the street and in or out of the drug store; one or two of the group drifted away, and newcomers took their places. An automobile drew up to the curb, was served by a negro lad; drove away. The clock on the courthouse struck nine measured strokes.

Soon, with a noise of starting engines, motor cars began to stream out of a side street and onto the square, and presently a flux of pedestrians appeared. It was the exodus from the picture show, and cars

one after another drew up to the curb with young
men and girls in them, and other youths and girls in
pairs turned into the drug store with talk and shrill
laughter and cries one to another, with slender bodies
in delicate colored dresses, shrill as apes and awkward, divinely young. Then the more sedate groups
—a man with a child or so gazing longingly into the
scented and gleaming interior of the store, followed
by three or four women—his wife and a neighbor or
so—talking sedately among themselves; more children—little girls in prim and sibilant clots, and boys
scuffling and darting with changing adolescent
shouts. A few of the sitters rose and joined passing
groups.

More belated couples came up the street and entered the drug store, and other cars; other couples
emerged and strolled on. The night watchman came
along presently, with his star on his open vest and a
pistol and a flashlight in his hip pockets; he too
stopped and joined in the slow, unhurried talk. The
last couple emerged from the drug store, and the last
car drove away. And presently the lights behind
them flashed off and the proprietor jingled his keys
in the door and rattled it, and stood for a moment
among them, then went on. Ten oclock. The Snopes
rose to his feet.

"Well, I reckon I'll turn in," he said generally.

"Time we all did," another said, and they rose also.
"Goodnight, Buck."

"Goodnight, gentlemen," the night watchman replied.

The Snopes turned into the first street. He went
steadily on beneath the spaced arc lights and turned
into a narrower street and followed it. From this
street he turned into a lane between massed honeysuckle higher than his head and sweet upon the night

air. The lane was dark, and he increased his pace. On
either hand the upper stories of houses rose above the
honeysuckle, with now and then a lighted window
among dark trees. He kept close to the wall and went
swiftly on. He went now between back premises;
lots and gardens, but before him another house
loomed, and a serried row of cedars on the lighter
sky; and he stole beside a stone wall and so came opposite the garage. He stopped here and sought in the
lush grass beneath the wall and stooped and raised a
pole, which he leaned against the wall. With the help
of the pole he mounted to the top of the wall and so
onto the garage roof.

But the house was dark, and presently he slid to
the ground and with the desperate courage of his despair he stole across the lawn and stopped beneath a
window. There was a light somewhere toward the
front of the house, but no sound, no movement, and
he stood for a time listening, darting his eyes this
way and that, covert and ceaseless as a cornered
animal.

The screen responded easily to his knife blade and
he raised it and listened again. Then with a single
scrambling motion he was in the room, crouching,
with his thudding heart. Still no sound, and the
whole house gave off that unmistakable emanation of
temporary desertion. He drew out his handkerchief
and wiped his mouth.

The light was in the next room, and he went on.
The stairs rose from the end of this room and he scuttled silently across it and mounted swiftly into darkness again and groped through the darkness until he
touched a wall, then a door. The knob turned under
his fingers.

It was the right room; he knew that at once: her
presence was all about him, and for a time his heart

thudded and thudded in his throat and fury and lust and despair shook him like a rag. But he pulled himself together; he must get out quickly, and he groped his way across to the bed and lay face down upon it, his head buried in the pillows, writhing and making smothered, animal-like moanings. But he must get out, and he rose and groped across the room again. What little light there was was behind him now, and instead of finding the door he blundered into a chest of drawers, and stood there a moment. Then with sudden decision he opened a drawer and fumbled in it. It was filled with a faintly scented fragility of garments, but he could not distinguish one from another.

He found a match in his pocket and struck it beneath the shelter of his palm, and by its light he chose one of the soft garments, discovering as the match died a packet of letters in one corner of the drawer. He recognised them at once and he threw the dead match to the floor and removed the letter he had just written from his pocket and put it in the drawer and put the other letters in his pocket, and he stood for a time with the garment crushed against his face; remained so for some time, until a sound caused him to jerk his head up. A car was coming up the drive, and as he turned and sprang to the window, its lights swept beneath him and fell full upon the open garage, and he crouched at the window in utter panic. Then he turned and sped to the door and stopped again crouching, panting and snarling in indecision.

He turned and ran back to the window. The garage was dark, and two dark figures were coming toward the house and he crouched within the window until they had passed from sight. Then, still clutching the garment, he climbed out the window

and swung from the sill for a moment, closed his eyes
and dropped.

There was a crash of glass and he sprawled in a
dusty litter, with other lesser crashes. He had fallen
into a shallow, glassed flower pit and he scrambled
out someway and tried to get to his feet and fell
again, while nausea swirled in him. It was his knee,
and he lay sick and with snarling teeth while his
trouser leg sopped slowly and damply, clutching the
garment he had stolen and staring at the dark sky
with wide, mad eyes. He heard voices in the house,
and a light came on in the window above him and he
dragged himself erect again, restraining his vomit,
and at a scrambling hobble he crossed the lawn and
plunged into the shadow of the cedars beside the garage, where he lay staring at the house where a man
leaned in a window, peering out and moaning a little
while his blood ran between his clasped fingers. He
drove himself onward again and dragged his bleeding
leg over the wall and dropped into the lane and cast
the pole down. A hundred yards further he stopped
and drew his torn trousers aside and tried to bandage
the long gash in his leg. But the handkerchief stained
over almost at once, and still his blood ran and ran
down his leg and into his shoe.

Once in the back room of the bank, he rolled his
trouser leg up and removed the handkerchief and
bathed the gash with cold water. It still bled, though
not so much, and he removed his shirt and bound it
as tightly as he could. He still felt an inclination toward nausea, and he drank long of the tepid water
from the lavatory tap. Immediately it warmed sa-
linely inside him and he clung to the lavatory, sweating, trying not to vomit, until the spell passed. His
leg felt numb and dead.

He entered the grilled cage. His left heel showed

yet a bloody print on the floor, but no blood ran from beneath the bandage. The vault door opened soundlessly; without striking a match he found the key to the cash box and opened it. He took only banknotes, which he stowed away in his inner coat pocket, but he took all he could find. Then he closed the vault and locked it, returned to the lavatory and wetted a towel and removed his heel prints from the linoleum floor. He passed out the rear door, threw the latch so it would lock behind him. The clock on the courthouse rang midnight.

In an alley between two negro stores he found the negro whom he had met at noon, with a battered Ford car. He gave the negro a bill and the negro cranked the car and came and stared curiously at his torn trousers and the glint of white cloth beneath. "Whut happened, boss? Y'aint hurt, is you?"

"Run into some wire," he answered shortly, and drove on. As he crossed the square he saw the night watchman, Buck, standing beneath the light before the postoffice, and cursed him with silent and bitter derision. He drove on and passed from view, and presently the sound of his going had died away.

He drove through Frenchman's Bend at two oclock, without stopping. The village was dark; Varner's store, the blacksmith shop (now a garage too, with a gasoline pump), Mrs Littlejohn's huge, unpainted boarding house—all the remembered scenes of his boyhood—were without life; he went on. He drove now along a rutted wagon road, between swampy jungle, at a snail's pace. After a half hour the road mounted a small knoll wooded with scrub oak and indiscriminate saplings, and faded into a barren, sun-baked surface in the middle of which squatted a low, broken-backed log house. His lights swept across its gaping front, and a huge gaunt hound descended from the porch and bellowed at him. He stopped and switched the lights off.

His leg was stiff and dead, and when he descended he was forced to cling to the car for a time, moving it back and forth until it would bear his weight. The hound stood ten feet away and thundered at him in a sober conscientious fury until he spoke to it, whereupon it ceased its clamor but stood yet in an attitude of watchful belligerence. He limped toward it, and it recognised him, and together they crossed the barren plot in the soundless dust and mounted the veranda. "Turpin," he called in a guarded voice.

The dog had followed him onto the porch, and it flopped noisily and scratched itself. The house consisted of two wings joined by an open hall; through the hall he could see sky, and another warped roof tree on the slope behind the house. His leg tingled and throbbed as with pins of fire. I got that 'ere bandage too tight, he thought. "Turpin."

A movement from the wing at his left, and into the lesser obscurity of the hall a shape emerged and stood in vague relief against the sky, in a knee-length night-shirt and a shotgun. "Who's thar?" the shape demanded.

"Byron Snopes."

The man leaned the gun against the wall and came onto the porch, and they shook hands limply. "What you doin', this time of night? Thought you was in town."

"On a trip for the bank," Snopes explained. "Just drove in, and I got to git right on. Might be gone some time, and I wanted to see Minnie Sue."

The other rubbed the wild shock of his head, then he scratched his leg. "She's a-sleepin'. Caint you wait till daylight?"

"I got to git on," he repeated. "Got to be pretty nigh Alabama by daybreak."

The man brooded heavily, rubbing his flank. "Well," he said finally, "ef you caint wait till mawnin'." He padded back into the house and vanished. The hound flopped again at Snopes' feet and sniffed noisily. From the river bottom a mile away an owl hooted with its mournful rising inflection. Snopes thrust his hand into his coat and touched the wadded delicate garment. In his breast pocket the money bulked against his arm.

Another figure stepped soundlessly into the hall, against the lighter sky; a smaller figure and even more shapeless, that stood for a moment, then came out to him. He put his arms around her, feeling her free body beneath the rough garment she had hastily donned. "Byron?" she said, "What is it, Byron?" He was trying to kiss her, and she suffered him readily, but withdrew her face immediately, peering at him. He drew her away from the door.

"Come on," he whispered. His voice was shaking and hoarse, and his body was trembling also. He led her to the steps and tried to draw her on, but she held back a little, peering at him.

"Let's set on the steps," she said. "What's the matter, Byron? You got a chill?"

"I'm all right. Let's git away where we can talk."

She let him draw her forward and down the steps, but as they moved further and further away from the house she began to resist, with curiosity and growing alarm. "Byron," she said again and stopped. His hands were trembling upon her, moving about

her body, and his voice was shaking so that she could
not understand him.

"You aint got on nothing under here but your
nightgown, have you?" he whispered.

"What?" He drew her a little further, but she
stopped firmly and he could not move her; she was as
strong as he. "You tell me what it is, now," she commanded. "You aint ready fer our marryin' yet, are
you?"

But he made no answer. He was trembling more
than ever, pawing at her. They struggled, and at last
he succeeded in dragging her to the ground and he
sprawled beside her, pawing at her clothing; whereupon she struggled in earnest, and soon she held him
helpless while he sprawled with his face against her
throat, babbling a name not hers. When he was still
she turned and thrust him away, and rose to her feet.

"You come back tomorrer, when you git over
this," she said, and she ran silently toward the house,
and was gone.

He sat where she had left him for a long time, with
his half-insane face between his knees and madness
and helpless rage and thwarted desire coiling within
him. The owl hooted again from the black river bottom; its cry faded mournfully across the land, beneath the chill stars, and the hound came silently
through the dust and sniffed at him, and went away.
After a time he rose and limped to the car and
started the engine.

FOUR

I

It was a sunny Sunday afternoon in October. Narcissa and Bayard had driven off soon after dinner, and Miss Jenny and old Bayard were sitting on the sunny end of the veranda when, preceded by Simon, the deputation came solemnly around the corner of the house from the rear. It consisted of six negroes in a catholic variety of Sunday raiment and it was headed by a huge, neckless negro in a Prince Albert coat and a hind-part-before collar, with an orotund air and a wild, compelling eye.

"Yere dey is, Cunnel," Simon said, and without pausing he mounted the steps and faced the deputation, leaving no doubt in the beholder's eye as to which side he was aligned with. The deputation halted and milled a little, solemnly decorous.

"What's this?" Miss Jenny demanded. "That you, Uncle Bird?"

"Yessum, Miss Jenny." One of the deputation uncovered his grizzled wool and bowed. "How you gittin' on?" The others shuffled their feet, and one by one they removed their hats. The leader clasped his across his chest like a congressional candidate being photographed.

"Here, Simon," old Bayard said. "What's this? What did you bring these niggers around here for?"

"Dey come fer dey money," Simon explained.

"What?"

"Money?" Miss Jenny repeated with interest. "What money, Simon?"

"Dey come fer de money you promised 'um," Simon shouted.

"I told you I wasn't going to pay that money," old Bayard said. "Did Simon tell you I was going to pay it?" he demanded of the committee.

"What money?" Miss Jenny repeated. "What are you talking about, Simon?" The leader of the deputation was shaping his mouth to words, but Simon forestalled him.

"Why, Cunnel, you tole me yo'self to tell dem niggers you wuz gwine pay 'um."

"I didn't do any such thing," old Bayard answered violently. "I told you that if they wanted to put you in jail, to go ahead and do it. That's what I told you."

"Why, Cunnel, you said it jes' ez plain. I kin prove it by Miss Jenny you tole me—"

"Not by me," Miss Jenny denied. "This is the first I heard about it. Whose money is it, Simon?"

Simon gave her a pained, reproachful look. "He tole me to tell 'um he wuz gwine pay it."

"I'm damned if I did," old Bayard stormed. "I told you I wouldn't pay a damn cent of it. And I told you that if you let 'em worry me about it, I'd skin you alive, sir."

"I aint gwine let 'um worry you," Simon answered soothingly. "You jes' give 'um dey money, en me en you kin fix it up later."

"I'll be eternally damned if I will; if I let a lazy nigger that aint worth his keep—"

"But somebody got to pay 'um," Simon pointed out patiently. "Aint dat right, Miss Jenny?"

"That's right," Miss Jenny agreed. "But it's not me."

"Yessuh, dey aint no argument dat somebody got to pay 'um. Ef somebody dont pay 'um dey'll put me in jail. And den whut'll y'all do, widout nobody to keep dem hosses fed en clean, and to clean de house en wait on de table? Co'se I dont mine gwine to jail, even ef dem stone flo's aint gwine do my mis'ry no good." And he drew a long and affecting picture, of high and grail-like principles, and patient abnegation. Old Bayard slammed his feet to the floor.

"How much is it?"

The leader swelled impressively in his Prince Albert. "Brudder Mo'," he said, "will you read out de total emoluments owed to de pupposed Secon' Baptis' church by de late Deacon Strother in his capacity ez treasurer of de church boa'd?"

Brother Moore in the rear of the group genuflected himself. Then ready hands pushed him into the foreground—a small ebon negro in sombre, overlarge black—where the parson majestically made room for him. He laid his hat on the earth at his feet and from the right-hand pocket of his coat he produced in the following order, a red bandana handkerchief; a shoe horn; a plug of chewing tobacco, and holding these in his hand he delved yet further, with an expression of mildly conscientious alarm. Then he replaced the objects, and from his left-hand pocket he produced a pocket knife; a stick on which was wound a length of dingy string; a short piece of leather strap attached to a rusty buckle, and lastly a greasy, dogeared notebook. He crammed the other things back into the pocket, dropping the leather strap, which he stooped and recovered, then he and the parson held a brief whispered conversation. He opened the notebook and fumbled the pages over, fumbled at them until the parson leaned over his shoulder and found the proper page and laid his finger upon it.

"How much is it, reverend?" old Bayard asked.

"Brudder Mo' will now read out de amount," the parson said. Brother Moore stared at the page and mumbled something in a weak, indistinguishable voice.

"What?" old Bayard demanded.

"Make 'im talk up," Simon said. "Cant nobody tell whut he sayin'."

"Louder," the parson rumbled, with just a trace of impatience.

"Sixty-sevum dollars en fawty cents," Brother Moore articulated at last. Old Bayard sat and swore for a time, then rose and tramped into the house, still swearing. Simon sighed and relaxed. The deputation milled again, politely, and Brother Moore faded briskly into the rear rank of it. The parson, however, still retained his former attitude of fateful and solemn profundity.

"What became of that money, Simon?" Miss Jenny asked curiously. "You had it, didn't you?"

"Dat's whut dey claims," Simon answered.

"What did you do with it?"

"Hit's all right," Simon assured her. "I jes' put it out, sort of."

"I bet you did," she agreed drily. "I bet it never even got cool while you had it. Who did you put it out to?"

"Oh, me and Cunnel done fix dat up," he said, "long time ago." Old Bayard tramped in the hall again, and emerged flapping a check in his hand.

"Here," he commanded, and the parson approached the railing and took it and folded it away in his coat pocket. Old Bayard glared at Simon. "And the next time you steal money and come to me to pay it back, I'm going to have you arrested and prosecute you myself, you hear? Get those niggers out of here."

The deputation stirred again, with a concerted movement, but the parson halted them with a commanding hand. He turned and faced Simon. "Deacon Strother," he said, "ez awdained minister of de late Fust Baptis' church, en recalled minister of de pupposed Secon' Baptis' church, en chairman of dis committee, I hereby reinfests you wid yo' fawmer capacity of deacon in de said pupposed Secon' Baptis' church. Amen. Cunnel Sartoris en ma'am, good day." Then he turned and herded his committee from sight.

"Thank de Lawd, we got rid of dat," Simon said, and he came and lowered himself to the top step, groaning pleasurably.

"And you remember what I said," old Bayard warned him. "One more time, now—"

But Simon was peering in the direction the church committee had taken. "Dar now," he said. "Whut you reckon dey wants now?" For the deputation had returned and it now peered diffidently around the corner.

"Well," old Bayard said violently. "What is it now?"

They were trying to thrust Brother Moore forward again, but he would not be thrust. At last the parson spoke.

"You fergot de fawty cents, whitefolks."

"What?"

"He says you lef' out de extry fawty cents," Simon shouted. Old Bayard exploded; Miss Jenny clapped her hands over her ears and the committee rolled its eyes in fearsome admiration while he soared to magnificent heights, alighting finally upon Simon.

"You give him that forty cents, and get 'em out of here," old Bayard finished. "And if you ever bring 'em back here again, I'll take a horsewhip to the whole lot of you."

"Lawd, Cunnel, I aint got fawty cents, en you knows it. Cant dey do widout dat, after gittin' de rest of it?"

"Yes you have, Simon," Miss Jenny said. "You had a half a dollar left after I ordered those shoes for you last night." Again Simon looked at her with pained astonishment.

"Give it to 'em," old Bayard commanded. Slowly Simon reached into his trousers and produced a half dollar and turned it slowly in his palm.

"I mought need dis money, Cunnel," he protested. "Seems like dey mought leave me dis."

"Give 'em that money!" old Bayard thundered. "I reckon you can pay forty cents of it, at least." Simon rose reluctantly, and the minister approached to meet him.

"Whar's my dime change?" he demanded, nor would he surrender the coin until the two nickels were in his hand. Then the committee departed.

"Now," old Bayard said, "I want to know what you did with that money."

"Well, suh," Simon began, "it wuz like dis. I put dat money out." Miss Jenny rose.

"My Lord," she said, "are you all going over that again?" And she left them. In her room, where she sat in a sunny window, she could still hear them—old Bayard's stormy rage, and Simon's bland and ready evasion rising and falling on the drowsy Sabbath air.

There was a rose, a single remaining rose. Through the sad, dead days of late summer it had continued to bloom, and now though persimmons had long swung their miniature suns among the caterpillar-festooned branches, and gum and maple and hickory had flaunted four gold-and-scarlet weeks, and the grass, where grandfathers of grasshoppers squatted sluggishly like sullen octogenarians, had been pencilled twice delicately with frost, and the sunny noons were scented with sassafras, it still bloomed. Overripe now, and a little gallantly blowsy, like a fading burlesque star. Miss Jenny worked in a sweater, nowadays, and her trowel glinted brightly in her earthy glove.

"It's like some women I've known," she said. "It just dont know how to give up gracefully and be a grandmamma."

"Let it have the summer out," Narcissa in her dark woolen dress, protested. She had a trowel too, and she pottered serenely after Miss Jenny's scolding brisk impatience, accomplishing nothing. Worse than Isom, because she demoralized Isom, who had immediately given his unspoken alliance to the Left, or passive, Wing. "It's entitled to its summer."

"Some folks dont know when summer's over," Miss Jenny rejoined. "Indian summer's no excuse for senile adolescence."

"It isn't senility, either."

"All right. You'll see, someday."

"Oh, someday. I'm not quite prepared to be a grandmother, yet."

"You're doing pretty well." Miss Jenny trowelled a tulip bulb carefully and expertly up and removed the clotted earth from its roots. "We seem to have pretty well worn out Bayard, for the time being," she continued. "I reckon we'd better name him John."

"Yes?"

"Yes," Miss Jenny repeated. "We'll name him John. You, Isom!"

The gin had been running steadily for a month, now, what with the Sartoris cotton and that of other planters further up the valley, and of smaller croppers with their tilted fields among the hills. The Sartoris place was farmed on shares. Most of the tenants had picked their cotton, and gathered the late corn; and of late afternoons, with Indian summer upon the land and an ancient sadness sharp as woodsmoke on the still air, Bayard and Narcissa would drive out to where, beside a dilapidated cotton house on the edge of a wooden ravine above a spring, the tenants brought their cane and made their winter supply of sorghum molasses. One of the negroes, a sort of patriarch among them, owned the mill and the mule that furnished the motive power. He did the community grinding and superintended the cooking of the juice for a tithe, and when Bayard and Narcissa arrived the mule would be plodding in a monotonous circle, its feet rustling in the dried cane-pith, drawing the long wooden beam which turned the mill into which one of the patriarch's grandsons fed the cane.

Round and round the mule went, setting its narrow, deerlike feet delicately down in the hissing cane-pith, its neck bobbing limber as a section of rubber hose in the collar, with its trace-galled flanks and flopping, lifeless ears, and its half-closed eyes drowsing venomously behind pale lids, apparently asleep with the monotony of its own motion. Some Cincinnatus of the cotton fields should contemplate the lowly destiny, some Homer should sing the saga, of the mule and of his place in the South. He it was, more than any one creature or thing, who, steadfast to the land when all else faltered before the hopeless juggernaut of circumstance, impervious to conditions that broke men's hearts because of his venomous and patient preoccupation with the immediate present, won the prone South from beneath the iron heel of Reconstruction and taught it pride again through humility and courage through adversity overcome; who accomplished the well-nigh impossible despite hopeless odds, by sheer and vindictive patience. Father and mother he does not resemble, sons and daughters he will never have; vindictive and patient (it is a known fact that he will labor ten years willingly and patiently for you, for the privilege of kicking you once); solitary but without pride, self-sufficient but without vanity; his voice is his own derision. Outcast and pariah, he has neither friend, wife, mistress nor sweetheart; celibate, he is unscarred, possesses neither pillar nor desert cave, he is not assaulted by temptations nor flagellated by dreams nor assuaged by visions; faith, hope and charity are not his. Misanthropic, he labors six days without reward for one creature whom he hates, bound with chains to another whom he despises, and spends the seventh day kicking or being kicked by his fellows. Misunderstood even by that creature (the nigger who drives him) whose impulses and mental processes most closely resemble his, he performs alien actions among alien surroundings; he finds bread not only for a race, but for an entire form of behavior; meek, his inheritance is cooked away from him along with his soul in a glue factory. Ugly, untiring and perverse, he can be moved neither by reason, flattery, nor promise of reward; he performs his humble monotonous duties without complaint, and his meed is blows. Alive, he is haled through the world, an object of general execration; unwept, unhonored and unsung, he bleaches his awkward, accusing bones among rusting cans and broken crockery and worn-out automobile tires on lonely hillsides, while his flesh soars unawares against the blue in the craws of buzzards.

As they approached, the groaning and creaking of the mill would be the first intimation, unless the wind happened to blow toward them. Then it would be the sharp, subtly exciting odor of fermentation and of cooking molasses to greet them. Bayard liked the smell of it, and they would drive up and sit for a time while the boy rolled his eyes covertly at them as he fed the mill, watching the patient unceasing mule and the old man stooped above the simmering pot. Sometimes Bayard got out and went over and talked to him, leaving Narcissa alone in the car, lapped in the ripe odors of the failing year and all its vague, rich sadness, her gaze brooding quietly upon Bayard and the old negro—the one lean and tall and fatally young and the other stooped with time, while her spirit went out in serene and steady waves, surrounding him unawares.

Then he would return and get in beside her, and she would touch his rough clothing but so lightly that he was not conscious of it, and they would drive back along the faint road, beside the flaunting woods, and soon, above turning oaks and locusts, the white house simple and huge and steadfast, and the orange disc of the harvest moon beyond the trees, halved like a cheese by the ultimate hills.

Sometimes they went back after dark. The mill was still then, its long motionless arm like a gesture across the firelit scene. The mule was munching somewhere in stable, or stamping and nuzzling its empty manger, or asleep standing, boding not of to-morrow; and against the firelight many forms moved. The negroes had gathered now: old men and

women sitting on crackling cushions of cane about
the blaze which one of their number fed with
pressed stalks until its incense-laden fury swirled
licking at the boughs overhead, making more golden
still the twinkling golden leaves; and young men and
girls, and children squatting and still as animals, staring into the fire. Sometimes they sang—quavering,
wordless chords in which sad monotonous minors
blent with mellow bass in passionless suspense and
faded along the quivering golden air, to be renewed.
But when the white folks arrived the singing ceased,
and they sat or lay about the crackling scented blaze
on which the blackened pot simmered, talking in
broken phrases murmurous with overtones ready
with sorrowful mirth, while in shadowy beds among
the dry whispering canestalks youths and girls murmured and giggled.

At last one of them, and sometimes both, stopped
in the "office" where old Bayard and Miss Jenny sat.
There was a fire of logs on the hearth now, and they
would sit in the glow of it—Miss Jenny beneath the
light with her lurid daily paper; old Bayard with his
slippered feet propped against the fireplace, his head
wreathed in smoke and the old setter dreaming
fitfully beside his chair, reliving proud and ancient
stands perhaps, or further back still, the lean, gawky
days of his young doghood, when the world was full
of scents that maddened the blood in him and pride
had not yet taught him self-restraint; Narcissa and
Bayard between them—Narcissa dreaming too in the
firelight, grave and still and serene, and young Bayard smoking his cigarettes in his leashed and moody
repose.

At last old Bayard would throw his cigar into the
fire and drop his feet to the floor, and the dog would
raise its head and blink and yawn with such gaping

deliberation that Narcissa, watching him, invariably yawned also. "Well, Jenny?"

Then Miss Jenny would lay her paper aside and rise. "Let me," Narcissa would say. "Let me go." But Miss Jenny never would, and presently she would return with a tray and three glasses, and old Bayard would unlock his desk and fetch the silver-stoppered decanter and compound three toddies with ritualistic care.

Once Bayard persuaded Narcissa into khaki and boots and carried her 'possum hunting. Caspey with a streaked and blackened lantern and a cow's horn slung over his shoulder, and Isom with a gunny sack and an axe, and four shadowy, restless hounds waited for them at the lot gate and they set off among ghostly shocks of corn, where every day almost Bayard kicked up a covey of quail, toward the woods.

"Where we going to start tonight, Caspey?" Bayard asked.

"Back of Unc' Henry's. Day's one in dat grape vine behine de cotton house. Blue treed 'im down dar las' night."

"How do you know he's there tonight, Caspey?" Narcissa asked.

"He be back," Caspey answered confidently. "He right dar now, watchin' dis lantern wid his eyes scrooched up, listenin' to hear ef de dawgs wid us."

They climbed through a fence and Caspey stooped and set the lantern on the ground. The dogs moiled and tugged about his legs with sniffings and throaty growls at one another as he unleashed them. "You, Ruby! Stan' still, dar. Hole up here, you potlickin' fool." They whimpered and surged, their eyes melting in fluid brief gleams, then they faded soundlessly and swiftly into the darkness. "Give 'um a little time," Caspey said. "Let 'um see ef he dar yit." From

the darkness ahead a dog yapped three times on a
high note. "Dat's dat young dawg," Caspey explained.
"Jes' showin' off. He aint smelt nothin'." Overhead
the stars swam vaguely in the hazy sky; the air was
not yet chill, and the earth was warm yet. They
stood in a steady oasis of lantern light in a world with
but one dimension, a vague cistern of darkness filled
with meagre light and topped with an edgeless can-
opy of ragged stars. It was smoking and emanating a
faint odor of heat. Caspey lifted it and turned the
wick down and set it at his feet again. Then from the
darkness there came a single note, resonant and low
and grave.

"Dar he," Isom said.

"Hit's Ruby," Caspey agreed, picking up the lantern. "She got 'im." The young dog yapped again,
with fierce hysteria, then the single low cry chimed
once more. Narcissa slid her arm through Bayard's
and they hurried on. "'Taint no rush," Caspey told
her. "Dey aint treed yit. Whooy. H'mon, dawg."
The young dog had ceased its yapping, but still at intervals the other one bayed her single timbrous note,
and they followed it. "H'mon, dawg."

They stumbled a little over fading plow-scars,
after Caspey's bobbing lantern, and the darkness
ahead was suddenly crescendic with short steady
cries in four keys. "Dey got 'im," Isom said.

"Dat's right," Caspey replied. "Le's go. Hold 'im,
dawg!" They trotted now, Narcissa clinging to
Bayard's arm, and plunged through rank grass and
over another fence and so among trees. Eyes gleamed
fleetingly from the darkness ahead, and another gust
of barking interspersed with tense and eager whimperings, and among stumbling half-lit shadows dogs
surged about them. "He up dar," Caspey said. "Ole
Blue sees 'im." He raised the lantern and set it upon

his head, peering up into the vine-matted sapling, and Bayard drew a flashlight from his jacket and turned its beam into the tree. The three older hounds sat in a tense circle about the tree, whimpering or barking in short spaced gusts, but the young one yapped steadily in mad, hysterical rushes. "Kick dat puppy still," Caspey commanded.

"You, Ginger, hush yo' mouf," Isom shouted; he laid his axe and sack down and caught the puppy and held it between his knees. Caspey and Bayard moved slowly around the tree, among the tense dogs; Narcissa followed them. "Dem vines is so thick . . ." Caspey said.

"Here he is," Bayard said suddenly, "I've got 'im." He steadied his light and Caspey moved behind him and stared over his shoulder.

"Where?" Narcissa asked.

"Dat's right," Caspey agreed. "Dar he is. Ruby dont lie. When she say he dar, he dar."

"Where is he, Bayard?" Narcissa repeated. He drew her before him and trained the light over her head, into the tree, and presently from the massed vines two reddish points of fire not a match-breadth apart, gleamed at her, winked out, then shone again.

"He movin'," Caspey said. "He young 'possum. Git up dar and shake 'im out, Isom." Bayard held his light on the creature's eyes and Caspey set his lantern down and herded the dogs together at his knees. Isom scrambled up into the tree and vanished in the vine, but they could follow his progress by the shaking branches and his panting as he threatened the animal with a mixture of cajolery and adjuration.

"Hah," he panted. "Aint gwine hurt you. Aint gwine do nothin' ter you but th'ow you in de cook-pot. Look out, mister; I'se coming up dar." He stopped; they could hear him moving the branches cautiously. "Here he," he called suddenly. "Hole dem dawgs, now."

"Little 'un, aint he?" Caspey asked.

"Cant tell. Cant see nothin' but his face. Watch dem dawgs." The upper part of the tree burst into violent and sustained commotion; Isom's voice whooped louder and louder as he shook the branches. "Here he comes," he shouted, and something dropped sluggishly and reluctantly from branch to branch, stopped, and the dogs set up a straining clamor, then fell again, and Bayard's light followed a lumpy object that dropped with a resounding thud to the earth and vanished immediately beneath a swirl of hounds. Caspey and Bayard leaped among them, and at last Narcissa saw the creature in the pool of the flashlight, lying on its side in a grinning curve, its eyes closed and its pink, baby-like hands doubled against its breast. She watched the motionless thing with a little loathing—such a contradiction, its vulpine, skull-like grin and those tiny, human-looking hands, and the long, rat-like tail of it. Isom dropped from the tree, and Caspey turned the two straining clamorous dogs he held over to him and picked up the axe, and while Narcissa watched in shrinking curiosity, he laid the axe across the thing's neck and put his foot on either end of the axe, and grasped the animal's tail . . . She turned and fled, her hand to her mouth.

But the wall of darkness stopped her and she stood trembling and a little sick, watching them as they moved about the lantern. Then Caspey drove the dogs away and Isom picked up the lumpy sack and swung it to his shoulder, and Bayard turned and looked for her. "Narcissa?"

"Here," she answered. He came to her.

"That's one. We ought to get a dozen, tonight."

"No," she said, shuddering. "No." He peered at her in the darkness.

"Not tired already, are you?"

"No," she answered, "I just . . . Come on; they're going."

Caspey led them on through the woods, now. They walked in a dry sibilance of leaves and crackling undergrowth. Trees loomed out of the darkness; above them, among the thinning branches, stars swam in the hushed, vague sky. The dogs were on ahead, and they went on over the uneven ground, sliding down into washes and ditches where sand gleamed in the pale glow of the lantern and the scissoring shadow of Caspey's legs was enormous, struggled up the other side.

"We better head away f'um de creek bottom," Caspey suggested. "Dey mought strike a 'coon, and den dey wont git home 'fo' day." He bore away toward the fields again. "H'mon, dawg." They went on. Narcissa was beginning to tire, but Bayard strode on with a fine obliviousness of that possibility, and she followed without complaint. At last, from far away, came that single ringing cry. Caspey stopped. "Le's see which way he gwine." They stood in the darkness, in the sad, faintly chill decline of the year, among the dying trees. "Whooy," Caspey shouted mellowly. "Go git 'im."

The dog replied, and they moved again, slowly, pausing at intervals to listen. The hound bayed again; there were two voices now, and they seemed to be moving in a circle across their path. "Whooy," Caspey called, his voice ebbing in falling echoes among the motionless trees. They went on. Again the dogs gave tongue, this time from a direction opposite that where the first one had bayed. "He ca'yin' 'um right back whar he come f'um," Caspey said. "We better wait 'twell dey gits 'im straightened out." He set the lantern down and squatted beside it, and Isom sloughed his burden and squatted also, and Bayard sat against a tree trunk and drew Narcissa down beside him. The dogs bayed again, nearer. Caspey turned his head and stared off into the darkness toward the sound.

"He headin' fer dat holler tree, aint he?" Isom asked.

"Soun' like it." They listened, motionless. "We have a job, den. Whooy." There was a faint chill in the air now, as the day's sunlight cooled from the ground, and Narcissa moved closer to Bayard. He took a packet of cigarettes from his jacket and gave Caspey one and lit his own. Isom squatted on his heels, his eyes rolling whitely in the lantern light.

"Gimme one, please, suh," he said.

"You aint got no business smokin', boy," Caspey told him. But Bayard gave him one, and he squatted leanly on his heels, holding the white cylinder in his black diffident hand. The dogs bayed again, mellow and chiming and timbrous in the darkness. "Yes, suh," Caspey repeated, "he headin' fer dat down tree."

"You know this country like you do the back yard, dont you, Caspey?" Narcissa said.

"Yessum, I ought to. I been over it a hund'ed times since I wuz bawn. Mist' Bayard do too. He been huntin' it long ez I is. Him and Mist' Johnny bofe. Miss Jenny send me wid 'um when de had dey fust gun; me and dat 'ere single bar'l gun I used to have to tie together wid a string. You member dat ole single bar'l, Mist' Bayard? But hit 'ud shoot. Many's de fox squir'l we shot in dese woods. Rabbits, too." Bayard was leaning against the tree. He was gazing off into the treetops and the soft sky beyond, his cigarette burning slowly in his hand. She looked at his bleak profile against the lantern glow, then she moved closer against him. But he did not respond, and she slid her hand into his. But it too was unresponsive, and again he had left her for the bleak and lonely heights of his frozen despair. Caspey was speaking again, in his slow, consonantless voice with its overtones of mellow sadness. "Mist' Johnny, now, he sho' could shoot. You 'member dat time me and you and him wuz—"

Bayard rose. He dropped his cigarette and crushed it carefully with his heel. "Let's move on," he said. "They aint going to tree." He drew Narcissa to her feet and turned and went on ahead of them. Caspey got up and unslung his horn and put it to his lips. The sound swelled about them, grave and clear and prolonged, then it died into echoes and so into silence again, leaving no ripple.

It was near midnight when they left Caspey and Isom at their cabin and followed the lane toward the house. After a while the barn loomed before them, and the house among its thinning trees, against the hazy sky. He opened the gate and she passed through and he followed and closed it, and turning he found her beside him, and stopped. "Bayard?" she whispered, leaning against him, and he put his arms around her and stood so, staring above her head into the sky. She took his face between her hands and drew it down, but his lips were cold and upon them she tasted fatality and doom, and she clung to him for a time, her head bowed against his chest.

After that she would not go with him again. So he went alone, returning anywhere between midnight and dawn, ripping his clothing off quietly in the darkness and sliding cautiously into bed. But when he was still, she would touch him and speak his name in the darkness beside him, and turn to him warm and soft with sleep. And they would lie so, holding each other in the darkness and the temporary abeyance of his despair and the isolation of that doom he could not escape.

2

"Well," Miss Jenny said briskly, above the soup, "your girl's gone and left you, and now you can find time to come out and see your kinfolks, cant you?"

Horace grinned a little. "To tell the truth, I came out to get something to eat. I dont think that one woman in ten has any aptitude for keeping house, but my place is certainly not in the home."

"You mean," Miss Jenny corrected, "that not one man in ten has sense enough to marry a decent cook."

"Maybe they have more sense and consideration for others than to spoil decent cooks," he suggested.

"Yes," young Bayard said, "even a cook'll quit work when she gets married."

"Dat's de troof," Simon, propped in a slightly florid attitude against the sideboard, in a collarless boiled shirt and his Sunday pants (it is Thanksgiving day) and reeking a little of whisky in addition to his normal odors, agreed. "I had to find Euphrony fo' new cookin' places de fust two mont' we wuz ma'ied."

Dr Peabody said: "Simon must have married somebody else's cook."

"I'd rather marry somebody else's cook than somebody else's wife," Miss Jenny snapped.

"Miss Jenny!" Narcissa reproved. "You hush."

"I'm sorry," Miss Jenny said immediately. "I

wasn't saying that to you, Horace: it just popped into my mind. I was talking to you, Loosh Peabody. You think, just because you've been eating off of us Thanksgiving and Christmas for sixty years, that you can come into my own house and laugh at me, dont you?"

"Hush, Miss Jenny!" Narcissa repeated.

"What's that?" Old Bayard, his napkin tucked into his waistcoat, lowered his spoon and cupped his hand to his ear.

"Nothing," young Bayard told him. "Aunt Jenny and Doc fighting again. Come alive, Simon." Simon stirred and removed the soup plates, but laggardly, still giving his interested attention to the altercation.

"Yes," Miss Jenny rushed on, "just because that old fool of a Will Falls put axle grease on a little bump on his face without killing him dead, you have to go around swelled up like a poisoned dog. What did you have to do with it? You certainly didn't take it off. Maybe you conjured it on his face to begin with?"

"Haven't you got a piece of bread or something Miss Jenny can put in her mouth, Simon?" Dr Peabody asked mildly. Miss Jenny glared at him a moment, then flopped back in her chair.

"You, Simon! Are you dead?" Simon removed the plates and bore them out, and the guests sat avoiding one another's eyes a little, while Miss Jenny behind her barricade of cups and jugs and urns and things, continued to breathe fire and brimstone.

"Will Falls," old Bayard repeated. "Jenny, tell Simon, when he fixes that basket, to come to my office: I've got something to go in it." This something was the pint flask of whisky which he included in old man Falls' Thanksgiving and Christmas basket and which the old man divided out in spoonsful as far as it would go among his ancient and homeless cronies on those days; and invariably old Bayard reminded her to remind Isom of what neither of them ever forgot or overlooked.

"All right," she answered. Simon reappeared, with a huge silver coffee urn, set it at Miss Jenny's hand and retreated kitchenward.

"How many of you want coffee now?" she asked generally. "Bayard will no more sit down to a meal without his coffee than he'd fly. Will you, Horace?" He declined, and without looking at Dr Peabody she said: "I reckon you'll have to have some, wont you?"

"If it's no trouble," he answered mildly. He winked at Narcissa, then he assumed an expression of lugubrious diffidence. Miss Jenny drew two cups, and Simon appeared with a huge platter borne gallantly and precariously aloft and set it before old Bayard with a magnificent flourish.

"My God, Simon," young Bayard said, "where did you get a whale this time of year?"

"Dat's a fish in dis worl', mon," Simon agreed. And it was a fish. It was three feet long and broad as a saddle blanket; it was a jolly red color and it lay gaping on the platter with an air of dashing and rollicking joviality.

"Dammit, Jenny," old Bayard said pettishly, "what did you want to have this thing, for? Who wants to clutter his stomach up with fish, in November, with a kitchen full of 'possum and turkey and squirrel?"

"There are other people to eat here beside you," she retorted. "If you dont want any, dont eat it. We always had a fish course at home," she added. "But you cant wean these Mississippi country folks away from bread and meat to save your life. Here, Simon." Simon set a stack of plates before old Bayard and he now came with his tray and Miss Jenny set two coffee cups on it, and he served them to old Bayard and Dr Peabody. Miss Jenny drew a cup for herself, and Simon passed sugar and cream. Old Bayard carved the fish, still rumbling heavily.

"I aint ever found anything wrong with fish at any time of year," Dr Peabody said.

"You wouldn't," Miss Jenny snapped. Again he winked heavily at Narcissa.

"Only," he continued, "I like to catch my own, out of my own pond. Mine have mo' food value."

"Still got your pond, Doc?" young Bayard asked.

"Yes. But the fishin' aint been so good, this year. Abe had the flu last winter, and ever since he's been goin' to sleep on me, and I have to sit there and wait until he wakes up and takes the fish off and baits my hook again. But finally I thought about tyin' one end of a cord to his leg and the other end to the bench, and now when I get a bite, I just give the string a yank and wake 'im up. You'll have to bring yo' wife out someday, Bayard. She aint never seen my pond."

"You haven't?" Bayard asked Narcissa. She had not. "He's got a row of benches around it, with footrests, and a railing just high enough to prop your pole on, and a nigger to every fisherman to bait his hook and take the fish off. I dont see why you feed all those niggers, Doc."

"Well, I've had 'em around so long I dont know how to get rid of 'em, 'less I drown 'em. Feedin' 'em is the main trouble, though. Takes everything I can make. If it wasn't for them, I'd a quit practicin' long ago. That's the reason I dine out whenever I can: every time I get a free meal, it's the same as a half holiday."

"How many have you got, Doctor?" Narcissa asked.

"I dont rightly know," he answered. "I got six or

seven registered ones, but I dont know how many scrubs I have. I see a new yearlin' every day or so." Simon was watching him with rapt interest.

"You aint got no extry room out dar, is you, Doctor?" he asked. "Here I slaves all day long, keepin' 'um in vittles en sech."

"Can you eat cold fish and greens every day?" Dr Peabody asked him solemnly.

"Well, suh," Simon answered doubtfully, "I aint right sho' erbout dat. I burnt out on fish once, when I wuz a young man, en I aint had no right stomach fer it since."

"Well, that's about all we eat, out home."

"All right, Simon," Miss Jenny said. Simon was propped statically against the sideboard, watching Dr Peabody with musing astonishment.

"En you keeps yo' size on cole fish en greens? Gentlemun, I'd be a bone-rack on dem kine o' vittles in two weeks, I sho'ly would."

"Simon!" Miss Jenny raised her voice sharply. "Why wont you let him alone, Loosh, so he can 'tend to his business?" Simon came abruptly untranced and removed the fish.

"Lay off of Doc, Aunt Jenny," young Bayard said. He touched his grandfather's arm. "Cant you make her let Doc alone?"

"What's he doing, Jenny?" old Bayard asked. "Wont he eat his dinner?"

"None of us'll get to eat anything, if he sits there and talks to Simon about cold fish and greens," Miss Jenny replied.

"I think you're mean, to treat him like you do, Miss Jenny," Narcissa said. She sat beside Horace; beneath the cloth her hand was in his.

"Well, it gives me something to be thankful for,"

Dr Peabody answered. "That I'm a widower. I want some mo' coffee, Jenny."

"Who wouldn't be, the size of a hogshead, and living on cold fish and turnip greens?" Miss Jenny snapped. He passed his cup and she refilled it.

"Oh, shut up, Aunt Jenny," young Bayard commanded. Simon appeared again, with Isom in procession now, and for the next few minutes they moved steadily between kitchen and dining room with a roast turkey and a cured ham and a dish of quail and another of squirrel, and a baked 'possum in a bed of sweet potatoes; and Irish potatoes and sweet potatoes, and squash and pickled beets, and rice and hominy, and hot biscuit and beaten biscuit and long thin sticks of cornbread, and strawberry and pear preserves, and quince and apple jelly, and blackberry jam and stewed cranberries.

Then they ceased talking for a while and really ate, glancing now and then across the table at one another in a rosy glow of amicability and steamy odors. From time to time Isom entered with hot bread, while Simon stood overlooking the field somewhat as Caesar must have stood looking down into Gaul, once he had it well in hand, or the Lord God Himself when he looked down upon His latest chemical experiment and said It is well.

"After this, Simon," Dr Peabody said, and he sighed a little, "I reckon I can take you on and find you a little side meat now and then."

"I 'speck you kin," Simon agreed, watching them like an eagle-eyed general who rushes reserves to the threatened points, pressing more food upon them as they faltered. But even Dr Peabody allowed himself vanquished after a time, and then Simon brought in pies of three kinds, and a small, deadly plum pud-

ding, and cake baked cunningly with whisky and
nuts and fruit and treacherous and fatal as sin; and at
last, with an air sibylline and gravely profound, a
bottle of port. The sun lay hazily in the glowing
west, falling levelly through the windows and upon
the silver arrayed upon the sideboard, dreaming in
hushed mellow gleams among its placid rotundities
and upon the colored glass in the fanlight high in the
western wall.

But that was November, the season of hazy, lan-
guorous days, when the first flush of autumn was
over and winter beneath the sere horizon breathed
yet a spell. November, when the year like a shawled
matron among her children dies peacefully, without
pain and of no disease. Early in December the rains
came and the year turned gray beneath the season of
dissolution and of death. All night and all day it
whispered upon the roof and along the eaves; the
leafless trees gestured their black and sorrowful
branches in it: only a lone stubborn hickory at the
foot of the park kept its leaves yet, gleaming like a
sodden flame against the eternal azure; beyond the
valley the hills were hidden within chill veils of it.

Almost daily, despite Miss Jenny's strictures and
commands and the grave and passive protest in Narcissa's eyes, Bayard went out with a shotgun and the
two dogs, to return just before dark, wet to the skin.
And cold; his lips would be chill on hers, and his
eyes bleak and haunted, and in the yellow firelight of
their room she would cling to him, or lie crying quietly in the darkness beside his rigid body with a
ghost between them.

"Look here," Miss Jenny said, coming upon her as
she sat brooding before the fire in old Bayard's den.

"You spend too much time this way; you're getting moony. Stop worrying about him: he's spent half his life soaking wet, yet he never had a cold that I can remember."

"Hasn't he?" she answered listlessly. Miss Jenny stood beside her chair, watching her keenly. Then she laid her hand on Narcissa's head, quite gently, for a Sartoris.

"Are you worrying because maybe he dont love you like you think he ought to?"

"It isn't that," she answered. "He doesn't love anybody. He wont even love the baby. He doesn't seem to be glad, or sorry, or anything."

"No," Miss Jenny agreed. The fire crackled and leaped among the resinous logs. Beyond the window the day dissolved endlessly. "Listen," Miss Jenny said abruptly. "Dont you ride in that car with him any more. You hear?"

"No. It wont make him drive slowly. Nothing will."

"Of course not. Nobody believes it will, not even Bayard. He goes along for the same reason that boy himself does. Sartoris. It's in the blood. Savages, every one of 'em. No earthly use to anyone." Together they gazed into the leaping flames, Miss Jenny's hand still lying on Narcissa's head. "I'm sorry I got you into this."

"You didn't do it. Nobody got me into it. I did it myself."

"H'm," Miss Jenny said. And then: "Would you do it over again?" The other didn't answer, and she repeated the question. "Would you?"

"Yes," Narcissa answered. "Dont you know I would?" Again there was silence between them, in which without words they sealed their hopeless pact with that fine and passive courage of women throughout the world's history. Narcissa rose. "I believe I'll go to town and spend the day with Horace, if you dont mind," she said.

"All right," Miss Jenny agreed. "I believe I would, too. Horace probably needs a little looking after, by now. He looked sort of gaunt when he was out here last week. Like he wasn't getting proper food."

When she entered the kitchen door Eunice, the cook, turned from the bread board and lifted her daubed hands in a soft dark gesture. "Well, Miss Narcy," she said, "we aint seed you in a mont'. Is you come all de way in de rain?"

"I came in the carriage. It was too wet for the car." She entered the kitchen. Eunice watched her with grave pleasure. "How are you all getting along?"

"He gits enough to eat, all right," Eunice answered. "I sees to dat. But I has to make 'im eat it. He needs you back here."

"I'm here, for the day, anyhow. What have you got for dinner?" Together they lifted lids and peered into the simmering vessels on the stove and in the oven. "Oh, chocolate pie!"

"I has to toll 'im wid dat," Eunice explained. "He'll eat anything, ef I jes' makes 'im a chocolate pie," she added proudly.

"I bet he does," Narcissa agreed. "Nobody can make chocolate pies like yours."

"Dis one aint turnt out so well," Eunice said, deprecatory. "I aint so pleased wid it."

"Why, Eunice! It's perfect."

"No'm, it aint up to de mark," Eunice insisted. But she beamed, gravely diffident, and for a few minutes the two of them talked amicably while Narcissa pried into cupboards and boxes.

Then she returned to the house and mounted to her room. The dressing table was bare of its intimate silver and crystal, and the drawers were empty, and the entire room with its air of still and fading desolation, reproached her. Chill, too; there had been no fire in the grate since last spring, and on the table beside the bed, in a blue vase, was a small faded bunch of flowers, forgotten and withered and dead. Touching them, they crumbled in her fingers, leaving a stain, and the water in the vase smelled of rank decay. She opened a window and threw them out.

The room was too chill to stop in long, and she decided to ask Eunice to build a fire on the hearth, for the sake of that part of her which still lingered here, soberly and a little sorrowful in the chill and reproachful desolation. At her chest of drawers she paused again and remembered those letters, fretfully and with a little brooding alarm, deprecating anew her carelessness in not destroying them. But maybe she had, and so entered again into the closed circle of her first fear and bewilderment, trying to remember what she had done with them. But she was certain she had left them in the drawer with her underthings, positive that she had put them there. Yet she had never been able to find them, nor had Eunice nor Horace seen them. The day she had missed them was the day before her wedding, when she packed her things. That day she had missed them, finding in their stead one in a different handwriting, which she did not remember having received. The gist of it was plain enough, although she had not understood some of it literally. But on that day, she read it with tranquil detachment: it and all it implied was definitely behind her now. And lacking even this, she would not have been shocked if she had comprehended it. Curious a little perhaps, at some of the words, but that is all.

But what she had done with those other letters she could not remember, and not being able to gave her moments of definite fear when she considered the possibility that people might learn that someone had thought such things about her and put them into words. Well, they were gone; there was nothing to do save hope that she had destroyed them as she had the last one, or if she had not, to trust that they would never be found. Yet that brought back the original distaste and dread: the possibility that the intactness of her deep and heretofore inviolate serenity might be the sport of circumstance; that she must trust to chance against the eventuality of a stranger casually raising a stray bit of paper from the ground . . .

But she would put this firmly aside, for the time being, at least. This should be Horace's day, and her own too; a surcease from that ghost-ridden dream to which she clung, waking. She descended the stairs. There was a fire in the living room. It had burned down to embers, however, and she put coal on it and punched it to a blaze. That would be the first thing he'd see when he entered; perhaps he'd wonder; perhaps he'd know before he entered, having sensed her presence. Then she considered 'phoning him, and she mused indecisively for a moment before the fire; then decided to let it be a surprise. But supposing he didn't come home to dinner. She considered this, and pictured him walking along a street in the rain, and immediately and with instinctive foreknowledge of what she would find, she went to the closet beneath the stairs and opened the door. It was as she had known: his overcoat and raincoat both hung there; the chances were he didn't even have an umbrella, and again irritation and exasperation and untroubled affection for him welled in her, and it was as it had been of old again, and all that had since happened to them rolled away.

Heretofore her piano had always been moved into the living room when cold weather came. But this year it stood yet in the smaller alcove. There was a fireplace here, but no fire had been lighted yet, and the room was chilly. Beneath her hands the cold keys gave forth a sluggish chord, accusing, reproving too; and she returned to the fire again and stood before it where she could see through the window the drive beneath its sombre, dripping trees. The small clock on the mantel behind her chimed twelve, and she went to the window and stood with her nose touching the chill glass and her breath misting it over. Soon, now: he was erratic in his hours, but never tardy, and every time an umbrella came into sight, her heart leaped a little. But it was not he, and she followed the bearer's plodding passage until he shifted the umbrella enough for her to see who it was and so did not see Horace until he was half way up the drive. His hat was turned down around his face and his coat collar was hunched to his ears, and as she had known, he didn't even have an umbrella.

"Oh, you idiot," she said and ran to the door and through the curtained glass she saw his shadowy shape come leaping up the steps. He flung the door open and entered, whipping his sodden hat against his leg, and so did not see her until she stepped forth. "You idiot," she said. "Where's your raincoat?"

For a moment he stared at her with his wild and diffident repose, then he said "Narcy!" and his face lighted and he swept her into his wet arms.

"Dont," she cried. "You're wet!" But he swung her from the floor, against his sodden chest, repeating Narcy, Narcy; then his cold nose was against her face and she tasted rain.

"Narcy," he said again, hugging her, and she ceased trying to free herself and clung to him. Then abruptly he released her and jerked his head up and stared at her with sober intensity.

"Narcy," he said, still staring at her, "has that surly black-guard . . . ?"

"No, of course not," she answered sharply. "Have you gone crazy?" Then she clung to him again, wet clothes and all, as though she would never let him go. "Oh, Horry," she said, "I've been a beast to you!"

"I was hoping," he said—they had eaten the chocolate pie and Horace now stood before the living-room fire, his coffee cup on the mantel, striking matches to his pipe—"that you might have come home for good. That they had sent you back."

"No," she answered. "I wish . . ."

"What?"

But she only said: "You'll be having somebody, soon." And then: "When is it to be, Horry?"

He sucked intently at his pipe; in his eyes little twin matchflames rose and fell. "I dont know. Next spring, I suppose. Whenever she will."

"You dont want to," she stated quietly. "Not after what it's all got to be now."

"She's in Reno now," he added, puffing at his pipe, his face averted a little. "Little Belle wrote me a letter about mountains."

She said: "Poor Harry." She sat with her chin in her palms, gazing into the fire.

"He'll have little Belle," he reminded her. "He cares more for her than he does for Belle, anyway."

"You dont know," she told him soberly. "You just say that because you want to believe it."

"Dont you think he's well off, rid of a woman who doesn't want him, who doesn't even love his child very much?"

"You dont know," she repeated. "People cant—cant—You cant play fast and loose with the way things ought to go on, after they've started off."

"Oh, people." He raised the cup and drained it, and sat down. "Barging around through a lifetime, clotting for no reason, breaking apart for no reason still. Chemicals. No need to pity a chemical."

"Chemicals," she mused, her serene face rosy in the firelight. "Chemicals. Maybe that's the reason so many of the things people do smell bad."

"Well, I dont know that I ever thought of it in exactly that way," he answered gravely. "But I daresay you're right, having femininity on your side." He brooded himself, restlessly. "But I suppose it's all sort of messy: living and seething corruption glossed over for a while by smoothly colored flesh; all foul, until the clean and naked bone." He mused again, she quietly beside him. "But it's something there, something you go after; must; driven. Not always swine. A plan somewhere, I suppose, known to Whoever first set the fermentation going. Perhaps it's just too big to be seen, like a locomotive is a porous mongrel substance without edges to the grains of sand that give it traction on wet rails. Or perhaps He has forgotten Himself what the plan was."

"But do you like to think of a woman who'll willingly give up her child in order to marry another man a little sooner?"

"Of course I dont. But neither do I like to remember that I have exchanged you for Belle, or that she has red hair and is going to be fat someday, or that she has lain in another man's arms and has a child that isn't mine, even though she did voluntarily give it up. Yet there are any number of virgins who love children walking the world today, some of whom look a little like you, probably, and a modest number of which I allow myself to believe, without conceit, that I could marry. And yet . . ." He struck another match to his pipe, but he let it go out again and sat forward in his chair, the pipe held loosely in his joined hands. "That may be the secret, after all. Not any subconscious striving after what we believed will be happiness, contentment; but a sort of gadfly urge after the petty, ignoble impulses which man has tried so vainly to conjure with words out of himself. Nature, perhaps, watching him as he tries to wean himself away from the rank and richly foul old mire that spawned him, biding her time and flouting that illusion of purifaction which he has foisted upon himself and calls his soul. But it's something there, something you—you—" He brooded upon the fire, holding his cold pipe. She put her hand out and touched his, and he clasped it and looked at her with his groping and wide intensity. But she was gazing into the fire, her cheek in her palm, and she drew his hand to her and stroked it on her face.

"Poor Horry," she said.

"Not happiness," he repeated. "I'm happier now than I'll ever be again. You dont find that, when you suddenly swap the part of yourself which you want least, for the half of someone else that he or she doesn't want. Do you? Did you find it?"

But she only said "Poor Horry" again. She stroked his hand slowly against her cheek as she stared into

the shaling ruby of the coals. The clock chimed
again, with blent small silver bells. She spoke without
moving.

"Aren't you going back to the office this afternoon?"

"No." His tone was again the grave, lightly casual
one which he employed with her. "I'm taking a holiday. Next time you come, I may have a case and
cant."

"You never have cases: you have functions," she
answered. "But I dont think you ought to neglect
your business," she added with grave reproof.

"Neither do I," he agreed. "But whatever else is
business for, then?"

"Dont be silly . . . Put on some coal, Horry."

But later he reverted again to his groping and
tragic premonitions. They had spent the afternoon
sitting before the replenished fire; later she had gone
to the kitchen and made tea. The day still dissolved
ceaselessly and monotonously without, and they sat
and talked in a sober and happy isolation from their
acquired ghosts, and again their feet chimed together
upon the dark road and, their faces turned inward to
one another's, the sinister and watchful trees were no
longer there. But the road was in reality two roads
become parallel for a brief mile and soon to part
again, and now and then their feet stumbled.

"It's having been younger once," he said. "Being
dragged by time out of a certain day like a kitten
from a tow sack, being thrust into another sack with
shreds of the first one sticking to your claws. Like
the burro that the prospector keeps on loading down
with a rock here and a rock there until it drops, leaving him in the middle of his desert, surrounded by
waiting buzzards," he added, musing in metaphors.
"Plunder. That's all it is. If you could just be

translated every so often, given a blank, fresh start, with nothing to remember. Dipped in Lethe every decade or so . . ."

"Or every year," she added. "Or day."

"Yes." The rain dripped and dripped, thickening the twilight; the room grew shadowy. The fire had burned down again; its steady fading glow fell upon their musing faces and brought the tea things on the low table beside them, out of the obscurity in quiet rotund gleams; and they sat hand in hand in the fitful shadows and the silence, waiting for something. And at last it came: a thundering knock at the door, and they knew then what it was they waited for, and through the window they saw the carriage curtains gleaming in the dusk and the horses stamping and steaming on the drive, in the ceaseless rain.

3

Horace had seen her on the street twice, his attention caught by the bronze splendor of her hair and by an indefinable something in her air, her carriage. It was not boldness and not arrogance exactly, but a sort of calm, lazy contemptuousness that left him seeking in his mind after an experience lost somewhere within the veils of years that swaddled his dead childhood; an experience so sharply felt at the time that the recollection of it lingered yet somewhere just beneath his consciousness although the motivation of its virginal clarity was lost beyond recall. The wakened ghost of it was so strong that during the rest of the day he roused from periods of abstraction to find that he had been searching for it a little fearfully among the crumbled and long unvisited corridors of his mind, and later as he sat before his fire at home, with a book. Then, as he lay in bed thinking of Belle and waiting for sleep, he remembered it.

He was five years old and his father had taken him to his first circus, and clinging to the man's hard, reassuring hand in a daze of blaring sounds and sharp cries and scents that tightened his small entrails with a sense of fabulous and unimaginable imminence and left him a little sick, he raised his head and found a tiger watching him with yellow and lazy contemplation; and while his whole small body was a tranced and soundless scream, the animal gaped and flicked its lips with an unbelievably pink tongue. It was an old tiger and toothless, and it had doubtless gazed through these same bars at decades and decades of Horaces, yet in him a thing these many generations politely dormant waked shrieking, and again for a red moment he dangled madly by his hands from the lowermost limb of a tree.

That was it, and though that youthful reaction was dulled now by the years, he found himself watching her on the street somewhat as a timorous person is drawn with delicious revulsions to gaze into a window filled with knives. He found himself thinking of her often, wondering who she was. A stranger, he had never seen her in company with anyone who might identify her. She was always alone and always definitely going somewhere; not at all as a transient, a visitor idling about the streets. And always that air of hers, lazy, predatory and coldly contemptuous. The sort of woman men stare after on the street and who does not even do them the honor of ignoring them.

The third time he saw her he was passing a store, a newly opened department store, just as she emerged at that free, purposeful gait he had come to know. In the center of the door sill was a small iron ridge onto

which the double doors locked, and she caught the
heel of her slipper on this ridge and emerged stumbling in a cascade of small parcels, and swearing. It
was a man's bold swearing, and she caught her balance and stamped her foot and kicked one of her
dropped parcels savagely into the gutter. Horace
retrieved it and turning saw her stooping for the others, and together they gathered them up and rose,
and she glanced at him briefly with level eyes of a
thick, dark brown and shot with golden lights somehow paradoxically cold.

"Thanks," she said, without emphasis, taking the
packages from him. "They ought to be jailed for
having a mantrap like that in the door." Then she
looked at him again, a level stare without boldness or
rudeness. "You're Horace Benbow, aren't you?" she
asked.

"Yes, that is my name. But I dont believe—"

She was counting her packages. "One more yet,"
she said, glancing about her feet. "Must be in the
street." He followed her to the curb, where she had
already picked up the other parcel, and she regarded
its muddy side and swore again. "Now I'll have to
have it rewrapped."

"Yes, too bad, isn't it?" he agreed. "If you'll allow
me—"

"I'll have it done at the drug store. Come along, if
you're not too busy. I want to talk to you."

She seemed to take it for granted that he would
follow, and he did so, with curiosity and that feeling
stronger than ever of a timorous person before a window of sharp knives. When he drew abreast of her
she looked at him again (she was almost as tall as he)
from beneath her level brows. Her face was rather
thin, with broad nostrils. Her mouth was flat though
full, and there was in the ugly distinction of her face

an indescribable something; a something boding and leashed, yet untamed. Carnivorous, he thought. A lady tiger in a tea gown; and remarking something of his thoughts in his face, she said: "I forgot: of course you dont know who I am. I'm Belle's sister."

"Oh, of course. You're Joan. I should have known."

"How? Nobody yet ever said we look alike. And you never saw me before."

"No," he agreed, "but I've been expecting for the last three months that some of Belle's kinfolks would be coming here to see what sort of animal I am."

"They wouldn't have sent me, though," she replied. "You can be easy on that." They went on along the street. Horace responded to greetings, but she strode on with that feline poise of hers; he was aware that men turned to look after her, but in her air there was neither awareness nor disregard of it, conscious or otherwise. And again he remembered that tiger yawning with bored and lazy contempt while round and static eyes stared down its cavernous pink gullet. "I want to stop here," she said, as they reached the drug store. "Do you have to go back to the store, or whatever it is?"

"Office," he corrected. "Not right away."

"That's right," she agreed, and he swung the door open for her, "you're a dentist, aren't you? Belle told me."

"Then I'm afraid she's deceiving us both," he answered drily. She glanced at him with her level, speculative gaze, and he added: "She's got the names confused and sent you to the wrong man."

"You seem to be clever," she said over her shoulder, "and I despise clever men. Dont you know any better than to waste cleverness on women? Save it for your friends." A youthful clerk in a white jacket approached, staring at her boldly; she asked him with contemptuous politeness to rewrap her parcel. Horace stopped beside her.

"Women friends?" he asked.

"Women what?" She stooped down, peering into a showcase of cosmetics. "Well, maybe so," she said indifferently. "But I never believe 'em, though. Cheap sports." She straightened up. "Belle's all right, if that's what you want to ask. It's done her good. She doesn't look so bad-humored and settled down, now. Sort of fat and sullen."

"I'm glad you think that. But what I am wondering is, how you happened to come here. Harry's living at the hotel, isn't he?"

"He's opened the house again, now. He just wanted somebody to talk to. I came to see what you look like," she told him.

"What I look like?"

"Yes. To see the man that could make old Belle kick over the traces." Her eyes were coldly contemplative, a little curious. "What did you do to her? I'll bet you haven't even got any money to speak of."

Horace grinned a little. "I must seem rather thoroughly impossible to you, then," he suggested.

"Oh, there's no accounting for the men women pick out. I sometimes wonder at myself. Only I've never chosen one I had to nurse, yet." The clerk returned with her package, and she made a trifling purchase and gathered up her effects. "I suppose you have to stick around your office all day, dont you?"

"Yes. It's the toothache season now, you know."

"You sound like a college boy now," she said coldly. "I suppose Belle's ghost will let you out at night, though?"

"It goes along too," he answered.

"Well, I'm not afraid of ghosts. I carry a few around, myself."

"You mean dripping flesh and bloody bones, dont you?" She looked at him again, with her flecked eyes that should have been warm but were not.

"I imagine you could be quite a nuisance," she told him. He opened the door and she passed through it. And gave him a brief nod, and while he stood on the street with his hat lifted she strode on, without even a conventional Thank you or Goodbye.

That evening while he sat at his lonely supper, she telephoned him, and thirty minutes later she came in Harry's car for him. And for the next three hours she drove him about while he sat hunched into his overcoat against the raw air. She wore no coat herself and appeared impervious to the chill, and she carried him on short excursions into the muddy winter countryside, the car sliding and skidding while he sat with tensed anticipatory muscles. But mostly they drove monotonously around town while he felt more and more like a fatted and succulent eating-creature in a suave parading cage. Sometimes she talked, but usually she drove in a lazy preoccupation, seemingly utterly oblivious of him.

Later, when she had begun coming to his house, coming without secrecy and with an unhurried contempt for possible eyes and ears and tongues—a contempt that also disregarded Horace's acute unease on that score, she still fell frequently into those periods of aloof and purring repose. Then, sitting before the fire in his living room, with the bronze and electric disorder of her hair and the firelight glowing in little red points in her unwinking eyes, she was like a sheathed poniard, like Chablis in a tall-stemmed glass. At these times she would utterly ignore him, cold and inaccessible. Then she would rouse and talk brutally of her lovers. Never of herself, other than to give him the salient points in her history that Belle had hinted at with a sort of belligerent prudery. The surface history was brief and simple enough. Married at eighteen to a man three times her age, she had deserted him in Honolulu and fled to Australia with an Englishman, assuming his name; was divorced by her husband, discovered by first-hand experience that no Englishman out of his native island has any honor about women; was deserted by him in Bombay, and in Calcutta, she married again. An American, a young man, an employee of Standard Oil company. A year later she divorced him, and since then her career had been devious and a little obscure, due to her restlessness. Her family would know next to nothing of her whereabouts, receiving her brief, infrequent letters from random points half the world apart. Her first husband had made a settlement on her, and from time to time and without warning she returned home and spent a day or a week or a month in the company of her father's bitter reserve and her mother's ready tearful uncomplaint, while neighbors, older people who had known her all her life, girls with whom she had played in pinafores and boys with whom she had sweethearted during the spring and summer of adolescence and newcomers to the town, looked after her on the street.

Forthright and inscrutable and unpredictable: sometimes she stayed an hour motionless before the fire while he sat nearby and did not dare touch her; sometimes she lay beside him while the firelight, fallen to a steady glow of coals, filled his bedroom with looming and motionless shadows until midnight or later, talking about her former lovers with a brutality that caused him hopeless and despairing anger and something of a child's hurt disillusion; speaking of them with that same utter lack of vanity and conventional modesty with which she discussed her body, asking him to tell her again that he thought her body beautiful, asking him if he had ever seen a match for her legs, then taking him with a savage and carnivorous suddenness that left him spent. Yet all the while remote beyond that barrier of cold inscrutability which he was never able to break down, and rising at last, again that other feline and inaccessible self and departing without even the formality of a final kiss or a Goodbye and leaving him to wonder, despite the evidences of her presence, whether he had not dreamed it, after all.

She made but one request of him: that he refrain from talking to her of love. "I'm tired of having to listen to it and talk and act a lot of childish stupidity," she explained. "I dont know anything about it, and I dont care to."

"You dont think there is any such thing?" he asked.

"I've never found it. And if we can get anything from each other worth having, what's the use in talking about it? And it'll take a race of better people than we are to bear it, if there's any such thing. Save that for Belle: you'll probably need it."

One night she did not depart at all. That was the night she revealed another feline trait: that of a prowling curiosity about dark rooms. She had paused at Narcissa's door, and although he tried to draw her onward, she opened the door and found the light switch and pressed it on. "Whose room is this?"

"Narcissa's," he answered shortly. "Come away."

"Oh, your sister's. The one that married that Sartoris." She examined the room quietly. "I'd like to have known that man," she said in a musing tone. "I think I'd be good for him. Marrying women, then leaving them after a month or two. Only one man ever left me," she stated calmly. "I was practically a child, or that wouldn't have . . . Yes, I'd have been just the thing for him." She entered the room; he followed and took her arm again.

"Come away, Joan."

"But I dont know," she added. "Maybe it's a good thing he's gone, after all. For both of us."

"Yes. Come away."

She turned her head and stared at him with her level inscrutable eyes, beneath the bronze disorder of her hair. "Men are funny animals," she said. "You carry so much junk around with you." There was in her eyes a cold derisive curiosity. "What do you call it? sacrilege? desecration?"

"Come away," he repeated.

Next day, in the gray December forenoon among the musty books in his office, the reaction found him. It was more than reaction: it was revulsion, and he held a spiritual stock-taking with a sort of bleak derision: for a moment, in company with the sinister gods themselves, he looked down upon Horace Benbow as upon an antic and irresponsible worm. It was worse; it was conduct not even becoming a college sophomore—he, who had thought to have put all such these ten years behind him; and he thought of his sister and he felt unclean. On the way home at noon he saw Harry Mitchell approaching, and he ducked into a store and hid—a thing Belle had never caused him to do.

He would not go to his room, where the impact of her presence must yet linger, and Eunice served his meal with her face averted, emanating disapproval and reproach; and he angered slowly and asked her the direct question. "Has Mrs Heppleton gone yet, Eunice?"

"I dont know, suh," Eunice answered, still without looking at him. She turned doorward.

"You dont know when she left?"

"I dont know, suh," Eunice repeated doggedly, and the swing door slapped behind her in dying oscillations.

But he would not mount to his room, and soon he was back down town again. It was a gray, raw day, following the two recent weeks of bright frosty weather. Christmas was not a week away, and already the shop windows bloomed in toy fairylands, with life in its mutations in miniature among cedar branches and cotton batting and dusted over with powdered tinsel, amid which Santa Claus in his myriad avatars simpered in fixed and rosy benignance; and with fruit and cocoanuts and giant sticks of peppermint; and fireworks of all kinds—roman candles and crackers and pinwheels; and about the muddy square fetlock-deep horses stood hitched to wagons laden with berried holly and mistletoe.

He was too restless to remain in one place, and through the short afternoon, on trivial pretexts or on no pretext at all, he descended the stairs and walked along the streets among the slow throngs of black and white in the first throes of the long winter vacation; and at last he realized that he was hoping to see her, realized it with longing and with dread, looking along the street before him for a glimpse of her shapeless marten coat and the curbed wild blaze of her hair, and the lithe and purposeful arrogance of her carriage, ready to flee when he did so.

But by the time he reached home in the early dusk the dread was still there, but it was only the savor of the longing, and without even pausing to remove his hat and coat he went to the telephone in its chill and darkling alcove beneath the stairs. And he stood with the chill receiver to his ear and watching the cloudy irregularity of his breath upon the nickel mouth-piece, waiting until out of the twilight and the chill the lazy purring of her voice should come. After a time he asked central to ring again, with polite impatience. He could hear the other instrument shrill again and he thought of her long body rising from its warm nest in her chair before a fire somewhere in the quiet house, imagined he could hear her feet on stairs nearer and nearer "Now. Now she is lifting her hand to the receiver now Now." But it was Rachel, the cook. Naw, suh, Miz Heppleton aint here. Yes, suh, she gone away. Suh? Naw, suh, she aint comin' back. She went off on de evenin' train. Naw, suh, Rachel didn't know where she was going.

It used to be that he'd fling his coat and hat down and Narcissa would come along presently and hang them up. But already bachelordom was getting him house-broke—accomplishing what affection never had and never would—and he hung his coat, in the pocket of which an unopened letter from Belle lay forgotten, carefully in the closet beneath the stairs, fumbling patiently with his chilled hands until he found a vacant hook. Then he mounted the stairs and opened his door and entered the cold room where between the secret walls she lingered yet in a hundred palpable ways—in the mirror above his chest of drawers, in the bed, the chairs; on the deep rug before the hearth where she had crouched naked and drowsing like a cat. The fire had burned out; the ashes were cold and the room was icy chill: outside, the graying twilight. He built up the fire and drew his chair close to the hearth and sat before it, his thin delicate hands spread to the crackling blaze.

4

. . . this time it was a Ford car, and Bayard saw its wild skid as the driver jerked it across the treacherous thawing road, and the driver's gaping mouth, and in the rushing moment and with brief amusement, between the man's cravatless collar and the woman's stocking wrapped about his head beneath his hat and tied under his chin, his Adam's apple like a scared puppy in a tow sack. Then this flashed past and Bayard wrenched the wheel, and the stalled Ford swam sickeningly into view again as the big car slewed greasily upon the clay surface, its declutched engine roaring. Then the other car swam away again as he wrenched the wheel over and slammed the clutch out for more stability; and again that sickening, unhurried rush as the car refused to regain its feet and the depthless December world swept laterally across his vision. Old Bayard lurched against him again: from the corner of his eye he could see the fellow's hand clutching at the edge of the door. Now they were facing the bluff on which the cemetery lay; directly over them John Sartoris' effigy lifted its florid stone gesture, and from among motionless cedars gazed out upon the valley where for two miles the railroad he had built ran beneath his carven eyes. Bayard wrenched the wheel again.

On the other side of the road a ravine dropped sheer away, among scrub cedars and corroded ridges skeletoned brittly with frost and muddy ice where the sun had not yet reached; the rear end of the car hung timelessly over this before it swung again, with the power full on, swung on until its nose pointed down hill again, with never a slackening of its speed. But still it would not come into the ruts again and it had lost the crown of the road, and though they had almost reached the foot of the hill, Bayard saw they would not make it. Just before the rear wheel slipped off he wrenched the steering wheel over and swung the nose straight over the bank, and the car poised lazily for a moment, as though taking breath. "Hang on," he shouted to his grandfather. Then they plunged.

An interval utterly without sound and in which all sensation of motion was lost. Then scrub cedar burst crackling about them and whipping branches of it exploded upon the nose of the car and slapped viciously at them as they sat with braced feet, and the car slewed in a long bounce. Another vacuum-like interval, then a shock that banged the wheel into Bayard's chest and wrenched it in his tight hands, wrenched his arm-socket. Beside him his grandfather lurched forward and he threw out his arm just in time to keep the other from crashing through the windshield. "Hang on," he shouted again. The car had never faltered and he dragged the leaping wheel over and swung it down the ravine and opened the engine again, and with the engine and the momentum of the plunge, they crashed on down the ravine and turned and heaved up the now shallow bank and onto the road again. Bayard brought it to a stop.

He sat motionless for a moment. "Whew," he said. And then: "Great God in the mountain." His grandfather sat quietly beside him, his hand still on the door and his head bent a little. "Think I'll have a cigarette, after that," Bayard added. He found one in his pocket, and a match; his hands were shaking. "I thought of that damn concrete bridge again, just as she went over," he explained, a little apologetically. He took a deep draught at his cigarette and glanced at his grandfather. "Y'all right?" Old Bayard made no reply, and with the cigarette poised, Bayard looked at him. He sat as before, his head bent a little and his hand on the door. "Grandfather?" Bayard said sharply. Still old Bayard didn't move, even when his grandson flung the cigarette away and shook him roughly.

5

Up the last hill the tireless pony bore him, and in the low December sun their shadow fell longly across the hardwood ridge and into the valley, from which the high, shrill yapping of the dogs came again upon the frosty windless air. Young dogs, Bayard told himself, and he sat his horse in the faint scar of the road, listening as the high breathless hysteria of them swept echoing across his aural field though the race itself was hidden beyond the trees. Motionless, he could feel frost in the air. Above him the pines, though there was no wind in them, made a continuous dry, wild sound; above them against the high evening blue, a shallow V of geese slid. There'll be ice tonight, he thought, thinking of black backwaters where they would come to rest, of rank bayonets of dead grasses about which the water would shrink soon in the brittle darkness, in fixed glassy ripples. Behind him the earth rolled away ridge on ridge blue as woodsmoke, on into a sky like thin congealed blood. He turned in his saddle and stared unwinking into the bloody west against which the sun spread like a crimson egg broken upon the ultimate hills.

That meant weather: he snuffed the motionless tingling air, hoping he smelled snow.

The pony snorted and tossed his head experimentally, and found the reins were slack and lowered his head and snorted again into the dead leaves and the delicate sere needles of pine at his feet. "Come up, Perry," Bayard said, jerking the reins. Perry raised his head and broke into a stiff, jolting trot, but Bayard lifted him out of it and curbed him again into his steady foxtrot. The sound of the dogs had ceased, but he had not gone far when they broke again into clamorous uproar to his left, and suddenly near, and as he reined Perry back and peered ahead along the quiet, fading scar of it, he saw the fox trotting sedately toward him in the middle of the road. Perry saw it at the same time and laid his fine ears back and rolled his young eyes. But the animal came on, placidly unawares at its steady, unhurried trot, glancing back over its shoulder from time to time. "Well, I'll be damned," Bayard whispered, holding Perry rigid between his knees. The fox was not forty yards away, yet still it came on, seemingly utterly unaware of the man and horse. Then Bayard shouted.

The fox glanced at him; the level sun swam redly and fleetingly in its eyes, then with a single modest flash of brown it was gone. Bayard expelled his breath: his heart was thumping against his ribs. "Whooy," he yelled. "Come on, dogs!" The dogs heard him and their din swelled to a shrill pandemonium and the pack swarmed wildly into the road in a mad chaos of spotted hides and flapping ears and tongues, and surged toward him. None of them was more than half grown, and ignoring the horse and rider they burst still clamoring into the undergrowth where the fox had vanished and shrieked frantically on; and as Bayard stood in his stirrups and peered after them, preceded by yapping in a yet higher and more frantic key, two even smaller puppies moiled out of the woods and galloped past him on their short legs, with whimpering cries and expressions of ludicrous and mad concern. Then the clamor died into hysterical echoes, and so away.

He rode on. On either hand were hills: the one darkling like a bronze bastion, upon the other the final rays of the sun lay redly. The air crackled with frost and tingled in his nostrils and seared his lungs with fiery, exhilarating needles. The road followed the valley; but half the sun now showed above the western wall, and among trees stark as the bars of a grate, he rode stirrup-deep in shadow like cold water. He would just about reach the house before dark. The clamor of the dogs swelled again ahead of him, approaching the road again, and he lifted Perry into a canter.

Presently before him lay a glade—an old field, sedge-grown, its plow-scars long healed over. The sun filled it with dying light, and he pulled Perry short upstanding: there, at the corner of the field beside the road, sat the fox. It sat there like a tame dog, watching the woods across the glade, and Bayard shook Perry forward again. The fox turned its head and looked at him with a covert, fleeting glance, but without alarm, and Bayard stopped again in intense astonishment. The clamor of the dogs swept nearer through the woods, yet still the fox sat on its haunches, watching the man with covert quick glances. It revealed no alarm whatever, not even when the puppies burst yapping madly from the trees. They moiled at the wood's edge for a time while the fox watched them. The largest one, evidently the leader, saw the quarry. Immediately they ceased their noise and trotted across the glade and squatted in a circle facing the fox, their tongues loll-ing. Then with one accord they all faced about and watched the darkening woods, from which and nearer and nearer, came that spent yapping in a higher key and interspersed with whimpering. The leader barked once; the yapping among the trees swelled with frantic relief and the two smaller puppies burst forth and burrowed like moles through the sedge and came up. Then the fox rose and cast another quick, covert glance at the horseman, and surrounded by the amicable weary calico of the puppies, trotted across the glade and vanished among the darkening trees. "Well, I'll be damned," Bayard said. "Come up, Perry."

At last a pale and windless plume of smoke stood above the trees, against the sky, and in the rambling, mudchinked wall a window glowed with ruddy invi-tation across the twilight. Dogs had already set up a resonant, bell-like uproar; above it Bayard could dis-tinguish the clear tenor of puppies and a voice shouting at them, and as he pulled Perry to a halt in the yard, the fox was vanishing diffidently but with-out haste beneath the back porch. A lean figure faced him in the dusk, with an axe in one hand and an arm-ful of wood, and Bayard said:

"What the devil's that thing, Buddy? That fox?"

"That's Ethel," Buddy answered. He put the wood down deliberately, and the axe, and he came and shook Bayard's hand once, limply, in the country fashion, but his hand was hard and firm. "How you?"

"All right," Bayard answered. "I came out to get that old fox Rafe was telling me about."

"Sure," Buddy agreed in his slow, infrequent voice. "We been expectin' you. Git down and lemme take yo' pony."

"No, I'll do it. You take the wood on in; I'll put

Perry up." But Buddy was firm, without insistence or rudeness, and Bayard surrendered the horse to him.

"Henry," Buddy shouted toward the house, "Henry." A door opened upon jolly leaping flames; a figure stood squatly in it. "Here's Bayard," Buddy said. "Go on in and warm," he added, leading the horse away. Dogs surrounded him; he picked up the wood and the axe and moved toward the house in a ghostly surge of dogs, and the figure stood in the door while he mounted the veranda and leaned the axe against the wall.

"How you?" Henry said, and again the handshake was limp; again the hand was firm and kind, harsher though than Buddy's hard young flesh. He relieved Bayard of the wood and they entered the house. The walls were of chinked logs; upon them hung two colored outdated calendars and a patent medicine lithograph. The floor was bare, of hand-trimmed boards scuffed with heavy boots and polished by the pads of generations of dogs; two men could lie side by side in the fireplace. In it now four-foot logs blazed against the clay fireback, swirling in wild plumes into the chimney's dark maw, and in silhouette against it, his head haloed by the fine shaggy disorder of his hair, Virginius MacCallum sat. "Hyer's Bayard Sartoris, pappy," Henry said.

The old man turned in his chair with grave, leonine deliberation and extended his hand without rising. In 1861 he was sixteen and he walked to Lexington, Virginia, and enlisted, served four years in the Stonewall brigade and walked back to Mississippi and built himself a house and got married. His wife's *dot* was a clock and a dressed hog; his own father gave them a mule. His wife was dead these many years, and her successor was dead, but he sat now before the fireplace at which that hog had been cooked, beneath the roof he had built in '66, and on the mantel above him the clock sat, deriding that time whose creature it had once been. "Well, boy?" he said. "You took yo' time about comin'. How's yo' folks?"

"Pretty well, sir," Bayard answered. He looked at the old man's hale, ruddy face intently and sharply. No, they hadn't heard yet.

"We been expectin' you ever since Rafe seen you in town last spring. Hyer, Henry, tell Mandy to set another plate."

Four dogs had followed him into the room. Three of them watched him gravely with glowing eyes; the other one, a blue-ticked hound with an expression of majestic gravity, came up and touched its cold nose to his head. "Hi, Gen'ral," he said, rubbing its ears, whereupon the other dogs approached and thrust their noses against his hands.

"Pull up a cheer," Mr MacCallum said. He squared his own chair around and Bayard obeyed, and the dogs followed him, surging with blundering decorum about his knees. "I keep sendin' word in to git yo' gran'pappy out hyer," the old man continued, "but he's too 'tarnal proud, or too damn lazy to come. Hyer, Gen'ral! Git away from thar. Kick 'em away, Bayard. Henry!" he shouted. Henry appeared. "Take these hyer damn dawgs out till after supper."

Henry drove the dogs from the room. Mr MacCallum picked up a long pine sliver from the hearth and fired it and lit his pipe, and smothered the sliver in the ashes and laid it on the hearth again. "Rafe and Lee air in town today," he said. "You could have come out in the waggin with them. But I reckon you'd ruther have yo' own hoss."

"Yes, sir," he answered quietly. Then they would know. He stared into the fire for a time, rubbing his hands slowly on his knees, and for an instant he saw the recent months of his life coldly in all their headlong and heedless wastefulness; saw it like the swift unrolling of a film, culminating in that which any fool might have foreseen. Well, dammit, suppose it had: was he to blame? had he insisted that his grandfather ride with him? had he given the old fellow a bum heart? And then, coldly: You were scared to go home. You made a nigger sneak your horse out for you. You, who deliberately do things your judgment tells you may not be successful, even possible, are afraid to face the consequences of your own acts. Then again something bitter and deep and sleepless in him blazed out in vindication and justification and accusation; what, he knew not, blazing out at what. Whom, he did not know: You did it! You caused it all: you killed Johnny.

Henry had drawn a chair up to the fire, and after a while the old man tapped his clay pipe carefully out against his palm and drew a huge, turnip-shaped silver watch from his corduroy vest. "Half after five," he said. "Aint them boys come yet?"

"They're here," Henry answered briefly, "Heard 'em takin' out when I put out the dawgs."

"Git the jug, then," his father ordered. Henry rose and departed again, and feet clumped heavily on the porch and Bayard turned in his chair and stared bleakly at the door. It opened and Rafe and Lee entered.

"Well, well," Rafe said, and his lean dark face lighted a little. "Got here at last, did you?" He shook Bayard's hand, and Lee followed him. Lee's face, like all of them, was a dark, saturnine mask. He was not so stocky as Rafe, and least talkative of them all. His eyes were black and restless; behind them lived something quick and wild and sad: he shook Bayard's hand without a word.

But Bayard was watching Rafe. There was nothing in Rafe's face; no coldness, no questioning—Was it possible that he could have been to town, and not heard? Or had Bayard himself dreamed it? But he remembered that unmistakable feel of his grandfather when he had touched him, remembered how he had suddenly slumped as though the very fibre of him, knit so erect and firm for so long by pride and by his unflagging and hopeless struggling against the curse of his name, had given way all at once, letting his skeleton rest at last. Mr MacCallum spoke.

"Did you go by the express office?"

"We never got to town," Rafe answered. "Axle tree broke just this side of Vernon. Had to uncouple the wagon and drive to Vernon and get it patched up. Too late to go in, then. We got our supplies there and come on home."

"Well, no matter. You'll be goin' in next week, for Christmas," the old man said, and upon a breath of vivid darkness Buddy entered and came and squatted leanly in the shadowy chimney corner.

"Got that fox you were telling me about hid out yet?" Bayard asked Rafe.

"Sure. And we'll get 'im, this time. Maybe tomorrow. Weather's changin'."

"Snow?"

"Might be. What's it goin' to do tonight, pappy?"

"Rain," the old man answered. "Tomorrow, too. Scent wont lay good until Wen'sday. Henry!" After a moment he shouted Henry again, and Henry entered, with a blackened steaming kettle and a stoneware jug and a thick tumbler with a metal spoon in it. There was something domestic, womanish, about

Henry, with his squat, slightly tubby figure and his mild brown eyes and his capable, unhurried hands. He it was who superintended the kitchen (he was a better cook now than Mandy) and the house, where he could be found most of the day, pottering soberly at some endless task. He visited town almost as infrequently as his father; he cared little for hunting, and his sole relaxation was making whisky, good whisky, in a secret fastness known only to his father and to the negro who assisted him, after a recipe handed down from lost generations of his dour and uncommunicative forbears. He set the kettle and the jug and the tumbler on the hearth, and took the clay pipe from his father's hand and put it on the mantel, and reached down a cracked tumbler of sugar and seven glasses, each with a spoon in it. The old man leaned forward into the firelight and made the toddies one by one, with tedious and sober deliberation. When he had made one around, there were two glasses left. "Aint them other boys come in yet?" he asked. Nobody answered, and he corked the jug. Henry set the two extra glasses back on the mantel.

Mandy came to the door presently, filling it with her calico expanse. "Y'all kin come in now," she said, and as she turned waddling Bayard spoke to her and she paused as the men rose. The old man was straight as an Indian, and with the exception of Buddy's lean and fluid length, he towered above his sons by a head. Mandy waited beside the door until they had passed, and gave Bayard her hand. "You aint been out in a long while, now," she said. "And I bet you aint fergot Mandy, neither."

"Sure I haven't," Bayard agreed. But he had. Money, to Mandy, did not compensate for some trinket of no value which John never forgot to bring her when he came. He followed the others into the frosty darkness again. Beneath his feet the ground was already stiffening; overhead the sky was brilliant with stars. He stumbled a little behind the clotted backs until Rafe opened a door into a separate building, upon a room filled with warmth and a thin blue haze in which a kerosene lamp burned steadily, and odors of food, and stood aside until they had entered. In the middle of the floor the table was laid, on it the lamp stood and at one end was placed a chair. The two sides and the other end were parallelled by backless benches. Against the further wall was the stove, and a huge cupboard of split boards, and a woodbox. Behind the stove two negro men and a half-grown boy sat, their faces shining with heat and with white rolling eyes; about their feet five puppies snarled with mock savageness at one another or chewed damply at the negroes' static ankles or prowled about beneath the stove and the adjacent floor with blundering, aimless inquisitiveness.

"Howdy, boys," Bayard said, calling them by name, and they bobbed at him with diffident flashes of teeth.

"Put dem puppies up, Richud," Mandy ordered. The negroes gathered the puppies up one by one and stowed them away in a smaller box behind the stove, where they continued to move about with scratchings and bumpings and an occasional smothered protest. From time to time during the meal a head would appear suddenly, staring over the box edge with blinking and solemn curiosity, then vanish with an abrupt scuffling thump and more protests, and moiling, infant-like noises rose again. "Hush up, dawgs! G'awn to sleep now," Richard would say, rapping the box with his knuckles. At last the noise ceased.

The old man took the chair, his sons around him, and the guest; some coatless, all collarless, with their dark, saturnine faces stamped all clearly from the same die. They ate. Sausage, and spare ribs, and a dish of hominy and one of fried sweet potatoes, and cornbread and a molasses jug of sorghum, and Mandy poured coffee from a huge enamelware pot. In the middle of the meal the two missing ones came in—Jackson, the eldest, a man of fifty-five, with a broad, high forehead and thick brows and an expression at once dreamy and intense—a sort of shy and impractical Cincinnatus; and Stuart, forty-four and Rafe's twin. Yet although they were twins, there was no closer resemblance between them than between any two of them. As though the die was too firm and made too clean an imprint to be either hurried or altered, even by nature. Stuart had none of Rafe's easy manner (Rafe was the only one of them that, by any stretch of the imagination, could have been called loquacious); on the other hand, he had much of Henry's placidity. He was a good farmer and a canny trader, and he had a respectable bank account of his own. Henry, fifty-three, was the second son.

They ate with silent and steady decorum, with only the barest essential words, but amicably. Mandy moved back and forth between table and stove.

Before the meal was finished a sudden bell-like uproar of dogs floated up and seeped, muted by the tight walls, into the room. "Dar, now." The negro Richard cocked his head. Buddy poised his coffee.

"Where are they, Dick?"

"Right back of de spring house. Dey got 'im, too." Buddy rose and slid leanly from his corner.

"I'll go with you," Bayard said, rising also. The others ate steadily. Richard got a lantern down from the cupboard top and lit it, and the three of them stepped out into the chill darkness across which the baying of the dogs came in musical gusts, ringing as frosty glass. It was chill and dark. The house loomed its rambling low wall broken by the ruddy glow of the window. "Ground's about hard already," Bayard remarked.

" 'Twont freeze tonight," Buddy answered. "Will it, Dick?"

"Naw, suh. Gwine rain."

"Go on," Bayard said. "I dont believe it."

"Pappy said so," Buddy answered. "Warmer'n 'twas at sundown."

"Dont feel like it, to me," Bayard insisted. They passed the wagon motionless in the starlight, its tires glinting like satin ribbons, and the long, rambling stable, from which placid munchings came, and an occasional snuffing snort as the lantern passed. The lantern twinkled among tree trunks as the path descended; the clamor of the dogs swelled just beneath them, and in a sapling just behind the spring house they found the 'possum, curled motionless and with its eyes tightly shut, in a fork not six feet from the ground. Buddy lifted it down by the tail, unresisting. "Hell," Bayard said.

Buddy called the dogs away, and they mounted the path again. In a disused shed behind the kitchen what seemed like at least fifty eyes gleamed in matched red points as Buddy swung the lantern in and flashed it onto a cage screened with chicken wire, from which rose a rank, warm odor and in which grizzled furry bodies moved sluggishly or swung sharp, skull-like faces into the light. He opened the door and dumped his latest capture in among its fellows and gave the lantern to Richard. They emerged. Already the sky was hazing over a little, losing its brittle brilliance.

The others sat in a semicircle before the fire; at the

old man's feet the blue-ticked hound dozed. They made room for Bayard, and Buddy squatted again in the chimney corner.

"Git 'im?" Mr MacCallum asked.

"Yes, sir," Bayard answered. "Like lifting your hat off a nail in the wall."

The old man puffed again. "We'll give you a sho' 'nough hunt befo' you leave."

Rafe said: "How many you got now, Buddy?"

"Aint got but fo'teen," Buddy answered.

"Fo'teen?" Henry repeated. "We wont never eat fo'teen 'possums."

"Turn 'em loose and run 'em again, then," Buddy answered. The old man puffed slowly at his pipe. The others smoked or chewed also, and Bayard produced his cigarettes and offered them to Buddy. Buddy shook his head.

"Buddy aint never started yet," Rafe said.

"You haven't?" Bayard asked. "What's the matter, Buddy?"

"Dont know," Buddy answered, from his shadow. "Just aint had time to learn, I reckon."

The fire crackled and swirled; from time to time Stuart, nearest the box, put another log on. The dog at the old man's feet dreamed, snuffed; soft ashes swirled on the hearth at its nose and it sneezed and woke, raised its head and blinked up at the old man's face, then dozed again. They sat without word or movement, their grave, aquiline faces as though carved by the firelight out of the shadowy darkness, shaped by a single thought and smoothed and colored by the same hand. The old man tapped his pipe carefully out upon his palm and consulted his fat silver watch. Eight oclock.

"We'uns git up at fo' oclock, Bayard," he said.

"But you dont have to git up till daylight. Henry, git the jug."

"Four oclock," Bayard repeated, as he and Buddy undressed in the lamplit chill of the lean-to room in which, in a huge wooden bed with a faded patchwork quilt, Buddy slept. "I dont see why you bother to go to bed at all." As he spoke his breath vaporized in the chilly air.

"Yes," Buddy agreed, ripping his shirt over his head and kicking his lean, race-horse shanks out of his shabby khaki pants. "Dont take long to spend the night at our house. You're comp'ny, though." Buddy's preparations for sleeping were simple: he removed his boots and pants and shirt and went to bed in his woolen underwear, and he now lay with only his round head in view, watching Bayard who stood in a sleeveless jersey and short thin trunks. "You aint goin' to sleep warm that-a-way," Buddy added. "You want one o' my heavy 'uns?"

"I'll sleep warm, I guess," Bayard answered. He blew the lamp out and groped his way to the bed, his toes curling away from the icy floor, and got in. The mattress was filled with corn shucks; it rattled beneath him, drily sibilant, and whenever he or Buddy moved at all or took a deep breath even, the shucks shifted with small ticking sounds.

"Git that 'ere quilt tucked in good over there," Buddy advised from the darkness, emitting his breath in a short explosive sound of relaxation and contentment. He yawned, audible but invisible. "Aint seen you in a long while," he suggested.

"That's right. Let's see, when was it? Two—three years, wasn't it?"

"Nineteen fifteen," Buddy answered. "Last time

you and him . . ." He ceased suddenly. Then he
added quietly: "I seen in a paper, when it happened.
The name. Kind of knowed right off 'twas him. It
was a limey paper."

"You did? Where were you?"

"Up there," Buddy answered. "Where them limeys
was. Where they sent us. Flat country. Dont see how
they ever drained it enough to make a crop, with all
that rain."

"Yes," Bayard said. His nose was like a lump of
ice. He could feel his breath warming his nose a little, could almost see the pale smoke of it as he
breathed; could feel the inhalation chilling his nostrils again. It seemed too that he could feel the planks
of the ceiling as they sloped down to the low wall on
Buddy's side, could feel the atmosphere packed into
the low corner, bitter and chill and thick, too thick
for breathing, like invisible slush; and he lay beneath
it . . . He was aware of the dry ticking of shucks beneath him and discovered so that he was breathing in
deep troubled draughts and he wished dreadfully to
be up, moving, before a fire, light; anywhere, anywhere. Buddy lay beside him in the oppressive, half-
congealed solidity of the chill, talking in his slow, in-
articulate idiom of the war. It was a vague, dreamy
sort of tale, without beginning or end and with
stumbling reference to places wretchedly pronounced—you got an impression of people, creatures
without initiation or background or future, caught
timelessly in a maze of solitary conflicting preoccupations, like bumping tops, against an imminent but
incomprehensible nightmare.

"How'd you like the army, Buddy?"

"Not much," Buddy answered. "Aint enough to
do. Good life for a lazy man." He mused a moment.
"They gimme a medal," he added, in a burst of

shy, diffident confidence and sober pleasure. "I aimed to show it to you, but I fergot. Do it tomorrow. That 'ere flo's too dang cold to tech till I have to. I'll watch a chance when pappy's outen the house."

"Why? Dont he know you got it?"

"He knows," Buddy answered. "Only he dont like it because he claims it's a Yankee medal. Rafe says pappy and Stonewall Jackson aint never surrendered."

"Yes," Bayard repeated. After a while Buddy ceased and sighed again, emptying his body for sleep. But Bayard lay rigidly on his back, his eyes wide open. It was like being drunk and whenever you close your eyes, the room starts going round and round, and so you lie rigid in the dark with your eyes wide open, not to get sick. Buddy had ceased talking; presently his breathing became longer, steady and regular, and the shucks shifted with sibilant complaint as Bayard turned slowly onto his side.

But Buddy breathed on in the darkness, steadily and peacefully. Bayard could hear his own breathing also, but above it, all around it, surrounding him, that other breathing. As though he were one thing breathing with restrained laboring, within himself breathing with Buddy's breathing; using up all the air so that the lesser thing must pant for it. Meanwhile the greater thing breathed peacefully and steadily and unawares, asleep, remote; ay, perhaps dead. Perhaps he was dead, and he recalled that morning, relived it again with strained and intense attention from the time he had seen the first tracer smoke, until from his steep side-slip he watched the flame burst like the gay flapping of an orange pennon from John's Camel and saw his brother's familiar gesture and the sudden awkward sprawl of his plunging body as it lost equilibrium in midair; relived it again as you might run over a printed tale, trying to remember, feel, a bullet going into his body or head that might have slain him at the same instant. That would account for it, would explain so much: that he too was dead and this was hell, through which he moved forever and ever with an illusion of quickness, seeking his brother who in turn was somewhere seeking him, never the two to meet. He turned onto his back again; the shucks whispered beneath him with dry derision.

The house was full of noises; to his sharpened senses the silence was myriad: the dry agony of wood in the black frost; the ticking of shucks as he breathed; the very atmosphere itself like slush ice in the vice of the cold, oppressing his lungs. His feet were cold, his limbs sweated with it, and about his hot heart his body was rigid and shivering and he raised his naked arms above the covers and lay for a time with the cold like a lead cast about them. And all the while Buddy's steady breathing and his own restrained and labored breath, both sourceless yet involved one with the other.

Beneath the covers again his arms were cold across his chest and his hands were like ice upon his ribs, and he moved with infinite caution while the chill croached from his shoulders downward and the hidden shucks chattered at him, and swung his legs to the floor, and his curling toes. He knew where the door was and he groped his way to it. It was fastened by a wooden bar, smooth as ice; he fumbled this out of its slots carefully and without noise. The door had sagged from the hinges and after the first jarring scrape, he grasped the edge of it in his chill fingers and raised it and swung it back, and stood in the door.

In the sky no star showed, and the sky was the sagging corpse of itself. It lay upon the earth like a deflated balloon; into it the dark shape of the kitchen rose without depth, and the trees beyond, and homely shapes like chill ghosts in the cold corpse-light—the woodpile; a farming tool; a barrel beside the broken stoop at the kitchen door, where he had stumbled, supperward. The gray chill seeped into him like water into sand, with short trickling runs; halting, groping about an obstruction, then on again, trickling at last along his unimpeded bones. He was shaking slowly and steadily with cold; beneath his hands his flesh was rough and without sensation, yet still it jerked and jerked as though something within the dead envelope of him strove to free itself. Above his head, upon the wooden roof, there sounded a single light tap, and as though at a signal, the gray silence began to dissolve. He shut the door silently and returned to bed.

In the bed he lay shaking more than ever, to the cold derision of the shucks under him, and he lay quietly on his back, hearing the winter rain whispering on the roof. There was no drumming, as when summer rain falls through the buoyant air, but a whisper of unemphatic sound, as though the atmosphere lying heavily upon the roof dissolved there and dripped sluggishly and steadily from the eaves. His blood flowed again, and the covers felt like iron or like ice; but while he lay motionless beneath the rain his blood warmed yet more, until at last his body ceased trembling and he lay presently in something like a tortured and fitful doze, surrounded by coiling images and shapes of stubborn despair and the cease-less striving for . . . not vindication so much as comprehension, a hand, no matter whose, to touch him out of his black chaos. He would spurn it, of course, but it would restore his cold sufficiency again.

The rain dripped on, dripped and dripped; beside him Buddy breathed placidly and steadily: he had not even changed his position. At times Bayard dozed fitfully: dozing, he was wide awake; waking, he lay in a hazy state filled with improbable moiling and in which there was neither relief nor rest: drop by drop the rain wore the night away, wore time away. But it was so long, so damn long. His spent blood, wearied with struggling, moved through his body in slow beats, like the rain, wearing his flesh away. It comes to all . . . Bible . . . some preacher, anyway. Maybe he knew. Peace. It comes to all.

At last, from beyond walls, he heard movement. It was indistinguishable, yet he knew it was of human origin, of people he knew waking again into the world he had not been able even temporarily to lose, people to whom he was . . . and he was comforted. The sounds continued, and at last and unmistakably he heard a door, and a voice which he knew that with a slight effort of concentration he could name; and best of all, that he could rise and go where they were gathered about a crackling fire. And he lay, at ease at last, intending to rise the next moment and go to them, putting it off a little longer while his blood beat slowly through his body and his heart was quieted. Buddy breathed steadily beside him, and his own breath was quiet now as Buddy's while the human sounds came murmurously into the cold room with grave and homely reassurance. It comes to all, it comes to all, his tired heart comforted him, and at last he slept.

He waked in the gray morning, his body weary and heavy and dull: his sleep had not rested him. Buddy was gone, and it still rained, though now it was a definite sound on the roof and the air was warmer, with a rawness that probed to the very bones of him; and in his stockings and carrying his scarred, expensive boots in his hands, he traversed the cold room where Lee and Rafe and Stuart slept, and found Rafe and Jackson before the living-room fire.

"We let you sleep," Rafe said, then he said: "Good Lord, boy, you look like a hant. Didn't you sleep last night?"

"Yes, I slept all right," Bayard answered. He sat down and stamped into his boots and buckled the thongs below his knees. Jackson sat at one side of the hearth; in the shadowy corner near his feet a number of small, living creatures moiled silently, and still bent over his boots Bayard said:

"What you got there, Jackson? What sort of puppies are them?"

"New breed I'm tryin'," Jackson answered, and Rafe approached with a half a tumbler of Henry's pale amber whisky.

"Them's Ethel's pups," he said. "Git Jackson to tell you about 'em after you eat. Here, drink this. You look all wore out. Buddy must a kept you awake, talkin'," he added, with dry irony.

Bayard accepted the glass and emptied it, and lit a cigarette. "Mandy's got yo' breakfast on the stove," Rafe added.

"Ethel?" Bayard repeated. "Oh, that fox. I aimed to ask about her, last night."

"Yes, Jackson aims to revolutionize the huntin' business, with her. Aims to raise a breed of animals with a hound's wind and bottom, and a fox's smartness and speed."

Bayard approached the shadowy corner and examined the small creatures with interest and curiosity.

"I never saw many fox pups," he said at last, "but I never saw any that looked like them."

"That's what Gen'ral seems to think," Rafe answered.

Jackson spat into the fire and stooped over the creatures. They knew his hands, and the moiling of them became more intense, and Bayard then noticed that they made no sound at all, not even puppy whimperings. "Hit's a experiment," Jackson explained. "The boys makes fun of 'em, but they haint no more'n weaned, yet. You wait and see."

"Dont know what you'll do with 'em," Rafe said brutally. "They wont be big enough for work stock. Better git yo' breakfast, Bayard."

"You wait and see," Jackson repeated. He touched the scramble of small bodies with his hands, in a gentle, protective gesture. "You cant tell nothin' 'bout a dawg 'twell hit's at least two months old, can you?" he appealed to Bayard, looking up at him with his vague, intense gaze from beneath his shaggy brows.

"Go git yo' breakfast, Bayard," Rafe repeated. "Buddy's done gone and left you."

He bathed his face with icy water in a tin pan on the porch, and ate his breakfast—ham and eggs and flapjacks and sorghum and coffee—while Mandy talked to him about his brother. When he returned to the house old Mr MacCallum was there. The puppies moiled inextricably in their corner, and the old man sat with his hands on his knees, watching them with bluff and ribald merriment, while Jackson sat nearby in a sort of hovering concern, like a hen.

"Come hyer, boy," the old man ordered when Bayard appeared. "Hyer, Rafe, git me that 'ere bait line." Rafe went out, returning presently with a bit of pork rind on the end of a string. The old man took it and rose, and hauled the puppies ungently into the light, where they crouched abjectly moiling—as strange a litter as Bayard had ever seen. No two of them looked alike, and none of them looked like anything else. Neither fox nor hound; partaking of both, yet neither; and despite their soft infancy, there was about them something monstrous and contradictory and obscene. Here a fox's keen, cruel muzzle between the melting, sad eyes of a hound and its mild ears; there limp ears tried valiantly to stand erect and failed ignobly in flapping points; shoebutton eyes in meek puppy faces, and limp brief tails brushed over with a faint, golden fuzz like the inside of a chestnut burr. As regards color, they ranged from pure reddish brown through an indiscriminate brindle to pure ticked beneath a faint dun cast; and one of them had, feature for feature, old General's face in comical miniature, even to his expression of sad and dignified disillusion. "Watch 'em, now," the old man ordered.

He got them all facing forward, then he dangled the meat directly behind them. Not one noticed it; he swept it back and forth above their heads; not one looked up. Then he swung it directly before their eyes; still they crouched diffidently on their young, unsteady legs and gazed at the meat with curiosity but without any interest at all and fell again to moiling soundlessly among themselves.

"You cant tell nothin' about a dawg—" Jackson began. His father interrupted him.

"Now, watch." He held the puppies with one hand and with the other he forced the meat into their mouths. Immediately they surged clumsily and eagerly over his hand, but he moved the meat away and at the length of the string he dragged it along the floor just ahead of them until they had attained a sort of scrambling lope. Then in midfloor he flicked the meat slightly aside, but without seeing it the group blundered on and into a shadowy corner, where the wall stopped them and from which there rose presently the patient, voiceless confusion of them. Jackson left his chair and picked them up and brought them back to the fire.

"Now, what do you think of them, for a pack of huntin' dogs?" the old man demanded. "Cant smell, cant bark, and damn ef I believe they kin see."

"You cant tell nothin' about a dawg—" Jackson essayed patiently.

"Gen'ral kin," his father interrupted. "Hyer, Rafe, call Gen'ral in hyer."

Rafe went to the door and called, and presently General entered, his claws hissing a little on the bare floor and his ticked coat beaded with rain, and he stood and looked into the old man's face with grave inquiry. "Come hyer," Mr MacCallum said, and the dog moved again, with slow dignity. At that moment he saw the puppies beneath Jackson's chair. He paused in midstride and for a moment he stood looking at them with fascination and bafflement and a sort of grave horror, then he gave his master one hurt, reproachful look and turned and departed, his tail between his legs. Mr MacCallum sat down and rumbled heavily within himself.

"You cant tell about dawgs—" Jackson repeated. He stooped and gathered up his charges, and stood up.

Mr MacCallum continued to rumble and shake. "Well, I dont blame the old feller," he said. "Ef I had to look around on a passel of chaps like them and say to myself Them's my boys—" But Jackson was gone. The old man sat and rumbled again, with enjoyment.

"Yes, suh, I reckon I'd feel 'bout as proud as he does. Rafe, han' me down my pipe."

All that day it rained, and the following day and the day after that. The dogs lurked about the house all morning, underfoot, or made brief excursions into the weather, returning to sprawl before the fire, drowsing and malodorous and steaming, until Henry came along and drove them out; twice from the door Bayard saw the fox, Ethel, fading with brisk diffidence across the yard. With the exception of Henry and Jackson, who had a touch of rheumatism, the others were somewhere out in the rain most of the day. But at mealtimes they gathered again, shucking their wet outer garments on the porch and stamping in to thrust their muddy, smoking boots to the fire while Henry was fetching the kettle and the jug. And last of all, Buddy, soaking wet.

Buddy had a way of getting his lean length up from his niche beside the chimney at any hour of the day and departing without a word, to return in an hour or six hours, or twelve or twenty-four or forty-eight, during which periods and despite the presence of Jackson and Henry and usually Lee, the place had a vague air of vacancy, until Bayard realized that the majority of the dogs were absent also. Hunting, they told Bayard when Buddy had been missing since breakfast.

"Why didn't he let me know?" he demanded.

"Maybe he thought you wouldn't keer to be out in the weather," Jackson suggested.

"Buddy dont mind weather," Henry explained. "One day's like another to him."

"Nothing aint anything to Buddy," Lee put in, in his bitter, passionate voice. He sat brooding in the

fire, his womanish hands moving restlessly on his
knees. "He's spent his whole life in that 'ere river
bottom, with a hunk of cold cawnbread to eat and a
passel of dawgs fer comp'ny." He rose abruptly and
quitted the room. Lee was in the late thirties. As a
child he had been sickly. He had a good tenor voice
and he was much in demand at Sunday singings. He
was supposed to be keeping company with a young
woman living in the hamlet of Mount Vernon, six
miles away. He spent much of his time tramping
moodily and alone about the countryside.

Henry spat into the fire and jerked his head after
the departing brother. "He been to Vernon lately?"

"Him and Rafe was there two days ago," Jackson
answered.

Bayard said: "Well, I wont melt. I wonder if I
could catch up with him now?"

They pondered for a while, spitting gravely into
the fire. "I misdoubt it," Jackson said at last.
"Buddy's liable to be ten mile away by now. You
ketch 'im next time 'fo' he starts out."

After that Bayard did so, and he and Buddy tried
for birds in the ragged, skeletoned fields in the rain,
in which the guns made a flat, mournful sound that
lingered in the streaming air like a spreading stain, or
tried the stagnant backwaters along the river channel
for duck and geese; or, accompanied now and then
by Rafe, hunted 'coon and wildcat in the bottom. At
times and far away, they would hear the shrill yapping of the young dogs in mad career. "There goes
Ethel," Buddy would remark. Then toward the end
of the week the weather cleared, and in a twilight
imminent with frost and while the scent lay well
upon the muddy earth, old General started the red
fox that had baffled him so many times.

All through the night the ringing, bell-like tones

quavered and swelled and echoed among the hills, and all of them save Henry followed on horseback, guided by the cries of the hounds but mostly by the old man's and Buddy's uncanny and seemingly clairvoyant skill in anticipating the course of the race. Occasionally they stopped while Buddy and his father wrangled about where the quarry would head next, but usually they agreed, apparently anticipating the animal's movements before it knew them itself; and once and again they halted their horses upon a hill and sat so in the frosty starlight until the dogs' voices welled out of the darkness mournful and chiming, swelled louder and nearer and swept invisibly past not half a mile away; faded diminishing and with a falling suspense, as of bells, into the darkness again.

"Thar, now!" the old man exclaimed, shapeless in his overcoat, upon his white horse. "Aint that music fer a man, now?"

"I hope they git 'im this time," Jackson said. "Hit hurts Gen'ral's conceit so much ever' time he fools 'im."

"They wont git 'im," Buddy said. "Soon's he gits tired, he'll hole up in them rocks."

"I reckon we'll have to wait till them pups of Jackson's gits big enough," the old man agreed. "Unless they'll refuse to run they own gran'pappy. They done refused ever' thing else excep' vittles."

"You jest wait," Jackson repeated, indefatigable. "When them puppies git old enough to—"

"Listen."

The talking ceased, and again across the silence the dogs' voices rang among the hills. Long, ringing cries fading, falling with a quavering suspense, like touched bells or strings, repeated and sustained by bell-like echoes repeated and dying among the dark hills beneath the stars, lingering yet in the ears crystal-clear, mournful and valiant and a little sad.

"Too bad Johnny aint here," Stuart said quietly. "He'd enjoy this race."

"He was a feller fer huntin', now," Jackson agreed. "He'd keep up with Buddy, even."

"John was a fine boy," the old man said.

"Yes, suh," Jackson repeated. "A right warm-hearted boy. Henry says he never come out hyer withouten he brung Mandy and the boys a little sto'-bought somethin'."

"He never sulled on a hunt," Stuart said. "No matter how cold and wet it was, even when he was a little chap, with that 'ere single bar'l he bought with his own money, that kicked 'im so hard ever' time he shot it. And yit he'd tote it around, instead of that 'ere sixteen old Colonel give 'im, jest because he saved his money and bought hit hisself."

"Yes," Jackson agreed, "ef a feller gits into some-thin' on his own accord, he ought to go through with hit cheerful."

"He was sho' a feller fer singin' and shoutin'," Mr MacCallum said. "Skeer all the game in ten mile. I mind that night he headed off a race down at Sam-son's bridge, and next we knowed, here him and the fox come a-floatin' down river on that 'ere drift lawg."

"That 'uz Johnny, all over," Jackson agreed. "Git-tin' a whoppin' big time outen ever' thing that come up."

"He was a fine boy," Mr MacCallum said again.

"Listen."

Again the hounds gave tongue in the darkness below them. The sound floated up upon the chill air, died into echoes that repeated the sound again until its source was lost and the very earth itself might have found voice, mournful and sad and wild with all regret.

Christmas was two days away, and they sat again about the fire after supper; again old General dozed at his master's feet. Tomorrow was Christmas eve and the wagon was going into town, and although, with that grave and unfailing hospitality of theirs, no word had been said to Bayard about his departure, he believed that in all their minds it was taken for granted that he would return home the following day for Christmas; and, since he had not mentioned it himself, a little curiosity and quiet speculation also.

It was cold again, with a vivid chill that caused the blazing logs to pop and crackle with vicious sparks and small glowing embers that leaped out upon the floor, to be crushed out by a lazy boot, and Bayard sat drowsily in a drowse of heat, his tired muscles relaxed in the cumulate waves of it as in a warm bath, and the stubborn struggling of his heart glozed over too, for the time. Time enough tomorrow to decide whether to go or not. Perhaps he'd just stay on, without offering that explanation that would never be demanded of him. Then he realized that Rafe, Lee, whoever went, would talk to people, would learn about that which he had not the courage to tell them.

Buddy had come out of his shadowy niche and he now squatted in the center of the semicircle, his back to the fire and his arms around his knees, with his motionless and seemingly tireless ability for sitting timelessly on his heels. He was the baby, twenty years old. His mother was the old man's second wife, and his hazel eyes and the reddish thatch cropped closely to his round head was a noticeable contrast to the others' brown eyes and black hair. But the old man had stamped Buddy's face as clearly as ever a one of the other boys, and despite its youth, it too was like the others—aquiline and spare, reserved and grave though a trifle ruddy with his fresh coloring and finer skin.

The others were of medium height or under, ranging from Jackson's faded, vaguely ineffectual lankness, through Henry's placid rotundity and Rafe's (Raphael Semmes he was) and Stuart's poised and stocky muscularity, to Lee's thin and fiery unrepose; but Buddy with his sapling-like leanness stood eye to eye with that father who wore his eighty-two years as though they were a thin shirt. "Long, spindlin' scoundrel," the old man would say, with bluff, assumed derogation. "Keeps hisself wore to a shadder totin' around all that 'ere grub he eats." And they would sit in silence, looking at Buddy's lean, jack-knifed length with the same identical thought, a thought which each believed peculiar to himself and which none ever divulged—that someday Buddy would marry and perpetuate the name.

Buddy also bore his father's name, though it is doubtful if anyone outside the family and the War Department knew it. He had run away at eighteen and enlisted; at the infantry concentration camp in Arkansas to which he had been sent, a fellow recruit called him Virge and Buddy had fought him steadily and without anger for seven minutes; at the New Jersey embarcation depot another man had done the same thing, and Buddy had fought him, again steadily and thoroughly and without anger. In Europe, still following the deep but uncomplex compulsions of his nature, he had contrived, unwittingly perhaps, to perpetrate something which was later ascertained by authority to have severely annoyed the enemy, for which Buddy had received his charm, as he called it. What it was he did, he could never be brought to tell, and the gaud not only failing to placate his father's rage over the fact that a son of his had joined the Federal army, but on the contrary adding fuel to it, the bauble languished among Buddy's sparse effects and his military career was never mentioned in the family circle; and now as usual Buddy squatted among them, his back to the fire and his arms around his knees, while they sat about the hearth with their bedtime toddies, talking of Christmas.

"Turkey," the old man was saying, with fine and rumbling disgust. "With a pen full of 'possums, and a river bottom full of squir'ls and ducks, and a smokehouse full of hawg meat, you damn boys have got to go clean to town and buy a turkey fer Christmas dinner."

"Christmas aint Christmas lessen a feller has a little somethin' different from ever' day," Jackson pointed out mildly.

"You boys jest wants a excuse to git to town and loaf around all day and spend money," the old man retorted. "I've seen a sight mo' Christmases than you have, boy, and ef hit's got to be sto'-bought, hit aint Christmas."

"How 'bout town-folks?" Rafe asked. "You aint allowin' them no Christmas a-tall."

"Dont deserve none," the old man snapped. "Livin' on a little two-by-fo' lot, jam right up in the next feller's back do', eatin' outen tin cans."

"Sposin' they all broke up in town," Stuart said, "and moved out here and took up land; you'd hear pappy cussin' town then. You couldn't git along without town to keep folks bottled up in, pappy, and you knows it."

"Buyin' turkeys," Mr MacCallum repeated with savage disgust. "Buyin' 'em. I mind the time when I could take a gun and step out that 'ere do' and git a gobbler in thirty minutes. And a venison ham in a hour mo'. Why, you fellers dont know nothin' about Christmas. All you knows is a sto' winder full of co-coanuts and Yankee-made popguns and sich."

"Yes, suh," Rafe said, and he winked at Bayard, "that was the biggest mistake the world ever made, when Lee surrendered. The country aint never got over it."

The old man snorted again. "I be damned ef I aint raised the damdest smartest set of boys in the world. Cant tell 'em nothin', cant learn 'em nothin'; cant even set in front of my own fire fer the whole passel of 'em tellin' me how to run the whole damn country. Hyer, you boys, git on to bed."

Next morning Jackson and Rafe and Stuart and Lee left for town at sunup in the wagon. Still none of them had made any sign, expressed any curiosity as to whether they would find him there when they returned that night, or whether it would be another three years before they saw him again. And Bayard stood on the frost-whitened porch, smoking a cigarette in the chill, vivid air while the yet hidden sun painted the eastern hills, and looked after the wagon and the four muffled figures in it and wondered if it would be three years again, or ever. The hounds came and nuzzled about him and he dropped his hand among their icy noses and the warm flicking of their tongues, gazing after the wagon, hidden now among the trees from which the dry rattling of it came unimpeded upon the soundless clear morning.

"Ready to go?" Buddy said behind him, and he turned and picked up his shotgun where it leaned against the wall. The hounds surged about them with eager whimperings and frosty breaths and Buddy led them across to a shed and huddled them inside and fastened the door upon their surprised protests. From another kennel he unfastened the young pointer, Dan. Behind them the hounds continued to raise their baffled and mellow expostulations.

Until noon they hunted the ragged, fallow fields and woods-edges in the warming air. The frost was soon gone, and the air warmed to a windless languor; and twice in brier thickets they saw redbirds darting like arrows of scarlet flame. At last Bayard lifted his eyes unwinking into the sun.

"I must go back, Buddy," he said. "I'm going home this afternoon."

"All right," Buddy agreed without protest, and he called the dog in. "You come back next month."

Mandy got them some cold food and they ate, and while Buddy went to saddle Perry, Bayard went into the house where he found Henry laboriously soling a pair of shoes and the old man reading a week-old newspaper through steel-bowed spectacles.

"I reckon yo' folks will be lookin' fer you," Mr MacCallum agreed. "We'll be expectin' you back next month, though, to git that 'ere fox. Ef we dont git 'im soon, Gen'ral wont be able to hold up his head befo' them puppies."

"Yes, sir," Bayard answered, "I will."

"And try to git yo' gran'pappy to come with you. He kin lay around hyer and eat his head off well as he kin in town."

"Yes, sir, I will."

Then Buddy led the pony up to the door, and the old man extended his hand without rising, and Henry put aside his cobbling and followed him onto the porch. "Come out again," he said diffidently, giving Bayard's hand a single pump-handle shake; and from a slobbering inquisitive surging of half-grown hounds Buddy reached up his hand.

"Be lookin' fer you," he said briefly, and together they stood and watched Bayard wheel away, and when he looked back they lifted their hands gravely. Then Buddy shouted after him and he reined Perry about and returned. Henry had vanished, and he reappeared with a weighted tow sack.

"I nigh fergot it," he said. "Jug of cawn pappy's sendin' in to yo' gran'paw. You wont git no better in Looeyvul ner nowhar else, neither," he added with quiet pride. Bayard thanked him, and Buddy fastened the sack to the pommel, where it lay solidly against his leg.

"There. That'll ride. So long."

"So long."

Perry moved on, and he looked back. They still stood there, quiet and grave and steadfast. Beside the kitchen door the fox, Ethel, sat, looking at him covertly; near her the half-grown puppies moved about in the sun. The sun was an hour above the western hills; the road wound on into the trees. He looked back again, the house sprawled its rambling length against the further trees, its smoke like a balanced plume against the windless sky. The door was empty again. He shook Perry into his easy, tireless foxtrot, the jug of whisky jouncing a little against his knee.

6

Where the dim, infrequent road to MacCallum's left the main road, rising, he halted Perry and sat for a while in the sunset. Jefferson, 14 miles. Rafe and the other boys would not be along for some time, yet, what with Christmas eve in town and the slow festive gathering of the county. Still, they may have left town early, so as to get home by dark; might not be an hour away. The sun's rays, slanting away, released the chill they had held prisoned in the ground during the perpendicular hours, and it rose slowly and gradually about him as he sat Perry in the middle of the road, and slowly his blood cooled with the cessation of Perry's motion. He turned the pony's back to town and shook him into his foxtrot again.

Darkness overtook him soon, but he rode on beneath the leafless trees, along the pale road in the gathering starlight. Already Perry was thinking of stable and supper and he went on with tentative, inquiring tossings of his head, but obediently and without slackening his gait, knowing not where they were going nor why, save that it was away from home, and a little dubious, though trustfully. The chill grew in the silence and the loneliness and the monotony of their progress. He reined Perry to a halt and produced the jug and drank, and fastened the sack to the saddle again.

The hills rose wild and black about him; no sign of any habitation, no trace of man's hand did they encounter. On all sides the hills rolled blackly away in the starlight, or when the road dipped into valleys where the ruts were already stiffening into iron-like shards that rattled beneath Perry's hooves, they stood about him darkly towering and sinister, feathering their leafless branches against the spangled sky. Where a stream of winter seepage trickled across the road Perry's feet crackled brittly in this ice, and Bayard slacked the reins while the pony snuffed at the water, and drank again from the jug.

He fumbled a match clumsily in his cold fingers and lit a cigarette, and pushed his sleeve back from his wrist. 11:30. "Well, Perry," his voice sounded loud and sudden in the stillness and darkness and the cold, "I reckon we better look for a place to hole up till morning." Perry raised his head and snorted, as though he understood the words, as though he would enter the bleak loneliness in which his rider moved, if he could. They went on, mounting again.

The darkness spread away, lessening a little presently where occasional fields lay in the vague starlight, breaking the monotony of trees; and after a time during which he rode with the reins slack on Perry's neck and his hands in his pockets seeking warmth between leather and groin, a cotton house squatted beside the road, its roof dusted over with a frosty sheen as of hushed silver. Not long, he said to himself, leaning forward and laying his hand on Perry's neck, feeling the warm, tireless blood there. "House soon, Perry, if we look sharp."

Again Perry whinneyed a little, as though he had understood, and presently he swerved from the road, and as Bayard reined him up he too saw the faint wagon trail leading away toward a low vague clump of trees. "Good boy, Perry," he said, slackening the reins again.

The house was a cabin. It was dark, but a hound came gauntly from beneath it and bayed at him and continued its uproar while he reined Perry to the door and knocked upon it with his numb hand. From within the house at last a voice, indistinguishable, and he repeated "Hello." Then he added: "I'm lost. Open the door. " The hound continued to bellow at him, and the door cracked upon a dying glow of embers, emitting a rank odor of negroes, and against the crack of warmth, a head.

"You, Jule," the head commanded. "Shut yo' mouf." The hound ceased obediently and retired beneath the house, growling. "Who dar?"

"I'm lost," Bayard repeated. "Can I sleep in your barn tonight?"

"Aint got no barn," the negro answered. "Dey's anudder house down de road a piece."

"I'll pay you." Bayard fumbled in his trousers with his numb hand. "My horse is tired out." The negro's head peered around the door, against the crack of firelight. "Come on, uncle," Bayard added impatiently, "don't keep a man standing in the cold."

"Who is you, whitefolks?"

"Bayard Sartoris, from Jefferson. Here," and he extended his hand.

"Banker Sartoris's folks?"

"Yes. Here."

"Wait a minute." The door closed. But Bayard tightened the reins and Perry moved readily and circled the house confidently and went on among frost-stiffened cotton stalks that clattered drily about his knees. As Bayard dismounted onto frozen rutted earth beneath a gaping doorway, a lantern approached, swung low among the bitten stalks and the shadowy scissoring of the man's legs, and he came up with a shapeless bundle under his arm and stood with the lantern while Bayard stripped the saddle and bridle off.

"How you manage to git so fur f'um home dis time o' night, whitefolks?" he asked curiously.

"Lost," Bayard answered briefly. "Where can I put my horse?"

The negro swung the lantern into a stall. Perry stepped carefully over the sill and turned into the lantern light again, his eyes rolling in phosphorescent gleams; Bayard followed and rubbed him down with the dry side of the saddle blanket. The negro vanished and reappeared with a few ears of corn and dumped them into the manger beside Perry's eager nuzzling. "You gwine be keerful about fire, aint you, boss?"

"Sure. I won't strike any matches at all."

"I got all my stock and tools and feed in here," the negro explained. "I cant affo'd to git burnt out. Insu'ance dont reach dis fur."

"Sure," Bayard repeated. He shut Perry's stall and drew the sack forth from where he had set it against the wall, and produced the jug. "Got a cup here?" The negro vanished again and Bayard could hear him in the crib in the wall opposite, then he emerged with a rusty can, from which he blew a bursting puff of chaff. They drank. Behind them Perry crunched his corn. The negro showed him the ladder to the loft.

"You wont fergit about no fire, boss?" he repeated anxiously.

"Sure," Bayard said. "Goodnight." He turned to mount. Again the negro stopped him and handed him the shapeless bundle he had brought out with him.

"Aint got but one to spare, but hit'll help some. You gwine to sleep cole, tonight." It was a quilt, ragged and filthy to the touch, and impregnated with that unmistakable odor of negroes.

"Thanks," Bayard answered. "Much obliged to you. Goodnight."

"Goodnight, whitefolks."

The lantern winked away, to the criss-crossing of the negro's legs, and Bayard mounted into darkness and the dry, pungent scent of hay. Here, in the darkness, he made himself a bed of it and lay down and rolled himself into the quilt, filth and odor and all, and thrust his icy hands inside his shirt, against his flenching chest. After a time and slowly his hands began to warm, tingling a little, but still his body lay shivering with weariness and with cold. Below him

Perry munched steadily and peacefully in the darkness, and gradually the shaking of his body ceased. Before he slept he uncovered his arm and looked at the luminous dial on his wrist. One oclock. It was already Christmas.

The sun waked him, falling in red bars through the cracks in the wall, and he lay for a time in his hard bed, with vivid chill upon his face like fresh city water, wondering where he was. Then he remembered, and moving, found that he was stiff with stale cold and that his blood moved through his arms and legs in small pellets like bird-shot. He dragged his legs from his odorous bed, but within his boots his feet were dead, and he sat flexing his knees and ankles for some time before his feet waked as with stinging needles. His movements were stiff and awkward, and he descended the ladder slowly and gingerly into the red sun that fell like a blare of trumpets into the hallway. The sun was just above the horizon, huge and red; and housetop, fenceposts, the casual farming tools rusting about the barnyard and the dead cotton stalks where the negro had farmed his land right up to his back door, were dusted over with frost which the sun changed to a scintillant rosy icing like that on a festive cake. Perry thrust his slender muzzle across the stall door and whinneyed at his master with vaporous fading puffs of frosty breath, and Bayard spoke to him and touched his cold nose. Then he uncovered the jug again and drank, and the negro with a milk pail appeared in the doorway.

"Mawnin', whitefolks. You g'awn to de house to de fire. I'll feed yo' hawss. De ole woman got yo' breakfus' ready." He was eyeing the jug and Bayard gave him another drink and picked up the sack. At the well he stopped and drew a pail of icy water and splashed his face.

A fire burned on the broken hearth, amid ashes and charred wood-ends and a litter of cooking vessels. Bayard shut the door behind him, upon the bright cold, and warmth and rich, stale rankness enveloped him. A woman bent over the fire replied to his greeting diffidently. Three pickaninnies became utterly still in a corner and watched him with rolling white eyes. One of them was a girl, in greasy, nondescript garments, her wool twisted into tight knots of soiled wisps of colored cloth. The second one might have been either or anything. The third one was practically helpless in a garment made from a man's suit of wool underclothes. It was too small to walk and it crawled about the floor in a sort of intense purposelessness, a glazed path running from either nostril to its chin, as though snails had crawled there.

Without looking at him the woman placed a chair before the fire, and Bayard seated himself and thrust his boots to the blaze. "Had your Christmas dram yet, aunty?" he asked.

"Naw, suh. Aint got none, dis year."

He swung the sack across his legs and set it on the floor. "Help yourself," he said. "Plenty in there." The three children squatted against the wall, watching him steadily, without movement and without sound. "Christmas come yet, chillen?" he asked them. But they only stared at him with the watchful gravity of animals until the woman returned and spoke to them in a chiding tone.

"Show de whitefolks yo' Sandy Claus," she prompted. "Thanky, suh," she added, putting a tin plate on his lap and setting a cracked china cup on the hearth at his feet. "Show 'im," she repeated.

"You want folks to think Sandy Claus dont know whar you lives at?"

The children stirred then, and from the shadow behind them, where they had hidden them when he entered, they produced a small tin automobile, a string of colored wooden beads, a small mirror and a huge stick of peppermint candy to which trash adhered and which they immediately fell to licking gravely, turn and turn about. The woman filled the cup from the coffee pot set among the embers, and she uncovered an iron skillet and forked a thick slab of sizzling meat onto his plate, and raked a grayish object from the ashes and dusted it off and put that too on his plate. Bayard ate his side meat and hoecake and drank the thin, tasteless liquid. The children now played quietly with their Christmas, but from time to time he looked up and found them watching him again. Presently the man entered with his pail of milk.

"Ole 'oman give you a snack?" he asked.

"Ye. What's the nearest town on the railroad?" he inquired. The other told him—eight miles away. "Can you drive me over there this morning, and take my horse back to MacCallum's some day this week?"

"My brudder-in-law bor'd my mules," the negro answered readily. "I aint got but de one span, and he done bor'd dem."

"I'll pay you five dollars."

The negro set the pail down, and the woman came and got it. He scratched his head slowly. "Five dollars," Bayard repeated.

"You's in a pow'ful rush, fer Chris'mus, whitefolks."

"Ten dollars," Bayard said impatiently. "Cant you get your mules from your brother-in-law?"

"I reckon so. I reckon he'll bring 'um back by dinnertime. We kin go den."

"Why cant you get 'em now? Take my horse and go get 'em. I want to catch a train."

"I aint had no Chris'mus yit, whitefolks. Feller workin ev'y day of de year wants a little Chris'mus."

Bayard swore beneath his breath, but he said: "All right, then. After dinner. But you see your brother-in-law has 'em back here in time."

"He'll be here: dont you worry about dat."

"All right. You and aunty help yourselves to the jug."

"Thanky, suh."

The stale, airtight room dulled him; the warmth was insidious to his bones wearied and stiff after the chill night. The negroes moved about the single room, the woman busy at the hearth with her cooking, the pickaninnies with their frugal and sorry gewgaws and filthy candy. Bayard sat in his chair and dozed the morning away. Not asleep, but time was lost in a timeless region where he lingered unawake and into which he realized after a long while that something was trying to penetrate; watched the vain attempts with peaceful detachment. But at last it succeeded: a voice. "Dinner ready."

The negroes drank with him again, amicably, a little diffidently—two opposed concepts antipathetic by race, blood, nature and environment, touching for a moment and fused within the illusion of a contradiction—humankind forgetting its lust and cowardice and greed for a day. Then dinner: 'possum with yams, more gray ashcake, the dead and tasteless liquid in the coffee pot; a dozen bananas and jagged shards of cocoanut, the children crawling about his feet like animals scenting food. He realized that they were holding back until he ate, but he overrode them; and at last (the mules having been miraculously returned by a yet incorporeal brother-in-law) with his depleted jug between his feet in the wagon bed, he looked once back at the cabin, with the woman standing in the door and a pale windless drift of smoke above its chimney.

Against the mules' gaunt ribs the broken harness rattled and jingled. The air was warm, yet laced too with a thin distillation of chill that darkness would increase. The road went on across the bright land. From time to time across the shining sedge or from beyond brown and leafless woods, came the flat reports of guns; occasionally they passed other teams or horsemen or pedestrians, who lifted dark restful hands to the negro buttoned into an army overcoat, with brief covert glances for the white man on the seat beside him. "Heyo, Chris'mus!" Beyond the yellow sedge and the brown leafless ridges the ultimate hills stood bluely against the immaculate sky. "Heyo."

They stopped and drank, and Bayard gave his companion a cigarette. The sun behind them now; no cloud, no wind in the serene pale cobalt. "Shawt days! Fo' mile mo'. Come up, mules." Between motionless willows, stubbornly green, a dry clatter of loose planks above water in murmurous flashes. The road lifted redly; pines stood against the sky. They crested this, and a plateau rolled away before them with its pattern of burnished sedge and fallow fields and brown woodland, and now and then a house, on into a shimmering azure haze, and low down on the horizon, smoke. "Two mile, now." Behind them the sun was a balloon tethered an hour above the trees. They drank again.

It had touched the horizon when they looked

down into the final valley where the railroad's shining threads vanished among houses and trees, and along the air to them distantly, there came a slow, heavy explosion. "Still celebratin'," the negro said.

They descended the final hill, among houses, in the windows of which hung wreathes and paper bells, and whose stoops were littered with spent firecrackers; and went along streets where children in bright sweaters and jackets sped on shiny coasters and skates and wagons. Again a heavy explosion from the dusk ahead, and they debouched into the square with its Sabbath calm, littered too with shattered scraps of paper. It looked like that at home, he knew, with men and youths he had known from boyhood lounging the holiday away, drinking a little and shooting fireworks, giving nickels and dimes and quarters to negro boys who shouted Chris'mus gif'! Chris'mus gif'! as they passed; and after dark, somewhere a dance, with holly and mistletoe and paper streamers, and the girls he had always known with their new bracelets and watches and fans amid warmth and lights and music and glittering laughter. A small group stood on a corner, and as they passed and preceded by a sudden scurry among the group, yellow flame was stencilled abruptly on the twilight and the heavy explosion reverberated in sluggish echoes. The mules quickened against their collars and the wagon rattled on.

There were lights within the houses now, behind the wreathes and the rotund bells, and through the dusk voices called with mellow insistence; children's voices replied, expostulant, reluctantly regretful. Then the station, where a 'bus and four or five cars stood aligned, and Bayard descended and the negro lifted down the sack.

"Much obliged," Bayard said. "Goodbye."

"Goodbye, whitefolks."

In the waiting room a stove glowed red hot and about the room stood cheerful groups, in sleek furs and overcoats, but he did not enter. He set the sack against the wall and tramped up and down the platform, warming his blood again. In both directions along the tracks green switch lights were steady in the dusk; a hands-breadth above the western trees the evening star was like an electric bulb. He tramped back and forth, glancing now and then into the ruddy windows, into the waiting room where the cheerful groups in their furs and overcoats gesticulated with festive though soundless animation, and into the colored waiting room, whose occupants sat patiently and murmurously about the stove in the dingy light. As he turned here a voice spoke diffidently from the shadow beside the door. "Chris'mus gif', boss." He took a coin from his pocket, and went on. Again from the square a firecracker exploded heavily, and above the trees a rocket arced, hung for a moment, then opened like a closed fist, spreading its golden and fading fingers upon the serene indigo sky without a sound.

Then the train came and brought its lighted windows to a jarring halt, and he picked up his sack again. And in the midst of a cheerful throng shouting goodbyes and holiday greetings to one another, he got aboard, unshaven, in his scarred boots and stained khaki pants, and his shabby, smoke-colored tweed jacket and his disreputable felt hat, and found a vacant seat and stowed the jug away beneath his legs.

FIVE

I

". . . and since the essence of spring is loneliness and a little sadness and a sense of mild frustration, I suppose you do get a keener purifaction when a little nostalgia is thrown in for good measure. At home I always found myself remembering apple trees or green lanes or the color of the sea in other places, and I'd be sad that I couldn't be everywhere at once, or that all the spring couldn't be concentrated in one place, like Byron's ladies' mouths. But now I seem to be unified and projected upon one single and very definite object, which is something to be said for me, after all." Horace's pen ceased and he gazed at the sheet scrawled over with his practically illegible script, while the words he had just written echoed yet in his mind with a little gallant and whimsical sadness, and for the time being he had quitted the desk and the room and the town and all the crude and blatant newness into which his destiny had brought him, and again that wild and delicate futility of his roamed unchallenged through the lonely region into which it had at last concentrated its conflicting parts. Already the thick cables along the veranda eaves would be budding into small lilac matchpoints, and with no effort at all he could see the lawn below the cedars, splashed with random narcissi among random fading jonquils and gladioli waiting to bloom in turn.

But his body sat motionless, its hand with the arrested pen upon the scrawled sheet, the paper lying upon the yellow varnished surface of his new desk. The chair in which he sat was new too, as was the room with its dead white walls and imitation oak woodwork. All day long the sun fell upon it, untempered by any shade. In the days of early spring it had been pleasant, falling as it now did through his western window and across the desk where a white hyacinth bloomed in a bowl of glazed maroon pottery. But as he sat musing, staring out the window where, beyond a tarred roof that drank heat like a sponge and radiated it, against a brick wall a clump of ragged heaven trees lifted shabby, diffident bloom, he dreaded the long hot summer days of sunlight upon the roof directly above him, remembered his dim and musty office at home, in which a breeze seemed always to move, with its serried undisturbed rows of dusty books that seemed to emanate coolness and dimness even on the hottest days. And thinking of this, he was again lost from the harsh newness in which his body sat. The pen moved again.

"Perhaps fortitude is a sorry imitation of something worth while, after all. To the so many who burrow along like moles in the dark, or like owls, to whom a candle-flame is a surfeit. But not those who carry peace along with them as the candle-flame carries light. I have always been ordered by words, but now it seems that I can even restore courage to my own cowardice by cozening it a little. I daresay you cannot read this as usual, or reading it, it will not mean anything to you. But you will have served your purpose anyway, thou still unravished bride of quietude." Thou wast happier in thy cage, happier? Horace thought, looking at the words he had written and in which, as usual, he was washing one woman's linen in the house of another. A thin breeze blew suddenly into the room; there was locust upon it, faintly sweet, and beneath it the paper stirred upon the desk, rousing him; and suddenly, as a man waking, he looked at his watch and replaced it and wrote rapidly:

"We are very glad to have little Belle with us. She likes it here: there is a whole family of little girls next door: stair steps of tow pigtails before whom it must be confessed that little Belle preens just a little; patronizes them. Children make all the difference in the world about a house. Too bad agents are not wise enough to supply rented houses with them. Particularly one like little Belle, so grave and shining and sort of irrelevantly and intensely mature, you know. But then, you dont know her very well, do you? But we both are very glad to have her with us. I believe that Harry " The pen ceased, and still poised, he sought the words that so rarely eluded him, realizing as he did so that, though one can lie about others with ready and extemporaneous promptitude, to lie about oneself requires deliberation and a careful choice of expression. Then he glanced again at his watch and scratched that out and wrote: "Belle sends love, O Serene." and blotted it and folded it swiftly into an envelope and addressed and stamped it, and rose and took his hat.

Thou wast happier in thy cage, happier . . . The corridor, with its rubber mat and identical closed doors expensively and importantly discreet; the stairway with its brass-bound steps and at each turning, a heavy brass receptacle in which cigarette butts and scraps of paper reposed upon tobacco-stained sand, all new, all smelling of recent varnish. There was a foyer of imitation oak and imitation marble; the street in an untempered glare of spring sunlight. The building too was new and an imitation of something else, or maybe a skillful and even more durable imitation of that, as was the whole town, the very spirit, the essence of which was crystallized in the courthouse building—an edifice imposing as a theatre drop, flamboyant and cheap and shoddy; obviously built without any definite plan by men without honesty or taste. It was a standing joke that it had cost $60,000, and the people who had paid for it retailed the story without anger, but on the contrary with a little frankly envious admiration.

Ten years ago the town was a hamlet, twelve miles from the railroad. Then a hardwood lumber concern had bought up the cypress swamps nearby and established a factory in the town. It was financed by eastern capital and operated by as plausible and affable a set of brigands as ever stole a county. They robbed the stockholders and the timber owners and one another and spent the money among the local merchants, who promptly caught the enthusiasm, and presently widows and orpahns in New York and New England were buying Stutz cars and imported caviar and silk dresses and diamond watches at three prices, and the town bootleggers and the moonshiners in the adjacent swamps waxed rich, and every fourth year the sheriff's office sold at public auction for the price of a Hollywood bungalow. People in the neighboring counties learned of all this and moved there and chopped all the trees down and built themselves mile after mile of identical frame houses with garage to match: the very air smelled of affluence and burning gasoline. Yes, there was money there, how much, no two estimates ever agreed; whose, at any one given time, God Himself

could not have said. But it was there, like that afflatus
of rank fecundity above a foul and stagnant pool on
which bugs dart spawning, die, are replaced in mid-
darting; in the air, in men's voices and gestures,
seemingly to be had for the taking. That was why
Belle had chosen it.

But for the time being Horace was utterly oblivious of its tarnished fury as he walked along the
street toward the new, ugly yellow station, carrying
his letter the words of which yet echoed derisively in
his mind   Belle sends love Belle sends love. He had
made acquaintances "In spite of yourself," Belle told
him harshly. "Thinking you are better than other
people." Yes, he had answered. Yes, with a weariness
too spent to argue with its own sense of integrity.
But he had made a few, some of whom he now
passed, was greeted, replied: merchants, another lawyer, his barber; a young man who was trying to sell
him an automobile. Naturally Belle would   Belle
sends love Belle sends   He still carried his letter in
his hand and glancing at the bulletin board on the
station wall he saw that the train was a little late, and
he went on down the platform to where the mail car
would stop and gave the letter to the mail carrier—a
lank, goose-necked man with a huge pistol strapped
to his thigh   Thou wast happier   The express
agent came along, dragging his truck   in thy cage,
happier   "Got another 'un today?" he asked, greeting Horace.

"What?" Horace said. "Oh, good afternoon."

"Got another 'un today?" the other repeated.

"Yes," Horace answered, watching the other
swing the truck skillfully into position beside the
rails   Happier   The sun was warm; already there
was something of summer's rankness in it—a quality
which, at home where among green and ancient trees

and graver and more constant surroundings, dwelt quietude and the soul's annealment, it had not even in July. Soon, soon, he said, and again he went voyaging alone from where his body leaned against a strange wall in a brief hiatus of the new harsh compulsions it now suffered. This will not last always: I have made too little effort to change my fellow man's actions and beliefs to have won a place in anyone's plan of infinity   In thy cage, happier?

The locomotive slid past, rousing him: he had not heard it, and the cars on rasping wheels, and from the door of the express car the clerk with a pencil stuck jauntily beneath his cap, flipped his hand at him. "Here you are, Professor," he said, handing down first to the agent a small wooden crate from which moisture dripped. "Smelling a little stout, today, but the fish wont mind that, will they?" Horace approached, his nostrils tightening a little. The clerk in the car door was watching him with friendly curiosity. "Say," he asked, "what kind of city fish you got around here, that have to have mail-order bait?"

"It's shrimp," Horace explained.

"Shrimp?" the other repeated. "Eat 'em yourself, do you?" he asked with interest.

"Yes. My wife's very fond of them."

"Well, I'll be damned," the clerk said heartily. "I thought it was some kind of patent fish-bait you were getting every Tuesday. Well, every man to his taste, I reckon. But I'll take steak, myself. All right, Bud; grab it."

Horace signed the agent's receipt and lifted the crate from the truck, holding it carefully away from himself. The smell invariably roused in him a faint but definite repulsion which he was not able to overcome, though Belle preferred shrimp above all foods. And it always seemed to him for hours afterward that the smell clung about his clothing, despite the fact that he knew better, knew that he had carried the package well clear of himself. He carried it so now, his elbow against his side and his forearm at a slight, tense angle with the dripping weight.

Behind him the bell rang, and with the bitten, deep snorts of starting, the train moved. He looked back and saw the cars slide past, gaining speed, carrying his letter away and the quiet, the intimacy the writing and the touching of it, had brought him. But day after tomorrow he could write again *Belle sends love Belle sends* Ah, well, we all respond to strings. And *She* would understand, it and the necessity for it, the dreadful need; *She* in her serene aloofness partaking of gods *Belle sends*

The street from curb to curb was uptorn. It was in the throes of being paved. Along it lines of negroes labored with pick and shovel, swinging their tools in a languid rhythm, steadily and with a lazy unhaste that seemed to spend itself in snatches of plaintive minor chanting punctuated by short grunting ejaculations which died upon the sunny air and ebbed away from the languid rhythm of picks that struck not; shovels that did not dig. Further up the street a huge misshapen machine like an antediluvian nightmare clattered and groaned. It dominated the scene with its noisy and measured fury, but against this as against a heroic frieze, the negroes labored on, their chanting and their motions more soporific than a measured tolling of far away bells.

His arm was becoming numb, but the first mark—a water plug—where he changed hands for the first time, was still a hundred yards away; and when he reached it and swapped the crate to the other hand, his fingers were dead of all sensation and his biceps was jumping a little within his sleeve. Which goes to prove the fallacy of all theories of physical training. According to that, every succeeding Tuesday he should be able to go a little further without changing, until by Christmas he would be able to carry the package all the way home without changing hands; and by Christmas ten years, all the way back to Gulfport, where they came from. Prize, maybe. More letters behind his name, anyway. C.S. Carrier of Shrimp. H. Benbow, M.A., Ll.D., C.S. Thou wast happier

The next mark was the corner where he turned, and he went on along the treeless street, between smug rows of houses identical one with another. Cheap frame houses, patently new, each with a garage and a car, usually a car that cost as much again as the house did. He reached the corner and changed hands again and turned into a smaller street, trailing spaced drops of melting ice behind him.

He lived on this street, and it was still open: motors could run on it, and he went on, dripping his trailing moisture along the sidewalk. With a motor car now, he could have Soon; perhaps next year; then things But naturally Belle would miss her car, after having had one always, a new one every year. Harry, and his passion for shiny wheels . . . which some would call generosity . . . "You lied to me. You told me you had plenty of money" Lied Lied took me away from my Well, it would be better now, with little Belle. And Harry would find . . . who functioned in movie subtitles, harshly: "What else do you want of mine? My dam blood?"

Man's life. No apparent explanation for it save as an opportunity for doing things he'd spend the rest of it not being very proud of. Well, she had her child again, anyway, he told himself, thinking how women never forgive the men who permit them to do the things which they later have any cause to regret; and remembering that day when, with little Belle's awkwardly packed suitcase in the rack overhead and little Belle primly beside him in a state of demure and shining excitement at the prospect of moving suddenly to a new town, he had shrunk into his corner like a felon until the familiar station and that picture of Harry's ugly dogged head and his eyes like those of a stricken ox, were left behind, he wondered if little Belle too would someday . . . But that last picture of Harry's face had a way of returning. It's only injured vanity, he argued with himself; he's hurt in his own estimation because he couldn't keep the female he had chosen in the world's sight. But still his eyes and their patient bloodshot bewilderment, to be exorcised somehow. He's a fool, anyway, he told himself savagely. And who has time to pity fools? Then he said God help us, God help us all, and then at last humor saved him and he thought with a fine whimsical flash of it that probably Belle would send him to Harry next for a motor car.

Man's very tragedies flout him. He has invented a masque for tragedy, given it the austerity which he believes the spectacle of himself warrants, and the thing makes faces behind his back; dead alone, he is not ridiculous, and even then only in his own eyes Thou wast happier   A voice piped with thin familiarity from beyond a fence. It was little Belle playing with the little girls next door, to whom she had already divulged with the bland naivete of children that Horace was not her real daddy: he was just the one that lived with them now, because her real daddy's name was Daddy and he lived in another town. It was a prettier town than this, while the little girls listened with respect coldly concealed: little Belle had gained a sort of grudging cosmopolitanish glamor, what with her uniquely diversified family.

At the next gate he paused, and opened it and entered his rented lawn where his rented garage stared its empty door at him like an accusing eye, and still carrying his package carefully away from him he went on between the two spindling poplars he had set out and approached his rented frame house with its yellow paint and its naked veranda, knowing that from behind a shade somewhere, Belle was watching him. In negligee, the heavy mass of her hair caught up with studied carelessness, and her hot, suspicious eyes and the rich and sullen discontent of her mouth Lied lied took me away from my husband: what is to keep The wild bronze flame of her hair Her Injury, yes. Inexcusable because of the utter lack of necessity or reason for it. Giving him nothing, taking nothing away from him. Obscene. Yes, obscene: a deliberate breaking of the rhythm of things for no reason; to both Belle and himself an insult; to Narcissa, in her home where her serenity lingered grave and constant and steadfast as a diffused and sourceless light, it was an adolescent scribbling on the walls of a temple. Reason in itself confounded If what parts can so remain . . . "I didn't lie. I told you; did what she would not have had the cowardice to do." What is to keep Ay, obscene if you will, but there was about her a sort of gallantry, like a swordsman who asks no quarter and gives none; slays or is slain with a fine gesture or no gesture at all; tragic and austere and fine, with the wild bronze flame of her hair. And he, he not only hadn't made a good battle; he hadn't even made a decent ghost. Thou wast happier in thy cage, happier? Nor oceans and seas . . .

"She had ghosts in her bed," Horace said, mounting the steps.

2

In January his aunt received a post card from Bayard mailed at Tampico; a month later, from Mexico City, a wire for money. And that was the last intimation he gave that he contemplated being at any stated place long enough for a communication to reach him, although from time to time he indicated by gaudy postals where he had been, after the bleak and brutal way of him. In April the card came from Rio, followed by an interval during which he seemed to have completely vanished and which Miss Jenny and Narcissa passed quietly at home, their days centered placidly about the expected child, which Miss Jenny had already named John. Miss Jenny felt that old Bayard had somehow flouted them all, had committed lese majesty toward his ancestors and the lusty glamor of the family doom by dying, as she put it, practically from the "inside out." Thus he was in something like bad odor with her, and as young Bayard was in more or less suspense, neither flesh nor fowl, she fell to talking more and more of John. Soon after old Bayard's death, in a sudden burst of rummaging and prowling which she called winter cleaning, she had found among his mother's relics a miniature of John done by a New Orleans painter when John and Bayard were about eight. Miss Jenny remembered that there had been one of each and it seemed to her that she could remember putting them both away together when their mother died. But the other she could not find. So she left Simon to gather up the litter she had made and brought the miniature downstairs to where Narcissa sat in the "office" and together they examined it.

The hair even at that early time was of a rich tawny shade, and rather long. "I remember that first day," Miss Jenny said, "when they came home from school. Bloody as hogs, both of 'em, from fighting other boys who said they looked like girls. Their mother washed 'em and petted 'em, but they were so busy bragging to Simon and Bayard about the slaughter they had done to mind it much. 'You ought to seen the others,' Johnny kept saying. Bayard blew up, of course; said it was a damn shame to send a boy out with curls down his back, and finally he bullied the poor woman into agreeing to let Simon barber 'em. And do you know what? Neither of 'em would let his hair be touched. It seems they hadn't licked all the enemy yet, and they were going to make the whole school admit that they could wear hair down to their heels, if they wanted to. And I reckon they did, because after two or three days there wasn't any more blood on 'em, and then they let Simon cut it off while their mother sat behind the piano in the parlor and cried. And that was the last of it."

The face was a child's face, and it was Bayard's too, yet there was already in it, not that bleak arrogance she had come to know in Bayard's, but a sort of frank spontaneity, warm and ready and generous; and as Narcissa held the small oval in her hand while the steady blue eyes looked quietly back at her and from the whole face among its tawny curls, with its smooth skin and child's mouth, there shone like a serene radiance something sweet and merry and wild, she realized as she never had before the blind tragedy of human events. And while she sat motionless with the medallion in her hand and Miss Jenny thought she was looking at it, she was cherishing the child under her own heart with all the aroused constancy of her nature: it was as though already she could discern the dark silver shape of that doom which she had incurred, standing beside her chair, waiting and biding its time. No, no she whispered with passionate protest, surrounding her child with wave after wave of that strength which welled so abundantly within her as the days accumulated, manning the walls with invincible garrisons. She was even glad Miss Jenny had shown her the thing: she was now forewarned as well as forearmed.

Meanwhile Miss Jenny continued to talk about the child as Johnny and to recall anecdotes of that other John's childhood, until at last Narcissa realized that Miss Jenny was getting the two confused; and with a sort of shock she knew that Miss Jenny was getting old, that at last even her indomitable old heart was growing a little tired. It was a shock, for she had never associated senility with Miss Jenny, who was so spare and erect and brusque and uncompromising and kind, looking after the place which was not hers and to which she had been transplanted when her own alien roots in a far away place where customs and manners and even the very climate were different, had been severed violently; running it with tireless efficiency and with the assistance of only a doddering old negro as irresponsible as a child.

But run the place she did, just as though old Bayard and young Bayard were there. But at night when they sat before the fire in the office as the year drew on and the night air drifted in heavy again with locust and with the song of mockingbirds and with all the renewed and timeless mischief of spring and at last even Miss Jenny admitted that they no longer needed a fire; when at these times she talked, Narcissa noticed that she no longer talked of her far off girlhood and of Jeb Stuart with his crimson sash and his garlanded bay and his mandolin, but always of a time no further back than Bayard's and John's childhood, as though her life were closing, not into the future, but out of the past, like a spool being rewound.

And as she would sit, serene again behind her forewarned and forearmed bastions, listening, she admired more than ever that indomitable spirit which, born with a woman's body into a heritage of rash and heedless men and seemingly for the sole purpose of cherishing those men to their early and violent ends, and this over a period of history which had seen brothers and husband slain in the same useless mischancing of human affairs, had seen the foundations of her life vanish as in a nightmare not to be healed by either waking or sleep from the soil where her forbears slept trusting in the integrity of mankind, and had had her own roots torn bodily and violently from that soil—a period at which the men themselves, for all their headlong and scornful rashness, would have quailed had their parts been passive parts and their doom been waiting. And she thought how much finer that gallantry which never lowered lance to foes no sword could ever find, that uncomplaining steadfastness of those unsung (ay, unwept, too) women than the fustian and useless glamor of the men that theirs was hidden by. And now she is trying to make me one of them; to make of my child just another rocket to glare for a moment in the sky, then die away.

But she was serene again, and her days centered more and more as the time drew nearer, and Miss Jenny's voice was only a sound, comforting but without significance. Each week she got a whimsical, gallantly humorous letter from Horace: these she read too with serene detachment—what she could decipher, that is. She had always found Horace's writing difficult, and parts that she could decipher meant nothing. But she knew that he expected that.

Then it was definitely spring again. Miss Jenny's and Isom's annual vernal altercation began, continued its violent but harmless course in the garden. They brought the tulip bulbs up from the cellar and set them out, Narcissa helping, and spaded up the other beds and unswaddled the roses and the transplanted jasmine. Narcissa drove into town, saw the first jonquils on the now deserted lawn, blooming as though she and Horace were still there, and later, the narcissi. But when the gladioli bloomed she was not going out any more save in the late afternoon or early evening, when she and Miss Jenny walked in the garden among burgeoning bloom and mockingbirds and belated thrushes where the long avenues of gloaming sunlight reluctant leaned, Miss Jenny still talking about Johnny; confusing the unborn with the dead.

Late in May they received a request for money from Bayard in San Francisco, where he had at last succeeded in being robbed. Miss Jenny sent it. "You come on home," she wired him, not telling Narcissa. "He'll come home, now," she did tell her. "You see if he dont. If for nothing else than to worry us for a while."

But a week later he still had not come home, and Miss Jenny wired him again, a night letter, to the former address. But when the wire was dispatched he was in Chicago, and when it reached San Francisco he was sitting among saxophones and painted ladies and middle-aged husbands at a table littered with soiled glasses and stained with cigarette ash and spilt liquor, accompanied by a girl and two men. One of the men wore whipcord, with an army pilot's silver wings on his breast. The other was a stocky man in shabby serge, with gray temples and intense, visionary eyes. The girl was a slim long thing, mostly legs apparently, with a bold red mouth and cold eyes, in an ultra smart dancing frock, and when the other two men crossed the room and spoke to Bayard she was cajoling him to drink with thinly concealed insistence. She and the aviator now danced together, and from time to time she looked back to where Bayard sat drinking steadily while the shabby man talked to him. She was saying: "I'm scared of him."

The shabby man was talking with leashed excitability, using two napkins folded lengthwise into narrow strips to illustrate something, his voice hoarse and importunate against the meaningless pandemonium of the horns and drums. For a while Bayard had half listened, staring at the man with his bleak chill eyes, but now he was watching something across the room, letting the man talk on, unminded. He was drinking whisky and soda steadily, with the bottle beside him. His hand was steady enough, but his face was dead white and he was quite drunk; and looking across at him from time to time, the girl was saying to her partner: "I'm scared, I tell you. God, I didn't know what to do, when you and your friend came over. Promise you wont go and leave us."

"You scared?" the aviator repeated in a jeering tone, but he too glanced back at Bayard's bleak arrogant face. "I bet you dont even need a horse."

"You dont know him," the girl rejoined, and she clutched his hand and struck her body shivering against his, and though his arm tightened and his hand slid down her back a little, it was under cover of the shuffling throng into which they were wedged, and a little warily, and he said quickly:

"Ease off, Sister: he's looking this way. I saw him

knock two teeth out of an Australian captain that just tried to speak to a girl he was with in a London joint two years ago." They moved on until the band was across the room from them. "What're you scared of? He's not an Indian: he wont hurt you as long as you mind your step. He's all right. I've known him a long time, in places where you had to be good, believe me."

"You dont know," she repeated, "I—" the music crashed to a stop; in the sudden silence the shabby man's voice rose from the nearby table:

"—could just get one of these damn yellow-livered pilots to—" his voice was drowned again in a surge of noise, drunken voices and shrill woman-laughter and scraping chairs, but as they approached the table the shabby man still talked with leashed insistent gestures while Bayard stared across the room at whatever it was he watched, raising his glass steadily to his mouth. The girl clutched her partner's arm.

"You've got to help me pass him out," she begged swiftly. "I'm scared to leave with him, I tell you."

"Pass Sartoris out? The man dont wear hair, nor the woman either. Run back to kindergarten, Sister." Then, struck with her sincerity, he said: "Say, what's he done, anyway?"

"I dont know. He'll do anything. He threw an empty bottle at a traffic cop as we were driving out here. You've got—"

"Hush it," he said. The shabby man ceased and raised his face impatiently. Bayard still gazed across the room.

"Brother-in-law over there," he said, speaking slowly and carefully. "Dont speak to family. Mad at us." They turned and looked.

"Where?" the aviator asked. Then he beckoned a waiter. "Here, Jack."

"Man with diamond headlight," Bayard said. "Brave man. Cant speak to him, though. Might hit me. Friend with him, anyway."

The aviator looked again. "Looks like his grandmother," he said. He called the waiter again, then to the girl: "Another cocktail?" He picked up the bottle and filled his glass and reached it over and filled Bayard's, and turned to the shabby man. "Where's yours?"

The shabby man waved it impatiently aside. "Look." He picked up the napkins again. "Dihedral increases in ratio to air speed, up to a certain point. Now, what I want to find out—"

"Tell it to the Marines, buddy," the aviator interrupted. "I heard a couple of years ago they got a airyplane. Here, waiter!" Bayard was watching the shabby man bleakly.

"You aren't drinking," the girl said. She touched the aviator beneath the table.

"No," Bayard agreed. "Why dont you fly his coffin for him, Monaghan?"

"Me?" The aviator set his glass down. "Like hell. My leave comes due next month." He raised the glass again. "Here's to wind-up," he said. "And no heel-taps."

"Yes," Bayard agreed, not touching his glass. His face was pale and rigid, a metal mask again.

"I tell you there's no danger at all, as long as you keep the speed below the point I'll give you," the shabby man said. "I've tested the wings with weights, and proved the lift and checked all my figures; all you have to do—"

"Wont you drink with us?" the girl insisted.

"Sure he will," the aviator said. "Say, you remember that night in Amiens when that big Irish devil, Comyn, wrecked the Cloche-Clos by blowing that

A.P.M.'s whistle at the door?" The shabby man sat smoothing the folded napkins on the table before him. Then he burst forth again, his voice hoarse and mad with the intensity of his frustrated dream:

"I've worked and slaved, and begged and borrowed, and now when I've got the machine and a government inspector, I cant get a test because you damn yellow-livered pilots wont take it up. A service full of you, drawing flying pay for sitting in two-story dance halls, swilling alcohol. You overseas pilots talking about your guts! No wonder you couldn't keep the Germans from—"

"Shut up," Bayard told him without heat, in his bleak, careful voice.

"You're not drinking," the girl repeated. "Wont you?" She raised his glass and touched her lips to it and extended it to him. Taking it, he grasped her hand too and held her so. But again he was staring across the room.

"Not brother-in-law," he said. "Husband-in-law. No. Wife's brother's husband-in-law. Wife used to be wife's brother's girl. Married, now. Fat woman. He's lucky."

"What're you talking about?" the aviator demanded. "Come on, let's have a drink."

The girl was taut at her arm's length, with the other hand she raised her glass and she smiled at him with brief and terrified coquetry. But he held her wrist in his hard fingers, and while she stared at him widely he drew her steadily toward him. "Turn me loose," she whispered. "Dont," and she set her glass down and with the other hand she tried to unclasp his fingers. The shabby man was brooding over his folded napkins; the aviator was carefully occupied with his drink. "Dont," she whispered again. Her body was wrung in her chair and she put her other hand out quickly, lest she be dragged out of it, and for a moment they stared at one another—she with wide and mute terror; he bleakly with the cruel cold mask of his face. Then he released her and rose and kicked his chair away.

"Come on, you," he said to the shabby man. He drew a wad of bills from his pocket and laid one beside her on the table. "That'll get you home," he said. But she sat nursing the wrist he had held, watching him without a sound. The aviator was discreetly interested in the bottom of his glass. "Come on," Bayard repeated, and he stalked steadily on. The shabby man rose and followed rapidly.

In a small alcove Harry Mitchell sat. On his table too were bottles and glasses, and he now sat slumped in his chair, his eyes closed and his bald head in the glow of an electric candle was dewed with rosy perspiration. Beside him sat a woman who turned and looked full at Bayard with an expression of harried desperation; above them stood a waiter with a head like that of a priest, and as Bayard passed he saw that the diamond was missing from Harry's tie and he heard their bitter suppressed voices as their hands struggled over something on the table between them, behind the discreet shelter of their backs, and as he and his companion reached the door the woman's voice rose with a burst of filthy rage into a shrill hysterical scream cut sharply off, as if someone had clapped a hand over her mouth.

The next day Miss Jenny drove in to town and wired him again. But when this wire was dispatched, Bayard was sitting in an aeroplane on the tarmac of the government field at Dayton, while the shabby man hovered and darted hysterically about and a group of army pilots stood nearby, politely noncommittal. The machine looked like any other bi-plane, save that there were no visible cables between the planes, which were braced from within by wires on a system of tension springs; and hence, motionless on the ground, dihedral was negative. The theory was that while in level flight dihedral would be eliminated for the sake of speed, as in the Spad type, and when the machine was banked, side pressure would automatically increase dihedral for manoeuverability. The cockpit was set well back toward the fin. "So you can see the wings when they buckle," the man who loaned him a helmet and goggles said drily. "It's an old pair," he added. But Bayard only glanced at him, bleakly humorless. "Look here, Sartoris," the man added, "let that crate alone. These birds show up here every week with something that will revolutionize flying, some new kind of mantrap that flies fine—on paper. If the C.O. wont give him a pilot (and you know we try anything here that has a prop on it) you can gamble it's a washout."

But Bayard took the helmet and goggles and went on across the aerodrome toward the hangar. The group followed him and stood quietly about with their bleak, wind-gnawed faces while the engine was being warmed up. But when Bayard got in and settled his goggles, the man approached and thrust his hand into Bayard's lap. "Here," he said brusquely. "Take this." It was a woman's garter, and Bayard picked it up and returned it.

"I wont need it," he said. "Thanks just the same."

"Well. You know your own business, of course. But if you ever let her get her nose down, you'll lose everything but the wheels."

"I know," Bayard answered. "I'll keep her up." The shabby man rushed up again, still talking. "Yes,

yes," Bayard replied impatiently. "You told me all
that. Contact," he snapped. The mechanic spun the
propeller over, and as the machine moved out the
shabby man still clung to the cockpit and shouted at
him. Soon he was running to keep up and still shouting, until Bayard lifted his hand off the cowling and
opened the throttle. But when he reached the end of
the field and turned back into the wind the man was
running toward him and waving his arms. Bayard
opened the throttle full and the machine lurched forward and when he passed the shabby man in midfield
the tail was high and the plane rushed on in long
bounds, and he had a fleeting glimpse of the man's
open mouth and his wild arms as the bounding
ceased.

There was not enough tension on the wires, he decided at once, watching them from the V strut out as
they tipped and swayed, and he jockeyed the thing
carefully on, gaining height. Also he realized that
there was a certain point beyond which his own
speed would rob him of lifting surface. He had
about two thousand feet now, and he turned, and in
doing so he found that aileron pressure utterly nega-
tived the inner plane's dihedral and doubled the
outer one, and he found himself in the wildest skid
he had seen since his Hun days. The machine not
only skidded: it flung its tail up like a diving whale
and the air speed indicator leaped thirty miles past
the dead line the inventor had given him. He was
headed back toward the field now, in a shallow dive,
and he pulled the stick back.

But only the wingtips responded by tipping
sharply upward; he flung the stick forward before
they ripped completely off, and he knew that only
the speed of the dive kept him from falling like an
inside out umbrella. And the speed was increasing: it

seemed an eternity before the wingtips recovered, and already he had overshot the field, under a thousand feet high. He pulled the stick back again; again the wingtips buckled and he slapped the stick over and kicked again into that skid, trying to check his speed. Again the machine swung its tail in a soaring arc, but this time the wings came off and he ducked his head automatically as one of them slapped viciously past it and crashed into the tail, shearing it too away.

3

That day Narcissa's child was born, and the following day Simon drove Miss Jenny in to town and set her down before the telegraph office and held the horses leashed and champing with gallant restiveness by a slight and surreptitious tightening of the reins, while beneath the tilted tophat and the voluminous duster, he swaggered, sitting down. Though he was sitting and you would not have thought it possible, Simon contrived by some means to actually strut. So Dr Peabody found him when he came along the street in the June sunlight, in his slovenly alpaca coat, carrying a newspaper.

"You look like a frog, Simon," he said. "Where's Miss Jenny?"

"Yessuh," Simon agreed. "Yessuh. Dey's swellin' en rejoicin' now. De little marster done arrive'. Yessuh, de little marster done arrive' and de ole times comin' back."

"Where's Miss Jenny?" Dr Peabody repeated impatiently.

"She in dar, tellygraftin' dat boy ter come on back hyer whar he belong at." Dr Peabody turned away and Simon watched him, a little fretted at his apathy in the face of the event. "Takes it jes' like trash," Simon mused aloud, with annoyed disparagement. "Nummine; we gwine wake 'um all up, now. Yessuh, de olden times comin' back again, sho'. Like in Marse John's time, when de Cunnel wuz de young marster en de niggers f'um de quawtuhs gethered on de front lawn, wishin' Mistis en de little marster well." And he watched Dr Peabody enter the door and through the plate glass window he saw him approach Miss Jenny as she stood at the counter with her message.

"Come home you fool and see your family or I will have you arrested" the message read in her firm, lucid script. "It's more than ten words," she told the operator, "but that dont matter this time. He'll come now: you watch. Or I'll send the sheriff after him, sure as his name's Sartoris."

"Yes, ma'am," the operator said. He was apparently having trouble reading it, and he looked up after a time and was about to speak when Miss Jenny remarked his distraction and repeated the message briskly.

"And make it stronger than that, if you want to," she added.

"Yes, ma'am," the operator said again, and he ducked down behind his desk, and presently and with a little mounting curiosity and impatience Miss Jenny leaned across the counter with a silver dollar in her fingers and watched him count the words three times in a sort of painful flurry.

"What's the matter, young man?" she demanded. "The government dont forbid the mentioning of a day-old child in a telegram, does it?"

The operator looked up. "Yes, ma'am, it's all right," he said at last, and she gave him the dollar, and as he sat holding it and Miss Jenny watched him

with yet more impatience, Dr Peabody came in and
touched her arm.

"Come away, Jenny," he said.

"Good morning," she said, turning at his voice.
"Well, it's about time you took notice. This is the
first Sartoris you've been a day late on in how many
years, Loosh? And soon as I get that fool boy home,
it'll be like old times again, as Simon says."

"Yes. Simon told me. Come away."

"Let me get my change." She turned to the operator, who stood with the yellow sheet in one hand and
the coin in the other. "Well, young man? Aint a dollar enough?"

"Yes, ma'am," he repeated, turning upon Dr Peabody his dumb, distracted eyes. Dr Peabody reached
fatly and took the message and the coin from him.

"Come away, Jenny," he said again. Miss Jenny
stood motionless for a moment, in her black silk dress
and her black bonnet set squarely on her head, staring at him with her piercing old eyes that saw so
much and so truly. Then she turned and walked
steadily to the door and stepped into the street and
waited until he joined her, and her hand was steady
too as she took the folded paper he offered.
MISSISSIPPI BOY it said in discreet capitals, and she
returned it to him immediately and from her waist
she took a small sheer handkerchief and wiped her
fingers lightly.

"I dont have to read it," she said. "They never get
into the papers but one way. And I know that he was
somewhere he had no business being, doing something that wasn't any affair of his."

"Yes," Dr Peabody said. He followed her to the
carriage and put his hands clumsily upon her as she
mounted.

"Dont paw me, Loosh," she snapped. "I'm not a

cripple." But he supported her elbow with his huge, gentle hand until she was seated, then he stood with his hat off while Simon laid the linen robe across her knees.

"Here," he said, and extended her the silver dollar and she returned it to her bag and clicked it shut and wiped her fingers again on her handkerchief.

"Well," she said, "thank God that's the last one. For a while, anyway. Home, Simon."

Simon sat with leashed magnificence, but under the occasion he unbent a little. "When you gwine come out en see de young marster, Doctuh?"

"Soon, Simon," he answered, and Simon clucked to the horses and wheeled away with a flourish, his hat tilted and the whip caught smartly back. Dr Peabody stood in the street, a shapeless hogshead of a man in a shabby alpaca coat, his hat in one hand and the folded newspaper and the yellow unsent message in the other, until Miss Jenny's straight slender back and the squarely indomitable angle of her bonnet had passed from sight.

But that was not the last one. One morning a week later, Simon was found in a negro cabin in town, with his grizzled head crushed in by a blunt instrument anonymously wielded.

"In whose house?" Miss Jenny demanded into the telephone. In that of a woman named Meloney Harris, the voice told her. Meloney . . . Mel . . . Belle Mitchell's face flashed before her, and she remembered: the mulatto girl whose smart apron and cap and lean shining shanks had lent such an air to Belle's parties, and who had quit Belle in order to set up a beauty parlor. Miss Jenny thanked the voice and hung up the receiver.

"The old gray-headed reprobate," she said, and she went into the office and sat down. "So that's what became of that church money he 'put out.' I wondered . . ." She sat stiffly and uncompromisingly erect in her chair, her hands idle on her lap. Well, that *is* the last one of 'em, she said. But no, he was hardly a Sartoris: he had at least had some shadow of a reason, while the others . . . "I think," Miss Jenny said, who had not spent a day in bed since she was forty years old, "that I'll be sick for a while."

And she did just exactly that. Went to bed, where she lay propped on pillows in a frivolous lace cap, and would permit no doctor to see her save Dr Peabody who called once informally and who sat sheepishly and mountainously for thirty minutes while Miss Jenny vented her invalid's spleen and the recurred anger of the salve fiasco upon him. And here she held daily councils with Isom and Elnora, and at the most unexpected times she would storm with unimpaired vigor from her window at Isom or Caspey in the yard beneath.

The child and the placid, gaily turbaned mountain who superintended his hours, spent most of the day in this room, and presently Narcissa herself; and the three of them would sit for rapt murmurous hours in a sort of choral debauch of abnegation while the object of it slept digesting, waked, stoked himself anew and slept again.

"He's a Sartoris, all right," Miss Jenny said, "but an improved model. He hasn't got that wild look of 'em. I believe it was the name. Bayard. We did well to name him Johnny."

"Yes," Narcissa said, watching her sleeping son with grave and tranquil serenity.

* * *

And there Miss Jenny staid until her while was up. Three weeks it was. She set the date before she went to bed and held to it stubbornly, refusing even to rise and attend the christening. That day fell on Sunday. It was late in June and jasmime drifted into the house in steady waves. Narcissa and the nurse, in an even more gaudy turban, had brought the baby, bathed and garnished and scented in his ceremonial robes, in to her, and later she heard them drive away, and the house was still again. The curtains stirred peacefully at the windows, and all the peaceful scents of summer came up on the sunny breeze, and sounds—birds, and somewhere a Sabbath bell, and Elnora's voice, chastened a little with her recent bereavement but still rich and mellow as she went about getting dinner. She sang sadly and endlessly and without words as she moved about the kitchen, but she broke off short when she looked up and saw Miss Jenny looking a little frail but fully dressed and erect as ever, in the door.

"Miss Jenny! Whut in de worl'! You git on back to yo' bed. Here," and Elnora crossed the kitchen, but Miss Jenny came firmly on.

"Where's Isom?" she demanded.

"He at de barn. You come on back to bed. I'm gwine tell Miss Narcissa on you."

"I'm tired staying in the house," Miss Jenny stated. "I'm going to town. Call Isom." Elnora protested still, but Miss Jenny insisted coldly, and Elnora called Isom from the door and returned, still portentous with pessimistic warnings, and presently Isom entered.

"Here," Miss Jenny said, handing him the keys. "Get the car out." Isom departed and Miss Jenny followed more slowly, and Elnora would have followed too, solicitous, but Miss Jenny drove her back to her kitchen; and unassisted she crossed the yard and got in beside Isom. "And you drive this thing careful, boy," she told him, "or I'll get over there and do it myself."

When they reached town, from slender spires rising among trees against the puffy summer clouds, church bells rang lazily upon the ebbing reaches of the sunny air. But at the edge of town Miss Jenny bade Isom turn into a narrow lane and they followed this and stopped presently before the iron gates to the cemetery. "I want to see if they fixed Simon all right," she explained. "I'm not going to church today: I've been shut up between walls long enough." Just from the prospect she got a mild exhilaration, like that of a small boy playing out of school.

The negro ground lay beyond the cemetery proper and its orderly plots, and Isom led her to Simon's grave. Simon's burying society had taken care of him, and after two weeks the mound was still heaped with floral designs from which the blooms had fallen, leaving a rank, lean mass of stems and peacefully rusting wire skeletons. Elnora, someone, had also been before her, and the grave was bordered with tedious rows of broken gaudy bits of crockery and of colored glass. "I reckon he'll have to have a headstone, too," Miss Jenny said aloud, and turning, saw Isom hauling his overalled legs into a tree, about which two catbirds whirled and darted in scolding circles. "You, Isom."

"Yessum," Isom answered and he dropped to the ground and the birds threatened him with a final burst of hysterical profanity, and followed her. They went on and into the white folks' section and passed now between marble shapes bearing names that she knew well, and dates in a stark and peaceful simplicity in the impervious stone. Now and then they were surmounted by symbolical urns and doves and surrounded by clipped tended sward green against the blanched marble and the blue, dappled sky and the black cedars from among which doves crooned endlessly reiterant. Here and there bright unfaded flowers lay in random bursts against the pattern of green and white; and presently John Sartoris lifted his stone back and his fulsome gesture amid a clump of cedars beyond which the bluff sheered sharply away into the valley.

Bayard's grave too was a shapeless mass of withered flowers, and Miss Jenny had Isom clear them off and carry them away. The masons were just beginning to lay the curbing around it, and the headstone itself sat nearby beneath a canvas cover. She lifted the cover and read the clean, new lettering: Bayard Sartoris. March 16, 1893—June 5, 1920. That was better. Simple: no Sartoris man to invent bombast to put on it. Cant lie dead in the ground without strutting and swaggering. Beside the grave was a second headstone; like the other save for the inscription. But the Sartoris touch was there, despite the fact that there was no grave to accompany it, and the whole thing was like a boastful voice in an empty church. Yet withal there was something else, as though the merry wild spirit of him who had laughed away so much of his heritage of humorless and fustian vainglory, managed somehow even yet to soften the arrogant gesture with which they had said farewell:

LIEUT. JOHN SARTORIS, R.A.F.
Killed in action, July 19, 1918.

'I bare him on eagles' wings
and brought him unto Me'

A faint breeze soughed in the cedars like a long sigh, and the branches moved gravely in it. Across the spaced tranquillity of the marble shapes the doves crooned their endless rising inflections. Isom returned for another armful of withered flowers and bore it away.

Old Bayard's headstone was simple too, having been born, as he had, too late for one war and too soon for the next one, and she thought what a joke They had played on him: denying him opportunities for swashbuckling and then denying him the privilege of being buried by men who would have invented vainglory for him. The cedars had almost overgrown his son John's and John's wife's graves. Sunlight reached them only in fitful splashes, dappling the weathered stone with brief stipplings; only with difficulty could the inscription have been deciphered. But she knew what it would be, what with the virus, the inspiration and the example of that one which dominated them all, which gave to the whole place in which weary people were supposed to rest, a hushed, orotund solemnity having no more to do with mortality than the bindings of books have to do with that of the characters, and beneath which the headstones of the wives whom they had dragged into their arrogant orbits were, despite their pompous genealogical references, modest and effacing as the song of thrushes beneath the eyrie of an eagle.

He stood on a stone pedestal, in his frock coat and bareheaded, one leg slightly advanced and one hand resting lightly on the stone pylon beside him. His head was lifted a little in that gesture of haughty arrogance which repeated itself generation after generation with a fateful fidelity, his back to the world and his carven eyes gazing out across the valley where his railroad ran and beyond it to the blue changeless hills, and beyond that. The pedestal and effigy were mottled with sessions of rain and sun and with drippings from the cedar branches, and the bold carving of the letters was bleared with mold, yet easily decipherable:

COLONEL JOHN SARTORIS, C.S.A.

1823   1876

Soldier, Statesman, Citizen of the World

*For man's enlightenment he lived
By man's ingratitude he died*

Pause here, son of sorrow; remember death.

This inscription had caused some furore on the part of the slayer's family, and a formal protest followed. But in complying with opinion, old Bayard had his revenge: he caused the line 'by man's ingratitude he died' to be chiselled crudely out and added beneath it: 'Fell at the hand of——Redlaw, Aug. 4, 1876.'

Miss Jenny stood for a time, musing, a slender, erect figure in black silk and a small uncompromising black bonnet. The wind drew among the cedars in long sighs, and steadily as pulses the sad hopeless reiteration of the doves came along the sunny air. Isom returned for the last armful of dead flowers, and looking out across the marble vistas where shadows of noon moved, she watched a group of children playing quietly and a little stiffly in their bright Sunday finery, among the tranquil dead. Well, it was the last one, at last, gathered in solemn conclave about the dying reverberation of their arrogant lusts, their dust moldering quietly beneath the pagan symbols of

their vainglory and the carven gestures of it in en-
during stone; and she remembered something Narcissa had said once, about a world without men, and
wondered if therein lay peaceful avenues and dwell-
ings thatched with quiet; and she didn't know.

Isom returned, and as she turned away Dr Peabody
called her name. He was dressed as usual in his
shabby broadcloth trousers and his shiny alpaca coat
and a floppy panama hat, and his son was with him.

"Well, boy," Miss Jenny said, giving young Loosh
her hand. His face was big-boned and roughly
molded. He had a thatch of straight, stiff black hair
and his eyes were steady and brown and his mouth
was large; and in all his ugly face there was reliability
and gentleness and humor. He was rawboned and he
wore his clothing awkwardly, and his hands were
large and bony and with them he performed delicate
surgical operations with the deftness of a hunter
skinning a squirrel and the celerity of a prestidigita-
tor. He lived in New York, where he was associated
with a surgeon whose name was a household word,
and once a year and sometimes twice he rode thirty-
six hours on the train, spent twenty hours with his father (which they passed walking about the town or
riding over the countryside in the sagging buckboard all day, and sitting on the veranda or before
the fire all the following night), took the train again
and ninety-two hours later, was at his clinic again.
He was thirty years old, only child of the woman Dr
Peabody had courted for fourteen years before he
was able to marry her. The courtship was during the
days when he physicked and amputated the whole
county by buckboard; often after a year's separation
he would drive thirty miles to see her, to be met on
the way and deflected to a childbed or a mangled

limb, with only a scribbled message to assuage the interval of another year. "So you're home again, are you?" Miss Jenny asked.

"Yes, ma'am. And find you as spry and handsome as ever."

"Jenny's too bad-tempered to ever do anything but dry up and blow away," Dr Peabody said.

"You'll remember I never let you wait on me, when I'm not well," she retorted. "I reckon you'll be tearing off again on the next train, wont you?" she asked young Loosh.

"Yessum, I'm afraid so. My vacation hasn't come due, yet."

"Well, at this rate you'll spend it at an old men's home somewhere. Why dont you all come out and have dinner, so he can see the boy?"

"I'd like to," young Loosh answered, "but I dont have time to do all the things I want to, so I just make up my mind not to do any of 'em. Besides, I'll have to spend this afternoon fishing," he added.

"Yes," his father put in, "and choppin' up good fish with a pocket knife just to see what makes 'em go. Lemme tell you what he did this mawnin': he grabbed that old lame hound of Abe's and operated on its shoulder so quick that Abe not only didn't know what he was doing, but even the dawg didn't. Only you forgot to look for his soul," he added.

"You dont know if he hasn't got one," young Loosh said, unruffled. "Dr Straud is trying to find the soul by electricity; he says—"

"Fiddlesticks," Miss Jenny snapped. "You better get a jar of Will Falls' salve and give it to him, Loosh. Well—" she glanced at the sun "—I'd better be going. If you wont come out to dinner—?"

"Thank you, ma'am," young Loosh answered. His father said:

"I brought him in to show him that collection of yours. We didn't know we looked that underfed."

"Help yourself," Miss Jenny answered. She went on, and they stood and watched her trim back until it passed from view.

"And now there's another one," young Loosh said musingly. "Another one to grow up and keep his folks in a stew until he finally succeeds in doing what they all expect of him. Well, maybe that Benbow blood will sort of hold him down. They're quiet folks, that girl; and Horace sort of . . . and just women to raise him . . ."

Dr Peabody grunted. "He's got Sartoris blood in him, too."

All of Narcissa's instincts had been antipathetic to him; his idea was a threat and his presence a violation of the very depths of her nature: in the headlong violence of him she had been like a lily in a gale which rocked it to its roots in a sort of vacuum, without any actual laying-on of hands. And now the gale had gone on; the lily had forgotten it as its fury died away into fading vibrations of old terrors and dreads, and the stalk recovered and the bell itself was untarnished save by the friction of its own petals. The gale is gone, and though the lily is sad a little with vibrations of ancient fears, it is not sorry.

Miss Jenny had arrived home, looking a little spent, and Narcissa had scolded her and at last prevailed on her to lie down after dinner. And here she had dozed while the drowsy afternoon wore away, and waked to lengthening shadows and a sound of piano keys touched softly from downstairs. I've slept all afternoon she told herself, rising. In Narcissa's room the child slept in his crib; beside him the nurse dozed placidly. Miss Jenny tiptoed out and descended the stairs and drew her chair out from behind the piano. Narcissa ceased.

"Do you feel rested?" Narcissa asked. "You shouldn't have done that."

"Fiddlesticks," Miss Jenny said. "It always does me good to see all those fool pompous men lying there with their marble mottoes and things. Thank the Lord, none of them will have a chance at me. I reckon the Lord knows His business, but I declare, sometimes . . . Play something." Narcissa obeyed, playing softly, and Miss Jenny sat listening for a while. But presently she began to talk of the child. Narcissa played quietly on, her white dress with its black ribbon at the waist vaguely luminous in the gloom. Jasmine drifted steadily in, and Miss Jenny talked on about little Johnny. Narcissa played with rapt inattention, as though she were not listening. Then, without ceasing and without turning her head, she said:

"He isn't John. He's Benbow Sartoris."

"What?"

"His name is Benbow Sartoris," she repeated.

Miss Jenny sat quite still for a moment. Twilight thickened slowly about them; Narcissa's dress was pale as wax. In the next room Elnora moved about, laying the table for supper. "And do you think that'll do any good?" Miss Jenny demanded. "Do you think you can change one of 'em with a name?"

The music went on in the dusk; the dusk was peopled with ghosts of glamorous and old disastrous things. And if they were just glamorous enough, there would be a Sartoris in them, and then they were sure to be disastrous. Pawns. But the Player and the game He plays—who knows? He must have a name for his pawns, though, but perhaps Sartoris is the name of the game itself—a game outmoded and played with pawns shaped too late and to an old dead pattern, and of which the Player Himself is a little wearied. For there is death in the sound of it, and a glamorous fatality, like silver pennons downrushing at sunset, or a dying fall of horns along the road to Roncevaux.

"Do you think," Miss Jenny insisted, "that because his name is Benbow, he'll be any less a Sartoris and a scoundrel and a fool?"

Narcissa played on as though she were not listening. Then she turned her head and without ceasing her hands, she smiled at Miss Jenny quietly, a little dreamily, with serene fond detachment. Beyond Miss Jenny's trim fading head the window curtains hung motionless without any wind; beyond the window evening was a windless lilac dream, foster-dam of quietude and peace.

Oxford, Miss
29 September 1927

end.

ABOUT THE AUTHOR

WILLIAM FAULKNER, born New Albany, Mississippi, September 25, 1897—died July 6, 1962. Enlisted Royal Air Force, Canada, 1918. Attended University of Mississippi. Traveled in Europe 1925-1926. Resident of Oxford, Mississippi, where he held various jobs while trying to establish himself as a writer. First published novel, *Soldiers' Pay*, 1926. Writer in Residence at the University of Virginia 1957-1958. Awarded the Nobel Prize for Literature 1950.

ABOUT THE EDITOR

DOUGLAS DAY, professor of English at the University of Virginia, is the author of *Swifter than Reason: The Poetry and Criticism of Robert Graves; Malcolm Lowry: A Biography;* and numerous articles in literary magazines.